DARK NIGHT GOLDEN DAWN

BOOK ONE
OF THE IMMORTAL ORDERS
TRILOGY

Dedication

To Doug, who proves over and over that love is an infinite well.

Sensitive Content

In this book, our main character, Harlow Krane, has been through a lot. She's struggled for a lot of her life with feelings of inadequacy. When the story opens, her abusive ex is moving on without her, causing her to confront much of what happened between them in these pages.

This is a story about Harlow's healing journey, as much as it is other things, and because of what she's been through there are references to: fatphobia, animal neglect, domestic and emotional abuse, depression and suicide. There are also brief mentions of homophobic behavior and child abuse, as well as quite a bit of fantasy violence.

While this is not a "dark" book, *per se*, it does not shy away from the kinds of topics that cause real harm, in real people's lives. While I always want my books to be an escape, this one is also about catharsis for the kinds of experiences that plague nearly every person I am close to. I have tried my hardest to pair these traumas with deep love, forgiveness when appropriate, and when not—well, you'll see.

But the bottom line is, if like so many of us, these are things you've been through yourself, please be cautious reading this story. Ultimately, I believe this is a story about healing and hope, but when you're deep in it, I know reading about these types of things can be triggering. If you're in a rough spot right now and you find something about all this inflammatory for your healing process, please, set this book aside and take care of you.

The Kranes and their friends will always be here, and Harlow would be the first to tell you that taking care of yourself is the most important part of healing. She has to learn that lesson herself in this book, but she and I would both say to put the book down if reading her story is doing more harm than good.

All my love.

Allison

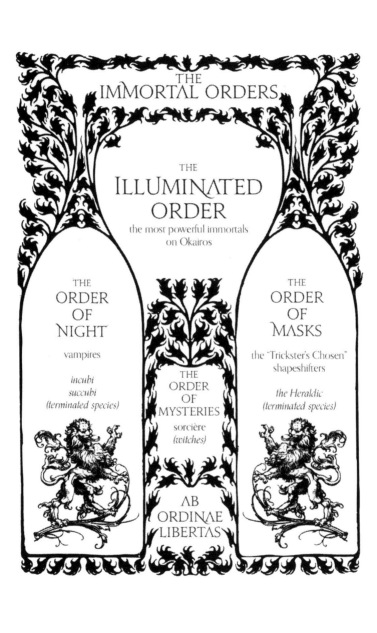

THE IMMORTAL ORDERS

THE

ILLUMINATED ORDER

the most powerful immortals
on Okairos

THE

ORDER
OF
NIGHT

vampires

incubi
succubi
(terminated species)

THE
ORDER
OF
MYSTERIES

sorcière
(witches)

ΛB
ORDINΛE
LIBERTΛS

THE

ORDER
OF
MASKS

the "Trickster's Chosen"
shapeshifters

the Heraldic
(terminated species)

PREFACE

"The Illuminated came to our world in the last days of the Empress Lofrata's reign, and for a time, we worshipped them as though they were gods. Soon enough, we learned they were not gods. They did not care for us, though they loved our world. No explanation was given regarding where they came from, or if they would ever leave.

Two thousand years have passed, and the Illuminated have surely changed the course of the world's history in ways we can scarcely imagine. Humans now share the world with not only the Illuminated, but their children begotten with our ancestors: vampires, witches and shapeshifters.

Though we live together in peace, as the Illuminated require, we would be foolish to claim this is a utopia. All of us live and die at their whim. As technology has advanced and the world has changed, the time of the Illuminated wanes and their numbers decrease, though their strangle-hold on power remains firm as ever."

Sofya Starkovski, *A Comprehensive History of the Illuminated and the Lower Orders*

CHAPTER ONE

Harlow Krane was doing her best not to check her phone. Her fingers itched with the desire to scroll through her socials, and the gossip sites, just to make herself miserable. It was six months ago all over again, when she and Mark broke up. Everyone was talking. Only now, they were talking because Mark had moved on—and she hadn't.

Since she and Mark separated, the gossips had declared Mark the wronged and she the wrong-doer. It made sense in many ways. The gossips were mostly run by humans, unlike the papers, which were all owned by the Illuminated. Of *course* they'd favor Mark's side of things. He was human—a human who'd *so* clearly moved on from his sorcière ex.

The texts Harlow received last night from her sisters had been unbearable. She shifted on the brass ladder she was perched on to take out her phone and read them again:

Thea: *We'll manage this tomorrow.*

So it was something to manage.

Meline: *Stay off your socials.*

She'd done so thus far, but now she desperately wanted to look.

Indigo, quickly following her twin: *Mark is out with a vampire princess. DON'T look at what they're saying about you.*

She knew it was indulging in some minor masochism, but she wanted to see. Wanted to feel the ache of knowing just how much of a loser everyone thought she'd become. Why was she like this?

Larkin: *I love you. Tell me if you're not okay? Okay?*

This was the only text she'd responded to, promising her youngest sister that she was all right, not checking her socials, and asking Larkin to tell the twins to mind their own business. Except social media *was* their business. They'd built a small social empire that had taken the bookstore, and all of Antiquity Row, from being an "Orders only" nook in Nuva Troi to being a *lifestyle*—a desirable destination for humans and immortals alike, with its charming cafes and old buildings.

And of course, the twins made their parents' bookstore, the Monas, the star of the show, the centerpiece of the cultural world of the Order of Mysteries, thereby making Harlow an object of interest to the gossips and socials alike. She'd never agreed to play such a role, but the twins' success had meant the success of their Order, and in a world ruled by the Illuminated, you took whatever success you could eke out, *and* whatever terrible side effects ensued as a result.

Harlow's disastrous love life being the talk of the town, and maybe even the country, was just one of those side effects. If she'd had her preference, she'd have spent her life in complete obscurity. She had no desire for anyone to know who she was or what she did with her life, and she certainly didn't want to think about what to do when she was the center of attention for all the wrong reasons.

She'd come into the bookstore early to avoid the inevitable barrage of strategizing that was coming as soon as Meline and Indigo scanned through the most important of the gossip apps,

Section Seven, over their coffee. Her phone began to buzz again, just as Mother entered the shop from the back office. Her sisters were up.

Aurelia Krane was looking at her own phone, as she floated a tea tray above her other hand, effortlessly using magic to keep it steady and aloft. "Your sisters are quite worried about you, the twins particularly so."

Harlow sighed from atop the brass ladder, slipping her phone back into her pocket and the last of the books she'd been shelving into place, and stepped down. Aurelia looked up as she guided the tea tray down onto the glass coffee table at the center of the shop's main floor showroom. This was the heart of the Monas, the place where Harlow and her four sisters grew up, the magic they would inherit. A world of esoteric knowledge, a legacy of books.

The two green velvet chesterfields that flanked the brass-rimmed glass coffee table hosted a variety of jewel toned cushions. Harlow pulled one down to sit on, onto the plush antique rug that bridged the two couches. She watched Aurelia carefully for signs that she would bring up the news about her on Section Seven, the twins' worries, anything about Mark. Instead, Aurelia was suspiciously placid, her bobbed silver hair shining in the weak springtime sunlight.

"A rare sunny day in Nuva Troi," Aurelia commented, setting her phone down.

"It's going to rain at ten," Harlow muttered as she poured the tea. Aurelia never beat around the bush unless she was uncomfortable. "Just say what you have to say, Mother."

Aurelia smiled, serene and wise, as always. "I *am* sorry about Mark, my darling. Are you holding up all right?"

Harlow sighed, taking a long sip of the Duke and Duchess tea her mother had brewed, the sharp scents of bergamot and lavender softening into rose and vanilla. It was perfect, as always.

She looked around the shop, at the warm white bookcases that stretched to the full height of the fifteen-foot ceilings, the grand staircase that took customers upstairs to the second and third floors, the ceiling, painted in rich oils and gold leaf to represent the heavens and Okairos' twin moons.

The Monas was her happy place, her true home, and she didn't want to talk about what happened with Mark here. Especially not after the nearly three years of turmoil her relationship with a human caused her family. It was the last of a long line of mistakes she'd been making for the past seven years, and Harlow's soul was brittle and fatigued.

She'd been back on solid ground with her family for the past few months and she wanted to keep it that way. This development with Mark threatened to put her back in a vulnerable spot, one she feared. Every time she felt like she was pulling things together, something unraveled her progress, and out of her small flock of sisters, she was the one who was always struggling, always lost. It was like her internal compass was missing and she couldn't find her place in the world.

"Of course," she said simply. "I'm always all right. You know that."

Aurelia raised her eyebrows, skeptically. "My dear girl, it's just us. Thea isn't in yet, and your Mama won't be down for a half-hour at least. She was running a bath when I left her."

Harlow wrinkled her nose at Aurelia. Mention of morning baths meant her parents spent the wee hours making love and it always made her want to scold Aurelia for telling.

"Don't wrinkle your nose at me, little bunny. You should be happy your mother and I still make enough of a ruckus that the neighbors text to ask if we might keep things down. Your mother had an orgasm so powerful…"

"Do not finish that sentence. *Please*. I beg you. I am happy you and Mama still have all the sex. But as someone who grew up listening to it, could you just *not*?"

Aurelia rolled her eyes. "Such a prude. Someday you'll meet someone who makes your toes curl so hard you'll think you'll explode when they look at you."

Harlow sighed. She'd felt that way about someone when she was much younger, and it ended so disastrously it had kicked off a domino effect of terrible decisions that were still ricocheting through her personal life, leaving a leaky mess everywhere she turned. She'd rather *not* feel that way again, if she was honest with herself.

"So, the human. Your sisters say something about news on the Section Seven app and the socials? Something about Mark and a vampire?"

Harlow groaned internally. Hearing her elegant, erudite mother discuss her humiliation on the gossips and socials made everything worse somehow. But she smoothed her face as well as she could. Of all the things she was bad at, pretending she was fine while her personal life burned around her was not one of them. She was an expert at *that*.

"Stop pretending you're not angry, Harlow. What good does it do to act this way?"

"I'm *not* mad. I don't care. You all just think I should because you would."

Aurelia lost her patience. "Harlow Andromeda Krane, I told you to drop the pretense."

Harlow cringed at the sound of the hunt in her mother's voice. The lupine snarl of a pack in pursuit of its quarry, the sound of the moon's song, and the goddess Akatei's power rang true in Aurelia's glamour. She glanced up at her mother, who appeared nearly ten feet tall and imposing as a divine being.

"Oh, stop that," she gasped, squeezing her eyes shut.

"Well, you wouldn't be honest." Aurelia returned to her usual self, serene as she smoothed her pants. "Be honest and I won't have to."

Harlow laughed. The dry humor in Aurelia's voice got her

every time. She was the parent who hated throwing her magical weight around. Selene wouldn't have hesitated, but Aurelia *had* tried to pry it out of her another way. She'd been trying for months to talk to her about Mark, despite how much she'd disapproved of their relationship.

Harlow took her mother's hand and Aurelia squeezed hard, reassuring her girl it was all right to let her guard down. "It's been six months, bun-bun. Surely you knew he would move on."

Harlow glared at her mother. "Of course I knew he would. It's *who* he moved on with that stings. Not because I care who he's with, but because it invites comparisons."

Aurelia nodded. "It is unfortunate he aligned himself with the Order of Night."

"Our whole affair was unfortunate. You and Mama were right about humans."

"We had very little problem with Mark's humanity, you know that, don't you?" Aurelia said softly.

This was an old wound, and Harlow suppressed the wince she felt coming on, but didn't quite succeed. Aurelia's hand covered her own. "It wasn't a good relationship, my darling."

Harlow rolled her eyes. "But you didn't like that Mark was human, did you?"

Aurelia sighed. "As we've discussed many times, what your mother and I worried about was his interest in sorcière secrets, in the Order at large... And his treatment of you. The way he tracked your every move... we worried about *that* most of all."

Aurelia said the last part quietly, tentatively. Harlow knew both her mothers had been concerned about Mark's incessant jealousy, his increasing demands on her time. By the time they'd broken up, she'd never gone anywhere alone. Even if she tried, he showed up with a kind of relentlessness that had worn her out so much she'd simply stopped going anywhere. The maters had been distressed by this, arguing that he was isolating her—dangerously so.

She stared into her teacup, feeling the sting of shame she always felt when she thought about how foolish she'd been about Mark. "It's over. We don't have to talk about it anymore."

A small sigh hissed from between Aurelia's lips. "We can talk about it for as long as you need to."

Harlow's gaze snapped to her mother's bright blue eyes. There was love and concern there, and real fear. She knew more about how things were with Mark than she'd expressed. Harlow didn't put it past her mothers to have used magic to find out what really happened between them, and that thought made everything worse.

Harlow couldn't escape the feeling that her legacy would be a trail of mistakes and apologies. This one though... this one was particularly bad because it didn't just hurt her, it had hurt her family, her Order, and now Mark's actions were an embarrassing reflection on all of them.

Aurelia gestured at her, waving her elegant hands imperiously. "You'd better look at the photos and have it done with."

Harlow nodded, pulling her phone out. When she unlocked it, the Section Seven app was already open. She scrolled past several posts about humans protesting procreation screenings in Nea Sterlis in breaking news. There it was, the first featured item in the lower Orders' gossip feed: Mark and a beautiful vampire princess, Olivia Sanvier, kissing and smiling for the cameras. One caption read, "Mark Easton, son of prominent tech mogul Alain Easton, and the new Lead Media Strategist for the Limen Publishing Group, levels up from a frumpy sorcière to a princess of the Order of Night!"

"Levels up?" The implication that she'd been a launch-point for Mark's social career stung. The frumpy comment stung as well, but it wasn't altogether inaccurate. She looked down at her ill-fitting trousers and the almost purposefully ugly blouse she was wearing. She'd stopped caring as much about what she looked like late in university, and at first it'd been freeing, confidence-building. Now it had turned into something else and she knew it. Frumpy indeed.

Aurelia read over her shoulder as she poured them both another cup of tea. "You aren't frumpy. What are they talking about?"

But then Aurelia glanced at her ensemble and her forehead wrinkled. It was as though she was seeing her child for the first time in a long time—through the world's eyes, rather than her own. It hurt Harlow's heart to feel her mother's scrutiny. She could practically hear Aurelia thinking, "What else have I missed?"

They liked Mark at first. Everyone had. He was handsome, funny, and smart. It wasn't until they'd been together for almost six months that the fighting started. The feeling that she was always doing something wrong, that every person she talked to threatened their relationship. Her life got smaller and smaller, until it was just her and Mark, against the world—or so she'd thought.

When he broke up with her and kicked her out of their apartment, Harlow was shocked. Six months later, she was still processing, and now there was *this*. Harlow scrolled down to a photo someone had snapped of her leaving the grocery store in a nearly identical outfit to the one she was wearing now, her hair in the kind of messy bun that looked terrible, instead of artfully mussed, the way she'd thought it looked when she threw her hair up.

Aurelia's jaw clenched, noticeably, as though she was suppressing all the things she wanted to say, and for that Harlow was eternally grateful. Selene had tried time and time again for the past few months to get Harlow to care about how she looked, but Harlow had resisted, getting pricklier each time Selene mentioned it. It wasn't just about keeping up appearances for Selene, who was the spitting image of Raia, goddess of fertility and sex. Mama was genuinely worried about her mental health, she knew that. Everyone was worried about her.

Harlow swallowed, and the act of doing so was difficult. She *was* frumpy these days. Dull really, on all counts. And who could compete with vampires? They were genetically predisposed to be attractive to humans, just like the Illuminated; everything about their biological makeup drew humans in. Not that she wanted to compete with Olivia Sanvier, or have Mark back, she didn't. But the socials drawing comparisons between them made it impossible for her *not* to.

Harlow frowned as she scratched at a tiny stain on her pants —where had that come from? She took a shaky breath, trying to push back the wave of insecurities threatening to wash over her. She wasn't an insecure person, but Section Seven could make anyone feel terrible about themselves, and Harlow was already in a bad place.

Aurelia smoothed her hair and kissed her forehead. "Humans. You know they glorify the Order of Night."

"I suppose." Harlow's feelings swirled with confusion.

She never understood the human need to identify with the Orders as though they were fan clubs they might join. Their love for the Order of Night was even more perplexing, since they were the Order of immortal creatures that threatened their safety the most directly. It didn't matter how many laws the Consortium of Immortals passed against non-consensual recreational bloodletting, the Order of Night was as dangerous to humans now as they were a thousand years ago, despite the monthly donations all humans were required to make to the Night's Own Blood Banks.

The comments about her on the write-up of Mark and

Olivia's date were brutal, many referring to Harlow in derogatory ways that made her stomach turn. Her cheeks reddened and she bit her bottom lip hard enough to draw blood. Her mother's cool fingers stroked her cheek, turning her face away from her phone. "That's enough, darling. Time to leave it be."

CHAPTER TWO

H arlow blinked back tears, feeling embarrassed. She took her mother's hand and kissed it. "I'm sorry."

Selene Krane descended the staircase, just as she apologized. Unlike Aurelia, who never failed to dress for work in a three-piece suit, Selene Krane was clad in one of her hundreds of dresses. This morning it was an orchid-colored velvet wrap dress, paired with knee-high heeled boots. Her dark blonde hair floated away from her face, and if she were human she wouldn't look a day over forty-five, even though she and Aurelia both were nearer to six hundred.

Harlow was always impressed by her mothers' style, but this morning, they were quintessential Selene and Aurelia, mistresses of the esoteric rare book trade, paragons of the Order of Mysteries, and her own dear parents.

"No apologizing, Harlow," Selene commanded, imperious as a goddess. "The human was a fool, and we are lucky to be rid of him."

This was as close as Selene would come to saying "I told you so," and for that much Harlow was grateful. Mama could hold a grudge, and she was glad to be so quickly on the other side of her temper.

Selene touched her daughter's honey-colored hair, so like her own, and kissed the top of her head. Harlow smelled her mother's familiar scent of violet, musk, and mysterious ancient woods. "The only thing to do now, dearest, is to meet someone else."

Harlow bristled at the suggestion. She wasn't ready to meet anyone new. It's why she hadn't moved back in with her parents when Mark kicked her out. She knew Selene would start trying to make matches for her and she wasn't ready to be paired yet. Fixing herself had been her top priority for the past six months and the project wasn't going as well as she'd hoped it would.

Aurelia sniffed softly and rose from the chesterfield to kiss her wife. "Perhaps we should let Harlow be."

Selene kissed Aurelia, a bit more passionately than Harlow was comfortable with witnessing, but that was the way of it with her parents. Five hundred years of marriage hadn't cooled their flame a bit.

"If we let Harlow be, she will turn into a dried up old hag. Is that what you want?"

Aurelia chuckled at Selene's forecast. "Now, now, my love. She's just seen the photos from last night. Let's not pronounce her a dried up old hag just yet. Let her adjust."

Harlow hated the way everyone in her family spoke about her like she wasn't sitting right there. It was the way of big families, and she dearly loved hers, but it was eternally annoying to have them discuss her as though she had no mind of her own.

"I am *fine*," she insisted. It was the wrong thing to say, if she'd wanted to be left alone.

"Wonderful!" Selene said with a warm but calculating smile. "Then you'll have no problem with joining us for the season." She said "the season" as though it were a proper noun, which of course it was in many ways.

"No!" Harlow moaned. "Please. It's so archaic. How can we

be the most powerful creatures on the planet and still be *selling* ourselves to one another? The humans moved past this centuries ago."

Selene and Aurelia sighed in unison. They'd borne Harlow's rants about this subject thousands of times. They were paired in their own season, long, long ago. They'd courted at a series of events specially designed to match children of the Illuminated and the lower Orders with socially compatible partners.

Harlow began to say something else, but Selene held up a finger. "Harlow, my love. Please. We've been over this many times and we stayed out of it while you dallied, but now it is time to do your duty to our family."

Dallied. As if she and Mark had been playing house, instead of in a deeply committed relationship. Harlow struggled not to grimace.

"It isn't as if marriages are forced upon anyone," Aurelia added. "We fell in love at our own season, as did our parents and siblings before us."

Harlow rolled her eyes. "But of course, you were pushed toward each other at every turn, weren't you? Your match was advantageous, with Mother's money and Mama's family properties. It was a business arrangement as much as love, wasn't it?"

Selene's passionate fury flashed in her large green eyes, the twins to her own, and Harlow was surprised she didn't pull the same kind of stunt Aurelia had earlier. "The fact that it was an advantageous pairing takes nothing away from how much I love your mother. Don't cheapen our love, or our traditions."

Guilt nipped at Harlow's poison tongue as she watched Selene fall dramatically into Aurelia's arms. It was true that by human standards the season was archaic and ridiculous, but nearly all the pairings resulted in long, loving romantic relationships, and those that didn't worked for other reasons. Polyamory was not uncommon amongst the Orders, and divorce was rare amongst those that paired during the season.

Harlow never knew whether it was because it stretched from spring into the blooming summer months, some of the most fortuitous times of the year to plant the seeds of love, or because the season itself, as a process, actually worked. Parents were absolutely forbidden from requiring a marriage if their children entered into a season, but of course they influenced their choices in every way they possibly could.

"I'm sorry." Harlow took Selene's hands and hugged both of her parents. "I know how much you love each other, and I do know the season works for many of our people. I just... I just wish I had more freedom in the matter."

Aurelia kissed both her cheeks before she gathered the tea tray up to brew a fresh pot. Selene's lips curved in a forgiving smile. "You have all the freedom in the world, Harlow. If you don't make a match, no one will blame you or find you lacking. Many pair outside the season, or do not bond at all. It is only an opportunity."

Harlow nodded. She had plenty to say about the matter, but she held her tongue. She knew both her parents would let it go completely if she didn't pair at all, but both Harlow and her eldest sister had been eligible to join the season for several years, and their mothers had never pressed them or encouraged it before.

Besides which, as much as she knew Selene had disapproved of her relationship with Mark, she was being uncharacteristically callous about moving on. Mama's *modus operandi* when it came to breakups was to spoil her girls until their hearts were fully healed, and if Harlow was honest with herself, she knew Selene didn't think she was "dallying" with Mark. She'd been just as worried as Aurelia was about how isolated she'd been when they were together, and now she was being altogether too glib. Something wasn't right.

Harlow glanced at the back office door, where she could hear Aurelia heating water for more tea. "Is everything all right? You and Mother have never suggested we join the season before, and all five of us are technically eligible now."

Selene's eyes darkened as she sank onto one of the chester-fields. For a moment, Harlow thought she might not answer her, but then something shifted in her countenance and Selene opened up to her second-eldest child. "Connor and Aislin McKay have their eye on this block again. We may not be able to hold out much longer. We need allies, or the Order of Mysteries will lose our foothold in the antiquities market. The Illuminated are making moves to take over."

Harlow gasped. "What?"

She hadn't realized things had gotten so bad, distracted as she'd been with Mark. The Monas was a fixture on Antiquity Row, six blocks of esoteric and occult shops and organizations that made up the backbone of the Order of Mysteries' income in Nuva Troi.

Besides which, Antiquity Row was an institution in the city —a *sorcière* institution. It was the place where anyone interested in ancient magics came to find rare goods, or just to be delighted by magic itself. The Kranes had owned the six-story building the Monas was housed in for nearly five hundred years. It was not only their business, but their home.

Selene sighed. "We were waiting to tell you. They say they don't want to change anything, just own all the property. Some families are thinking of selling. They're offering quite a lot."

"Damn them. Just another entitled Illuminated family thinking they own the world."

Aurelia returned from the office with another pot of tea. She glanced at Selene, and Harlow saw the look of sorrow that passed between them. They were afraid of losing the Monas, and maybe Antiquity Row completely. She felt a squeeze of pressured panic grip her heart.

"Hush, Harlow," Selene soothed with a hug. "They won't

get it. Not if we present a united front. Perhaps there are other things we might offer them."

"Other things? Like what?"

Aurelia and Selene both looked uncomfortable. "We were going to talk with you and your sisters about this later today..."

"Spit it out, mothers."

Out the window the shadow of clouds loomed. The sunny morning was over, and Harlow felt the incoming darkness acutely, as though it were more than just the usual Avril weather in Nuva Troi.

"I'm sure you've heard the rumors about the Illuminated," Selene said conspiratorially. "That they've been having trouble as of late... conceiving."

Of course Harlow had heard that, as well as the speculation that the Order of Mysteries might be the perfect solution to their problem—or to be specific, that pairing eligible Illuminated with those of the most powerful sorcière families might be the solution. Typically, Orders didn't mix much, but it didn't mean they *couldn't*. Anyone paying attention had heard the speculation, or rather read it, as it was all the back-channel gossips wrote about, even though Section Seven wouldn't touch it.

Aurelia gave Selene a cautionary look, but Mama barreled into her next statement with her usual verve. "Finn McKay is home from Nea Sterlis. I'm told he has two graduate degrees from Aphelion, a Masters in business and what was the other one, pet?"

Harlow wrinkled her nose in annoyance. Aphelion University was the most prestigious college in the country. There wasn't a better school in Nytra and of course Finn McKay had two degrees from there, while Harlow had been too afraid to even apply, and had simply gone to the University of Nuva Troi. Apparently today was a day for rubbing it in that all her exes were doing amazing things... Not that Finn was her ex. Not exactly, anyway.

"Public policy of some kind, I believe," Aurelia said absently, not taking her eyes from Harlow.

"Yes, something like that. He's back and I have it on good authority that both he and Alaric Velarius will join the season this year."

Understanding of Selene's implication hit Harlow like a punch in the gut. "No, you can't possibly think..."

Selene shrugged. "Why shouldn't the Krane girls pair with the most eligible Illuminated bachelors? If they want sorcière wives, surely any of you would be more than good enough for them."

Harlow's breath shuddered through her lungs at the thought of Finn McKay. Memories of stormy eyes and dark, unruly hair threatened to drag her into a past that she wouldn't, couldn't return to. Not here, not now. Not ever. That had been the start of everything falling apart, time and time again.

To tamp down the panic that threatened to take over she spoke quickly, hoping reason might curb this ridiculous idea before it went further. "You're the ones who always said the Illuminated world is dangerous. That they're too powerful for their own good. And weren't we *just* talking about how no one is forced to do anything during the season?"

"I know, I know," Aurelia said, in what Harlow assumed was meant to be a calming tone. "And if none of you are interested in them, that will be just fine."

Selene opened her mouth to say something, probably that it was *not* just fine, but Aurelia shook her head. "None of you have to do anything you don't want to, but an alliance with the McKays and others like them would increase the sorcières' power and standing in the Orders. Surely you cannot deny that."

Harlow shrugged. She couldn't deny it, but she did think it rather hard that she and her sisters were to be offered up like prizes to the Illuminated. She knew better than to say such a thing to her parents though. The thought that a pairing might be made between Finbar McKay and one of her sisters made her ill.

No. That simply would not do. Her mothers might not understand the danger someone like Finn posed to her sisters, but she did, all too well. Harlow wasn't going to let any of them be hurt by a self-centered, arrogant prick like him, and if she had to sabotage the entire season to keep him away from her sisters, she would.

CHAPTER THREE

Harlow was saved from needing to respond by her eldest sister's entrance. Thea Krane was a vision. No one could deny that she took after Aurelia in both looks and intelligence. Tall, statuesque, and graceful, she was the one her mothers should have been coaxing to align with the Illuminated. Perhaps they'd already convinced her.

Harlow was well aware that she'd been left out of family business, as well as Order business, while she reacclimated to sorcière society. After nearly two years living amongst humans, the sorcière were wary of her. It was to be expected, she supposed, but she wished things were different.

She missed being invited to rituals. Seventeen hells, she'd be grateful to be invited to one of the "witch and bitch" coffee dates she used to turn her nose up at. But most of her old friends had stopped speaking to her, and since her magical talent hadn't emerged yet, it made it even easier to avoid her. She wasn't sure how to gain people's trust again; she barely felt like she could trust herself most days. Her lack of magical prowess had a lot to do with that.

Octobre had come and gone, taking her twenty-fifth

birthday with it, and still she was stuck doing the equivalent of party tricks while most sorcière her age had manifested their true magical talents in ways that made them special. Selene and Aurelia cautioned her that her time living with humans may have stunted her progress, to be patient, but it made her feel like a failure all the same.

Thea kissed their mothers sweetly, taking off her coat and depositing it in the back office. Perfect Thea. If she weren't Harlow's best friend in the world, it would be easy to hate her sister. In addition to being so beautiful she was often mistaken for one of the Illuminated, she was brilliantly talented in the deep magics.

Her artistry had manifested on her twenty-third birthday, the ideal age for a prodigy, and now that she was twenty-seven, she created some of the most beautiful artwork Harlow had ever seen. Paintings, sculptures—her personal works were stunning. Here at the shop, she used her talent to restore the most precious of the ancient books the maters took in.

When Thea returned from the back office she asked after everyone's plans for the day. When no one responded to her she pulled her dark brown hair back into a low chignon and raised her perfectly groomed eyebrows. "What's going on?"

Selene poured herself a cup of tea. "We were telling Harlow about the season. She is not thrilled."

Thea laughed. "Of course she isn't. That's our Harlow." Her sister hugged her close, whispering, "It won't be so bad, pal. Just come to the events. You don't have to talk to anyone if you don't want to."

Harlow looked into her sister's luminous brown eyes, nodding. "Fine, fine. I'll come."

She wasn't going to tell Thea that she would go to these events primarily to keep her sisters from being sold off to Finn McKay. She and Thea were close, but they had differing opinions about how to change the Orders' outdated traditions. Thea thought subtlety and transforming things from within was the best method, and Harlow thought they should burn it all down.

There was no use in arguing; she could give in now or give in later, but Selene wore the look that told Harlow she wouldn't stop until she agreed to join the antiquated pairing ritual. She sighed deeply, then asked, "When is the first event? I suppose I'll need to secure an adequate wardrobe if I'm going to participate."

Aurelia and Selene both looked as though they'd collapse from the relief of not having to convince their second-eldest further, but Thea's eyes glittered with suspicion. Harlow rolled her eyes and lifted her shoulders when Thea pinched her.

Selene shot them a look that screamed, *Behave*, before beginning her instructions to Harlow. "The opening ceremony is tomorrow evening at the Grove, as it always is, followed by the garden party at the Statuary this weekend. For the opening ceremony you won't need anything new, as we'll dress for ritual. You may wear the pallyra you already have. Is it clean?"

"Of course it is." The heavy ceremonial robe was always clean, since she was never invited to important rituals anymore. At least she didn't need to worry about that. Harlow shifted uncomfortably. She knew it was time for the season, of course, but she'd lost track of the exact date it began. Tomorrow felt very soon. Too soon.

Selene nodded, then added, "You don't have to wear anything elaborate to the Statuary party. It's a casual event."

A laugh bubbled in her throat. *A casual event.* Nothing was casual when the Illuminated and all three of the lower Orders were involved. She wracked her brain. Her penchant for vintage might serve her well, but she needed to call in an expert if she was going to get through this without the gossips tearing her to pieces, and the socials... that would be the worst. All the people she *knew* talking about her return to immortal society. Her stomach soured and she swallowed hard, trying to keep her throat clear of the bile threatening to rise. The season's events would be covered relentlessly online and in print, and since she and Mark were already a story, she knew she'd be a target for the whole season.

Selene sensed her concern. "I'll transfer money into your account, darling. Get whatever you need. Perhaps you might ask Enzo to help you."

Harlow smiled in response to cover the anxiety wringing her stomach into knots. Enzo Weraka ran one of the most prestigious ateliers in Nuva Troi and they'd been the best of friends for most of their lives. Until Mark anyway. They hadn't talked in a while, not like they used to. Selene deposited Harlow's phone in her lap as she trailed back up the grand staircase. "Better text him now. I'll make calls about the money."

Harlow waited until she heard the door to the residence click shut, two stories above the shop, before turning to Aurelia and Thea, who'd begun shelving new books. "Are the sillies participating in the season too?"

Aurelia frowned. "I've asked you not to call your sisters that."

Thea shook her head, pursing her lips in disapproval. Of course, Thea always had her best manners on, even when it was just their family. Harlow's eyelashes fluttered in frustration. "Well? Will they?"

Aurelia nodded. "Yes. They are eligible to participate, and all three of them wish to attend the events."

"Even Larkin?" Harlow could hardly imagine her youngest sister, who was barely twenty, wanting to be paired.

Larkin was a quiet girl, studious and musically inclined, who had never shown an ounce of interest in lovers. Unlike the twins, Indigo and Meline, who had been obsessed with romance from the time they could form words, Larkin had never cared.

Aurelia smiled, her eyes warming at the thought of her youngest. "I think Larkin is hoping to make friends, more than anything else. And the season is a wonderful opportunity for that as well."

"Sure," Harlow said, barely concealing the ultra-dry note of sarcasm in her voice as she shot a text to Enzo. *The maters have convinced me to join the season.*

Before he could answer, she added: *Anything in my size in your treasure trove that I can wear to the Statuary this weekend?*

And then, because she'd missed him horribly and wished they could be the way they were before Mark: *Please tell me you're going to these things too. I won't make it without you.*

She waited, feeling shaky and impatient, hoping he'd respond. She'd drifted apart from everyone that mattered when she and Mark had moved in together, but since the breakup, she'd heard from Enzo a few times and they'd made halfhearted plans to have dinner that neither had followed through on.

After what felt like eons, her phone vibrated in her hands. *Client here. Come by at lunchtime?*

She sighed with relief and shot back immediately. *See you at one.*

Enzo hearted her response and she tucked her phone into the pocket of her frumpy pants, feeling some measure of relief. Enzo would take care of her clothes, and maybe their friendship could get back on track in the process.

Selene returned, with Larkin, Meline and Indigo in tow. All three still lived at home and they swept into the shop like a wave of buoyant energy, especially the twins, who both kissed her and asked if she was all right. They were like the sun and the moon, identical but for their hair. Meline was tow-headed, her hair so fair it might be silver, and Indigo's was darker even than Thea and Larkin's. The worry that poured off the three of them told her they knew the true depth and breadth of what the gossips and socials were saying about her. Akatei bless them though, they didn't say a word. Larkin squeezed her arm as she pushed a cart of new books ready to be restocked past her.

Meli was on the phone and computer simultaneously already, scheduling the various Order of Mysteries events that would take place at the shop in the early evenings in the coming week. Indigo unlocked the front doors, and a ray of weak sunshine pushed through the clouds as the first customer arrived. As everyone got to work for the day, Harlow's heart swelled. The seven of them were a well-oiled machine, working in perfect harmony.

Her mothers were the perpetual hosts, solving literary conundrums and matching people with books they never imagined they needed. No one left the Monas unsatisfied or without a sense that they'd come in contact with the Mysteries. Customers ranged from the lower Orders to curious humans, and Aurelia and Selene were as much a part of the attraction to the Monas as the books themselves. Harlow and Thea set about their work in restoration and curation, in the third-floor workroom, and the morning passed quickly in companionable quiet.

The workroom was Harlow's sanctuary. Shelves of new acquisitions lined the walls, with two large library tables at the center of the room. One was for Thea's restorative work, and the other for Harlow's cataloguing. Until her magical abilities manifested fully, she was in charge of making detailed notes about each of the acquisitions and Thea's restorations for the Order of Mysteries' records, before any of the volumes were distributed for sale, or for the Order's private collections, which were vast troves of magical knowledge.

For the most part, while the Orders socialized with one another, they remained quite separate when it came to governance and sharing knowledge. The outward reasoning was that each was specifically talented in one area of the world beyond humans' perception, and that it was best to cultivate those talents, rather than water them down with frequent intermixing. Anyone with half a brain understood this was the Illuminated's way of keeping them from forming meaningful coalitions. With just enough tension strung taut between each of the lower Orders, the Illuminated never had to worry about them rising up together.

That had only happened once, eighteen hundred years ago, during the War of the Orders. Those that had risen against the Illuminated had made a valiant effort, but were crushed within two years of the war's start. Though there had been perpetual peace since that time, the Illuminated made it clear that resistance against them would result in far more dire consequences now than it had then. They'd developed and controlled the only weaponry allowed on Okairos, and their vast financial and securities organizations made it all but impossible to push back, even a little. They liked to think of themselves as a benevolent oligarchy, but in truth, they were no better than the human mafia in most ways. And of course, they controlled even those heinous criminals.

The Illuminated controlled everything. Even this store, which they could take in an instant, though the maters had owned this property for hundreds of years. If they wanted it, they could have it. If they wanted one of the sorcière to marry Finn McKay or Alaric Velarius and restart their gene pool, they could have that too. But Harlow was determined that neither she, nor her sisters, would be the sorcières entangled with them.

Alaric might not be so bad; in fact, of all the Illuminated, he was one of the best. And his parents were as kind as the older Illuminated could be. But Finn McKay was ruthless, intimidating and cold. Harlow knew that all too well. The words of a first edition copy of *Lore of the Lilu* swam in front of her eyes.

Why won't you talk to me?

What would I have to say to you?

Harlow tried to shut out the memory of how those beautiful slate-grey eyes had narrowed at her. How he'd turned and walked away, without so much as a look back, as her heart had crumbled to ash. She clutched the buttons of her ugly blouse, as though she could stop it from happening if she gripped hard enough. But nothing could change the fact that Finn McKay couldn't be trusted.

With a deep breath, Harlow attempted again to focus on noting the quality of the text and images in *Lore of the Lilu,* but nothing she read stuck. Usually, the topic of the Order of Night's most taboo creatures would fascinate her. Tales of the infamous incubi and succubi and their many fantastical abilities had terrified Harlow and her sisters as children. She turned a few more of the fragile pages. A beautifully macabre illustration of an incubus turning a screaming sorcière into a succubus as a gallery of vampires watched sent shivers down Harlow's spine. She tried for another ten minutes to read the essays within the book, but despite its salacious topic, *Lore of the Lilu* was remarkably boring.

It was nothing like the stories Thea had told her when they were small, of incubi who could steal a sorcière's heart and turn them into a soulless monster. Harlow shivered at the memory. Even vampires were afraid of the incubi, but, incredibly, this collection of essays had reduced these impossibly strong creatures to a catalogue of physical attributes and hypothetical ways to kill them. That was of no interest; there hadn't been a case of incubism or succubism since the War of the Orders. Unlike vampires, who were humans who had been turned by the magic in vampire venom, the incubi were near-impossible to sire, and they were the only ones who could turn sorcière to succubi. Both species of the Order of Night had died out long ago.

Harlow sighed and slid *Lore of the Lilu* off its cradle and into its polyethylene sleeve, then turned her attention to watching Thea work at restoring something that resembled a bestiary. Her sister's hands pulled shimmering strands of magic from the air around the book. Thea's elegant fingers moved deftly as she wove reality to fit her vision, and a particularly lovely illumination of a gryphon began to emerge from the page.

"What book is that?" Harlow asked.

Thea glanced up. "It's a first edition of *The Heraldic Order,* not particularly rare, or old, but the illuminations were done in an early modern style."

Harlow watched as the words describing the Heraldic shifters became clearer.

"Can you even imagine what a world with gryphonic shifters must have been like?" Harlow asked.

Thea shook her head. "It's tragic, I think."

"Fucking Illuminated," Harlow swore, whispering it, even here in the privacy of the workroom. They'd executed immortals who'd joined the humans in the War of the Orders, including the Heraldic Order, which had consisted of shifters whose alternae were dragons, gryphons, alicorns and the like. Nowadays, most of the Trickster's Chosen could only shift into common animals. Nothing that threatened the Illuminated.

Thea sighed, but made no other remark. Harlow pulled her stool up to her sister's table, watching her continued work. "Nonetheless, your work is beautiful as ever. That looks nearly new."

Thea looked pleased at Harlow's praise. "Thank you, pal. It's really coming along. I should finish this one today." She glanced at the little clock on the windowsill. "Oh! Don't you need to be at Enzo's soon? You'd better get going!"

Harlow nodded. "You're right. I've got to go."

She grabbed her purse and slipped her phone inside, before escaping down the back stairs, sliding into her aubergine coat with a generous shawl collar. She tied the sash hurriedly as she rushed into the chilly spring afternoon.

The crunch of dried leaves, leftover from the winter, made a satisfying noise under her feet on the cobblestone of the courtyard as she hurried into the back alley to the shortcut that would take her to Enzo's atelier a few streets over.

The thick hedgerows of dawn viburnum gave off a scent of

vanilla and lilac that infused the alleyways of the Row, and Harlow couldn't help but slow her pace to breathe in the scent of renewal. Of life starting again. She rounded the corner, turning onto Mulberry Street, letting the feeling sink in, wondering if with all that was going wrong it was wise to feel this way. Just as she was beginning to feel foolish for letting hope kindle in her, a text came through from Selene.

Money's in your account. Have Enzo secure enough attire to get you to the Solstice Gala. Spare no expense.

She responded, *Thank you so much*, feeling grateful, but also frustrated at the amount of money a season would cost their family. Five girls, all needing dozens of garments and accessories, though her sisters were likely more equipped to weather the social season than she was. Her time navigating the upper echelons of human society with Mark had been less demanding on her wardrobe.

The Orders were extravagant when it came to clothes, but rigid about what was appropriate. There were dozens of rules to remember about color, motif, and fabric, whereas humans mostly cared about what they thought looked good and the newest trends. Thea once called the human obsession with "meaningless disposability" disgraceful, and it was one of her observations about them that Harlow completely agreed with.

Harlow sent another text to Selene to remind her that she would need her share of the family jewelry brought out of the safeguarded vault for the season and they were having a lively exchange about Harlow's propensity to lose things when Harlow stumbled into a wall of muscle.

"Careful there," the wall rumbled in a voice so deep she felt it in her toes.

Harlow looked up from her phone and was transported to the past. She was seventeen, and her entire body flooded with heat when she met the long-lashed eyes staring into hers. Finn McKay's hands steadied her, kept her from falling. His face was stony, serious as ever as he gazed down at her, but she saw the corner of his mouth twitch, as though he suppressed a smile.

The square jaw, the sensual lips, the broad shoulders and muscled chest were all enough to make her knees weak, but his eyes did her in. Eyes the color of a stormy sea, and so expressive she saw their history flash through them as they stared into hers. Then they went carefully blank, and his expression reformed into something cultivated and smooth, aloof, but alluring, and Harlow hated the way her breath caught looking at him.

He'd once described himself as "everyone's type," which was infuriatingly accurate. Their entire lives, people had been obsessed with everything he said, wore or did. He was the son of the richest, if not most powerful, Illuminated family in Nuva Troi, after all. But it wasn't just that, it was the aura of danger that always clung to him.

Unlike Alaric Velarius, whose mother was the arch-chancellor of the Illuminated Order and whose family was widely respected, the McKays were known for their vicious business practices and dealings in the hidden underworld of Nytra. Of course the fact that his family were some of the most terrifying Illuminated on Okairos only increased his allure for most people. She ripped herself out of the swoon her body had involuntarily dragged her into to glare at Finn as she pushed away from him.

"Watch where you're going, McKay," she muttered above the sound of her pounding heart. She prayed futilely to Akatei that he couldn't hear it, though she knew well enough that he could.

He laughed, dry and arrogant as ever, only compounding the fact that she knew he knew the effect he was having on her. "You're the one who ran into me, Krane. What are you doing here? Thought you ran around with humans these days."

The sneer in his voice grated on her nerves, flustering her. "Mark and I broke up."

"Right." He drew the word out to several dry syllables, and she couldn't tell if he was being snide or thoughtful. Probably snide, she decided when he kept talking. "I read something this morning about his level-up."

Harlow pushed past him, cheeks burning with humiliation, especially as his eyes drifted over her decidedly *frumpy* ensemble. Something like concern flared in those silvery-blue eyes, as though he regretted his comment. He grabbed her arm to stop her, then dropped it when she flinched. "Hey, I'm sorry."

Harlow looked up, infuriated by the way she had to tilt her head to look at him, his stupid floppy hair and the way his broad chest filled out the white t-shirt he wore under the leather jacket she knew he bought at a flea market when they were fifteen. She hated that she remembered that day perfectly.

"Sorry about what?" she bit out. He had plenty to be sorry for, that was certain.

He hesitated, gauging how angry she was. "About you and Mark. I was sorry to hear you broke up. He seemed nice."

Harlow's heart stopped beating for half a second, she was sure of it. It was a lie. No one thought Mark seemed nice. Mark wasn't nice. He was smart and charismatic, yes. But no one thought he was nice. Certainly not the Illuminated, who tended to despise humans who'd managed to carve out a bit of power and prestige for themselves in a world where they were meant to remain little more than well-cared-for livestock. The Eastons were just the kind of humans people like the McKays hated.

Some horrible part of her thought he *did* sound genuinely sorry, like the Finn she used to know. The one who listened when something was wrong and never judged her. The one who she'd spent hours talking to as a kid. But she knew better than to be suckered into thinking *that* Finn was here in this moment. That Finn was gone for good, washed away like flotsam at high tide. He'd been lost to her since she was seventeen years old, and he wasn't ever coming back.

"Whatever." It was an ineffective comeback, but Harlow couldn't think of anything better to say. She pushed past him and as she started to open the door to Enzo's atelier, she thought she saw his shoulders slump slightly. He turned and all the arrogance she knew and hated was plain on his face.

"See you at the Grove tomorrow." He strode away and she didn't like it one bit that her traitorous body paused to watch him go.

CHAPTER FOUR

"He's a dick, but that ass is worth watching," purred a voice in her ear.

She turned to find Enzo in the doorway of his shop, and threw herself into his arms for a hug. He smelled expensive, like vetiver and sun-kissed citrus, and he looked like a fever dream, dressed in a magenta suit, his eyes lined with gold. His silky black hair was tied back in a bun, and his rich brown skin was radiant, even in the vernal gloom that had descended over the afternoon.

"Come in, come in. The remodel is finally done and I want you to see what I've done with the place."

Harlow didn't miss the way Enzo's eyes carefully slid over her clothes, his face the bland neutral mask of a true professional. Her thoughts threatened to take her back to the sidewalk and Finn McKay, but she shoved them down. She was here to have Enzo help her find her way back to herself, after all, and if they could find their way back to one another in the process, so much the better. It was time to begin a new phase, one where she was a credit to her Order, her family, and her friends, instead of the perpetual mess she'd been for the past few years.

She took Enzo's hands in hers, trying to project all the feelings she'd been shoving down about losing her best friend to the surface, hoping that Enzo's talent as an empath would help him understand her sincerity. "I should have come before."

Harlow wanted to apologize a hundred ways, to say how sorry she was for letting things get so bad. Her mouth opened and closed, unsure of how to begin.

He drew her into another hug. "I should have asked you to come sooner."

Harlow felt all the tension leave her body. She and Enzo had been friends since before even she and Finn, since their parents had been close for ages. The distance of the last two years had been a strain, but in that one hug, she felt she was forgiven.

There hadn't been fights or conflict when she'd moved in with Mark, just worry and tension about his growing control over her. Everyone in her life within the lower Orders had warned her about the human obsession with magic and the world of those descended from the Illuminated. They'd warned her that Mark's interests might not be entirely focused on her, but on her status in the Order of Mysteries, as her mothers were on the high council of sorcière.

And there was always the subtle concern over what Harlow wasn't saying about things between her and Mark. Enzo had been the most worried, knowing better than anyone how long it had taken for her to recover from her only other true relationship, and he'd made no secret of how concerned he was with Mark's behavior. Harlow hadn't listened to any of her family or Enzo about the warning signs, and had been frustrated that they'd been right in the end.

Now, six months outside Mark's influence, she saw all too clearly how foolish she'd been. He'd isolated her slowly and carefully, until he thought she'd do anything he asked. When she wouldn't give up her Order's secrets, he'd kicked her out of their home, and the life she thought they were building together, cutting her off completely.

Putting things back together had been an exercise in humility. Harlow made amends to her family first, slowly over the last few months. She'd gone back to her work at the Monas, after a hiatus working in a human bookstore that Mark had approved of, and that had helped things with her sisters. Her mothers had been the first to welcome her back, no questions asked. But she hadn't known how to tell Enzo he was right about Mark, maybe because he was the only one who'd known her, who'd been to their apartment, who'd actually *tried* to see what she saw in Mark and who'd still seen the truth of the situation.

That all seemed far away now, as she stepped into Enzo's atelier. Burnished wooden racks of vintage and antique clothing mixed with Enzo's own couture creations throughout the light-filled space. The walls were painted midnight blue, and an enormous vase of curly willow branches and fragrant eucalyptus graced a round pedestal table at the center of the room. Plush, patterned rugs in deep ruby reds covered the slate floors and an enormous crystal chandelier gave the entire shop an air of luxurious artistry.

Wooden mannequins modeled Enzo's most exquisite creations, gowns of unparalleled beauty, touched with his magic in every stitch. He and Thea were very similar in that both their artistic proclivities were strong before their magic took hold, and now that they were in their mid-twenties, their artistry was amplified by their magical abilities, a natural extension of themselves.

Harlow wished she knew how her magic would manifest. She could do basic spells of protection, glamours of all kinds, and had an extensive education in magical lore, history, and craft, of course. As a sorcière, this was the way she grew up, learning the ways of mystery, and how to bend the filaments of magic, that held aether itself, to her will. But her own special ability, the way her own magic would carve the path of her life, refused to make itself known.

"Oh, Enzo," she breathed, pushing her own disappointment aside to be happy for her friend. "It's perfect."

He grinned, his straight white teeth dazzling as dimples punctuated his joy. She clasped his arm, filled with true happiness. It was easy to be happy for Enzo; she loved him, and being here, feeling their bond reforming itself moment by moment, was just what she needed. Harlow had tried so hard when she was with Mark to forget how much she missed Enzo and her sisters, but she never could.

Shame filled her for how she'd treated them, but she tried to push it aside, deflect it before he caught on. "I see your name a lot in Section Seven."

"Attached to all the most stylish socialites of the Orders, of course," he laughed.

It was true, he dressed the most elegant members of the lower Orders, and the Illuminated were some of his best clients. "I doubt I can afford your custom gowns these days, but I'm here for whatever vintage you can armor me in. I've been roped into the season."

Enzo pulled her onto the soft leather couch at the center of the shop. "The maters are finally insisting? Is it because of the McKays' interest in the Row?"

Of course he already knew. The gossip was out and it would make this whole thing even worse. She nodded. "Are you dressing Finn? Was he the client?"

Enzo grimaced. "Yes... Are you mad?"

"No, no. Of course not. Business is business and the Illuminated are good customers, even the McKays."

"Harls... I know you don't want to hear this, but I think Finn's changed."

A long silence passed between them.

"You're right. I can't hear that. You know what he did. How he hurt me."

"I do. I'll never forget it. He hurt me too, you know? But he's been here four times since he's been back from Nea Sterlis and he seems different. Like the old Finn. We even went for coffee last week. He asked about what types of guys I was interested in these days and offered to introduce me to a few of his friends he thought I might pair well with during the season. He wasn't just being nice either. He was... like he used to be."

Harlow swallowed hard. The three of them had been so close in school, and then one day Finn snapped, and Harlow and Enzo weren't good enough for him anymore. She shook off the memories before she could fall into that abyss.

"Did he apologize? Did he explain himself? Did he say why he spent our entire sixth year making our lives a living hell?"

Enzo cupped her cheeks in his hands. The familiarity of the gesture warmed Harlow's heart. "First of all, Petra is the one who did most of the misery-making, so let's put the blame for that where it belongs. Second, I didn't ask him to explain or apologize. I don't have to."

He was right. Petra Velarius had done most of the work to turn Harlow and Enzo into social pariahs, but Finn had done nothing to stop her. He'd just walked away from them both and never looked back, until now, apparently. A sob caught in her throat as Enzo's words fully sunk in; he hadn't asked *her* to apologize either. One of his many gifts was his deep empathy, his magical ability to see what was on people's hearts. He'd forgiven her instantly, as soon as he recognized the apology that welled in her; she'd felt it happen.

"I wish I had your abilities," she said, understanding his change of heart when it came to Finn, but not able to trust it herself. The McKays were poisonous vipers, and even if Finn wasn't aligned with what they were doing now, he wasn't innocent either. "But I can't trust him. You understand?"

Enzo nodded. "I do. It was different with the two of you. I get it."

She took his hands and squeezed. "I am just really, *really* happy to have your help getting ready for this. You know how nervous these things make me."

Enzo grinned again. "You will be beautiful at every event. I'll do everything I can to make your season perfect, right?"

"I don't need to be perfect. Just presentable."

Enzo rolled his eyes. "Come on, Harls. It's just you and me. Admit it, you want to slay them all with your devastating curves. Especially after Section Seven called you frumpy this morning."

His tone was matter-of-fact, not judgmental. She knew he was seeing what Selene and Aurelia did—her outer appearance as a reflection of her inner turmoil. Harlow bit her bottom lip. "I do, a little, but here's the budget."

She pulled up the amount she had to work with on her phone and Enzo barely glanced at it. "You're good."

"What? That's barely enough for two of your couture gowns, let alone a season's worth of wardrobe."

"Come here."

He pulled her off the couch and back towards an area of the shop where a desk sat in a corner nook flanked by tall bookcases, all full of books about costuming and fashion throughout the centuries. There were several marble pedestals arranged in front of the tall windows, which displayed some of the books with illustrations. One particularly beautiful one depicted different pallyra, showing off the ceremonial robes of the Immortal Orders in all their glory. Harlow stood gaping at the spectacular collection of rare books.

Enzo touched her arm, guiding her toward the book of pallyra designs. "Your sister finished my collection last year, for the remodel, and it's so popular with clients that they wrote an article about it in the Times. Apparently, I have the most extensive collection of books on fashion history in the country."

Harlow smiled. "Thea is so good at sourcing collectors' material."

"I don't think you understand, Harlow. She tipped off the Times. My business has tripled since the article. They've been calling me fashion's greatest scholar, which is true, but still bizarre to read in print. I'm dressing your entire family for the season on whatever budget you can afford. Your family means the world to me, they always have."

He took her by the hips and guided her in front of a floor-length gilded mirror. "You're going into this season with a killer wardrobe. I won't have it any other way. In fact, come look at what I've put together for you already. I have a few options for the Statuary party I think you'll love."

Enzo showed her to a rack with her name on it, full of jewel tones that would set her skin and hair aglow. Most of the clothes were for daytime events and he began the work of measuring her for the gowns she'd need for Solon Mai and the Solstice Gala, helping her onto a platform so he could have access to her limbs. She tried to chat with him, while he did so, but he hushed her.

"I won't be able to keep my numbers straight if you talk, so zip it."

She did as he asked, grateful for everything he was doing for her. Grateful to Thea and her parents for always treating Enzo like family, and that they all loved him as dearly as she did. His parents had been killed in a horrific train accident when they were in secondary school and the maters had welcomed him to every family dinner, brunch and high holiday celebration after that so he'd never be lonely in the huge townhouse they'd left him.

When he was finished measuring he helped her down from the platform. Tears pricked the corners of her eyes; she'd missed Enzo so much it hurt sometimes, and spending this time together made the ache in her heart sharper. She looked him straight in his dark brown eyes and tried to be brave. "I made a lot of mistakes when you were honest with me about Mark and I regret them all. You have always been a good friend to me, my best friend aside from Thea, and I am sorry for shutting you out."

Enzo nodded solemnly, accepting her apology with his signature grace. "Are you okay? *Really?*"

Harlow knew he already knew the answer. That she wasn't okay. That some days she worried she was too damaged to go on, that no one would ever be able to love or respect someone as foolish as she was. That she feared that she was the kind of person who simply *attracted* bad people.

Enzo cupped her face in his hands. "Harls, you know that's not true, don't you?"

He didn't often let on that his empathy sometimes worked a little like mind-reading, as he knew it made people uncomfortable. But now, Enzo's eyes were soft with love for her, apparently caring little for whether or not his supernatural ability to read her creeped her out. Harlow averted her eyes, wiping hot tears away.

"You had other partners between Finn and Mark that were good to you. What about Kate Spencer?"

Harlow smiled. Katerina Spencer had been a supremely good girlfriend for the few short months they'd had together. When she'd moved back to Nea Sterlis to help her sire open a new winery and transferred to Aphelion, Harlow had been sad to see her go, but they'd only dated for a few months and she'd understood. She'd met Mark just a few days later. "She left me too."

Enzo rolled his eyes. "That was different and you know it. What happened with Mark wasn't your fault. It was his. I wish you could see that."

"I'm sorry for everything that happened between us," she whispered, wanting to avoid talking about Mark more. "I should have handled things differently. Especially when I came home. I needed time to sort things through."

Enzo squeezed her arm. "I know, Harls. You didn't have to say it."

Her head tilted to the side. "I didn't *have* to say it, but you should expect better from me."

"Fair enough." He squeezed her hands hard. "Want me to help bring the first round of things to your new place?"

Harlow shifted her weight uncomfortably. "I know you're busy, with things starting up tomorrow and everything..."

Enzo's chiseled brow furrowed. "Why don't you want me to see your apartment?"

Harlow looked at the herringbone pattern in the expensive wood floors, tracing it with the toe of her shoe. "It's... It's... Not very nice. But it's what I could afford when Mark kicked me out."

Her best friend's jaw clenched. "Why would you think I'd care about that kind of thing?"

Harlow shrugged, not saying what was in her head. The sorcière cared about how things looked. They were Nuva Troi's aesthetes. And her apartment did not give evidence that she was from one of the Order of Mysteries' oldest and most prestigious families. She loved it, but she knew that others would not, and she didn't think she could stand it if Enzo hated it.

"I'm coming over. Don't argue." He picked up an armful of clothes and began packing them for transport. The command in Enzo's voice reminded her that *he* was the true heir to the arch-chancellor's position. That when he came of age, Aurelia would step aside and he would head the Order. She couldn't help but smile.

"Wear comfortable shoes. It's a climb."

CHAPTER FIVE

"It's no wonder your ass looks so good," Enzo laughed, lagging half a flight behind her. "This is a workout."

Harlow paused, shifting the bulk of the clothes she carried slightly. "It's a bit of a hike, I know. And the building could use some work... I'm sorry the elevator was out. It's like that sometimes..."

"Harlow, stop. I like it."

She squinted slightly, but like most empaths, Enzo rarely lied.

"Really. I love these green walls, and the layers of peeling paint are actually very charming."

There was no hint of sarcasm in his voice, to her surprise. He saw what she did in this place: worn beauty. The Illuminated didn't allow much to fade on Okairos. It was one of the many double binds of their rule. The world was well-kept, beautiful, and in many ways safe, but its people weren't free. Places like this building, that showed their age, were extremely rare.

They walked the last few flights in silence. The building was owned cooperatively, and when the last owner of the penthouse had died, none of the tenants could agree on who should buy it next. Preserving the structure of the building had been important to the board, as well as not washing away the building's history with magic. They'd been looking for someone who wouldn't go to the Illuminated to complain about the layers of age that had failed to be restored. When they'd first read Harlow's application and seen her name they rejected her, but when they'd heard she'd lived two years among humans, they'd allowed her an interview.

When the board finally let her in to see the apartment, she'd emptied her meager savings that day. To her, the place was perfect, but she knew it wasn't what most people she knew would have chosen. Now, her heart fluttered nervously as she pressed her palm to the cool metal plate that scanned her DNA. The locks made a soft *snick* sound as the security system recognized her and the door opened softly.

Behind her, Enzo gasped. "Oh, Harlow. Now I *completely* understand..."

She saw it again for the first time, through Enzo's eyes. The exposed brick peeking through the crumbling white plaster. The ancient black steel-paned windows that arched towards the soaring ceilings, and the view of Ambracia Bay from the terrace that filled the undressed windows. There wasn't much in the way of walls, only the bathroom was contained—and there was barely a kitchen. Only a stove, a fridge and an ancient stepback hutch remained, as the former tenant's children had stripped the place of anything of value when clearing her estate. Harlow's few possessions sat in boxes still, except for her bed and a few nearly-empty wrought iron racks for clothes.

"You could use some furniture... and a real kitchen," Enzo mused. "But I love it."

He dropped his armful of clothes on her bed and pushed open the double doors that lead to the terrace. "This is unreal," he gasped, looking out at the blue water of the bay. The sun was peeking out from the clouds, gearing up to give Nuva Troi a rare sunset over the bay.

She joined him outside, smiling. "Do you want to change it all? Make it shiny and new again?"

Enzo shook his head. "No. I love this. I love seeing the history of the building in all its glorious layers." His eyes closed for a moment and Harlow could feel the threads of magic shifting around them. He was probing the building. "It's structurally sound. The sorcière here have done good work to make sure the building is safe, while allowing the aesthetic features to age naturally. It's absolutely genius."

Harlow grinned. "I thought so too, to be honest. It's unlike anything I've ever seen."

"The Illuminated cannot tolerate age..." he murmured as he wandered back inside. "It's a shame, really. Age and decay are nothing to fear. Everything about this place is beautiful."

Harlow didn't answer. They'd been over this a million times in their youth, questioning why the Illuminated were the way they were, dreaming of a better world. Enzo started to unpack the zippered bags they'd brought her new clothes upstairs in, but she shooed him away.

"You've done enough. I'll hang them. Do you want something to drink? I have..." she peered into her fridge. "Water or some oat milk."

"Not even a kettle for tea?"

She grimaced at him. "Of course I have tea and a kettle. What do you want?"

"Something dark and smoky."

She smirked. "You sure you're talking about tea?"

Enzo laughed. "It was very nearly a single entendre. But I do want some tea."

Harlow took a smoky black tea blend with a hint of vanilla out of the hutch and started the water to boil as Enzo slipped off his shoes and settled onto her bed. "Your linens are lovely."

She nodded. The fresh white bedclothes had been her gift to herself when she moved in. They were soft and silky, with half a dozen pillows piled like clouds to nest in while she watched the ubiquitous Nuva Troi rain or the rare sunset. Enzo did just that now, and when she handed him a steaming mug of tea, she snuggled in close next to him.

"So, are you seeing anyone?" she asked.

He shook his head. "No, I've been so focused on finishing the atelier I haven't had time for that. I cleaned out the townhouse too. It's rented now."

"How's that feel?" Enzo's parents' home had been a haven for all when Clarissa Weraka was arch-chancellor of the Order of Mysteries. The Werakas had been some of the few sorcière who believed in a world without such strict delineations between the four species of humanoid creatures who populated Okairos and their home had been full of joyful parties and quiet respite from the busy world in equal turn.

"At a certain point, it got easier. When everything was in boxes, one day it was just *things*. It had become a time capsule, you know?"

She nodded. After Enzo's parents died he hadn't changed a thing in their five story townhouse in Uptown.

"I was afraid to move anything for so long. I just kept the dust off things. But the longer I let it sit, the worse things got inside." Enzo patted his heart. "Last year, I walked downstairs and was afraid to make coffee. I was afraid that if I moved another mug the last memories of my mother would disappear."

Harlow looped her arm through Enzo's and he rested his head on her shoulder, assuming a pose they'd sat in thousands of times since childhood. Her mind's eye saw Clarissa bustling around her kitchen, dark tresses piled on her head, her sculpted face bursting into laughter as she made breakfast for Enzo, Maurice, and Harlow. Harlow had eaten hundreds of breakfasts at Enzo's as a child. When Clarissa and Maurice died, Enzo wasn't the only one to lose his family. Clarissa and Maurice were Aurelia and Selene's closest friends, and Enzo their godchild.

Harlow's chest shuddered at the memories. "I should have been there to help you."

Enzo nodded. "I wish you had been. I...I should have called you. It's not all your fault, you know. I made mistakes too. Gods, I needed you though."

Tears trailed down both of their cheeks and Harlow felt Enzo's arm tighten around hers as he sipped his tea.

Enzo's voice was shaky when he said, "I should have fought harder for you to come home, Harls. I saw his heart, what he was like, and I wasn't as supportive as I should've been."

"You tried to be..."

He cut her off. "A little. I tried a little. But my mother wouldn't have liked that I let things go so easily, Harlow. If you're not ready to meet someone new, maybe the season isn't the best idea..."

Now Harlow cut Enzo off, her voice struggling through the sharp pain clenching her throat. "It's okay. I'm ready. I need to get back into the swing of Order life and prove to everyone they can trust me. It'll be the easiest way to move on." Enzo nodded, understanding the depth of Harlow's emotions, probably better than she did. "As bad as Mark was, I'm worse. I thought I deserved it all—all his anger, his jealousy—I thought I caused it. And even though my head knows that's not true now, my heart doesn't." It was the first time Harlow had admitted this to anyone, even herself.

"Then is this really the time to get into a new relationship?"

Harlow shrugged. "It's been six months. Things are getting better, and my family needs me. The Order needs me. I need to be a part of our world again, Enzo."

He kissed her forehead. "I completely understand, but what are you going to do if they want you to pair with Finn?"

Harlow shook her head. "As long as it's me, not my sisters, I'll do whatever it takes."

"Harlow," Enzo said, drawing her name out several syllables longer than it was, but he didn't say anything else.

No one understood duty to the Order of Mysteries better than Enzo. He shook his head, but didn't respond to the thoughts that were probably broadcasting themselves at a shout from inside her head. Like Thea, Enzo believed in the magic of the season, that it drew the right people together and matched them perfectly, so long as they showed up with open hearts, willing to find love. Harlow wasn't sure that was anything more than lore, and an open heart certainly wasn't going to solve anything between her and Finn.

The rain started up again, obscuring the last of the sunset. Enzo drained his cup and slipped his shoes back on, taking his cup to the kitchen sink. "Let's get these clothes hung up and order some food, okay? No more sad talk right now."

Harlow smiled. She could do that. She typed their order into her Dined, Dealed, Delivered app for delivery of fancy burgers and parmesan fries from the pack-owned pizza joint, Gastro Lupo, around the corner. Enzo unzipped the wardrobe bags they'd used to transport the clothes and they began hanging them together in companionable silence. When they began chatting again it was to gossip about the newest hit television show, *Knight's Children*, a *very* loosely historical drama about medieval vampire knights.

Enzo was complaining about the intricacies of inaccurate portrayal of medieval costuming and makeup when the burgers arrived. The rain broke long enough for them to eat on the terrace on two plastic chairs Harlow had found in the dumpster out back. When the last fry had been consumed and Harlow was sure she'd burst, Enzo kissed her forehead.

"You know how to get to the Grove, right?" He asked as he dragged her up from the terrace tile.

Harlow nodded as she walked him to the door. "The invitation will come at the eleventh hour and act as a portal..." Harlow rolled her eyes. "And then I'll be in our super secret ritual spot in the woods somewhere, right?"

Enzo shook his head. "You might try taking this a little more seriously."

"I might," she laughed as he ran down the steps. She closed the door. "I might."

CHAPTER SIX

When she turned back to her empty apartment, it felt lonely for the first time. It wasn't that she hadn't felt sad here before—she'd rarely felt anything else since she moved in—but she'd also valued her solitude while she'd grieved the loss of her relationship with Mark. Tonight, for the first time, she wished she had furniture and a TV or stereo, instead of just her phone. She wished she had her boxes of books and art, packed away in the Monas' attic. All things Mark had insisted she give up when she'd moved in with him.

A phantom movement caught her eye, but when she turned nothing was there. A shiver slipped deep into the secret parts of her, rattling her to her core. It might be one of the building's many ghosts, but in her heart she knew it was something worse: the memory of what she'd abandoned. Harlow tried her best never to think about the giant black cat Mark forced her to leave behind, but tonight it was impossible not to. She missed Axel so much her heart nearly burst with guilt. The helpless feeling she got any time she allowed herself to think of him squeezed her lungs until she could barely breathe.

Harlow left the double doors to the terrace open, letting the chilly spring air fill her lungs as she blinked tears away. It was pouring again and the rain made the view of the city below and the bay look like a painting. She climbed in bed, knowing she couldn't escape the looming loneliness that crept in, filling her with grief. The witchlights that floated above her bed went out with a quiet word and Harlow stared into the dim darkness of her nearly empty apartment.

Mark hadn't wanted anything that reminded Harlow of her "old life" when they'd moved in together, emphasizing that they were building a life together outside of the Orders. When he kicked her out, she hadn't had much to take with her except her clothes. Keeping Axel had been his cruelest move though. Mark didn't even like the feline; he'd kept him to spite her, and she'd been too ashamed to tell anyone that she'd left her baby behind.

Harlow couldn't escape the knowledge that the emptiness of her apartment was a half-hearted punishment for failing with Mark, as was her general failure to dress in ways that made her feel good, or feed herself nourishing food. She hadn't been taking care of herself, because when she'd chosen Mark, that was supposed to prove to everyone that she could do things differently than the other sorcière, and that she would succeed at it. That the years she'd spent wasting herself at uni were over, and she was making a new life for herself.

Except nothing worked out the way she'd planned. Things ended with Mark. She never applied to grad school. Her magic never deepened or grew. She was lost, adrift in all the things she'd done wrong. Every time she tried to make things better, it seemed like they just got worse instead. So she'd opted to do nothing for herself. She was practicing what she considered neutral neglect, trying to keep her head down and not make anything in her life worse than it needed to be.

She'd seen a therapist for exactly one month and when they'd asked her to name something she'd done right since she was seventeen she came up blank. Harlow knew the therapist was trying to help, that they thought this question might help her see that she hadn't *actually* done everything wrong. But her failure to come up with a satisfactory answer sent her into a spiral of shame that lasted for weeks. She'd never gone back. What was the point?

Harlow tossed and turned for a few minutes, trying to get to sleep, but she couldn't relax. It felt like beetles were crawling under her skin. She opened up her phone and scrolled through Section Seven until she found posts that would prove she deserved the punishment she was doling out to herself. There they were, both of them, fortuitously grouped together, one right after the other.

Mark Easton Leaves the Antiquity Row Dud Behind For Good. There was a photo of Mark helping Olivia out of a black town car. Olivia's dress was so short that Harlow could see her panties, which was probably the point. Jealousy roiled in her gut. It was the worst kind of jealousy, because it wasn't even that she wanted Mark back.

No, she genuinely wanted Mark to move on, and quickly. Just not with someone who looked like *that*. Everywhere Harlow had curves, Olivia was lithe and sensual in a way Harlow knew she couldn't pull off. In the last days of their relationship, Mark had made many comments about how unattractive he found her, saying she'd "let herself go," more than once. It stung that he'd found someone so easily that fit every qualification that Harlow could not. Even now, as much as she resented him, she wrestled with the fact that she wanted him to want her back, for her to be the one who rejected him, not the pathetic way things had ended.

She took a deep breath, trying to interrupt the spiral of shame she was headed down. *Next.*

She'd already caught sight of the telltale stormy eyes, but as she scrolled up her stomach did somersaults. *Illuminated Playboy Finbar McKay Returns to Nuva Troi With Prize.*

Harlow snorted; apparently the "prize" was Petra Velarius. At the very least it pleased her that Petra would be absolutely horrified not to have her actual name published alongside Finn's, but Section Seven was alarmingly sexist at times, to provoke people into loudly complaining, sharing stories on all their socials about the publication's retro attitudes. It was all an act to get more engagement.

Neither Finn nor Petra looked dressed for a night on the town. In fact, they were both wearing jeans and sweaters, as though they'd been to a coffee shop together. And she knew for a fact that he hadn't returned to Nuva Troi *with* Petra. She'd been here all along, working at her parents' investment firm. Still, it grated Harlow's nerves to see them together.

She did the thing she was always promising herself she wouldn't and started to scroll through the comments on the post. Most were humans, speculating that Petra and Finn would be the season's "it" couple. People talked about them like they were characters in a TV show or book, saying they "shipped" them together.

A text came through from Meline that blessedly blocked her view of Petra's sour expression. *If you're reading Section Seven, don't believe everything you read. Finn and Petra were at a family dinner at Umbra. They cropped Alaric out of the pic.*

I wasn't looking at it, she typed back.

Indi says to tell you that you're a big liar-liarface and that you wouldn't've texted back so fast if you weren't. CAUGHT!

Mind your own business, sillies.

You ARE our business, came a text from Indigo, popping up in front of Meline's. *Get off socials and go to sleep.*

Harlow sent the twins both a series of black heart emojis and then tossed her phone aside, resisting the urge to go back and read the posts she'd skipped earlier about the protests in Nea Sterlis. There had been more pushback from humans as of late against the restrictive laws that treated them as objects, rather than people. She couldn't say she blamed them, but she wasn't sure what to do; the Illuminated proved time and again that they were too powerful to resist. Harlow groaned into her pile of pillows, angry that she'd let herself get so worked up. There was no way she was going to sleep now.

"Lux," she muttered and the soft witchlights illuminated.

Harlow got up to look at the clothes she and Enzo had hung together. Her pallyra was ready for tomorrow evening and she couldn't help but feel excited to wear the embroidered, floor-length robe. She stroked the soft, heavy black fabric, tracing the dark flourishes that bled into the cranes and wolves that represented her family's lineage. Tomorrow wouldn't be so bad, as the opening night of the season was more about the ritual than socializing, as she understood it.

The Statuary party gave her pause though. She stared at the dress Enzo had picked out for her to wear to the party held in one of Nuva Troi's many elegant public gardens. As an outdoor event, it was expected that the attendees would dress casually, but what that meant was hard for Harlow to tease out, especially when she looked at what she'd be wearing.

She ran her fingers down the decadent fabric of the dress for the Statuary party. It was a deep, dark blue, with a high neck and a buttoned bodice that she was to leave slightly undone to reveal the lace trim of the vintage bustier she would be wearing underneath. The hem of the dress fell to her knees, and there were a pair of tall black stack-heeled boots that tied with satin laces to wear with it. It all seemed the opposite of casual to her, especially when combined with the gorgeous slate-grey wool frock coat she was to wear over the dress.

But Enzo had assured her that this was what was considered a "casual" look for the season. That the tailored high-waisted pants and blouses were suitable for morning and early afternoon events, but nothing after two o'clock. After two, day dresses were the only acceptable option, and between five and nine, cocktail dresses, and after that only evening gowns. The additional rules about colors, jewelry and ornamentation were baffling to her, despite her love of clothes.

The ritual of it all was mysterious, and she had to admit she was feeling a bit lured by the siren song of jewel tones on the racks in front of her. She ran her hands over the luxurious fabrics. When she'd unpacked the rest of her clothes, ones that had largely had Enzo's touch in one way or another over the years, she saw that her wardrobe was one she recognized as a sorcière of the Order of Mysteries.

"Not frumpy at all," she whispered to her wardrobe, thinking of the terrible Section Seven post.

No, now she would finally feel like she was dressed as *herself*, rather than dipping into human trends, or the other Orders' fashions. She couldn't help but feel proud. She'd always loved her people's ways, their deep commitment to using their magics to enrich the arts and academic pursuits. The Order of Mysteries made the world a more beautiful, more intelligent place, and she loved that aspect of her heritage, even if she wasn't directly contributing to it yet.

Completely unwelcome thoughts about Finn began to creep back in now that she was idle. She pushed away thoughts about him and Petra and instead considered what Enzo said about him changing, about the way he'd looked today. Older, but still beautiful in that perpetually mussed way he had, his eyes glowing, if faintly, with immortal power. And the dangerous pull of him was the same as it had ever been, wicked in its intensity.

She flopped onto her bed and closed her eyes, feeling his hands on her, steadying her. Feeling their slick skin slip against each other, further in the past. The feel of his mouth on her neck so long ago as they'd kissed in his car. The way the backseat of the Woody, his sturdy SUV, had felt like the whole world as they'd ground against one another in a feverish wave of lust that had been building between them for years. Her fingers slid into her pants at the memory of his hands in the same spot, her pleasure mounting as she remembered the way his face looked when his fingers had stroked the crotch of her panties, finding them drenched with her desire for him.

It was no different now, but instead of remembering the teenagers they'd been, her mind supplanted the people who'd run into one another on the street today. The memory of that night mixed with the fantasy of fucking him now. Her body heated, responding to her touch as her imagination replaced teenage Finn with the adult she'd been so furious with this afternoon.

Her breath came in short gasps as she rubbed tight circles around her swollen clit, imagining Finn pushing her dress up as she straddled him in the backseat of the SUV, pushing her panties aside as he slid effortlessly inside her. The thought of him filling her so easily was incongruent with the memory of how they'd fumbled through their single sexual encounter, but she didn't much care. That night, awkward as it had been, had been perfect, a promise of learning together, that their passion would carry them into the kind of sexual prowess that would leave them both satisfied for centuries. It wasn't that she hadn't had good sex after Finn; she had, perhaps even better. It was that she'd never felt quite as deeply for a lover as she had for him that night—she never *let* herself feel that way.

But now she felt too much, other emotions clouding whatever pleasure she might have gleaned from mixing the memory and the fantasy of him. The feel of him driving into her, moaning words of devotion in her ears, grew ever more distant as she failed to bring herself to climax. Harlow's head fell back as a moan escaped her lips, frustration mixing with the elusive power of the memory. The fantasy slipped away far too quickly, which inevitably brought about thoughts of everything that followed from what happened in real life. The months of sorrow. The worry that clouded both her parents' eyes every time they looked at her.

Harlow sat up gasping, yanking her hand from her body. She marched herself into the bathroom and turned the shower on cold. There would be no thinking of Finn McKay and that one perfect night, the one that ruined everything. And there *certainly* would be no fantasizing about him now.

If she was going to do this, honor her family's wishes and complete the season, she was not allowed to think of him that way, *ever*. She shed her clothes and stepped into the water, letting the freezing streams cool her hot skin and drag her back, firmly, into the present, where she promised herself she would stay.

Chapter Seven

Though the thick fabric of the pallyra was heavy, it wasn't warm enough for a cold spring night in the sacred Grove. She'd only been there for the high holy days, the turn of the wheel, never for any of the other rituals that all four of the Immortal Orders conducted there. Her participation in Solon Mai rituals of years past told her that she'd need to layer well underneath her ceremonial outwear, so she'd slipped on a pair of leggings and a sweater and planned to wear comfortable boots when she heard her phone buzz. It was Enzo.

Wear something hot under your frippery tonight, we're invited to the Velarius afterparty.

She sighed, thinking of opting out, but another text came through just as she was about to suggest her favorite pub, the Three Besoms, instead. Thea this time.

I know Enzo is texting you about the Velarius party. You're going. Dress appropriately. Jeans are fine, but for Aphora's sake, wear a nice sweater or one of those vintage jackets you love. No UNT sweatshirts.

There was a pause while the little dots cascaded, indicating that Thea was sending another text.

I mean it. Wear something beautiful, Harlow. Show them who you are.

Thea texted like she was writing a formal letter, and though it made Harlow's heart race to think about mingling with all the people from her past who'd made her miserable in school, she texted both her sister and Enzo back to assure them she'd dress appropriately.

Show them who you are.

Who was she, anyway? There was nothing wrong with dressing down, but her frumpy clothes weren't who *she* was. She'd been purposely hiding herself. Her throat clamped closed. Letting herself be seen felt dangerous, but maybe she could live dangerously. Maybe to get through this, she would have to. Harlow yanked off her cozy boots and leggings and pulled on a pair of wide legged jeans.

Wear something hot.

Next, she discarded the sweater in favor of an expensive, cream-colored henley with a black bra underneath. To keep warm, she slipped on a black shearling-lined vest, and then unbuttoned her shirt one button more than she usually would. She slipped the gold medal she always wore, depicting Akatei's three faces, back on and felt instantly better, protected by the Order of Mysteries' patron goddess.

Her phone told her it was 10:48. The invitation would arrive at the eleventh hour, so she didn't have much time for hair and makeup. She wished she hadn't frittered the day away reading a new romance novel, but it was what it was. She had just enough time for a simple glamour. It was all she could manage with her limited magical abilities anyway.

Harlow went to the bathroom and while she looked in the mirror, pulled strands of magic from the air and wove them around her until her lashes were darkened and longer, 'til the dark circles under her eyes disappeared and her long honey colored hair curled away from her face. She gave her already high cheekbones a boost and left her nose alone, adding a faint blush to her pale cheeks.

A sound of paper scraping the wide planks of the wooden floor outside the bathroom caught her attention. The envelope she was waiting for slid under the front door and flew towards her, of its own accord.

"Ridiculous," she muttered, plucking it from the air as she slid on her pallyra, fastening the thick fabric with nearly invisible metal hooks.

She opened the envelope to read what she assumed would be a charming inscription, but instead found a long list of small-print legalese about consenting to participate in the season. Her eyes floated over the bloated verbiage until she found instructions at the bottom of the page that directed her to speak the Illuminated Order's motto for Okairos aloud and press her thumb to the page to indicate consent.

Ab ordine libertas. From order comes freedom. She begged to differ, especially when it came to the Illuminated's ideas of "order," but she said the phrase aloud and pressed her left thumb to the page. Sharp pain lanced through her skin and she felt momentarily emptied out of all energy as she was transported from her apartment to a clearing in the forest.

Above her, Okairos' twin moons waxed to near fullness, lighting the enormous redwood trees that surrounded her with uncanny light. The woods were silent, though she knew they must be full of others like herself. She staggered a bit, feeling hollow; she'd never felt that way after portaling. Harlow glanced at her thumb—there was no trace of a wound, but a distinct feeling of unease lingered inside her. Perhaps it was just anxiety about the evening ahead.

A lantern sat at her feet. Harlow saw nothing to indicate what she was supposed to do next, so she picked it up, pressing her fingers to Akatei's medallion for comfort. The light from the lantern dissipated a bit, tiny globules of light falling to the forest floor and floating like fireflies along the path ahead of her, into the dark forest.

Harlow took a step forward and the effect intensified. The short train of her pallyra dragged the ground behind her, her billowing sleeve flowing prettily as she held the lantern aloft, and she felt like a true sorcière for the first time in a long while. She was meant to follow the trail of lights, she supposed. The woods were eerily quiet as she walked, and though she peered deep into the darkness, she saw no other lights, no other indication that the forest was full of this season's participants.

The faint sense of unease occurred to her again. Something just beyond her understanding pressed at her senses. She tried to use her second sight, but found she could not. In a moment of panic, Harlow struggled to feel the threads of magic around her, the most basic skill a sorcière had, but felt nothing at all. Her heart began to pound louder with every step she took.

Somewhere in the distance, a shrill scream pierced the air. Cold fear laced her blood. That was no animal, it was a *person*. She halted, trying to pinpoint the location of the scream, but it was as though it came from everywhere. Just as suddenly as it began, it stopped, and the air was thick with magic. She felt the threads around her sing to life again, full to bursting with aethereal power so potent it threatened to overwhelm her. Then there was a great contraction in the air and she was nearly knocked to her knees, the breath sucked roughly from her lungs.

When she could breathe freely again, the threads of magic around her felt the same as they always did. Sounds of the forest at night time, rustling pine needles in the breeze, an owl in the distance all echoed in her ears. And voices. When Harlow looked around, she saw trails of light through the forest, indicating there were dozens of people in the forest, making their way to the Grove, just like her.

This was strange magic, like none she'd ever felt or seen, and she'd seen a lot of fantastic magic in her twenty-five years. She kept following the trail of bobbing lights until she spotted Enzo and Thea, walking together a bit away from her. Ahead she could see the clearing where the ritual would take place. She gathered the train of her pallyra up in her arms and waded through the dense brush until she reached them.

They both reached out to kiss her cheeks and Thea strung an arm through hers as they huddled together.

"Hi," Harlow murmured quietly. "That was odd, wasn't it?"

The two of them looked mildly confused.

"What was odd?" Enzo asked. "Using the portal?"

Thea nudged her in the side, playfully. "You haven't been out here in a while, have you? Snapping from one place to another can be disorienting."

Her sister was right, of course; she hadn't been to a ritual or portaled since she moved in with Mark, but that wasn't it. Enzo and Thea smiled at her, gently, sweetly. Both were perfectly calm. They hadn't had the same experience she did. Harlow sensed that this was neither the time nor the place to explain. "Yeah, I guess I haven't portaled in a while. I felt a little sick after."

Thea smiled sympathetically. "Are you feeling better now, pal?"

Harlow nodded and the three of them walked together in thoughtful silence toward the Grove. As they neared the clearing, the air changed, growing cold and viscous. Harlow felt the individual strands of magic, distended and thick with too much aether. Her brow furrowed as she pushed through them, feeling them scrape against her spirit body uncomfortably. The part of her that, as a sorcière, was always just beyond the material world cringed at the unnatural feeling of bloated aethereal threads. The trails of bobbing lights floated in a spiral to the night sky and all around the clearing, as more and more of this season's participants and their families gathered in the clearing.

Enzo took her elbow, and Thea led the way through the crowd to where Selene and the sillies stood together. Aurelia was standing on a low stone dais in front of a pair of wooden effigies decorated in purifying herbs, with the other leaders of the Immortal Orders. Merhart Lear, the arch-chancellor of the Trickster's Chosen, stood next to her, locs of their snow-white hair twisted into a crown atop their dark head, the emerald green of the Order of Masks' pallyra setting off the cool undertones in their skin beautifully. Lear was one of the few snow leopard shifters and their feline intelligence was evident as they chatted amiably with Aurelia. Berith Sanvier, leader of the Order of Night, stood apart from them, eyes narrowed in annoyance.

The Order of Night had no use for unions between themselves or other Orders for the purposes of procreation, but they participated in the season to broker unions of power. Harlow had to admit that not all vampires were bad, nor were they *inherently* evil; Katerina Spencer was one such example, along with her House. But Berith and the House of Remiel were something different.

Berith was said to be one of the first vampires, not sired by venom but born from a union between the first of the Illuminated and a human who carried the extremely rare Gene-V. And he was the Order of Night's king, rumored to have killed tens of thousands of humans in his long life. His moonstone eyes were cold in contrast to his crimson pallyra as he gazed out over the growing crowd. When Pasiphae Velarius, the arch-chancellor of the Illuminated, joined the other three leaders on the dais, Berith squirmed as the glowing light of her eyes fell upon him.

"Someday that will be you up there," Selene said to Enzo as she hugged his shoulders proudly as any parent.

"Not for another hundred years or so," he mumbled, looking slightly embarrassed when she kissed his cheek. The arch-chancellor of the Order of Mysteries was required to have completely matured into their magic, something that usually took at least a century.

Meline and Indigo giggled, while Larkin looked slightly

bewildered by the crowd. Harlow moved to stand behind her younger sisters. She wasn't sure if it was what happened in the woods, or some deeper instinct, but something about this gathering didn't feel safe. Someone brushed against her back and when she turned, she found Finn McKay standing behind her. His pallyra was gold, as all the Illuminated's ceremonial garb were, and its color did nothing for his pale skin. It was one of the few times she'd ever seen him look bad in something.

His stormy eyes lit softly in the dark, but were narrowed in suspicion as he looked at the dais. She forgot herself and asked the question on her lips. "What's wrong?"

He glanced down at her, as if noticing she was there for the first time. "Getting here was strange."

She was about to ask him what he meant when Pasiphae began talking. Unlike Finn, the gold of her pallyra set off her brown skin and glossy black hair beautifully. "Welcome friends. Welcome to the seventeen *hundredth* season."

The crowd murmured a greeting back to her. Seventeen hundred years of this. The Illuminated had started this tradition a mere hundred years after the War of the Orders, after they had finished exterminating those that stood against them—the season was a show of goodwill, according to them. Harlow fought to keep the sneer off her face. She felt Finn shift behind her as more people crowded into the clearing. His chest bumped into her back and she felt his hands on her arms, bracing them both as the space in the Grove tightened, constricted by the surge of the crowd.

"Sorry," he breathed, his mouth uncomfortably close to her ear. Heat flooded her abdomen, gathering at her core in a way that made her want to scream. How dare her body betray her this way?

Harlow had space to step closer to her family, to give him more room, but she stayed stubbornly rooted in place. She told herself it was because she wasn't going to move for him, but part of her knew she enjoyed the heat pooling between her legs, the heavy weight of her breasts, so apparent now that he was touching her. When the crowd settled, his hands disappeared. He stepped backwards, a shock of cold air hitting her back, but she could still feel the heat of him like she was an asteroid drawn into his orbit—she couldn't quite step away.

Pasiphae was talking about duty now. The Orders' duty to the world, to humans especially, to maintain safety and order, to ensure the freedom and prosperity the world now experienced, would continue through the strength and cooperation of the four Orders. Harlow could hardly hear the words. Her body tuned itself to Finn's. She could hear each breath he took, and her chest rose and fell in time with his.

And she knew, because she knew how sensitive the damn Illuminated's senses were, that he could hear the way her heart beat faster, feel the synchronized breaths they were taking, and could likely scent the wet desire gathering between her legs.

"Unbelievable," he growled as he yanked her close to him, one hand spreading possessively across her abdomen as he pinned her to him, his other arm shielding her from some oncoming threat.

Harlow didn't have time to wonder at the close contact. A vampire stumbled into them hard as Finn's arm warded her from the impending collision. Harlow stifled a cry as she crumpled into Finn's embrace at the impact. Vampires got their physical strength from the Illuminated though, and it only took Finn's outstretched arm to push the creature away from her.

"So sorry," the vampire slurred. "Had a bit too much of a drunk co-ed before I came. My first season...." She hiccupped slightly and wiped a trickle of blood from the corner of her mouth.

Harlow wondered if the co-ed had survived the encounter, as the vampire disappeared into the crowd. It took a lot to make a vampire drunk, and if she'd been drinking only from the co-ed, they were very likely dead. The utter helplessness she felt at this realization was frustratingly familiar, as was the rapidity with which her mind put it aside. There was nothing she could do. As long as the Illuminated's control over Okairos went unchallenged, there was nothing anyone could do about individual acts of violence like this.

Finn's arm lingered around her waist longer than was necessary, his fingers spreading over her belly as though he wanted to caress every soft curve of her body. Her breath caught in her chest and she felt his lungs stop in time with hers.

"Are you all right?" he whispered. The arm he'd used to shield her lowered slowly, as though he was afraid something else might threaten her and that hand, the one that pinned her against him, only pressed harder, as though he was as desperate as she was to drink in the electric heat passing between them.

She nodded, unable to form words. No one had seen the encounter, it happened so fast, but Enzo glanced back at her, noticing the trajectory of Finn's hand, which was moving tantalizingly lower by the second. Enzo winked at the two of them. *Winked*.

Finn's hands fell away and he pushed her upright so quickly she nearly fell forward into Thea, who seemed determined not to look back, even though Enzo was elbowing her suggestively. Harlow glanced back at Finn, only for a second. It was a mistake. His gaze was fixed on her, his expression full of so much longing she felt it reverberate through her, tingling in all the best, worst spots, until her toes involuntarily curled inside her boots. His lips parted, as though he too was remembering the way it felt to be deep inside her, and then the mask fell.

The open look in his eyes shuttered and his expression was dry arrogance again as he backed away. "See you at Alaric's," he muttered, his beautiful upper lip curling slightly.

She hated him. She wanted him. She *hated* him more.

Pasiphae's speech was ending and she lifted her hands and shouted, "*ab ordine libertas.*"

The crowd echoed her and the effigies burst into flame with the heat of Pasiphae's power. In the moment of combustion, time slowed, and dark shadows clouded Harlow's vision. She didn't know why exactly, but she turned to look back at Finn—he was still backing away, but he too was suspended in time, while the rest of the crowd moved normally.

Nausea flooded Harlow's body, bile burning her throat. She felt unnaturally bound and helpless. Her movements slowed as she turned, as some unknown force restricted her movement. Finn's eyes met hers before he turned away, and they glowed with intense light. As time sped up again he looked back over his shoulder and nodded once.

Whatever just happened, he saw it too—or rather, he sensed the same thing she did. The wrongness of it. Whatever was happening here was more than it seemed. Harlow had always hated the idea of the season, and now she feared it.

CHAPTER EIGHT

Hot drinks were served and people mingled, but Harlow stuck close to Enzo and Thea. Meline and Indigo disappeared into the crowd with their massive group of friends, but Harlow noticed that Larkin stayed with Selene, her eyes betraying the panic she was feeling. Harlow watched as Selene had a brief, quiet conversation with her youngest sister. When Larkin nodded, Selene smiled and motioned to her and Thea.

"I'll go see what's up," Harlow said.

Thea and Enzo were busy talking to a small group of sorcière that Harlow knew by sight, but hadn't gone to school with. They were some of the few sorcière that moved to Nuva Troi from elsewhere; all were musicians and artists of some kind or other, and one was a celebrated model. Thea nodded as she broke away from their little group. No one had asked her even one question, so enamored as they were with Thea and Enzo.

That was fine with her, but she'd hated the way their eyes skimmed over her, as if they were trying not to look at her. She knew everyone read Section Seven religiously. They'd all seen her humiliated several times now since she and Mark broke up; the most recent posts just happened to be the worst since Mark was clearly flourishing and she wasn't.

"I'm not feeling very well," Selene said. "Larkin is taking me home to watch movies in bed."

"Scary movies," Larkin said, a mischievous glimmer in her green eyes.

"We will settle on a psychological thriller," Selene said definitively, the same mischievousness in her countenance. "Tell Li-li that we're leaving, all right darling?"

Harlow nodded, smiling at Selene's nickname for Aurelia. "Of course, Mama." She squeezed Larkin's hand. "See you tomorrow, pal?"

Larkin smiled bravely. "Yes, I'm going to be at the Statuary party. Definitely."

She sounded like she was trying hard to convince herself of the idea and Harlow's worries about Larkin being too young to be at a season renewed, but it would be decidedly unfair to keep her from the festivities, if that's what she wanted. Harlow knew all too well that sometimes you just had to try things to find out what was right for you and what wasn't.

Aurelia was chatting with a few members of her book club when Harlow found her. She patted Harlow's arm and smiled at the news that Selene and Larkin had gone home, barely pausing her conversation. Harlow's heart ached at the way the sorcière her mother spoke to simply ignored her, as though she did not exist. She'd known these witches her entire life, and now their gazes drifted over her like she was a ghost, something best ignored. When Harlow returned to the group surrounding Thea and Enzo, they were waiting for her. "We're going to the Velarius party now. You ready?"

Harlow nodded and she took Thea and Enzo's outstretched hands. None of their magic was mature enough to portal significant distances on their own, but as their powers had already manifested some time ago both Thea and Enzo could manage a trip across town and had just enough magic to bring her along. The others in the group blinked out of sight and Harlow drew a sharp breath in, closing her eyes and focusing her tiny bit of power so that it added to Thea and Enzo's. They would direct their travel, all she had to do was lend them her energy and wait.

When she opened her eyes, she felt fine. Nothing like she had when she entered the Grove. The realization struck her again that something had been wrong with magic at the opening ceremony, but she tried to brush it off. She looked around, taking in her surroundings to distract herself. They were standing behind a blossoming cherry tree in a rooftop garden in fashionable Midtown from the look of things below. This wasn't the Velarius estate in Uptown. "Where are we?"

Thea smiled a bit too sweetly. "This is Alaric's place."

Harlow narrowed her eyes at the familiarity with which her sister referred to Alaric Velarius. "You've been here before?" she asked, suspicion edging her voice sharply.

Thea laughed. "No, silly. But he did invite me and Enzo both. In an email."

Enzo nodded. "He did. He writes lovely emails."

Harlow shook her head. It was true that Alaric Velarius was a nice person, but he was heir to the Velarius fortune, and more importantly to his mother Pasiphae's seat as arch-chancellor of the Immortal Orders. One day, he would very literally rule not just Nytra, but all of Okairos.

She supposed it didn't really matter what she thought, so she kept her mouth shut and let them draw her into the party. Both of them shed their pallyra quickly and she handed hers to Thea, smiling sheepishly. Thea pulled at threads of magic and all three of their ceremonial robes disappeared.

"Back home where they belong," Thea said with a soft clap of her hands.

She was elegant in a long-sleeve black bodysuit and skinny jeans tucked into thigh-high black boots. Medallions of Akatei and Aphora both hung around her neck and her fingers were adorned with half a dozen gold rings. Enzo was dressed in an understated black button-down and peacock-blue jeans, with loafers. They both looked incredible.

Enzo shook his head, wrestling Harlow out of her fuzzy vest. "No to this. Send it home, Thea."

Her sister did as ordered, grinning as Enzo flicked another button of her shirt open. The lace of her bra was showing now. Harlow sighed as Thea's fingers wove magic rapidly, fixing her hair and makeup, she assumed.

It was the kind of profligate use of magic that made humans wary of them: needless, ridiculous, extravagant. It wasn't that humans couldn't learn to use magic; in theory they could. It wouldn't be as easy for them as it was for the sorcière, but anyone could do magic if they learned how. But it was as illegal to teach humans magic as it was for them to learn, and they rightfully resented the sorcière more than the other Orders as a result, despite the fact that the law was made by the Illuminated. She'd empathized with that resentment since she was a child, and it had been one of the things Mark said he'd loved about her most.

As though reading her mind, Enzo shook his head. The practical boots she'd chosen disappeared before she could protest. He yanked a pair of stack-heeled boots out of the aether and had them on her, while Thea sent the others home.

"*Now* you're ready," Enzo declared as he turned her toward the mirrored windows of Alaric's apartment. She looked good. Everything in the outfit strategically hugged her curves, fitting and flaring so her legs looked a mile long and her chest was tastefully exposed.

"Okay," she said quietly. "I look kind of..."

"Hot," Thea finished for her. "You look hot, Harlow. Not frumpy, miserable, or any of the other things all the socials have been saying. You look like *you*."

Harlow's lips curled slightly, but she felt every muscle in her contract at the thought of the party beyond the cover of the tree. Out there, music was playing and she heard people talking and she knew as soon as they walked in, they'd be talking about her, pitying her.

"Let's go," Enzo said as he took her hand. "Rip the bandage right off, okay?"

She nodded and followed them down the pea gravel path that was littered with petals from the dozens of blooming cherry trees that dotted the rooftop garden. A bar was set up near the doors to Alaric's place. This was nothing like her penthouse, which was tiny in comparison. It was, like most things the Illuminated coveted, both old and new at the same time. Everything was beautiful, nothing showed a hint of age, even though much of Alaric's furniture and decor were likely vintage, mixed with precious antiquities.

Just as she'd expected, heads turned as they walked through the group of familiar faces, but most eyes lingered on her sister and Enzo. And just like at the Grove, the rest slid over her as though she were invisible. For that, she supposed she ought to be grateful. Only one gaze rested on her. She shook her head; Finn McKay was glowering at her from under a tree.

He wasn't alone. A slender, blonde vampire was flirting with him. He nodded absently as she talked, his eyes never leaving Harlow. The vampire followed his gaze and then she was glaring at Harlow as well.

"Excuse me," Harlow said to Thea and Enzo as the vampire stalked off in a fiery huff. Finn didn't seem to notice that his companion had disappeared. Similarly, if Thea and Enzo said anything to her as she left them, she didn't hear them. She tried to convince herself that it was because she and Finn McKay needed to have a word, not because they were drawn to one another like opposing ends of a magnet.

"You noticed something was off at the Grove, didn't you?"

she asked before she'd even reached him. She knew he could hear her as she neared. He stood so still, it was unnatural.

The intensity of his eyes drifting over her set her heart to pounding as he leaned harder against the tree. "No pleasantries then. I like it."

She rolled her eyes. "What did you see?"

He shrugged, looking bored. Too bored. He was putting on an attitude, wearing it like a coat. She could feel the eyes at her back and he could probably hear everything people were whispering, but she was grateful she could not. His face stayed carefully aloof, but his voice lowered significantly. "It isn't what I saw. It's what I heard."

He took out his phone and fiddled with something. The music changed to a popular club song and got significantly louder. "I'm in charge of the noise this evening," he said. "Better that we're not overheard."

She nodded once, but didn't turn. She wouldn't give them the satisfaction. "A scream. Did you hear a scream?"

She saw the look of real worry in his eyes as he nodded, though the rest of his face didn't move from that insufferable expression of bored annoyance. Everything about him said he couldn't care less about social conventions, and yet he still managed to look perfectly put together. His slouchy vintage band t-shirt draped across his muscular chest, and he'd had the audacity to wear low-slung grey sweatpants and sneakers. Everyone else was dressed to the nines in their "casualwear"— and Finbar McKay was dressed in sweats. Only he could get away with something like that.

"You've made quite the sartorial shift," he remarked, his eyes running over her body again. Something about it felt appraising, rather than lewd, like he was checking her over for wounds after a battle. She didn't like the way her heart grasped onto the idea that he might care how she was faring.

The tone he used confused the way he looked at her. Harlow

couldn't tell if he was being sarcastic or not—if he was insulting her, or simply making an observation. She wasn't sure how to react, so she glared. "None of your business, McKay."

He laughed, his eyes crinkling at the corners in a way that nearly melted her resolve to keep hating him. "Right. Got it, Krane. But if you don't want it to be my business, you might try buttoning another button." She turned her glare into a glower and he threw his hands up. "I'm just saying. That's a very eye-catching shirt."

He said the words, but his eyes were locked on hers. In fact, though he'd clearly appraised her, his focus hadn't lingered anywhere but her eyes since she'd noticed him watching her. It was far too intimate.

As he shoved his hands back into his pockets she caught a clearer view of the tattoo around his left arm. As she'd walked up, it had looked like a beautifully rendered sleeve of black line art; now she saw the details of the image on the inside of his forearm more clearly. A snake wound around a sword and a horns up moon in the background. Lilacs bloomed behind the sword, encircling his forearm. The sight of the flowers stopped her breath.

It had been a spring night, in early Mai; the windows had been down in the car and the scent of lilacs drifted in, her favorite flower. The memory of him above her, pushing her hair away from her face as he'd whispered that he... No. No. *No.* This was *not* allowed. She had forbidden herself to think about that night and she would stick to it. The lilacs on his arm meant nothing. It was a coincidence, nothing more. Plenty of people liked lilacs.

She broke the connection between them by stepping away. He cleared his throat and shifted his stance against the tree. A bloom flushed his cheeks that matched her own.

"What do you think it was?" she asked, changing the subject. "The scream?"

He shrugged, conspicuously turning his arm so the inside of his muscular forearm didn't show again. "I really don't know. Nothing good. Did your sense of magic just... disappear?"

She nodded. "Yes, and then everything kind of contracted and then it all came back."

"Until the ceremony. Something happened when the effigies combusted. I know you felt it too."

Harlow started to answer, but the change in his expression caught her attention. The interest that lit in his eyes when she was talking died and he was no longer affecting boredom; now his expression was something else entirely, though she couldn't tell what. She turned slowly to find Petra Velarius standing behind her with a bottle of sparkling wine and two glasses. Her sleek ebony hair was pulled into a ponytail so tight it looked like it would give her a headache, and the black sweater dress she was wearing was so fitted Harlow could count her ribs.

Finn pushed off the tree and walked past her without a second glance. "Later, Harls," he said quietly as he passed her.

Petra heard, her head snapping over her shoulder, her dark eyes narrowed into a glare. Petra Velarius was stunning no matter what, but Harlow suspected she glared so much because she knew it made her look even more beautiful.

"Later, McKay," Harlow murmured as they walked away.

She wasn't sure what to make of the conversation, but she understood one thing: whatever they'd seen and heard, Finn didn't want Petra, or anyone else, to know about it. This was curious.

There was a bench a few steps away from Finn's tree and she sank into it, hoping to wait out the rest of the party here in peace. She wasn't to be so lucky. One of the Trickster's Chosen approached her. Their facial structure reminded her a bit of Merhart Lear, and like Merhart they wore their long hair in locs, pulled into an elegant bun at the back of their head.

Harlow couldn't help but think Enzo would be impressed

with their outfit, as they were wearing a midnight blue satin flight suit, with a pattern of golden swallows and clouds embroidered onto it. The collar was flipped up and the suit was unbuttoned halfway down their muscled chest.

When they smiled at Harlow, offering her a glass of iced tea, she felt an empathic connection snap between them. "You're a chameleon," she breathed, amazed to be meeting such a rare shifter by coincidence. Most of the Order of Masks had one animal form they could shift into at will, but chameleons could change into *anything* living, even other people, and they were notoriously empathic.

They grinned, dimples pressing into the cool-toned, dark skin of their face. "I'm Riley Quinn," they answered. "And it's good to finally meet you."

"Finally?" she asked, accepting the iced tea gratefully, noticing that Riley sipped a glass of their own.

"I'm a friend of Kate Spencer's. She says hi by the way."

Harlow nodded, blushing slightly. It was nice that Kate still talked about her. That explained the iced tea. Most people outside her family didn't know she didn't drink much anymore, but Kate knew, as they'd kept in touch sporadically over the years. "Do you want to sit?"

Riley grinned again. "Thanks, you're the only person I know here, except Alaric and Finn, and they're both busy."

Harlow laughed. "And you don't really even know me."

Riley bumped her shoulder with theirs. "I do though. Katie talks about you a lot."

"*Katie*?" She'd never heard anyone refer to Katerina Spencer that way before. She was too enigmatic, too epic for diminutives, in Harlow's opinion.

Riley laughed again. It was a nice sound. "I think I bring out her softer side. She deserved a nickname."

"That's something I'd like to see," Harlow said. Kate was notoriously wild and brash, Harlow's complete opposite. Their short affair had led her to believe they'd probably be better off as friends than lovers, but that hadn't dulled Kate's allure. "Well, if she's been talking about me lately, I'm nervous to know what you must think of me."

Riley's perfectly groomed eyebrows raised incredulously. "What do you mean? Katie thinks the world of you. I've never heard her say a bad word about you."

Something about that made tears well up in Harlow's eyes. She knew it wouldn't be the same if Riley knew Mark, and knowing that Kate spoke well of her touched her deeply. Maybe Enzo was right, she wasn't the asshole-magnet she thought she was.

"Well," she said, her voice rough with emotion. "I don't have a bad word to say about her either."

"I get it," Riley said. "Your relationship was complicated. The way it ended was complicated."

"True," Harlow said, resisting the urge to say more. Chameleons were tricky; their empathy made it all too comfortable to say things you'd never say to anyone else. They'd just met and they were already talking about exes. She couldn't help but be suspicious.

"Why have I never met you before?" she asked. "I'm sure I'd have heard of someone as obviously stylish as you."

Riley's laugh was drier now. "You're smart to be cautious, Harlow. I already liked you from what I'd heard about you. Now I like you more."

She noticed they didn't answer her question, but she didn't press it. Something about Riley Quinn was too intriguing to pass up. She didn't want to ruin the organic feel of their conversation. "Well I haven't heard anything about you and I like you too. Are you, by any chance, interested in meeting a renowned fashion historian and famous designer?"

"*Please* tell me you're talking about Enzo Weraka, because *yes*, yes I am. Finn said he'd introduce me, but I know Enzo's really your friend, and I admire his work so much. Did you read his article in Couture Review last autumn about aethereal iconography in pre-Illuminated fabrics and pottery? It was fascinating."

It was Harlow's turn to grin, though she noted that Riley mentioned Finn. She tucked that away for later, focusing on the realization that the magnificent shifter before her was obviously interested in her best friend for all the right reasons. She loved it when people saw the same genius she did in Enzo. "I think I see him at the bar. Come with me."

When she introduced them, she hardly heard the pleasantries they exchanged. The sparks flying between them were so obvious. She waited for a polite amount of time before asking, "Where's Thea?"

Enzo looked around. "Dancing, I thought. But I don't see her."

Harlow took a small step out of Riley and Enzo's cloud of flirtation to shoot her sister a text. *Where are you? I'm ready to head home.*

One flashed back immediately. *Ran into a friend from uni. Probably going to have a long talk at a coffee shop. Catch up tomorrow?*

Sure thing, she responded, then interrupted Riley and Enzo. "I'm going to take off."

Enzo looked momentarily distraught, but she shook her head as he took her hand. "I'm fine. Just tired and ready to turn in."

He kissed her cheek and she his, whispering, "Careful with your heart. I think Riley Quinn's a bit of a personality."

Enzo hugged her tightly. "Get home safe, love."

"It was so nice to meet you," Riley said with another dazzling smile.

She nodded, looking back once as she left to check on Enzo. He and Riley were already slow dancing and she shook her head with a smile. Someone who believed in the magic of the season as much as Enzo did deserved a little romance. She made her way back down the path littered with cherry blossoms and found the elevator, slipping out of the party without taking a second to look for Finn and Petra. She didn't want to know what they were up to.

The entire day had been a lot. Harlow needed time, space and possibly a big order of parmesan fries to process. So she went home, and put herself straight to bed. The first event of the season was over, and she deserved the rest.

CHAPTER NINE

The next morning, Harlow treated herself to a pineapple-coconut smoothie from the coffee shop around the corner, and then began to get ready for the Statuary party. She was exhausted from the night before, but she played an audiobook version of her favorite volume of children's folklore to distract herself from turning it all over in her head again.

She'd already spent the night dreaming about it, there was no need to go over it again. After she'd bathed she dressed, in between texts from her sisters and the maters, all checking in about the previous night. She shot off a few to Enzo as well, and when he finally answered he confirmed that he had not taken Riley home, but that he was hoping to see them again soon. A smile stretched across Harlow's face. Introducing them had been a good idea.

She stood in front of the ancient mirror that hung behind her front door. The glass was spotty, but it gave her a clear enough view of herself to make sure she looked all right. The dress Enzo chose nipped and flared in all the right places to make Harlow feel like an old film star. She'd been skeptical about unbuttoning the dress to reveal the lace of the bustier, but it gave the ensemble an elegantly alluring flair that kept it from being matronly.

Harlow managed a glamour on her hair that tamed her waves into large, loose curls that curved away from her face in a fashionable way that looked a bit undone. She did her makeup by hand, the human way, because she liked to. It was something she'd learned from Kate in uni and she'd kept doing it, even though she could get the same effect in mere seconds from a glamour.

The ritual of painting her face calmed her, soothed her frayed nerves and focused her scattered mind, which kept trying to go over the events at the Grove just one more time. Harlow preferred a somewhat natural look for daytime, but it still took the kind of effort that satisfied her. She set the entire look with glamour, to make sure none of her hard work would disappear in the hours that would follow, but she was pleased with the effect as she washed her hands. Harlow snapped a quick selfie in the mirror and sent it to Enzo and her sisters for approval. When no one had any objections, she walked downstairs to the car that was waiting to take her to the Statuary.

As they drove through the city, Harlow pressed her head against the cool window of the cab, drinking Nuva Troi in. Outside, the glittering neighborhoods of uptown melted into the rainy afternoon like watercolor paintings. Here, the buildings were centuries old, with enormous walled gardens that hid the estates from the view of the road.

Below, modern steel and glass rose shining in the drizzle, glowing before the ocean beyond. Everywhere, dark forest contrasted with the lights of the sprawling metropolis. Harlow's heart swelled with love for Nuva Troi. Despite its many flaws, she loved this city. Its dark beauty made her feel at home in a way no other place ever had.

The sky was grey and a perpetual drizzle threatened the rest of Nuva Troi, but the Statuary remained dry as a bone, due to the Illuminated's efforts to make the afternoon event perfect. The human cabbie shook his head as she paid him, suspicious of the magic that changed the weather for one part of the city but not the rest, she assumed.

Harlow couldn't say she blamed him. She too thought it was ostentatious to use magic for something as trivial as keeping party guests from getting rained on, but it was the way of the Illuminated to make certain the events of the season were perfectly executed. Harlow texted both Thea and Enzo to tell them she'd arrived and then wandered into the gardens.

The Statuary was a monument to "great" Illuminated warriors and politicians, as well as being the city's second largest botanical garden. Everywhere, a riot of flowers bloomed, filling the air with the heady scent of lilacs, roses, and the blooms from the jacaranda trees that lined the path that led to the center of the garden. Beyond the trees, the afternoon was ablaze with gold, purple and deep indigo flowers, as well as glossy green leaves everywhere she turned.

Many of the flowers wouldn't bloom naturally until later in the spring or early summer, but the Illuminated had used magic to ensure the entire Statuary was awash with color and scent. The effect was utterly enchanting, but also formidable. Forcing flowers to bloom ahead of season was an intimidating show of dominion to anyone who truly understood the way magic and nature interacted.

To speed up a growing season, literally thousands of factors had to be managed. It was complex magic that went against the aethereal order, the natural force of nature and magic working in concert. To do such a thing, in addition to keeping the rain away from the Statuary with a degree of ease that Harlow knew wouldn't drain the Illuminated in charge of these aspects of the party in the slightest, was a message to the lower Orders.

It was a reminder that everything in this world belonged to

the Illuminated. Everyone else existed at their whim. That included the lower Orders, who even with their combined power, inherited from their Illuminated ancestry, never stood a chance of resisting them. And so traditions like the season, started by the Illuminated to control the lower Orders, went on as though they were *enjoyable*.

Harlow wasn't well-versed in the deeper lore of the season, but she knew the tradition started after the War of the Orders to tempt the lower Orders into forming alliances with one another, rather than with humans, which would expand their numbers. Of course, because the Illuminated were generally good at whatever they put their minds to, especially when they worked as a group, it was successful. It helped that their resources were limitless, their magic unsurpassed.

Aside from the Order of Night, which procreated through infecting humans with their venom, the Order of Mysteries and Order of Masks had eventually been convinced to pair within their own groups over humans, and true societies had formed within the Orders, strengthening the traditions the Illuminated started as the Orders made them their own.

It had never been forbidden to form unions with humans, but after the season had grown in popularity, those pairings were fewer and farther between than before. The lower Orders became suspicious of human motives, and the humans were as fascinated with the lower Orders as they'd been with the Illuminated, creating stark societal stratification between the groups. The Illuminated got their way yet again, by exerting their wealth and influence over the lower Orders. It was how it had always been for two thousand years. The Illuminated shaped society as they saw fit and everyone else simply followed along.

It helped that they were excellent at throwing a party. Harlow resented the Illuminated's unchecked power over the world, and the lower Orders in particular, but she had to admit they knew what they were doing in that regard. Soft, sultry music floated through the air and all paths led towards the center of the gardens, where vast quantities of food were laid out on tables and people were milling about socializing.

Harlow saw plenty of people she knew, and would rather not speak to, but she located Enzo and Thea quickly. Thea looked lovely as ever in a creamy white and tan plaid coat that caused her pale skin and dark hair to glow ever so slightly. She looked like Aphora, goddess of the sea and moon, had descended to attend the first party of the season, and everywhere, people were staring at her, whispering.

"Where are the maters and the sillies?" Harlow asked as Enzo handed her a mug of steaming lavender tea.

"Not arrived yet," Thea said, looking slightly uncomfortable as the people around them whispered. "Is there something wrong with the way I look?"

Her expression was so genuinely pained, so nervous, that Enzo and Harlow burst into a fit of laughter. "No, darling," Enzo said when he was able to breathe again. "They're stunned by how beautiful you are. You're outshining the Illuminated."

Thea blushed, which only served to make her prettier, in Harlow's opinion. Through the crowd, she saw a tall, dark figure notice the effect. He was the same as he'd been in secondary school in many ways but older, less lanky, and still so beautiful it hurt to look at him. She hadn't seen him at all last night, at his own home, so it was a little surprising to see him now.

"Don't look," Harlow whispered. "But Alaric Velarius is coming this way."

Thea did not do as she was told. She looked directly at the Illuminated man who was pushing through the crowd towards them and her cheeks flushed further. Harlow noticed that his eyes emitted a faint glow, and the grin that spread over his face was full of dangerous joy. Was it possible that Alaric Velarius was already *in love* with her sister?

Enzo elbowed her. "He's going to make her a target for the entire season if he isn't careful."

Harlow shook her head, almost imperceptibly. She'd never been through a season herself, but she knew the stories. When the swan of the season was marked so early, the competition could get vicious. And Alaric Velarius was arguably the most eligible bachelor in all four Orders. Harlow had a feeling Thea's competition was about to be *very* angry.

The crowd parted for Alaric and Harlow saw he carried two cut glass flutes of rose cordial. She looked at her sister's empty hands and knew. He was going to hand her one of those glasses and every person that had been hoping they had a chance with Alaric Velarius, Okairos' prince of princes, would be crushed.

It happened in nearly slow motion from her perspective. His eyes were locked on Thea's as he greeted the three of them. As he approached, his dark skin glowed softly in the green gloom of the garden and his eyes shone with appreciation for her sister, along with the usual light of the Illuminated that seemed brighter when they experienced strong emotions.

"It's been a while," he said to Thea, his sonorous voice sounding a bit unsure.

"Yes," she replied.

He held out the flute of cordial to her sister, as Harlow knew he would, and when Thea's slender fingers curled around it, they brushed his, their eyes never faltering from the other's gaze. Harlow had a brief moment where she was tempted to make a gagging noise, but then she saw the narrowed eyes of those who'd hoped to have a chance with him.

She hoped he meant this, this small-seeming but monumental gesture. Otherwise Thea's season would be over before it began. If he decided on someone different, or this gesture wasn't meant to be as meaningful as everyone had clearly already determined it was, the jealous vipers that were now seething around them would destroy Thea's chances at anyone else.

Harlow needn't have worried that Alaric didn't know the impact he was making. As Thea took the flute from him Harlow heard him whisper, "Gods, Thea. I missed you. You look beautiful."

Her sister looked down at her cordial and smiled as he swept her cheek with a kiss so sweet and chaste several people in the crowd gasped. The first kiss of the season had been laid, and Thea Krane was its beneficiary. She was the season's blooming rose, and now everyone knew it.

Harlow tried her best not to smirk, but hardly succeeded. Enzo nudged her again and she thought he was agreeing with her that Thea's success had been incredibly satisfying to watch, but she realized too late that he was warning her. He'd been looking at something over her shoulder—she'd assumed it was the jealous onlookers, but the deep voice that sent shivers down her spine brought her back to the horrifying reality of the moment.

"Hey, Harls."

CHAPTER TEN

She turned slowly to face Finn McKay. He was dressed in a pair of slim fitting grey wool slacks, a white t-shirt, and a soft-looking navy blazer with the collar turned up. He was flouting tradition by not wearing a collared shirt, but she doubted anyone would care. His hair was freshly cut and yet still looked as though he'd just rolled out of bed.

Do not think of Finbar McKay rolling out of bed, she chided herself.

"Hello, Finbar." Her voice was chilly, as she tried to tamp down the incredible rush of heat she got from looking at him.

He winced. "Harls, don't call me that."

"Stop calling me 'Harls' and I'll call *you* something else."

He narrowed his eyes at her, then one corner of his mouth quirked up in that horribly smug, sensual way he had of smiling. "As you wish, Ms. Krane."

"If I had *my* wish, you'd be anywhere but here, McKay."

Thea hissed softly in disapproval and Alaric's face was strangely twisted with pain, as though she'd hurt *his* feelings. The crowd was listening, Harlow knew, and it was likely a misstep to be so rude to the heir to the McKay fortune, but she couldn't seem to stop herself. The way he'd just walked off with Petra in the middle of their conversation last night had stung more than she realized.

Finn blinked a few times and then nodded, taking a place next to Alaric, rather than her. The rest of them began to chat idly and slowly the crowd lost interest. Harlow felt the tension in the air relax, as people began to tend to their own business.

But Harlow did not relax. In fact, her body tensed so rigidly she thought her muscles might explode and she struggled to keep her breath even. Enzo and Finn were discussing one of Finn and Alaric's friends from Nea Sterlis who wouldn't arrive until just before the Solstice Gala, but Harlow couldn't follow their conversation. Her throat was dry and her mug was empty.

She murmured something about getting another drink and moved away, swiping a glass of rose cordial off a table, and wandered into the boxwood maze. She knew the maze would be occupied later in the party by the first sets of lovers to pair off. But now, while everyone was getting to know one another in the context of the season, it was blessedly empty.

A shiver ran through her. The air was a bit too chilly here to be drinking something cool. She turned to make her way back to the party to find hot tea instead, and saw him seated on a stone bench, as though waiting for her. "Are you following me, McKay?"

He rolled his eyes and pulled a pack of cigarettes out of his jacket pocket. "Don't flatter yourself, Krane. I just hate this bullshit. You know that better than anybody."

She did know that. They'd made fun of the season endlessly in secondary school, calling it a desperate way to find love. Now, here they both were, neither of them paired, both expected to make an advantageous match. Both the kinds of desperate actors they'd once derided.

"So why come?" She didn't know why she asked.

He looked up and she saw the kind of pain in his eyes she

remembered from when they were children. The kind that spoke of the cruelty of his parents, their ruthless ways. The kind that had brought them together, originally, because she and Enzo were the only ones who knew how bad they were, how much they hurt him.

He pulled a cigarette from the pack, lighting it with a brief pull on the threads of magic surrounding them, then took a deep drag. The smoke wasn't toxic smelling like some of the stuff humans smoked. It smelled of woodfire, dark honey and cloves, expensive. "You know why I'm here."

His voice was wary, no trace of his usual arrogance, or the swagger she'd come to know in the months after their friendship ended. She was tempted to read something deeper into his words, something beyond the obligation she knew he felt he owed his parents. The freshly cut hair and clean shaven face showed that he cared about *something* here, despite his obvious attempt to appear as though he didn't. She'd never seen him look so much like he was conforming to the Illuminated's stuffy sense of style.

Something nipped at her suspicion, making her wonder if it were possible he'd cleaned up because he knew he'd see *her*. Not that she cared about that kind of thing. She actually preferred him the way he usually was, longer hair, the merest hint of a beard. Her skin heated at a random memory of a video she'd seen on socials of him at the beach, walking out of the waves carrying his surfboard, water dripping off his bare chest.

Harlow shoved her reaction down deep and lashed out to get herself in line. "Still doing everything mommy and daddy say, I see."

As she swept past him, out of the maze, she heard the sharp intake of his breath. It was a low blow, and perhaps he deserved it, once. *But it has been nearly seven years,* a little voice whispered in her heart, *does he still deserve it now?* She wasn't willing to stay in the maze and find out. He'd hurt her by walking off last night, and that hurt compounded years of pain—pain that had only started because of him—and now his family was trying to destroy her family's livelihood. She wanted nothing to do with him.

The rest of the party was mind-numbingly boring and while Finn still primarily socialized with Alaric, Thea, and Enzo, he stayed well away from her. That was fine. It was all just fine. When Petra arrived to wrap herself around Finn, Harlow decided to find somewhere else to be.

Petra's satisfied smile was enough to make her regret giving up ground, but she didn't feel confident enough to stand up to her. Enzo looked concerned, as though he'd follow, but she shook her head slightly. He shouldn't have to lose his place in what was the most highly coveted circle at the party because she couldn't stand to be near both Petra and Finn at the same time.

Harlow spent an hour trying to find the maters and her sisters in the vast gardens, as her phone had run out of battery life, but could only locate Larkin. Her youngest sister sat alone at a wrought iron table, staring at her hands, her dark hair in her face.

"Hey, pal. Where's everyone else?"

Larkin looked up at her, her green eyes and heavy brows a mix of both their mothers. "They all found people to talk to."

"And what about you? Why are you alone?"

Larkin shrugged, examining her fingernails. "I don't think I understand all this very well."

Harlow sat down on the bench next to her and sighed. "Me either."

Larkin shook her head. "I know what *you* mean, but that's not what *I* mean."

This caught Harlow's attention. "Parse that out for me, pal."

"*You* mean that you don't understand all the frivolity. You think this is ridiculous and hate the forced nature of the season and the way the Illuminated control us."

Larkin's eyes were bright and intelligent, her words incisive. Harlow nodded. "That's a good approximation of how I feel. Sure."

"But *I* don't understand how to flirt."

Harlow started to say something sisterly and encouraging, but Larkin shook her head. "I don't understand *why* either. Why flirt? Why run off into the maze together? Why, Harlow? Why does any of that seem appealing?"

Harlow began to understand better. She pulled a piece of her sister's dark brown hair playfully, thinking of how she'd never liked romances, or to play romantic pretend games as a littling. "I don't know how to explain it. It's all a feeling I don't quite understand myself."

"What's wrong with me that I don't feel that way at all, ever?" Larkin's voice was full of such despair, such sorrow, that Harlow's heart cracked.

"Nothing, pal. Nothing at all." A tear rolled down Larkin's face and Harlow wiped it away. "Got your phone? Mine's out of battery."

Larkin nodded and handed her phone over. Harlow texted the maters and Thea. *It's Harlow, my phone's out of batt. Taking Larkin home. Tell Enzo I'm not going out this evening.*

Harlow didn't wait for a reply. She didn't want one. "Let's get out of here. Go home, order pizza and watch a movie."

Larkin wiped another tear from her face. "A scary movie, okay?"

"Scary as you please," Harlow agreed, knowing Selene hadn't indulged her last night and they'd probably watched a slew of mysteries instead.

They made their way out of the garden to where a line of cabs should be waiting, but none were there. Harlow groaned; it was too early. The cabs wouldn't arrive for another hour or two. She started to ask Larkin for her phone again when Finn McKay walked out of the garden gates holding his car keys, smoking another of his expensive cigarettes. He was leaving.

He didn't see them standing there. She had to make a quick decision. His name was out of her mouth before she could change her mind. "Finn?"

When he heard her, his head snapped around. It took him seconds to see Larkin's miserable face and her worried eyes. He'd been halfway down the block when she called to him, but he reached her side in seconds, the cigarette gone from his hand.

"Are you okay?" He sounded concerned.

Harlow wasn't sure what to say.

He seemed at war with himself for a moment, then before she could answer he asked, "Do you need a ride?"

There were a thousand reasons to say no, but her sister's hunched shoulders were all she needed. "I'd be grateful if you could help us get out of here."

He nodded and gestured to the street. "My car's parked this way. I'll take you home."

Harlow put her arm around Larkin and followed Finn to a dark green vintage sports car. "Will we all fit?" she asked sarcastically.

He grimaced at her. "It has a backseat."

"I'll sit in back," Larkin said, quietly interrupting.

He opened the doors and pushed back the camel-colored front seat so she could get in and then helped her inside. Harlow was surprised at how gentle he was with Larkin, and the soft tone of his voice as he showed her where the seatbelt was. For someone who struck fear and awe into most people, he could be surprisingly considerate.

The ride through the city was quiet. He cracked a window and started to light another cigarette. Before she could think better of her actions, she snatched it out of his fingers. The current that snapped between them was electric.

"Hey," he snapped, glaring at her sidelong as he watched traffic.

"Just because you can't get lung cancer doesn't mean you should smoke this shit. If it's illegal for humans, maybe you should lay off too."

She rolled down her window a crack, rolling her eyes at the old crank lever, and tossed the cigarette out.

"And now you've littered, Krane," he said, the sharp edge of his deep voice tempered by humor. "Now who should be following the rules better? Isn't littering illegal for humans too?"

Larkin snorted softly in the back seat and Harlow spun so fast to glare at her sister that her seatbelt choked her.

"Careful there, kitten," Finn murmured. "Don't hurt yourself.

She crossed her arms across her chest and sighed. "Don't call me kitten."

"Don't call you kitten, don't call you Harls." Finn shook his head, making eye contact with Larkin in the backseat via the rearview mirror. Both of them were laughing at her.

Harlow fought the urge to laugh along with them. Finbar McKay was not her friend, he was not her prospective lover, he was a problem. One she needed to solve, and quickly, as they were almost home. Harlow only spoke again to tell him how to get into the courtyard. When he stopped, there was awkward silence.

"Thanks for the ride," Harlow said, her hand on the door handle.

"Do you want to order pizza and watch a scary movie with us?" Larkin asked from the back seat. It was the first thing she'd said in twenty minutes.

Harlow's eyes went wide. Her heart tumbled as he grinned, peeking into the back at Larkin. When he answered she didn't know whether to cheer or scream. "Yeah. I'd love that. Thanks for asking."

CHAPTER ELEVEN

Harlow followed them into the house, up the four flights of stairs that led to the residence above the bookstore. The staircase wall was papered in a rich tapestry-style that depicted stags and cranes, representative of her mothers' combined heritage. Harlow let her fingers drag over the wallpaper as she had as a child, thinking she might feel the feathers or fur come to life under her touch.

She watched Finn's eyes take in every part of her childhood home as they entered. The plush rugs, the natural objects and copious amounts of art. The cozy furniture and rich, colorful palette. She'd told him about it dozens of times as children, but he'd never come here. Of course, neither of their parents had approved of their friendship, and so they mostly saw each other at school and parties.

Larkin said something about changing out of her dress and they were left alone in the living room. Harlow plugged her phone in and turned to ask him why he'd wanted to come inside, but his expression was so open, and so unlike the cold version of him she'd grown used to, that her words died in her mouth.

He swallowed hard as she made eye contact. "I always

wanted to come here. It's just like you said, better even. This place feels like a real home."

She nodded. It was true, her mothers had elegant taste, but never sacrificed comfort or the ability to gather with their family. There were three long couches in a u-shaped arrangement in the great room, and a television that was magicked to look like an oil seascape when not in use. The walls were painted a deep green, and the couches were overstuffed, with dozens of pillows and blankets ready to snuggle into. Round brass lamps with empire shades cast warm pools of light on the blue rugs. For a moment, she saw it all from his perspective.

Everywhere there was evidence of the women who called this home. Dozens of framed photographs gilded the library table behind the couches. Tables were strewn with notebooks, scrunchies, and novels stuck with bookmarks. Someone's slippers and a pair of wool socks peeked out from under one of the couches. This was where seven people who genuinely loved one another gathered frequently.

She knew there were no spaces like it in his family's home. He'd said as much when they were younger. Harlow started to say something but he shook his head again. "Please don't ask me to explain myself tonight, Harls. Just let me order pizza?"

Part of her wanted to say no, was tempted to tell him to get out, but there was such a soft look of need in his eyes that she couldn't manage the unkind words on her tongue. "Fine. I'm going to change clothes too. You know what I like on pizza. Larkin only likes cheese."

He nodded and she slipped out of the great room while he dialed his phone, a look of subtle joy on his face that bothered her. She went up one floor to Larkin's room and knocked.

"Come in," Larkin called.

She was wearing sweats and had removed all the makeup she'd worn at the party. Harlow had to admit that she looked more herself this way, more comfortable and real. And happier.

She didn't look the way Harlow always looked when she wore sweats, frumpy and miserable. She looked like Larkin, like the essence of Larkin, athletic and fresh. And cheeky as seventeen hells. The little silly was grinning her head off like she'd gotten away with murder.

"Why did you ask him in?" Harlow asked sharply.

"For the same reason you brought me home. He needed it."

Harlow closed her eyes. *He* needed it. "What about me?"

Larkin shook her head, smiling. "You needed it too. I remember how you used to talk about him. Whatever happened between you, you should fix it."

"It's complicated, pal."

Larkin shrugged. "I may not understand why people fall in love, or how, but I know what two people in love look like."

Harlow threw a stuffed bunny at Larkin. "We are not in love."

"You were though," Larkin said, wise as a sage as she caught the threadbare rabbit. "And maybe you will be again."

"Fat chance."

"I've always thought that expression sounded like it meant there was a really good chance that said thing was about to happen," Larkin mused. "Plus, he seems nice. I don't know why you've said so many mean things about him."

Larkin was too young to remember the way he'd shattered her. Too young to remember her broken heart. And she'd never told the sillies everything, only Thea and Enzo. Larkin only remembered that once he'd been Harlow's friend and then for some reason he wasn't.

"I'm gonna go change."

"Mama packed you and Thea's spare things in cold storage when the attic closets got moths, remember?"

"Damnit. Thanks for reminding me."

She left Larkin and went to her parents' room, a vibrant peach palace of decadent love. Harlow dug through Selene's drawers until she found the only thing she hoped wouldn't make her look like she was trying to seduce someone, a pair of lavender cashmere drawstring joggers and a matching sweater with a wide neck. When she changed, the sweater fell off one shoulder in an alluring way she'd rather avoid, but Selene didn't own clothes that *weren't* alluring and nothing of Aurelia's would fit her.

"Damn you, Mama," she said as she looked in the mirror. She looked sexy, like she wanted to be touched, which was of course the point of this outfit. Selene was in perpetual seduction mode, even after hundreds of years of marriage.

"No wonder the two of them are always doing it," she muttered as she shut off the light.

In the great room, she found Larkin and Finn arguing over which horror movie to watch. They were laughing, talking about directors and their favorite actors. She'd forgotten he loved movies, that horror was one of his favorite genres.

The door buzzed and Larkin jumped up. "I'll get the pizza."

Finn handed her several bills. "No change, okay?"

Larkin nodded, grinning at the big tip he was going to give. Her sister was very interested in tipping well and he'd clearly impressed her.

When they heard her feet on the stairs, his gaze turned to Harlow, slowly as though he was afraid to look at her. "You look..."

"Ridiculous," Harlow finished for him, grabbing her phone from the charger. "I had to borrow something from Selene and all her casual clothes look like she's about to seduce Aurelia. Believe it or not, this was the best I could find."

"I was going to say you look beautiful," he muttered, not taking his eyes off the screen as he scrolled through the horror section.

Harlow was stunned. He'd never said anything like it to her. Not even before, and certainly not with that quiver in his hands. He tried to hide it, but she saw. His hands were shaking. Akatei blessed them, and Larkin came back with the pizza before she had to think of something to say. The three of them sat on the floor in front of the coffee table, and Larkin chose a ghost story.

Harlow checked her phone. There were messages from the maters asking for an update on how Larkin was doing. She texted back to let them know they were home safe and that she planned to spend the night.

She apologized again to Enzo for abandoning him, and got a text back that said he hoped she had a great night. A winky emoji followed and she texted a question mark back.

I saw who took you home. Update me on everything tomorrow.

Thea said she'd be home in a few hours, that Alaric was taking her out for a late dinner, but that she planned to spend the night at home, rather than her own place. Before she could text back, Larkin plucked her phone from her fingers.

"Watch the movie, please," the little tyrant commanded, tossing her phone aside. Eventually, Larkin moved to the couch and covered up with a blanket, but Harlow was glued in place.

She was acutely aware of both the moment Larkin fell asleep and Finn's warm body next to hers. He was sitting close enough to touch. The film got scarier. It wasn't a gory slasher film, but a tense ghost story, a thriller. Harlow knew the jump scare was coming, felt her body go taut and then startle as the ghost appeared for the first time. Her fingers brushed Finn's involuntarily and he took her hand.

"I forgot that you hate scary movies," he whispered.

She tried to even her breathing, but he ran his thumb down the center of her palm in a way that was far from innocent. Warmth flooded her belly as his eyes grazed over her bare shoulder, at the bustier that was practically exposed by the sweater's wide neck.

Every nerve in her body screamed for his touch, betraying her heart. Harlow closed her eyes and she felt the whisper of his breath on her face. Then nothing. He let go of her fingers and moved ever so slightly away from her. Her heart dropped with disappointment, traitorous disappointment.

Then she heard it: Larkin's breathing was irregular. She was awake, but pretending to sleep. She glanced at Finn and saw his lips curl into a smile, a real one, not that smug one he'd worn at the party. He'd known before she had, that preternatural Illuminated sense of hearing telling him Larkin had woken.

When the movie ended, Larkin was awake and she said goodnight quickly. Harlow knew she wasn't going to bed. Her littlest silly was going to get the talking to of her life when Finn left. He helped to take the leftover pizza boxes into the kitchen. When Harlow turned away from the huge fridge he was smiling wistfully, leaning against the island, arms crossed.

"This is almost how I imagined it would be."

"Almost?" she asked, as though in a dream. Only the little lamp on the counter was on, making the kitchen cozy and dark.

Finn pushed away from the island, the muscles in his chest flexing. Sometime during the movie he'd taken his jacket off, and the t-shirt he wore was practically sinful, it looked so good on him. He moved slowly, deliberately, giving her a chance to move away. She told herself she stayed in one spot because this was better than one of her sisters being the object of his attention, or worse, *his parents'* attention. But the deeper voice inside her spoke the truth: she knew he'd never make a single move on any of her sisters.

The ferocity of his attention spoke volumes. He was nearly touching her now. Her breath quickened when one long arm snaked around her waist as he pulled her to him. She didn't think, didn't allow herself to think, but raised her chin to be kissed as she leaned into him, pressing her palms into the solid, warm bulk of his chest.

He tugged on her gently, bringing her closer and she responded, wrapping her arms around his neck. He smelled so good, and the way his body warmed hers was decadent, indulgent, and oh so dangerous.

Finn's mouth was soft against her skin as he bent to kiss her cheekbones. "I wanted this so much when we were in school. To come here, to watch a movie with your sisters and hold your hand. To kiss you in the kitchen. To be a normal couple."

"Then why did you ruin it all?" she asked, the words slipping out, even as she leaned into the heat of his chest.

"Godsdamn it, Harls," he growled, letting her go. The cold air that filled the space between them shocked her system.

Before she could ask him again, he was gone, using that supernatural speed to leave her standing alone in the kitchen, her chest feeling flayed open as though she were seventeen again, heart freshly broken. She slid to the floor, shaking with the sobs she'd shoved down for seven years.

Chapter Twelve

"Harlow?" Larkin's voice was gentle. How long had she been sitting here? "Are you okay? Did he hurt you?" Now her sister was panicked.

"No, pal. He didn't hurt me. Well, maybe my feelings, but that was a long time ago."

Larkin pulled her up off the marble floor. "Come on. Come to my room."

Harlow nodded, wiping her face with the tissue Larkin handed her and following her sister to her room. Larkin's room was lit by a host of floating witchlights, and her bed had a canopy with dark grey linen curtains. Her walls were papered with old sheets of music and her violin was out, as though she might play at any moment.

Harlow let her little sister tuck her into bed and then crawl in next to her, curling up against her shoulder. "Thought I was supposed to be comforting you," she muttered.

"You can, if you want... I had fun until he made you cry. I didn't think that's what would happen, not from the way you were looking at each other."

Harlow didn't reply. She just let the tears slip down her face.

Larkin tucked her cold feet under Harlow's legs. "What's the story between you?"

It was a simple question, but there were no easy answers. Mostly because Harlow didn't really know what happened. "We were good friends from the time we were ten. His family moved here that year, and Finn, Enzo and I became inseparable."

"How old was I?" Larkin asked.

Harlow smiled faintly as she counted back. Larkin always asked how old she was whenever Thea or Harlow told a story about their past. She seemed fascinated with the idea that there was so much history she'd missed, being the baby. "About three, I guess?"

"That explains why I don't remember."

Harlow swiped a quick kiss on top of Larkin's dark head. "His parents didn't like that we were close. They wanted him to have more Illuminated friends, so we could only socialize at school or at events where all four Orders gathered. And even then, they made it clear that they disapproved."

Larkin scoffed. "And now they think one of us should marry him."

"Yeah. A bit hypocritical."

"What else is new?" Her sister sounded almost as jaded as she did. Larkin poked her side. "Finish the story."

"By the time we were in secondary school, right before uni, we both knew we were in love, that maybe we'd always been in love, but we knew we couldn't be together. His parents wouldn't allow it and they're the McKays. They always get their way."

Larkin nodded and looped her arm through Harlow's, holding her hand. Harlow smiled. Larkin was so sensitive. She knew the awful part of the story was coming.

"Anyway, one night Finn took me to see an exhibit. He loved to draw and one of his favorite artists was showing at a gallery downtown. So we went, just the two of us."

"Where was Enzo?"

Harlow hugged her littlest sister. "On a date of his own."

"So, you went to the art exhibit. What happened after?"

Harlow blushed. "We drove around for a while, and then... We stopped, and... Things went too far, I guess."

"You had sex?" Larkin sounded surprised.

"Yes, it had been building between us for a while. We'd kissed a few times and never talked about it. And that night things went further. It was my first time."

"Was it really bad? You look like you're going to cry again."

"No, it was wonderful. One of the best nights of my life."

Larkin wiped tears from Harlow's face. "What went wrong?"

"I don't know. But the next day he was different. Cold. Within a month he was downright mean to both me and Enzo. He cut us both out. Do you know Alaric's cousin Petra?"

Larkin nodded.

"He started hanging around her and her crowd."

"Was Alaric friends with them?"

"Not really. He's Thea's age, a year older, actually. He had his own friends and eventually Finn ran around with them instead."

"With the uni kids?"

"Yes, and that was better. When he was friends with Petra, they were really hard on me and Enzo. Well, she was anyway, and he did nothing to stop it. He didn't participate, but he just stood there whenever she bullied me and Enzo. Me especially."

"I remember that part. You coming home every day, broken looking and exhausted. I remember hearing the maters saying they thought they'd have to send you away, but then things got better. Was that when he became friends with Alaric?"

Harlow wasn't sure if Larkin actually remembered that, or if the twins had told her about it enough times that she thought she did. "Yeah, I guess so. Alaric is a good person. Maybe he was a better influence on Finn. I don't know. When we all went to university, I tried to leave it behind, let it go, but it ate me up inside for years. I made a lot of mistakes at uni because I couldn't let it go."

"Then you met Mark."

"Well, I saw a lot of other people in between, but yeah, Mark was the first person I really loved after Finn."

Larkin grimaced, as though she thought Mark was a bad follow-up. "And now Finn's back and everyone wants you to pair."

"I guess." Harlow felt as though the breath had been knocked out of her as she sunk down into the pillows of Larkin's bed.

"Does that seem a little wild to you?" Larkin peered over at her. "Like, *really* wild?"

"Yeah, pal. Shut off the lights, okay? I think I'm done for the day."

"Nyx," Larkin whispered and the witch lights went out, and Harlow was left with a head full of memories and a bruised heart.

CHAPTER THIRTEEN

H arlow smelled breakfast before she was fully awake, the familiar sounds of a weekend morning at home filling her ears and making her drowsy. She opened her eyes and was supremely confused. Instead of the huge attic bedroom she shared with Thea until she was eighteen, she was someplace else.

"I got you tea," Larkin chirped, pressing a warm mug into her hands.

"Oh, right, I slept in here." Harlow took the mug and sipped gratefully as she sat up, propping herself up in the enormous pile of pillows Larkin slept amongst. "What's with the tea service?"

Larkin wrinkled her nose. "Everyone is in the kitchen interrogating Thea about her dinner with Alaric."

Harlow sunk deeper into the pillows and pushed back the covers. "Get in. We don't need to participate in that."

Larkin smiled and cuddled in. Harlow loved the twins fiercely, as she loved all her sisters, but they were an intense pair, and if they had Selene on their side, the scene in the kitchen was bound to be more than she wanted to deal with just now.

Besides, Larkin had slipped out of discussing the reason they left the party last night.

"So, pal. You cleverly avoided having to talk to me last night. Want to fill me in on what's going on with you?"

Larkin tucked her face into Harlow's shoulder, like she had when she was a little girl. "It's hard to explain."

"Give it a try."

"I know what romance *is*. I even kind of like to read about it or watch TV shows with it, but I just don't... feel it."

"Not ever? With anyone?"

Larkin shook her head. "It's not a matter of who, it's just that I don't feel like that about people."

"What about sex?"

Larkin shook her head. "I don't really get that either. I fooled around with the people I dated in secondary and sometimes it felt nice, but all the stuff the books talk about? I just didn't feel it. Do you think something's wrong with me?"

Harlow threw an arm around her sister and hugged her. "No, pal. I don't. Lots of people feel that way; humans are better at talking about it than the Orders. Since we're so obsessed with pairing, we don't talk about what it's like when someone doesn't want to."

Larkin nodded. "That makes sense I guess. I just feel like the odd one out."

Harlow's arm tightened around her sister. "I think you'll find other people like you and when you do, it'll help you understand yourself better."

"Really? Do you know any?"

Harlow laughed. "Probably. I'll think about it and ask Enzo, if that's all right. I think one of his friends from uni felt similarly about things. Would you like to talk to her if that's the case?"

Larkin nodded. "Enzo always has nice friends."

"Do you want to keep going to the season parties?"

Larkin blanched. "No, but I think Mama will be mad."

"She won't. I promise. Just tell her and Mother how you feel. They'll understand, pal."

"You think the sex queens will get this? They've been in love forever."

They giggled together and Harlow set her empty mug down to wrap her other arm around her youngest sister. "They've also *lived* forever. They get a lot of stuff we don't give them credit for."

When Harlow said it, she realized how true it was, and how lucky they were to have such good parents. All Finn's troubles with his own family were a thought away. She tried to brush it off, but something bothered her about how he'd acted the night before, so happy to be here, and then gone the instant she'd questioned him about why he'd abandoned her.

Selene poked her head in. "So that's where my cashmere sweatsuit went. Time for waffles, my darlings."

Harlow gave Larkin a meaningful look as she climbed out of bed. "Talk to her. I'll send Mother in."

Selene looked concerned and Harlow kissed her cheek as she passed. "I love you, Mama."

Selene pulled her back before she got out the door, into a massive hug. "I love you too, dear girl. I'm so glad my babies are all home."

Harlow grinned and sent Aurelia to Larkin's room as she entered the kitchen. The twins were already planning a lazy day of a family movie marathon, taking their waffles into the living room. Only Thea was left in the kitchen.

"So, Alaric Velarius, and you're the swan of the season."

Thea blushed. "No one is saying that."

Harlow grabbed Thea's phone, clicked open the Section Seven app and scrolled down past news of a human celebrity's party. Then she flipped the phone around to show her sister the headline.

Sorcière heiress the swan of the Orders' mating season.

Thea looked horrified. "Oh dear. Mating season?"

Harlow shrugged as she piled waffles on her plate. "The app is run by humans, what do you expect? Plus, it's not altogether inaccurate."

"Crudely put," Thea said ruefully, closing her phone.

"So, is he serious about you?" Harlow cut right to the chase. She had no desire to question her sister after the morning she'd probably already had.

Thea's smile was small, but joyful. "Yes."

"And you're serious about him?"

Thea nodded, looking pleased.

Harlow ate her waffles. "Sounds good."

Thea started to say something, then seemed to think better of it. "Was Finn here last night?"

"I don't want to talk about it."

"Harlow..."

"Leave it." Harlow's voice was sharp as she pushed away from the table. Explaining things to sweet, sensitive Larkin was one thing, but she couldn't talk about this more today. "I've gotta go home."

Thea grabbed her hand. "Please don't go. We're supposed to have a movie marathon and eat junk food all day. It won't be the same if you go."

"I can't talk about him," Harlow rasped, her voice rough with unshed tears. "Please, don't make me."

"Fine," Thea said, guiding her back into her chair. "Finish your waffles."

Harlow did, as her sister watched in perfect silence.

THE REST OF THE WEEKEND SLIPPED BY IN DOMESTIC bliss. The maters tended to the shoppers and the girls took shifts helping, but mostly they lay about enjoying themselves. When

Sunday night came, Harlow dreaded going home to her near-empty apartment.

"Why don't you move back in?" Aurelia suggested, as though reading her mind.

They'd been reading together in the study for over an hour, but Harlow was distracted by thoughts of her lonely apartment. "I can't."

Aurelia put down her book. "Why not?"

Harlow mirrored her mother and shook her head. "I just can't."

"You hate your apartment."

Harlow *loved* her apartment, but that would be hard to explain to Aurelia, who liked everything in her life to be just so. "I need to be there for a while. It was so good to be here this weekend, to be with all of you and to forget about everything that's wrong, but I need my own place."

"Tell me why." Aurelia's expression suggested a willingness to listen.

Harlow sighed. "Because I have things I need to work out, and if I stay here, you and Mama will work the magic you work without even thinking, and I'll feel better and forget that I need to sort myself out."

"Would that be so bad? To let us help you? To feel better after everything that happened with Mark?"

Harlow got up and kissed Aurelia's cheek. "It wouldn't be if I'd actually work out all the bullshit going on in my head, but I won't. I'll just keep putting it off."

"What's going on up there, bun-bun?" Aurelia tapped Harlow's forehead.

Harlow sat at Aurelia's feet, rested her head on her lap, and thought about her mother's question. "I feel like I can't do anything right."

"Is this about your magic? You know your talent will manifest soon enough. Your time with humans simply delayed things.

Now that you're back with us, safe in the lower Orders, things will right themselves."

Harlow didn't answer. Aurelia was usually very perceptive, but she and Mama had been skirting around asking what really happened with Mark for six months. All Harlow had told them was that it was over and her new address.

Aurelia tipped Harlow's head up so their eyes met. "What happened with Mark, bun?"

She took a shaky breath, remembering what she'd told Larkin about their parents understanding the world better than they gave them credit for. "You were all right. He was hurting me."

Aether surged in the threads of magic around Aurelia, dark and menacing, a reminder that her mother was a force to be reckoned with. Harlow shook her head. "Not physically. But the way he talked to me... It was confusing. Even now, I know he was manipulating me, but I can't shake the feeling I'm the one who was wrong."

Her mother's eyes narrowed in fury. "I will kill him."

Harlow believed it. "That would only get us in trouble with the Consortium. It's not against the law to make someone believe you're the only person they can trust. He twisted everything anyone said to me in so many ways... I thought for a long time that you all hated me."

"We were *afraid* for you, my darling," Aurelia said, pressing a kiss to her forehead. "You changed so much in such a short time. We weren't sure how to address it without making things worse. Mama and I know we made a mistake. We should have gotten you out of there sooner."

Harlow bit her lip, trying not to cry. "I wouldn't have gone, and if you'd have forced me, you'd have proven him right. The worst part is that he knew it. He knew he had me fooled."

Threads of magic sputtered with power, sizzling around

Aurelia's fingertips. She drew them back from Harlow. "I'm sorry, bun. I'm finding it difficult to control myself."

Harlow took her mother's hands and kissed them, letting the little sparks of power fizzle out against her skin. "I didn't know how much he'd fooled me until the day he kicked me out."

"Why did he do it? If he had you fooled, why did he let you go?"

Harlow couldn't meet Aurelia's gaze. "I don't really know."

The magic flared around Aurelia's fingertips again. "What does *that* mean?"

"I don't remember the last night very well. There's a kind of blank spot in my memory. I remember some of the fight we had, that he pushed too far about Order secrets, but I can't remember the particulars... and then everything goes blank until I woke up here the next day."

Something broke in Aurelia's eyes as Harlow met them. "Darling girl, I am so sorry. I didn't know."

Harlow took one last wobbly breath. "And I left a friend behind."

Aurelia's brow wrinkled. "Who?"

Harlow's shoulders slumped with the burden of her guilt. "I adopted a street cat when he forced me to quit my job at the shelter. The only part of our argument I remember is that he took Axel from me. I've texted him dozens of times, trying to get him back, but he doesn't answer." She choked on a sob. "I don't even know if he's okay."

"My sweet girl." Aurelia stroked her hair. "We'll get Axel back, I promise you that." Aurelia's tone was reassuring, but it wouldn't make up for the months she'd let her ragamuffin baby stay with Mark.

Harlow stared at her hands. "The whole thing made me feel like I don't deserve to have good things happen to me. I can't seem to take care of myself, or care what happens to me unless I think about you all."

Aurelia's fingers stopped. "What do you mean?"

"Somewhere along the way I stopped believing I was worthy of my own love."

Aurelia took a sharp breath in and held it, as though she were afraid she'd say the wrong thing. But she continued to stroke Harlow's honey-gold hair, letting her speak.

"I need time to sort all of this out. I know all the ways he made me feel were a ploy to find out Order secrets. You all were right about him. But the stuff he said to me about myself—it felt real. It still does. I have to find a way to get the inside of my head back under my control. Being alone gives me the space to do that."

"Okay, bun. You know Mama and I will help you, don't you? Whatever you need."

"I know. Thank you. You and Mama are so good to us..." she hesitated, not wanting to ruin the tender moment, but as long as they were discussing the hard stuff, she might as well ask. "What do the McKays *really* want from us? Why are you and Mama so worried?"

Aurelia's brow furrowed and Harlow thought she might not answer. But then Aurelia let go of whatever was holding her back. "Things are bad with the Order of Night. The humans' fascination with them is causing problems. We need strong alliances to get them back in line."

"Are they making more vampires?"

Aurelia nodded, her face grave. "And it's not just that, though that is bad enough. They are killing more indiscriminately, though we've managed to keep it quiet so far."

Harlow thought of the vampire in the Grove and how open she'd been about draining a UNT co-ed. The thought of the Order of Night being out of control was chilling. Aurelia continued, "The Illuminated haven't been doing much to stop them, and you know the Order of Masks... The shifters hate to take a side without all the evidence, so that's left the council trying to form alliances with the Illuminated.

"But the Illuminated have been too busy creating more wealth to be interested in the Order of Night, perhaps to compensate for how clear it is that they're no longer reproducing the way they once did. They're consolidating power, which means we should be too."

Finally, Harlow understood the scope of her family's worries about her relationship with Mark, given his fascination with the lower Orders, and the push towards having all five girls in the season. She was sickened to know the Order of Night was being so reckless and that the Illuminated didn't care, but she wasn't surprised. The lower Orders existed in a delicate balance between the unrivaled power of the Illuminated and the massive numbers of humans. The vampires' callous indiscretion could be the end of the lower Orders if they weren't more careful.

"What are we going to do?" Harlow breathed, head reeling with the information.

Aurelia sat back in her chair, shaking her head. "Many things we won't like, I suspect."

The answer was vague, but Harlow didn't get the sense that her mother was being evasive, only frustrated. She wouldn't be this worried about the season and alliances with the Illuminated if this was all there was to the problem. The Order of Mysteries was always navigating power struggles like these.

"What does all this have to do with all of us participating in the season?"

Her mother's head fell to the side, resting on her fist as she frowned. She was contemplating how much to tell Harlow, that much was clear. Harlow's stomach turned. The worry in her eyes was telling. "Mother, what does this have to do with the McKays and Finn? What aren't you telling us?"

Aurelia's chin quivered. Harlow's chest tightened to see her typically serene mother in such consternation. She swallowed hard and drew courage up from some unknown spot inside her. It was better to know than not. "What have they offered?"

"They're offering to back off from buying up the Row, and they'll support us with the Order of Night, get the other high families of the Illuminated Order to force them to fall in line."

They wouldn't offer so much if there wasn't something they wanted in return. "In exchange for what?"

"An heir. They seem certain that you, in particular, could produce one with Finn. I'm not sure why, but they're utterly convinced."

Harlow felt dizzy, suddenly sick to her stomach. "Does he know? Finn, I mean. Is he a part of this?"

Aurelia shook her head, distressed. "I don't know, my darling. I won't ask you to do anything you don't want to, but I don't see how we'll avoid a true disaster with the humans if they don't help us. We'll lose everything. *Everything.*"

"Oh," Harlow sighed, sinking onto Aurelia's footstool. Her proud mother wept in front of her, thin shoulders shaking with furious grief. There was no sign of the flickering aether now, just Aurelia's surrender to her helplessness against the Illuminated's machinations. Harlow's chest constricted sharply with each sob that wracked her mother's frame.

"Mommy," she whispered as her arms went around Aurelia. "Mommy, don't cry."

"I can't help it, my girl. It's shameful to ask you to even consider this, especially after everything you just told me about Mark. I can't ask you to do this. The McKays are hideous, vulgar. Cruel."

"Shhhh," Harlow soothed. "They are, but Finn isn't like that. I'll talk to him."

"No," Aurelia sobbed. "No, Harlow. Don't do it. Oh, my darling, I'm so sorry."

"Mommy," Harlow pleaded. "Mommy, please don't cry. I'll fix things, I promise."

She looked up to see Selene in the doorway, face white as a sheet, clutching her chest, tears streaming down her face at the sight of her strong, proud wife breaking down in her second-eldest's arms.

Harlow motioned to Selene. "Mama, come take her. I have to go."

Selene rushed to Aurelia, replacing Harlow's arms with her own. "I don't want you to worry, either of you. I am going to fix this."

Selene caught her hand. "She's right, my love. Don't do anything rash."

"Finn is different. I'll fix this. Please let me go."

Selene nodded, and Harlow kissed them both, and then went home to think.

CHAPTER FOURTEEN

Harlow paced the floors of her apartment until the downstairs neighbors pounded on their ceiling. She hopped onto the bed to relieve them from her nervous noise. Her thoughts swirled uncontrollably. She needed to sort things out, figure out a way to stop all this and get things back on track with the Order. More than that, she had to find a way to keep her family safe from the McKays. She might be a ruined specimen of a witch, but she wouldn't see her sisters sacrificed to them, nor would she see her parents turned out of their home.

There had to be something that unwound all of this—something that would set the Kranes and maybe even the entire Order of Mysteries free. It was a tangled knot of issues, and she had no idea where to start untangling it. Her head dropped into her hands in frustration.

Start at the beginning, she thought. But where *was* the beginning?

The night in the Grove. The scream in the forest, and the fact that as far as she knew, she and Finn were the only ones to hear it. Somehow, in all this, they were connected. She didn't want to think about the almost-kiss in the kitchen, or the way Finn's hands had felt on her when he pulled her out of the drunk vampire's way in the Grove, but she did.

It was hard to read him, but if she was honest with herself she knew he still cared for her, and after the things he'd said at her parents' she knew a part of him longed for something she could give him, but that he couldn't seem to have on his own: family. She'd always wondered what she could possibly have to offer Finn McKay, and now she understood; he had the world at his feet, but she had family.

Though she loathed the thought of giving his parents anything they wanted, her family was what was most important. She'd made her decision before she'd even left her parents' house. There wasn't anything left to do but try to get him to agree. She texted Enzo.

Do you have Finn's number?

...

Yes, why?

I need to call him.

Call me first.

I don't have time for this tonight. I'll tell you everything over brunch tomorrow. Promise.

Finn's contact info came through, with a message. *You most certainly will. Eleven. My place.*

Harlow took a deep breath and then called. The phone rang several times, so long she thought she'd get his voicemail, but then he picked up.

"Who's this?" His voice was sleepy. She looked at the clock: nine-thirty. He was asleep at nine-thirty? Shouldn't he be out partying?

"Harlow."

He was immediately alert. "Harls? What's wrong?"

She had to say it or she'd lose her nerve. "Can you meet me at our spot by the river?"

"Are you all right?" He sounded awake now, a bit panicked even.

"Yes. I just need to talk to you."

"Okay." His voice was hesitant. "I can be there in twenty. Do you need a ride?"

"No, I'll see you there."

She hung up and breathed, then changed into leggings and a sweater, sneakers, and a puffer vest to ward off the humid chill in the air. Then she scrambled down the stairs before she could think better of what she was about to do.

Harlow made the walk to Riverside Park in short order. She infused her vest with a tiny bit of magical warmth just for good measure as she folded herself up on a bench to wait. The pine trees in the park whispered in the cold nighttime air, and the scent of freshly mowed grass filled her nose as she waited. Chilly as it was in Nuva Troi, it was still spring and things were beginning to grow again.

"I wish you'd let me drive you," Finn said as he sat down next to her.

He was too close, but she'd sat at the end of the bench and there was nowhere to scoot away from his tantalizing heat. "I'm fine."

"You're clearly not."

She sighed and threw back her head in a silent scream, shaking her fists at the wind. It felt a little embarrassing to lose her cool, but it also made her feel marginally better.

He bumped her shoulder with his. "See. Not fine. What's up?"

The gesture was friendly, too friendly. Maybe that would make things easier. Gods above, she didn't want to be having this conversation. She didn't know any way to begin that might soften the blow of her questions, and she wasn't sure she wanted to. "Did you know about the offers your parents have been making mine?"

She watched his face carefully, wishing she had Enzo's talent for empathy. His eyes darkened with confusion. "No, what do you mean?"

She gave it to him straight, no sugar-coating. "Apparently, if I bear your child they'll stop harassing the Order of Mysteries about buying up the Row and help us to keep the Order of Night from destroying our tenuous alliances with the humans. *Apparently*, the vampires are killing them again and your parents won't help until I make a baby with you."

He sprang away from her, so fast it caught her by surprise. It was easy to forget the Illuminated were different from the rest of the Orders, that they were more like gods than the creatures of the lower Orders—until one of them moved like that or did magic. Then it was easy to remember that they ruled the world with an ironclad grip for a reason.

Fury burned in Finn's eyes. "They..." he appeared to be struggling to breathe. "Said what?"

Harlow was tempted to shrink back. When Mark got angry with her, when his fury rose the way Finn's did now, she always had. But tonight she felt reckless and she let her sharp tongue fly. "Oh, you heard me. Did you know they've been planning this? How long has this been going on?"

She braced for retaliation, for cruel words about her and her family's inferiority. But he didn't react like Mark did to her moments of bravery, with that cold, devious anger that smelled like danger. No, Finn was as distressed as she was. He paced like a caged animal, and for all his bulk and preternatural grace, she wasn't afraid. He was objectively one of the most terrifying people in Nytra, and yet, she was not afraid.

This surprised her. When Mark was angry, she was *always* afraid, frozen with cold terror, waiting to make her next wrong move, because all her moves were wrong when she and Mark argued. But something about Finn's reaction comforted her, as enraged as he seemed. It was clear he wasn't angry at her.

But why should he be? she thought to herself. *It's his family that's done something wrong.*

It hadn't ever mattered who was wrong with Mark. It was always Harlow's fault. Her heart clenched as the depth of the comparison she was making hit her. How had she missed this reality when she lived with Mark? The unfairness of his anger had never occurred to her. Even when she resisted it, deep down, she'd believed it was her fault for mouthing off. For making him mad.

The sound of Finn's voice brought her back to the present moment. He knelt before her. "I didn't know. Harls, I promise. I knew they had some harebrained scheme about you. They've been hinting, but we don't talk much since... Well, ever..." He was out of breath, panicking. "And I knew something was up with the Order of Night, but I thought it was being handled. The sorcière can't keep them in check on their own. Obviously, we need to help. There's too many humans... If they decided to stand against us... Gods, Harlow..."

His eyes were wild as he got up. He began to pace again and she saw the way his hands shook as he moved. On a strange whim, she caught one of them as he passed her. "Finn. *Finn.*"

He stopped and knelt in front of her again, his head bowed as though he were a penitent, or a knight to his lady. Her heart thumped a little too hard at the thoughts that his position before her brought up. Finn's voice was determined when he spoke. "I will stop this. I promise."

"How?" The question was simple, but it seemed to break him. He curled into a rather large ball at her feet.

"I don't know. I'll think of something."

She knew it would come to this when she left her parents' house. A part of her had always known it would come down to this when she agreed to take part in the season— that her family's fortune would depend on the two of them. It was what his parents wanted, and they *always* got what they wanted. There wasn't any way out of this, not really. They were trapped, both of them, stuck in inescapable patterns, no matter how much they wanted things to change.

Harlow sighed. "You don't have to. I'll do it."

Finn's head shot up. "You'll do *what*?"

"Have the baby. Give you an heir."

"Pair with me? *Bond* with me?"

She shrugged. "If that's what it takes."

He looked as though he would vomit. "Absolutely not."

"I'm that repulsive to you? Is there someone else?"

He stood, backing away from her in horror. "NO," he shouted.

When she shrank away he looked confused for a moment. Then understanding flickered in his eyes. Some recognition of her reaction, deep within himself. He crouched down again, making himself small in front of her, bowing his head. Finn McKay, one of the most powerful Illuminated in all Okairos, bowed before her, making himself innocuous to soothe her. *What was happening here?*

Harlow's blood rushed through her veins as he gingerly took her fingers into his hands, giving her every opportunity to pull away. When he spoke, his voice was as soft and gentle as it was deep. "No. There's no one else."

He looked up, straight into her eyes and there was not a shred of deceit in them. By now, Harlow knew what manipulation looked like, and there wasn't a trace of its poison on him. "Gods Harlow, do you think I'd really force you into something like that?"

Harlow tried to claw past all the complicated feelings swirling in her chest. Finn McKay might not be fooling her right now, but he was still her enemy. Still one of the Illuminated. He could not be fully trusted. She needed to get the control back in this conversation. "It's not forcing if I accept."

He carefully placed her hands back in her lap and stepped

away from her. "Well, I don't. Accept that is. I won't be that to you, and fuck you for trying to convince me to be a part of this."

"Fuck *me*? Are you kidding?" There was that sharp tongue of hers again, just begging to make him angry, egging him on, daring him to turn on her. Daring him to transform into the monster she expected.

But he didn't turn into anything. He stayed infuriatingly *Finn*. He pushed his hands through his dark hair, taking breath after shuddering breath, eyeing her warily. For a moment she saw herself the way he did. Yet another person pushing him to do something he clearly didn't want to do. She could understand that at least, being with her was a nightmare—it was one of the things Mark told her about herself that she truly believed. She wrecked people, and she would hurt Finn too before all this was over; and part of her wanted to, wanted vengeance for how he'd hurt her. She was the monster here, not him.

But Harlow couldn't care about that. She'd already made her decision. She would do whatever it took to keep her sisters from having to make alliances like this one, and she'd keep her Order from losing the little power that was theirs. If the McKays wanted her, they could have her. The baby was another story, but she'd find a way around that later.

His breath steadied and his eyes cleared. "We need to delay my parents' plans so we can figure things out."

Harlow nodded, relieved that he would at least help her. "What do you have in mind?"

He covered his face with his hands and took a few deep breaths. "The Solon Mai event is next weekend. At it, we'll convince everyone we're falling for each other and by Solstice, I'll ask for your hand."

"Okay, I think that was my plan. You just said it nicer—without all the baby stuff."

He shrugged. "It could work to buy us some time anyway."

She rolled her eyes. "Is anyone going to believe we went from hating each other to cozying up at Solon Mai?"

His eyes widened. "You hate me?"

A cold breeze bit into her skin, making her eyes water. "I don't know. I used to."

When she looked up, there was something like despair on his face for a moment. Then it cleared and he was collected as ever. "There's season-sponsored cocktail parties all week this week. We can plan to be at the same ones and you know... warm up to each other again."

"And then what? My family's whole life is on the line here. We need to have a better plan than this."

He slid onto the bench next to her, sitting further away this time. "Hopefully, by Solstice I can convince my parents to do the right thing, leave the Row alone and help with the Order of Night. I'll find something else they want and give it to them. I'll go work for my dad if I have to. You won't have to go through with it and then... I don't know, we'll have a terrible fight and break up."

She sat frozen, listening. It was a decent plan. Not the most brilliant plan of all time. Some would say faking a relationship was an old trick, but it might work. "And what if they don't comply? What if they won't do any of it 'til I breed with you?"

"Holy Raia, Mother of all. The mouth on you."

She looked at him, eyes hard, expecting to see reproach in his expression or the kind of anger that meant he'd punish her for days with the silent treatment. Instead, she found desire, awe, something like pride. His hand drifted towards her, then fell before making contact.

"Well?" she demanded, flustered by the way her heart beat faster every time she pushed him and he didn't react a thing like Mark would have. "What's your plan if none of it works?"

"Then I'll consider your way. But my way will work."

She had her doubts, but at least he'd agreed.

"We'll have to convince everyone," she murmured. "Even Alaric and Thea."

He slid closer and flopped against her with a familiarity that both comforted and scared her. "Especially them. They're the two worst liars I know."

She nodded and got up before things could get too intimate. All of this was confusing, more confusing than she'd anticipated. "See you this week. I'll text you about the parties I want to attend. Not too many though."

He nodded. "One should be enough, and maybe coffee somewhere the Section Seven people like to get photos... Maybe the new place on Eighty-eighth and Vine? The one with the succulent wall everyone on socials likes?"

"Sure. Whatever you want." The whole thing was starting to make Harlow sick. She wanted to go home.

"Should we... talk about things?"

Harlow was already walking away. "What things?" she asked without turning.

"You know what things, Harls."

"No," she said firmly as she walked away.

He trailed behind her as she walked home. He made no secret of following her, but he stayed a block back, and was staring at his phone every time she looked over her shoulder. She raced up the stairs to the terrace to see if he'd waited. He was standing by the street lamp, looking up. She waved, managing a wry smile. He nodded and then walked into the misty dark of the night.

Harlow knew they'd have to talk about it all eventually. One way or another that conversation was coming, but she would do whatever it took to keep her family and her Order from losing what was theirs, and she couldn't have her feelings for Finn McKay screwing that up. She tossed and turned long into the night, worrying herself into shaky, dreamless sleep.

CHAPTER FIFTEEN

S omeone was hammering Harlow's head with a mallet, beating her senseless. She thrashed, fighting them off, but they'd bound her in some sort of sack. A strangled scream, her own, woke her. She was tangled in her sheets, and someone was knocking loudly on her door. She glanced at her phone.

Seven missed calls from Enzo.

It was 11:45.

She'd slept through brunch.

And also apparently, three missed calls from the maters, one from Thea, two from Larkin, and a text message from Finn from ten minutes ago.

She read the text as she stumbled to the door. *I'm all in for Solon Mai and this week, if you still are.*

I am, she replied, then flung open the door to let Enzo in.

He was dressed in a tracksuit she recognized from *Elegante Magazine* as one he'd designed himself. The fabric was printed with dozens of golden snow leopards, with red stripes on the arms and legs, and his hair was in a ponytail.

"I like your outfit," she said as she wiped sleep from her eyes. "Sorry I missed our date. Finn and I were up late."

"If you spill quickly, I won't strangle you for missing brunch," Enzo said, perching on her kitchen counter.

Harlow knew from experience it was best to comply immediately. She yawned as she filled the kettle with water. "Well, you know he took me and Larkin home from the Statuary party, right?"

Enzo nodded as she put the kettle on the stove. He wasn't going to say a word until she'd told him everything. *Close to the truth as you can get it*, she reminded herself. She hated to lie to Enzo, but too much was on the line.

"He stayed and we watched a movie... and there were sparks. But I kind of freaked out. I called him to see if we could try to work things out and we talked for a long time."

"And?"

She poured hot water over a pot of Empress Grey leaves, sprinkling lavender buds and a spoonful of honey in for good measure. It wasn't Duke and Duchess, but it was close enough.

"And I think we're in a better place. We'll see how things go."

"Did he apologize for everything?"

She shook her head. "No, but I think you're right that he's changed."

That was all the truth at least. She hadn't really lied, not yet. She *did* think he'd changed. It's why she'd called him at all, why she'd come up with this terrible plan. Because deep in her heart, she knew there were worse things than being paired with Finn McKay, even if he didn't love her, even if his parents were *his parents*. Like the Order of Night destroying the balance of the world. That would definitely be worse.

Her phone vibrated. Finn. Enzo saw and smiled. "What's Mr. McKay have to say this morning?"

Harlow read the text and blushed.

"Well?"

"He says he hopes you have something indecent planned for my Solon Mai gown."

"That's *exactly* what he said?" Enzo asked with a grin.

Harlow glanced at the text again. "Verbatim."

That was a lie. The text actually said, *Good. Wear something to the Solon Mai ball so indecent that I'd be an idiot not to fuck you on the spot.*

But she couldn't quite bring herself to say that out loud. So she lied. And she'd be lying further if she said that every bone in her body hadn't threatened to turn to jelly when she'd read it. As for her text back, all she could manage was, *Will do.* She was fighting the urge to cringe. Why couldn't she think of better things to say to him? Snappy, clever things?

"I have *ideas*. Will you come to the atelier today? I'm scrapping my old plan for something different."

Harlow texted the maters to tell them she was all right, and going to be fitted for her Solon Mai dress. "Yes, do you want to go now? I have the day off from work."

Enzo laughed. "I bet you do, princess. Let's go."

He sat on the bathroom counter and chatted to her about Riley Quinn as she showered. Apparently, they were just in from Nea Sterlis, which was why she'd never met them before. "They're gorgeous and smart as hell. I'm in so much trouble. My mother would have loved them."

"What do they do for the Order of Masks, any good dirt on them?" Harlow asked as she rinsed her hair.

"That's the funny thing. Riley's not a member of the Order of Masks."

"What?" Harlow peeked out from the shower curtain. "A Rogue?"

Enzo nodded. "A little dangerous."

"Your mother would *not* have loved that."

Enzo smiled wickedly. "But I do."

"You are delighted with this, aren't you?" Harlow flicked water at her friend, who grinned.

"Oh, absolutely. I've always wanted to date an agent of the Rogue Queen."

"So Riley works for her? She's real?"

"Quite real, and yes."

Enzo handed her a towel when she stuck her hand out. "And you're seeing them again when?"

"Riley's coming with me to the Solon Mai ball. By then, it should be our fifth date."

Harlow wrapped herself in a fluffy robe and combed out her hair, then glamoured it dry, with a touch of makeup.

"Most excellent," Enzo said when she came out of the bathroom, and handed her clothes to wear. "Let's get you fitted for something wholly indecent. Something that will make Finn McKay lose his mind."

Harlow gave Enzo a shaky smile and got dressed.

SEVERAL HOURS LATER AND THE DRESS WAS NEARLY pieced together. Enzo wiped a bit of perspiration off his brow and snapped some photos. "I can finish the rest without you. Do you like it?"

Harlow nodded, hardly recognizing herself in the mirror. The dress was beyond what she could have imagined herself. It conformed perfectly to the Solon Mai standard: ball gowns must be floor length, long sleeved, and always black. Lace or damask were the only approved fabrics. By most stretches of the imagination, this would lead gowns to be rather staid, but in Enzo's capable hands, the dress was wickedly extravagant.

The dress required that Harlow wear a strapless bodysuit

that matched the color of her skin perfectly, giving the impression that she was completely nude under the transparent gown. The silky fabric mimicked the patterns of the most intricately woven lace, with none of the usual itch, making her tantalizingly touchable. The bodice fit close and had a high neck, but the skirt swept away from her hips suggestively.

Tiny reflective threads woven into the pattern of the lace shimmered slightly when she moved, giving the dress a subtle glow, rather than the flash of sequins. It was perfectly tasteful, yet wildly sensual at the same time.

"Something's not quite right," Enzo mused, pulling strands of magic from the air around the dress, weaving his vision into reality for the gown. The lace pattern emerged further to look like hundreds of wings, rather than the floral motif he'd started with.

"There," he breathed. "I think that's it."

Harlow could barely speak.

Enzo grinned, snapping a few more photos and then unpinned her from the gown. "I'll get the finish work done shortly."

"What should I do with my hair and makeup?" Harlow murmured, watching the fabric move in Enzo's hands as she changed back into her clothes.

"Nothing fussy. Since you will already appear to be nearly nude, I'd go for something loose. Already mussed."

Harlow smiled. "You are a gift, you know that?"

Enzo repinned the dress to the mannequin in Harlow's size. "Oh, I know."

Harlow scanned through the titles of the books on Enzo's shelves. "Have you ever thought about writing a book?"

He looked up from his work, his dark eyes slightly surprised. "Yes, how did you know?"

Harlow shrugged. "You're just so talented, and the way your

magic manifested was so brilliant. I hope you'll write lots of books. The world should know more about you."

Enzo hugged her fiercely. "Thank you for saying that, Harlow. It means a lot. Now go! I have half a dozen dresses to finish."

She kissed him goodbye, and left feeling thoughtful.

CHAPTER SIXTEEN

H er conversation with Enzo made her think about her own magic as she walked through the vibrant atmosphere of Mulberry Street. Her entire life, she'd been surrounded by talented sorcière. People with innate gifts so strong, even before their magic manifested, that it was obvious what their magical abilities would mature into. She wasn't like that.

Harlow couldn't identify a single talent of her own. It wasn't that she was mediocre; she was perfectly competent at many things, but unlike the other sorcière she knew, she wasn't particularly good at any *one* thing. She had lots of passions, many talents, and as such was at a complete loss as to how her magic would mature, and the sorcière she would settle into. It made her feel like a flake.

She headed toward the Monas. She wanted to do some reading for the rest of the afternoon. The maters had a collection on manifestation; surely she could find the answers she sought and jumpstart her stalled progress. A nasty voice inside her reasoned that if her problems could be solved with books, she'd already have solved them. Harlow steeled herself against the voice, pulling her coat tighter around her body.

As she made her way through the crowded streets of the Row, a cold, hard body knocked into her shoulder, pushing her off course. She looked behind her to find Olivia Sanvier scowling at her. She was even lovelier in person than she was in photos, with shoulder length red hair, pale skin, and the kind of lips that made her black lipstick look elegantly gothic, rather than foolish. The intensity of the hatred the vampire was projecting was startling.

Harlow tried to move aside. "Oh, sorry. I must not have seen you."

The vampire mirrored her movements with eerie accuracy, blocking her way. "Watch where you're going, witch."

Harlow felt the throb of her heartbeat in her veins acutely, as a chill slid into her bones. She was surprised by the tone the encounter was headed. She'd only met Olivia socially a few times, and they had been utterly unremarkable. Aside from the fact that Olivia was seeing Mark now, Harlow couldn't think of any reason for her to be so hostile. She'd been jealous of exes before, but this was something else, something visceral. Surely this couldn't all be about Mark, could it?

And like she'd summoned him just by thinking his name, Mark appeared, stepping out of a store that primarily sold divination tools, with a large shopping bag in his arms.

"Harlow," he said with a tight smile. "It's nice to see you. Liv, this is Harlow Krane."

Olivia rolled her eyes. "We've met. She ran right into me. She's as clumsy as you said."

Harlow's cheeks burned with embarrassment. Of course Mark had been talking badly about her. That certainly wasn't a shock, but everything about this encounter thrummed with an undercurrent that warned her to stay alert.

"Not really a surprise though, with all that body. She must

run into things all the time." Olivia laughed and took Mark's free hand in hers. The gesture was possessive, and the air around her crackled with feral energy. Olivia Sanvier was a dangerous vampire, as petty as she was powerful, apparently.

Mark laughed, a cruel sneer on his lips, but added nothing, turning sharply away from her in abject dismissal. Harlow felt as though she would crumple into the sidewalk, flat under their feet. She couldn't remember a time in the recent past that she'd felt so small. But then, she'd been back among the only people she was sure she could trust. Now, cowering here in front of Mark, she remembered too acutely what the last few months of their relationship had been like—the constant derision, interspersed with briefer and briefer periods of intense passion.

"Well, good to meet you," Harlow said, unsteady on her feet as they passed her.

Olivia sneered, her fangs showing and her stony eyes fierce. "See you again soon, witch. Don't worry, I'm taking *good care* of your little kitty."

Something splintered into dozens of jagged pieces inside Harlow as she watched them hail a cab and head uptown, towards the House of Remiel. Mark glanced at her from the back seat, a smug glint in his eyes. What had Olivia meant by that? She'd never heard of vampires feeding off animals, but of course they *could*. They had blood, after all. *Would Mark let Olivia hurt Axel?*

Deep in her gut, she knew he would. He'd let the House of Remiel's princess do whatever in seventeen hells she wanted to get what *he* wanted: more power. It was the only thing he'd ever been interested in, she understood in a sickening, enlightening moment. From the day they met, until the day he kicked her out, all he'd ever wanted was more power. He'd never wanted *her* at all.

For a moment, she understood it. Though the lower Orders were ruled just as stringently as the humans by the Illuminated, they were not their victims in the same way. But Mark was something else. Rich and powerful in his own right, he was exempt from things like the monthly blood donations required of other humans, and she knew the Eastons had never undergone the kinds of rigorous screenings most humans suffered in order to qualify to procreate. He'd had as much power as she had growing up, perhaps more, because his family was so much wealthier than hers. He'd never wanted justice or equality between the creatures of Okairos, not the kind she dreamed of.

How had she been so foolish? How had she ever believed he wanted the same things she did? How had she been so easily seduced by a few carefully constructed conversations in the beginning that never amounted to anything? How had she let things get so bad that she'd leave Axel with him?

Something bloomed deep within her as she hailed a cab of her own, something fierce and primal, protective. The fibers of magic in the air around her snapped, as though she'd done something to alter reality, but she was too focused on her plan to pay much attention. Her vision focused sharply and all her senses heightened in a way that made her feel like a cat stalking prey.

Harlow gave the cabbie Mark's address. He'd taken her key back, but it didn't matter. Today was the day she was taking Axel, and the final shreds of her self-respect she'd left behind, back. The elite human sector downtown in Greenvale Slope was as lovely and well-kept as any of the Orders' sectors, but Harlow barely registered the scenery. Something inside her was writhing, changing, begging to be let out. She paid the cabbie without speaking a word and swept into the building she'd lived in for nearly two years.

Salvatore, the human doorman, waved to her as she passed, looking worried. She knew he'd be too afraid to stop her, and as she expected, he was dialing the phone at his desk as the elevator doors closed. She had at least a half-hour, given traffic at this time of day, to get Axel and get out before Mark could make it back to this side of town. She closed her eyes, waiting for the elevator to reach the fourteenth floor.

Harlow floated out of the elevator, as if in a dream. She wasn't sure if it was the shock of coming face to face with Mark and Olivia, or if she was finally losing it, but her vision was blurry and she could have sworn magic crackled around her from elsewhere, beyond the threads that made up everything on Okairos. She would have to consider that later. Right now, she had only one goal.

"I'm coming, baby boy," she murmured, though she wasn't exactly sure how she would achieve that. Some force in her, whatever bloomed on Mulberry Street, urged her on.

From somewhere inside the apartment, she heard Axel howling in response. He could hear her. Absolute fury overcame her and her vision went completely dark for a moment. Her eyes shot open to the sound of the door flying past her, into the hallway. She'd just torn it off its hinges. That was something new, but she would have to think about that later. Someone had opened the door to their apartment, so now she probably needed to worry about the city guard, in addition to Mark returning.

"Axel?" she whispered, not wanting to step foot inside her former prison. For that's what it had been after he'd persuaded her to quit her job at the human bookstore: a prison.

Inside, the sounds of frantic yowling and a loud thud echoed through the cold hallways. Axel was shut up somewhere. Whatever new power seethed in her propagated at an unbelievable rate, filling her to the brim with an undulating force begging to be let out.

Harlow stepped inside the apartment, her skin prickling as a flood of memories threatened to wash her new confidence away. The dynamic force of the power in her fluctuated, changing by the moment. Harlow rode the waves of it as best she could, and found that she sailed along the currents of the storm within her with ease. There was no danger of her losing control now.

"Axel. Baby boy, where are you?" she called. The sound of her voice was alien, deep and resonant, shaking the walls and doors.

The volume of Axel's yowling increased and there was another loud thud. He was locked in the hall bath. She ran down the tiled hallway, willing her fear to subside enough to carry her through this. Harlow yanked on the door, which always stuck a little, and it flew open, releasing the stench of feline urine and feces. Mark hadn't been regularly cleaning up after the cat, and the bathtub was full of waste. Harlow tamped down her rage, focusing on searching for Axel. Her eyes met two golden pools of wrath.

Axel was sitting on the counter, enraged by his captivity, but clean enough, given the circumstances. His usually silky coat was dull though, and the fur around his middle sank into the impression of his ribs—not much, but enough for Harlow to know he hadn't been eating enough. Mark and Olivia would pay for this, but not until she got him away, made sure he was safe. Tears streamed down her face as she opened her arms. Axel cried, the piteous sound breaking Harlow's heart, as he jumped into her arms, clinging tightly to her.

He'd been a sleek, muscular eighteen pounds when Mark kicked her out, and now he was skinny and far too light. She held him close as she ran for the hallway and the stairs, everything behind them a blur. Harlow refused to look back, knowing that her window of time to escape without question was narrowing. As she went, the elevator showed that a car was coming up and she didn't want to be on this floor when it arrived.

"Hold on, baby boy," she cautioned. "We're going home."

The cat nuzzled against her face, purring happily, which shattered her heart even further as she raced down flight after flight of stairs. It was impossible to imagine how he could be so happy to see her when she left him behind. It didn't matter now. All that mattered was getting him out of here.

A shout rang out from the flights above her; the city guard she supposed. Footsteps clattered down behind her and she ran faster, but they were gaining and she had several more flights to go—and then what? She hadn't asked the cabbie to stay, and even if she had, they wouldn't have run from the city guard for her.

She'd be caught and they might even make her give Axel back to Mark. Somewhere, deep inside, a voice reminded her that was unlikely to happen, that her mothers were important people, that Finn might even help her, but the protective instinct that drove her on overrode that logic. The same instinct bade her to halt, suggesting something she didn't even know was possible. But she wouldn't question it, not now, with Axel in her arms and freedom just a few flights of stairs away.

"Hold tight," she warned Axel, who stared murderously up at the guards clambering down the stairs.

Aether crackled around her, flowing through the threads of magic she pulled at with her free left hand, holding Axel close with her right. Midnight blue shadows spilled from her fingers as she wove sigils of protection, the most basic she knew. It was all she could think of to do, but when she'd finished, nothing happened. The threads of magic didn't shift the way they were supposed to. In fact, nothing happened.

She'd somehow pulled a door off its hinges on her way in, but couldn't do a simple protection spell? What was wrong with her?

The most basic tenet of magic occurred to her then: magic is will, woven into reality. The aether was the power, but magic, at its core, was a matter of will. Harlow felt something stirring within her, and her spirit eye snapped open in the limen, the world between all worlds, where her spirit form flew as if on giant wings towards the heart of the limen, where all magic came from. It was full of inky blue shadows, just like the ones that came from her. They seemed to sing when they saw her coming. Power coursed through her spirit form, into her material body.

Harlow blinked and was back in the stairwell. The city guard was nearly upon them, their feet pounding the metal stairs. She didn't have time to think, but she glanced down at the shadows swirling around her and whispered a plea, "Protect us."

By Akatei's grace, the shadows dancing at her fingertips came alive and the aether crackled once more as the shadows billowed out of her, filling the stairwell, until the light from the fluorescents disappeared entirely. The sounds of the guards' shouts muffled to a dull roar as Harlow walked calmly down the remaining flight of stairs, out the back door and onto the concrete stairs that led to the alley. She pressed her hand to the closed door, more shadows flowing from her touch, and wished she knew a way to lock the door.

Something vibrated softly under her hand, and a lock appeared and turned of its own accord, looking as though it had always been there. A key appeared in her hand and she tucked it into her purse, clutching Axel tight, relief edging each breath she took. She couldn't explain what was happening with her magic, but they were almost free.

As she turned to walk down the steps she felt her second sight engage. A glassy wall, opaque and treacherous, rose up before her. She and Axel had been here before, the night she and Mark split up.

"I don't have time for this now," she breathed, holding Axel just a bit tighter.

Her second sight refused to disengage and Harlow had the distinct sense that she was falling, as if in a dream. The shadows that had filled the stairwell flooded her mind's eye now, pulling her back into the reality outside her connection to the aether.

Thank you, she thought to herself. Whatever it was, this primal force was helping her. The glass wall was gone and she could move again. Inside the building, she heard the city guard shouting, pulling on the door. They would go around the building eventually. If she didn't want to be caught, she had to leave now.

Harlow walked as calmly as she could out of the alley onto the street, and hailed another cab, stepping into it with only a quick glance behind her. No one followed as the cab pulled away, and the shadows had disappeared.

"Don't usually let animals in the cab, miss," the cabbie remarked as he pulled into traffic.

"I understand," Harlow said, clinging to Axel. "I'll pay extra."

The cabbie glanced at her in the rearview mirror. "You two running from something bad?"

Harlow met his gaze in the mirror, and she saw the fear that she'd been suppressing surface in her reflection. "My ex."

He nodded then, understanding in his gentle brown eyes. There were still good people in the world. People who would help someone in trouble, just because they recognized that kind of fear. The cabbie's voice was calm when he said, "Let's get you two home then."

"Thank you," Harlow murmured, giving him the Monas' address. She buried her face in Axel's fur and wept silently with relief. "Let's go home," she whispered to her cat, who still clung to her, purring softly in her ear.

CHAPTER SEVENTEEN

arlow paid the cabbie extra, just as she'd promised, even though he hadn't charged her anything for bringing Axel. He watched her closely from the cab until she pushed the front door of the shop open, waving to him to let him know she was fine. The cab pulled away from the curb and Harlow stumbled inside the Monas. As she did, the impact of what she'd done hit her, wooziness flooding her limbs. She was surprised to find the shop empty of customers. What time was it?

Harlow tripped on the edge of the rug at the front door, righting herself quickly, but shaky on her feet. Larkin looked up from the register as Harlow stumbled toward the couches at the center of the main floor showroom. Axel leapt from her arms onto one of the green couches. She met his lamp-like eyes as she crumpled to the ground.

"Mama!" Her youngest sister's scream filled her ears as she tried to sit up, to reach her cat.

Selene came rushing out from the back and helped her onto one of the couches at the center of the showroom floor. Axel leapt into Harlow's lap, hissing protectively at Selene. Mama raised her eyebrows at the cat, and her voice was sharp when she issued her command. "Lock the doors, Larkin. We're closed."

Larkin did as she was told. "Is there anyone else here?"

Selene shook her head after a moment of appraisal, using her magic to probe the shop. "I don't think so. Go get Li-li. Now."

Larkin disappeared. Harlow was dizzy, but Axel's weight comforted her. "What's wrong with me?" Her words were clumpy in her mouth, which felt dry and swollen.

Selene held up one of Harlow's hands, showing it to her. All of her fingers were deepest midnight blue, as though she'd dipped them in a vat of ink. "Has this ever happened before?"

Harlow shook her head.

"What happened before you came in? Tell me everything, in detail."

Aurelia appeared, with Larkin and Thea. "The twins are double checking that we're alone. Dear gods, is that what I think it is?"

She was looking at her fingers, not Axel. Harlow was sure Mother knew what a cat was. That struck her as funny, and she giggled, stroking Axel's back, which was heartachingly bony.

Selene shushed her wife, sparing only a glance for the cat. "Tell me everything that happened, Harlow."

"I saw Mark, and the vampire princess. She threatened to hurt Axel... So I went and got him." Her head was cloudy, and she was having trouble remembering exactly what had happened.

"Keep talking," Selene urged. "Then what?"

"I made the door fly off. Then the city guarffs came... the city guarf. The city *guard*... Yes, that's it. They came and the shadows ate them up and then I locked them in the building! A nice human drove me howl. *Home*."

She felt inebriated. That was what this feeling was. Aurelia examined her stained fingers, showing Thea. "Get the Merkhov text and something for this cat to eat. The fourth volume from the new shipment—for the book, not the cat food. Get the cat some kind of meat."

Thea nodded, apparently knowing the book Aurelia referenced, and having some idea of how to feed a cat. Thea was so smart. The smartest smarty there had ever been probably, except for Mother, and maybe scientific geniuses. Harlow's mind swirled with the train of thoughts that careened wildly off course.

"I feel drunk," Harlow said, her voice fuzzy-sounding in her ears.

"We don't need the Merkhov to confirm this," Selene said softly. "I thought my grandmother was the last of them, but this is just like what she described, down to the stained fingers. I made her tell me how it happened to her the first time—when we decided to have children... so I'd know the signs."

Aurelia nodded. "I believe you, but I don't think having the Merkhov on hand will hurt. Larkin, please go make a very strong pot of tea. Your sister is going to need something bracing."

Larkin did as she was bid. Selene helped Harlow into a more upright position, gripping her chin tightly in her fingers. "Look at me. Did you use any magic? Do anything with it?"

Harlow bobbed her head vigorously. Too vigorously. Now her vision swam. "Yes, I made a lock for the door and filled the stairwell with shadows. *Beautiful* shadows... They came out of my *hands*! I got him back, my baby boy. Isn't he such a good boy?"

Aurelia laughed softly at Harlow's babbling, then grew serious as she spoke to her wife. "Her heart is so big; she did all this for the cat. Is this why this happened?"

Selene shook her head as Axel flexed his paws against Harlow's leg and then nestled into her side for a nap. "Perhaps. Sometimes feelings of protectiveness or heightened stress can trigger it. Li-li, this explains why she's such a late bloomer.

Striders typically don't come into their power until they're twenty-five or six. Sometimes later."

Annoyance prickled at the corners of Harlow's awareness. "Stop talking about me. I'm right here." She felt a mug press into her hands.

Larkin smiled at her gently. "Drink up."

Selene nodded, urging her on. "It won't always be like this, bun. A Strider's initial manifestation is typically a bit dramatic. It's addled you a bit. Drink your tea."

"Tea solves everything," Larkin whispered.

Axel darted forward from his spot next to Harlow and she opened her eyes more fully to watch him eat from a plate of plain chicken. She sipped from the warm mug slowly; Larkin was right, tea did solve everything. Thankfully, everyone stopped speaking while she drank.

Thea returned with a thick leather-bound book that looked as though it had sustained terrible water damage. She already had it open when she handed it to Aurelia. Mother nodded as she read a few pages, and then handed the book to Selene.

Harlow started to feel more like herself, the wooziness wearing off slowly as she sipped the fragrant Duke and Duchess tea, breathing in the comforting scent of lavender, vanilla and rose. She flexed her fingers. They ached slightly, but the inky stain was starting to fade.

Axel finished eating and then climbed into her lap, turned thrice, and then curled his nose into his long tail. His soft, rhythmic purrs soothed her further as she stroked his fur, which was in poor shape after six months with Mark. They'd fix all that —there were veterinary experts in the Order—she'd make sure he saw the best ones, sorcière who'd fix him up, and fit him with his own protective sigil that would keep anyone from harming him again.

Her mind drifted back to the conversation at hand. What the maters were saying was perplexing, but something deep within her warmed to the ideas they discussed. It all made a certain kind of sense.

"What's a Strider?" she asked when she'd drained her mug.

Larkin was reading the book now, her eyebrows raised, her open mouth covered with one hand. "A bridge between the aether and Okairos," she murmured from behind her hand.

Meline and Indigo came downstairs. "There's no one here. We swept twice," Indigo said softly to Selene. Even though the wards were set up to indicate such things with a high degree of accuracy, the maters had instilled a value in their girls not to solely depend on magic. Magic, like all things, was fallible.

Meline read over Larkin's shoulder. "Harlow can use pure magic? She doesn't have to weave threads or use spells?"

Selene shrugged. "That's what Grandmama always said. Spells and weaving didn't work for her once she'd manifested. She had to do everything by instinct. She was one of the last of a line of sorcière that could access magic at its source. I haven't heard of another coming into power for years, but that's not surprising. The Illuminated don't like them much, as you might imagine; it's likely they hide, if any still exist."

All of her sisters spoke at once. Harlow couldn't make out one vein of the conversation, let alone a quarter dozen. She was trying to parse out the idea that she would no longer be able to do spells, or weave threads of magic in the ways she was used to, but they were all *so noisy*. It had happened to *her*, and no one had asked her how *she* felt about it.

"Stop. Talking. *About*. Me," Harlow hissed. Strands of magic around her snapped and she watched her fingers stain with dark, inky magic. Her vision darkened slightly, as though she'd slipped sunglasses on. Axel's ears swiveled, but he did not move. In fact, he seemed even more relaxed.

Everyone quieted as they turned to look at her.

"Oh Harlow," Thea breathed. "You're divine."

Indigo nodded. "The embodiment of Akatei."

"Hush, don't be blasphemous," Meline cut her off. But Meline switched her phone's screen to front-camera and showed Harlow her face, as though she held up a mirror. Harlow's eyes had gone completely dark, pinpricks of galaxies being born or dying lighting from deep within. And the filaments of magic swirling around her fingers undulated in formless waves, like liquid shadow, rather than the usual iridescent strands she was used to seeing.

"Put that down," Harlow commanded her sister. Her voice sounded strange, like hers, but something more. So it hadn't just been the apartment's acoustics. Meline put the phone down instantly. It was the fastest she'd seen one of the twins obey, ever.

"Harlow, calm down," Aurelia said, taking Harlow's dark blue fingers in hers. "We'll explain everything. Girls, could you give me and Mama a few minutes with your sister?"

Slowly, her sisters dispersed. Harlow watched Thea usher them upstairs, and she knew exactly which step her eldest sister sat on in the stairwell to eavesdrop. It wasn't her heightened senses that told her this, though she thought they might be able to capture such an image, but rather years of sisterly experience. She'd sat on that step with Thea, dozens of times, listening to what went on in the shop below, when she was supposed to be abed.

The familiar childhood memory of eavesdropping with Thea on Order meetings brought her back to herself. She felt the magic recede and her vision cleared to show her a matched set of worried mothers. Axel sighed deeply in his sleep, turning on his side so she could rub his soft belly fur. "So, are you going to explain what's happening to me now?"

Selene draped an arm around her and hugged her. "Your magical talent has manifested, my love. And it's a bit different than we expected it might be."

"Though perhaps we should have seen the signs earlier," Aurelia mused as she flipped through the pages of the Merkhov book, which had no title, only a damaged black leather cover. A mild mildew scent floated up from the pages, confirming that it had either been damaged by water or stored someplace damp. "It says here that Striders often tend to feel displaced and misunderstood."

Something heavy lifted from Harlow's heart. "Really?" Her head was starting to clear.

Aurelia nodded. "Yes, it also says that Striders tend to be competent, and even good at many things before their magic matures, which can further confuse them. I am so sorry, Harlow, I should have hunted this book down sooner, knowing that your great-grandmother was a Strider herself."

"But what is a Strider? Why can't I weave threads or use spells?"

Selene's smile was gentle. "Because you don't need them, my love. What happened when you protected yourself and Axel from the guard, when you actually tried to use magic?"

Harlow remembered the way her spirit body had flown. "I went to the limen in my spirit body—but it was different than it typically is. I think I had wings."

Aurelia seemed to be tracking what she said in the book, nodding. "The limen is where all aethereal power comes from, it's the heart of magic."

Axel settled against her, purring deeply. "That's what you meant when you said I could use magic at its source. I'm using liminal magic."

Selene made a humming noise. "Not exactly. The limen is rather large, a world unto itself, with its own magical rules. To use what we typically term 'liminal magic' you would have to be a creature of the limen itself. You are simply drawing magic from its most potent source, rather than through the threads of reality. There is no conduit between you and your power."

Harlow stared at the herringbone pattern of the wood floor beneath her feet. A hundred competing feelings rattled around inside her. She wasn't sure if she wanted to laugh or cry.

Aurelia passed the book to Selene, pointing to a particular passage. "It says here that the lineage sometimes skips two to three generations, but that Striders are typically born into times when their powers are needed most."

Selene closed the book without reading the passage Aurelia indicated. "Harlow? Are you all right?"

"Sure, Mama. I'm fine. I'm always fine."

Selene cupped Harlow's face in her warm hands. "My darling, that is not true. No one is always fine."

Harlow shrugged, looking anywhere but at either of her parents. She wanted to drag Axel off her lap and hug him tightly to her chest, but he looked so peaceful that she let him be. "So what does this all mean? How do Striders use magic if they don't use spells or weave threads? I assume it's a bit different from the rest of you, since I don't know anyone whose manifestation made their fingers turn colors."

Aurelia's smile was wide. "Each Strider's process is a little different, so there's no methods, no spells. She must learn to trust herself, her intuition. And then, Harlow... A Strider's power is as strong as her will. There are limits, of course, but each Strider must find the edges of her magic on her own."

That sounded a bit frightening. "So no one can teach me?"

Selene shook her head. "No, dearest, I'm afraid not."

There was a rustle of footsteps on the stairs, and a flurry of whispers. "Just come in here," Selene called.

Larkin and Thea rushed into the room. Thea clasped a second book to her chest. "Larkin found this. It's the companion to the Merkhov book, a collection of facsimiles of the texts Merkhov worked with primarily to write her book. Look at this."

Larkin set up a cradle on the coffee table and they gathered round to look at the facsimile of a triptych. The writing underneath each image was indecipherable, written in glyphs Harlow had never seen before. The images themselves were difficult to make out, because of the damage to the book, but she could make out scales in the first two and bodies that looked like snakes. The third seemed to depict something else entirely.

"They almost look like the humans' alchemical illuminations," Selene murmured. "Merkhov's book isn't about alchemy though. It is about navigating the limen, and those who move between. Thea, can you do anything about the images?"

Meline and Indigo peeked through the door to the back stairs. "Can we come in?"

Selene motioned to them and somehow all seven of the Krane women piled onto one couch together. Selene stroked Harlow's hair as Thea worked. Axel jumped onto the back of the couch, stretching his long body out contentedly, resting his chin on Harlow's shoulder as he too watched the oldest Krane sister manipulate reality.

Thea pulled strands of magic quickly, hands darting here and there as she wove them together with expert grace. "I hadn't planned to start either of these texts until next month. I will get to it immediately, but... yes, there... That's better."

The first illumination in the triptych was beautiful. It depicted two snakes, each consuming the other's tail, encircling a semi-transparent sphere that encased a giant egg. The upper snake's body had likely been gilded in the original manuscript, while the intensity of the lower snake's dark blue hue was probably derived from lapis. The originals had to have been extremely costly to produce.

"The color of the snake," Larkin gasped, grabbing Harlow's hands. "It looks familiar, doesn't it?"

Selene's mouth pressed into a grim line as she gazed at the metallic gleam of the upper snake's body. Thea continued her work and shortly the first image was much clearer, showing that the gilded snake emitted light, while the lower snake did not.

Selene stared into her wife's eyes for a long time before Aurelia shook her head, worry creasing her brow.

"What is it?" Harlow asked as Aurelia stared off into the distance. "What do you think this represents?"

"A union," Selene said softly. "Your mother believes this represents a union."

"Of who?" Indigo murmured as Thea sank to the floor in front of Selene. Everyone shifted slightly as Larkin joined her, spreading out a bit more. Larkin poured her eldest sister a cup of tea, and Thea sipped gratefully. The maters were suspiciously quiet.

"The gilded snake represents the Illuminated, doesn't it?" Meline asked, though it hardly sounded like a question. "And the blue snake may depict a Strider. It's not the pure blue of a lapis ink. They must have mixed it with something else to get the darker hue. Maybe tumsole or a bit of vermillion?"

It was a mistake to think that Indigo and Meline only cared about society happenings and their socials. They were as well versed in manuscript production as any of the Kranes.

As if to prove this fact, Indigo nodded at her sister thoughtfully. "Two snakes, locked in what... a destructive cycle? But they're protecting the egg... What do you think the other two images show, Thea?"

Thea shrugged. "I'm a little tired from the rapid-restoration, pal. I'll keep working on the other two and then I guess we'll see."

"I suspect they depict what will happen if a Strider and one of the Illuminated procreate," Aurelia replied bitterly.

Selene let out a deeply held breath in an angry hiss, and Harlow's heart began to pound. If the original triptych represented some sort of indicator about what would happen if a Strider procreated with one of the Illuminated it could explain the McKays' interest in her pairing with Finn. "Do you think the

McKays have seen this? Do they know what I am? What book is this originally from?"

"I don't know the answers to any of those questions, darling." Aurelia shook her head as the collective tension held between the seven of them filled the room. "I think until we know more, we should keep this between us."

"If the McKays have seen this..." Harlow mused, the possibilities endless and terrifying. "Maybe they know more than we do already."

Meline looked thoughtful, her knack for thinking through complex social problems in overdrive. "That's possible, of course, but if you want the upper hand, you need to act as if you don't know."

Indigo nodded at her twin. "Exactly. And if you want to draw them out, find out what they know, you should start making nice with Finn."

Harlow narrowed her eyes at the twins. This was her plan, of course, but the two of them were excellent social strategists. It made sense to hear them out. "Why?"

Meline shifted out from under Indigo's legs. "Because if they think they're getting their way, they're likely to let their guard down. Right now, they're vigilant, trying to get the two of you together. If they think they're winning, they might show their hand."

"Do you think Finn knows what this is all about?" Larkin asked, eyes worried. Harlow read her easily; Larkin liked Finn and didn't want to be disappointed in him.

Meline and Indigo shrugged in unison. "It's hard to say. There are pros and cons to both sides. If he regularly defies them, probably not. They'd want to keep their motives a secret as long as possible."

Thea looked uncomfortable. Harlow kicked her lightly. "You have secret-face, Thea."

Everyone turned to look at the eldest Krane sister. "Alaric

told me some things. Many of them are irrelevant to this conversation and private..." She was clearly flustered. "But if I had to make a guess, he doesn't know. Finn hates his parents. Isn't that right, Harlow?"

Harlow nodded. "He does. But he's desperate for their approval."

Thea's face revealed she had more to say.

Aurelia looked annoyed. "Spit it all out, Thea, for Goddess-sake."

"It's not mine to tell. All I'll say is that I don't think Finn would help his parents hurt Harlow." She took Harlow's hand. "You need to talk to him, pal. You need to let him tell you what happened before uni."

"She can't tell him all this," Meline screeched. "He might be the enemy here."

Harlow untangled herself from her family's arms. "Thank you for your thoughts. If it's okay, I think I'm going to go home. I need a few days to myself. I'll see you all at the Metro for the Solon Mai ball."

Selene kissed her cheek. As protective as she was of her children, she always knew when to let them have space. "We'll be here, love."

Harlow nodded, and kissed her family goodbye, one by one and then slid into her coat. "Come on, Axel," she murmured as the black cat leapt from the back of the couch to follow her. "Let's go home."

CHAPTER EIGHTEEN

Harlow knew Thea would follow, so she walked slowly, waiting in the alley for her sister. She scooped Axel into her coat, whispering to him that he'd had a big day and should let her carry him home. Soon enough, the sound of hurried footsteps signaled Thea's approach. She was pulling her coat on and extending an umbrella to fend off the rain that hung in the air, rather than fall in heavy drops.

"Hey pal, thanks for waiting." Thea's smile didn't reach her eyes.

Harlow ducked under the umbrella and looped her free arm through Thea's, taking in her heady orchid and wood scent. "You want to walk us home?"

Thea gripped her arm, to steady herself or Harlow, she didn't know. "That would be good."

They walked in silence for a while. Axel purred softly against Harlow's chest, content to curl against her as they walked. Thea seemed deep in thought, and Harlow knew better than to rush her sister while she was working out the right way to say something. She'd speak when she was ready.

"Finn told Alaric about your plan. He was worried he couldn't pull it off alone. Alaric wasn't supposed to tell me..."

Harlow sighed. "But he did."

Thea sounded uncomfortable. "Yes."

"Are you going to tell Alaric about me being a Strider?"

"No! Harlow, I would never. You're my sister and... Do you really think I would?"

Harlow shrugged. "I guess I don't know much about how close you are. Why doesn't Finn think he can pull this off alone? I'm sorry it's such a stretch for him to pretend to be interested in me."

Thea stopped, yanking Harlow around to face her under the umbrella with unusual force. Her eyes burned with intense frustration. "Is that what you think? That he needs tips on how to *fake* being in love with you?"

"What else am I supposed to think?" Harlow's voice was an octave or two higher than usual, the shrill sound of her words grating on her nerves. Axel grumbled at the decibel of her voice from inside her coat.

Thea shook her head and stepped back, leaving Harlow in the rain that was falling in earnest now. "You need to talk to him. Hear him out about what happened between you."

"Why can't *you* just tell me?"

Thea was already walking back towards the Monas. She didn't stop as she called over her shoulder, "It will be better if you talk to him. In person, preferably." She stopped and turned around. "Tell him everything, Harlow. I mean it. *Everything.*"

That was in direct violation to what the twins had suggested. Harlow watched her sister disappear into the falling darkness, wondering what Thea knew that the twins did not, and then trudged home. The stairs to her apartment felt even steeper with Axel in her jacket. He seemed to sense her slowing down and jumped out, racing up the stairs ahead of her. When she unlocked the door he ran inside, excited to look around, and then sat down hard.

"Not much here, huh?" Harlow said. "Lots to look at out on the terrace though."

She opened the door for him and he immediately went outside and curled up in one of the plastic chairs Harlow had placed under the narrow awning that provided a bit of shelter from the rain. He purred happily, as if to say, "This will do," and then promptly fell asleep.

Harlow tossed her phone on the bed and changed out of her wet clothes and into a pair of silk pyjamas Enzo had tucked into one of the bags of clothes they'd taken home. She found an empty box that could make do for a litter box, tearing up a newspaper to substitute for litter, and called Axel into the bathroom, where she tucked the box behind her sink.

"Can you go there 'til we get some litter?"

He bumped his head against her leg, agreeing. They went to the kitchen together and she got out a bowl for water and pulled a chicken breast out of the fridge, cutting it up and placing it on a plate next to the bowl on the floor. Axel ate a few bites and then hopped onto her bed, meowing plaintively. She obliged him, climbing into bed and nestling into the pile of pillows as he curled into a ball, warm and cozy in the blankets.

Tears clouded Harlow's vision as she stroked his back. After so many months of feeling unbearably lonely, she could hardly believe her little friend was here now. Safe. They were *both* safe. No one could enter the apartment without her express desire for them to do so. This was the secret of this building, the reason she'd been interested in it in the first place. The wards were second-to-none, built straight into the bones of the building itself, complex and customizable, making this a veritable fortress. Mark couldn't get to either of them here.

As Axel's tiny feline snores drifted into the air, mixing with the sounds of the rain on the terrace, Aurelia's words ran through her head on repeat: *each Strider's process is a little different, so there's no methods, no spells. She must learn to trust herself, her intuition.*

She lit the candles on her bedside table with a quick twist of the threads near them, then got comfortable, focusing narrowly on her breath. She listened to the sounds of her apartment, of Axel snoring, and allowed them to disappear from her notice. Her eyes relaxed and her vision softened until her second sight engaged.

Harlow felt for the filaments of magic that surrounded her, the fibers of reality that wove gracefully together to build the world as she knew it. They were in everything, glowing strong in her, as a living being, and slightly faded in inanimate objects, but still they lit softly at her notice, as they always had. Now though, she saw the other side to the light, the shimmering darkness from which the threads of power grew and conducted aether into the whole of Okairos.

She was certain she was seeing between, into the limen, beyond reality into the source of magic itself. She allowed her second sight to focus on that fertile shadow. It called to her, its sweet song growing louder in her ears as her fingers reached for it, almost involuntarily. She felt a stab of self-doubt, worried about doing this on her own, and the shadows shrank from her.

Harlow was tempted to cringe, tempted to stop. Her fear was there before her, nearly tangible in its magnitude. For the first time in a long time, she knew exactly what to do. She felt her fear and doubt acutely, every sharp, ragged edge. Instead of pushing them away as she usually did, she welcomed them. Tucked them into her heart, like she would joy or comfort, and began to hum a noteless song of promise.

"I will not abandon you," she murmured.

The shadows swirled at her vow, growing in size and shimmering grace. They swirled towards her outstretched fingers in liquid slow motion. When they made contact, she was full for the first time of what felt like limitless power. Every filament of reality sang before her, begging to be shaped, changed, loved, *made*. All because the source of the light, the fertile dark, had settled within her heart.

"I'll never leave you," she said, a bit louder now. "I'll never turn away."

She knew now that she wasn't speaking only to the living shadow, staining her fingers with its potent power, but also her*self*, *her* darkness.

"You are mine, and I am yours," she promised the darkness, and its song was a pledge in return. If she would not turn away, if she would take it in and keep it always, it would also keep her. The liquid shadow danced over her skin, then over Axel's fur. She watched in awe as her vision shifted, showing her the sources of all Axel's little hurts, his weakened bones and muscles, the growing malnutrition he was suffering from.

Her heart ached with desire for him to be made whole and well again. Before her eyes, that desire was made real, inside first and finally in the sheen of his fur as he stretched out on the bed, rolling onto his back. His golden eyes opened slightly and he sighed deeply, as though he were comfortable for the first time in ages. Harlow's shadows danced with joy at her success. The rush of pleasure, joy and bittersweet sadness she felt all at once threatened to overwhelm her.

She did not shrink back. She did not turn away. There in the dark, she too was made whole, forged anew. The candles flared. The shadows drank her in and she swallowed them down. Harlow Krane was more herself than she had ever been, and now she was becoming something more than she had ever been before.

Chapter Nineteen

Harlow spent the next two days practicing with the shadows. Soon she could manipulate reality in much the same way as her parents and Thea could, but instead of pulling power from the tapestry of magic surrounding her, she used it at its source. The difference was subtle at first, but she sensed as she worked that a profound ability lay beyond what she could immediately understand.

She created furniture for herself, then made it disappear. Decorated the entire apartment, then tore it down, banishing all evidence of what she could do from her sight. Eventually, she settled on making up a litter box for Axel. Her real accomplishment was fashioning an enormous cat tree from scrap wood she found in the basement, which she transformed into gnarled manzanita branches that made the apartment feel like an enchanted forest. The feline climbed into it immediately to look out the windows.

The only thing she could not change was herself. Any time she tried to do more than a basic glamour to enhance her beauty, the shadows refused, as if in disapproval, though there was something else behind the refusal—a sense that she was not ready yet, that there were other steps to take first. Aside from that, her imagination was her only limit, or so she thought. Then she attempted to create a living being from nothing. Just a moth, nothing larger like a mammal.

The shadows shrank back, and she felt the wrongness of it. She spoke aloud to them, apologizing, and then spent time in deep meditation communing with the source of magic as best she could. It didn't use words to communicate, but she felt its desire as though it were speaking. She didn't understand the power yet, but her affinity with it grew by the hour. As time went on, she understood that she could not create new life from nothing, but she could breathe new life into what was already available to her.

Harlow thought she had an excellent handle on things, for a beginner anyway, when she built a miniature replica of the house she'd dreamed of living in since she was a witchling from a cardboard box that she found in the trash. An irrepressible grin spread over her face, gazing at the gardens she built for it, when her phone buzzed. Annoyed by the interruption, she stepped away from her creation to check her phone.

It was a text from Finn. *Ready for tonight? We should go to the thing at the White Oak, unless you want to go somewhere else.*

Worry coursed through her, and fear. Not about the cocktail party, or even Solon Mai. They could manage that. But afterwards. The conversation she knew they had to have. So many scenarios ran through her mind, and all of them scared her. The ones the secret parts of her longed for scared her the most.

The White Oak is fine, she texted back, forcing herself to be brave. *I'll be there at 7.*

When she turned back to her tiny dreamhouse, it was gone. She felt for the shadows and they did not respond. Her heart pounded. She'd made so much progress so quickly. Why was this happening now? She glanced at her phone and wondered.

The shadows didn't like fear. Or maybe it was that she wasn't able to wield them properly when she was afraid? She sat down to try to figure it out, but her mind flooded with memories. Finn smiling that half smile when she talked about her dreams as he sketched. His arms around her at a party, secret kisses. Laughing 'til her sides ached over jokes only the two of them found funny.

She pushed away the thoughts of the night it all ended and let the way his demeanor changed the day after fill her mind's eye. The way his gaze slid over her in the hallways at school, like she wasn't even there. When she'd begged to talk to him, he'd laughed, and asked what *she* could have to talk with *him* about in an emotionless tone that had crushed her heart so fast she hadn't seen what was coming.

And the months after. It wasn't just Petra's bullying. It was the way he looked away from both her and Enzo. The calls he never returned. The way she'd felt more lonely and desperate than she'd imagined possible. He'd left her empty, broken, a shell of her former self, and she'd spent the following years filling herself with as many lovers as possible. Kate Spencer had been a brief respite from those times, but then she'd gone back to Nea Sterlis and Harlow's desperation returned. The drugs, the booze, anything to stop her from feeling the emptiness Finn left behind.

And then one night Mark Easton had held her hair back as she puked in a bush like it was the most natural thing in the world. He'd wiped Harlow's mouth with his shirt and taken her home. When they fucked it was the most alive Harlow had ever felt, and Mark was *proud* of her. Proud to be with her. Or at least he had been at first. Harlow thought that feeling could last forever. But of course it hadn't. Being with Mark had made everything worse.

Could she ever stop operating from this place of fear? The hurt she felt was so deep, so impenetrable, she didn't know if she could ever reach the end of it. Something soft as silk brushed her hands. The shadows flit between her fingers, winding up her arms as though they wanted to comfort her.

"Thank you," she whispered.

The darkness in her sang in response and she let the notes wash over her. Surrounded by her beautiful dark magic, Harlow closed her eyes and dipped into the fluid sadness, letting herself sink deep into it for the first time in years.

Harlow didn't know how long she disappeared for, but when she came to Axel was licking her fingertips and it was nearly six thirty. She'd have to hurry if she wanted to meet Finn at the White Oak on time. First, she called for a car, then texted Enzo to find out what she was supposed to wear, and groaned when the answer was all too simple: *The little black dress. Heels.*

She knew the one and had been dreading it. Once she had smoked out her eyes with black shadow she pulled it on, whispering a prayer to Aphora that she'd look all right. When she checked herself in the mirror, she smiled. She actually liked it.

"What do you think?" she asked Axel, who merely yawned and settled into the blankets for a long nap.

The black velvet wrapped around her in soft folds that hugged her hips and waist, propelling her bust into prominence via the low neckline of the dress. Long sleeves covered her arms —it was still too cold for shorter sleeves at night— and the dress fell to just below her knees, so she wouldn't have to worry about accidentally flashing anyone. When she stepped into the simple black pumps she smiled again. She could walk in these. Enzo had thought of everything.

Harlow fed Axel and then hurried downstairs to catch her car. The driver, a human in their mid-fifties, greeted her and then returned to listening to an art history podcast, leaving Harlow to her own devices as they wound through the city. She was nervous about leaving Axel for the evening, but knew he'd be fine on his own. Before things had gone so wrong with Mark, he'd always been fine by himself.

Besides, Larkin had promised to check in on him. Harlow knew she was being overly anxious, but she texted her youngest sister one more time to remind her. There was a near-instantaneous reply: *I'm already headed to your place with a pizza and a ginormous box of toys and stuff Mama bought him. She's not-so-secretly in love with your cat. Stop worrying and have fun, catmom.*

Harlow shot off a thank you and closed her eyes, taking deep breath after deep breath, and before she knew it they'd reached the White Oak. It was Nuva Troi's most prominent whiskey bar, located in a renovated warehouse in Midtown. It was always trendy, but tonight it was lit with witchlights, music floating onto the street.

She was alone tonight, which was both good and bad. The maters and the twins had gone to a big party down by the wharf that seemed tailored to the season's slightly younger crowd and their parents, and Enzo and Thea were attending a party in Uptown. Something at one of the wineries' tasting rooms. She was glad she didn't have to go to that—she'd rather drink whiskey if she had to drink at all.

As the car drove off, she lingered for an extra moment outside, feeling nervous.

"Going in?"

She turned to find Alaric standing next to her, dazzling her with his casual beauty. "Yes, are you?"

He grinned. "Nope. I got my wires crossed with your sister and thought she was coming here, but she said she was going to that thing at Cask & Vine. Wishful listening on my part, I guess. *I don't really like wine.*" He whispered the last sentence conspiratorially, as a goofy smile spread across his face.

Harlow smiled. It was impossible not to be charmed by him.

"Finn's inside already, and I happen to know that my cousin is at the wharf party tonight."

Harlow chuckled. "Well, at least there's that."

He squeezed her shoulder. "Gotta dash. Can't keep my girl waiting."

Harlow didn't have time to think of something else to say. He'd disappeared.

CHAPTER TWENTY

She'd never been to the White Oak. It was a favorite among the Order of Masks, owned by a wealthy wolf pack from Nea Sterlis, and it had opened when she and Mark were together—but they never came to this side of town. They never went anywhere in the last months of their relationship where Harlow might run into anyone she knew. She'd thought at the time that it was because he wanted her to himself, but now she saw it differently. He'd wanted her alone, weak, and pliable. She shook off the thought of the argument they'd had about coming to the White Oak's opening as she stepped inside the bar.

As she took it all in, she understood why Finn wanted to come here. Not only was the building beautiful with its exposed brick walls and the dozen enormous crystal chandeliers that hung from the ceiling, but the White Oak hadn't closed the bar down to the public for the party, only devoted their main floor to it.

The upper bar was still open and it was full of gawking humans, and some photographers she recognized as Section Seven staff, as well as a bevy of freelance paparazzi. She resisted the urge to pull the neckline of her dress up, or fade into the shadows. She steeled herself against what she knew was coming: the posts on the gossips, the chatter on the socials.

Photos would be taken and shared without her consent. People would speculate about her motives, talk about her and Finn, her and Mark, all of it in ways she wouldn't be able to control or ignore. The feeling that she was making herself a target in this dress, coming here with Finn, this *was* the plan. This was what she needed to do for her family.

The music shifted and Harlow's heart dropped into her stomach. The song was one she'd put on every playlist as a teenager. The one that made her think of him—and he had to know it—this song had been playing *that* night. This whole damn album on repeat. When she tore her eyes from her shoes, the bartender was grinning at her.

"He said you might need this." The shifter gave Harlow a decidedly lupine grin and pushed a glass of whiskey towards her. "It's our best, and Finn knows what he's talking about."

Harlow took the glass and sipped, wondering how the bartender got on a first name basis with Finbar McKay. The whiskey was good. Deep, complex, smoky. She was in so much trouble. She threw back the whole glass, even though shots hadn't been her thing in quite some time. She eyed the bartender, who was short, with an athletic build and short black hair, shaved on the sides.

Her sparkling brown eyes crinkled with amusement as she poured Harlow another finger of whiskey. "I hear you don't even need this stuff to fuck him."

Harlow raised her eyebrows. "And you would know?"

The bartender laughed, a rough, joyful sound. "He wishes. I don't swing that way though."

Harlow laughed with her. "I wish I didn't."

The bartender rested her elbow on the bar, smirking roguishly. "If you change your mind about Finn, stay after the party."

Harlow bit her lip, stifling the giggle that was bubbling up from her chest. "If he can't behave, I might."

"You won't, but it was fun talking to you." The bartender nodded to someone behind Harlow and when she turned, Finn was standing in the middle of the room, his gaze intense as his eyes found hers. He was on the phone, but as their attention locked onto one another, he said goodbye and hung up, sliding his phone into the pocket of his jeans as he drank her in. Something coiled tight and low in Harlow's belly woke, warmth creeping through her in slow, fiery licks.

Then he was next to her and if the bartender stayed to hear what he'd say to her, she didn't know, because the smell of smoky oud wood and rich, golden amber, so familiar in its exhilarating nature, distracted her to the point that she nearly lost her good sense. He leaned against the bar, his body close enough that she could feel its heat, but far enough away for propriety.

"You trying to kill me with that dress, Harls?"

She struggled to find the words she wanted, and sharper, uglier ones came out instead. "You're immortal. It'd be harder than I'd like to kill you."

He laughed as the music swelled, and it was impossible not to remember their last night together. Not with this song playing, not with him standing so close to her. His body hovering over hers, the sweet pain of him inside her. The way he'd pushed her hair out of her face as he told her he loved her.

"You trying to kill me with this song, McKay?"

He swallowed hard, his throat bobbing. "I didn't ask them to play it." His fingers skimmed her hip. "But I'm not sorry they are."

It was her turn to swallow. He was too good at this. If she wasn't careful, she'd fall for him for real, and she couldn't let that happen. She looked at the wide rustic planks of the wood floor. If he was going to play this way, she could too. When she raised her eyes, she did so slowly, taking a small step closer.

"Do you think about it? That night?" she asked so softly only he would hear her. To anyone watching, she knew it would look like they were flirting. Well, not *flirting* exactly, but definitely courting.

She watched his chest heave as he struggled to breathe naturally. "Yes."

His fingers pressed into the soft curve of her hip and she slid a hand up the buttons of his crisp white shirt. He'd actually dressed up for this. "How much?"

"I try not to... but a lot."

She made a soft humming noise as she took another step closer, looking up at him through her lashes. "Me too. I think about the way it felt to run through the rain. We were soaking wet."

A low rumble vibrated through his chest and his eyes lit softly; he was reacting to her, just the way she'd hoped he would. The photographers upstairs saw too and got out their cameras. She tugged gently on his shirt. The collar was open and he wasn't wearing a tie, so she slipped a finger inside, caressing his skin lightly.

He looked good, but she didn't like this buttoned-up look he'd been trotting out to the season events. Something in her wished for his usual leather jacket and messy hair. Hells, she missed the way he'd painted his nails when they were in secondary. Those were dangerous thoughts—she needed to stay on track here. It would be best if she stayed in control and *he* was off balance.

She lifted her face, parting her lips, pleased with the way his eyes tracked even the smallest of her movements. "I think about the way it felt to have you so deep inside me I forgot we were two people."

"You really are trying to kill me," he murmured, his voice rough.

"And I think about how you pushed my wet hair from my

face and moved in me, so gentle and slow... You told me you loved me. Do you remember that?"

He nodded, his thumb drifting to her face, grazing her bottom lip, as the fingers that had pressed into her hip strayed to the small of her back, pulling her so close she could feel his desire for her stirring. He was going to kiss her. What's worse, she wanted him to. Her lips ached to feel his.

Her wounded heart spoke before her mutinous body could act. "You fucked me, told me you loved me, and then you acted like nothing happened between us." The words fell from her lips in a honeyed tone that did nothing to mask the anger burning in her chest. The cameras on the balcony wouldn't catch that, but he would.

She felt the flinch he didn't show as she stepped even closer, her breasts pressing hard into his chest. "Remember that, McKay. Remember that you broke me into a million pieces. Remember that you let that vicious princess Petra Velarius make my life a living hell for a year. Remember that I can *never* fully trust you."

"I know," he said, breathless. "Believe me. I know."

She looked at him now, really looked. His storm-grey eyes were dark with some version of sadness, maybe grief. A kernel of guilt burrowed into her heart. She'd actually hurt him, which for some reason, she hadn't expected. Just like she hadn't expected for this moment to feel so terrible. For years after what happened between them, she'd imagined working him up the way she had just now, only to decimate him, destroy him the way he'd destroyed her.

But this didn't feel good. She didn't feel like she'd won anything. In fact, she had the distinct feeling that she'd lost something that had become very precious to her in recent months—her self-respect. This wasn't how she treated people. This was how *Mark* treated people. Harlow recoiled from the thought, horrified. She started to say she was sorry, but couldn't form the vulnerable words, much as she wanted to.

"We should go," she said, softening her tone in lieu of an apology. "If they think we're leaving together it will be on everyone's socials in minutes. That's what we want, right?"

He cleared his throat and she wondered if he could hear the unspoken apology she'd wanted to voice. "If they think I took you home, they'll call you all sorts of terrible things and no one will take this seriously."

Godsdamn him, he was right. She imagined Indigo and Meline rolling their eyes at her lack of foresight. Harlow sighed. "I shouldn't have said all that."

His hand was still on the small of her back, though his arm had tensed significantly. Now, it relaxed a measure and she stepped back a little, but not so far away that his hand would be dislodged.

His head dipped and he wore a contrite expression. "I probably shouldn't have moved things forward so quickly. I don't know how to do this with you. It feels good, and then bad... We should talk about what happened between us."

Her heart skipped a terrifying beat. "Not here, not tonight."

He shook his head. "No. On Solon Mai though, all right? After the ball."

She nodded, glancing at the balcony to the upper bar. The music had changed, thank Aphora, though the White Oak was apparently playing nostalgic favorites tonight. A different bartender than before asked if they wanted anything else.

Finn shook his head. "Can I get my check?"

"What are you doing?" she whispered. "I thought leaving was a bad idea."

"Follow along, please."

She raised her eyebrows, suspicious.

"You can choose not to trust me. I deserve that. But please, just follow along."

She watched while he left an enormous tip and signed his name, taking his card back and putting it in his wallet. Then he took her hand, kissing her palm. His lips were warm and soft against her skin and the kiss was slow and sweet as his eyes met hers.

"They'll follow," he murmured, as he leaned close enough for his lips to brush the shell of her ear. "Now laugh and nod, like I just asked you to do something fun."

She did as he asked and he led her out of the bar, still holding her hand. Sure enough, the photographers scrambled to follow. "They'll catch up," he said when they reached the sidewalk.

His eye met hers as his fingers laced tighter through her own. The heat coiled in her belly slithered with pleasure, loosening again, sending warmth lapping across the sweetest aching spots. She tore her eyes from his, asking, "Where are we going?"

His mouth lifted in that rare, signature Finbar McKay smile that girls in secondary had claimed dropped panties in an instant. The memory brought her attention to her own undergarments, which were decidedly damp from their encounter inside the bar, to her horror. His voice was smooth, gloriously honeyed with some unknown pleasure. "You'll see."

They walked down the street, still holding hands. In this area, there were bars and restaurants everywhere. Fancy places she didn't usually go. Places the Times reviewed constantly, on repeat, like there wasn't other food in the city. When Finn stopped, it wasn't in front of any of those places. It was in front of a human street vendor.

"Finn McKay," the man said with a smile. He was middle-aged, with pale skin, red hair, and fantastic dimples. "What'll it be for you and the goddess tonight?"

Finn grinned. "Hey, Brennan. Can we get two giant waffle cones, with vanilla bean ice cream and chocolate sprinkles?"

"You don't want one to share?" Brennan asked, grinning deviously. Harlow wondered how often Finn brought dates to

Brennan's cart. She could just imagine how charming it would seem to all the high society immortals he'd been linked with in the past. Her heart stammered, unsure. That wasn't a fair assumption. And why should she care who he brought where?

Finn shook his head. "Nope, we're not at the sharing stage yet, but vanilla bean with sprinkles is Harls' favorite."

The words struck her hard, slamming into her, a truckload of memories she'd worked hard to repress since things went wrong between them. After every test she failed, every time she disappointed Selene, all the times she'd embarrassed herself trying out for plays she never got into, he'd brought her vanilla bean ice cream, her favorite, and a bottle of sprinkles to shake onto every bite. Her chin threatened to quiver, so she bit her bottom lip hard.

When Brennan handed the big cones over, he also gave them wooden spoons. As they walked away, she heard, rather than saw the photographers following. They'd catch up soon.

"I should have been there to give this to you when some asshole treated you like shit in secondary."

She looked up at him and started to say he didn't need to say anything else tonight, but he shook his head. His words came out in a tumble. "I shouldn't have been that asshole. I've done a lot of work on myself since back then, and maybe I don't deserve your forgiveness, but I hope at least when I explain things on Solon Mai, you'll get any closure you still need..."

"Okay."

He looked down at her, his brow furrowed in surprise. "What?"

She didn't want to hold grudges or act out in ways that made her feel like a monster. That path was dangerous. Harlow wasn't the least bit sure that she could trust Finn, and she was positive they weren't starting anything real, but she could hear him out and let this go for good. She could try to heal, and then start over. She didn't know how that would work with everything she'd committed to doing for the Order and her family, but she was finally willing to try.

"Okay," she said, so quietly she was afraid he might not hear her. "We'll talk. I'll get closure, and then we'll figure out what to do next."

His face was open and she saw how surprised he was. How hope lit softly in his face, flickering weakly as a candle in a windstorm. "Yeah?"

Harlow nodded as she took a big bite of the ice cream, and started walking towards the subway. She didn't want to be the one to douse that light. Not tonight, even though she knew anything more than this between them was utterly impossible. "Yeah. Wanna ride to my stop with me?"

Finn smiled. "I do."

Behind them, the sound of cameras followed until they disappeared into the subterranean stairway.

CHAPTER TWENTY-ONE

The days after the White Oak party were a riot of news about Harlow, Thea, and the Illuminated men courting them. Section Seven and the socials all but quit talking about Mark and Olivia. Instead, photos of her at the whiskey bar, and on the street with Finn, circulated everywhere, along with commentary about her clothes, about how long she and Finn had known one another and if she or Thea were to be considered the season's swan.

The nearly unanimous conclusion was that despite the entertaining showing she and Finn put on as a couple, the glamor of Thea and Alaric's fairytale match was too good to pass up. Their burgeoning love story was all anyone following the season closely—which according to Indigo and Meline was literally millions of people—were talking about. Harlow spent the entire morning in bed cuddling Axel, catching up on gossip sites and socials, drinking tea and laughing to herself at all the speculation.

A few times, she'd thought of texting some of the funnier memes people were making about her and Finn to him, but she refrained. They'd reached a truce the night of the White Oak party, but she still didn't completely trust him. She was almost certain he wasn't in league with his parents, but she didn't know if they could even be friends, let alone anything more.

Still, the realization that she wanted closure and to move on from their sad past remained, and that was enough for her. That and getting his parents off the Order of Mysteries' back for good. She had to remember that was the real goal here, not making herself feel better.

An alarm went off on her phone, reminding her to get going. She'd promised to get ready for the Solon Mai ball with Enzo and her sisters at his place, and she'd been trying to take a nap with Axel but had gotten sucked into her phone. She hadn't slept well all week, between monitoring socials and practicing with her shadow magic. Harlow hoped to Aphora that Thea could glamour away the dark circles under her eyes.

The alarm rang again, insistently. Harlow shut it off and fed Axel, who was fast asleep, sprawled out on her bed. She kissed him and he purred, but did not wake. He was doing much better, sleeping comfortably now and eating regularly. He'd even started to play with the toys Larkin had brought over, to Harlow's surprise. Axel had never been interested in toys before, but perhaps that was because he'd known what she hadn't at the time—that they hadn't been safe at Mark's.

She gathered her things and went downstairs to hail a cab, which was blessedly easy to do. She fell into the back seat, feeling drained and anxious about the evening ahead. The ever-present spring drizzle in Nuva Troi draped the world in a comforting blanket of grey and she dozed a little in the back seat.

When they came to a stop on Mulberry Street, she paid the cabbie, tipping generously, and entered the atelier from the back. Enzo's parents had owned the entire building, and at one time rented out the top floors as office space. Now, Enzo resided here, above the shop.

Harlow pressed her palm to the metal plate next to the door, as Enzo had instructed her to do, and it opened—a stunning bit of magical tech that must have cost Enzo a fortune. Her own combination of lock and wards worked similarly to let in who she wanted to, and keep out anyone else, but this single piece of tech seemed to do it all in one go. Her eyes narrowed slightly as the door opened and a soft voice said, "Welcome, Harlow Krane."

The muffled sound of blaring pop music from upstairs suffused the stairwell. Harlow took a deep breath; they were already having a good time and she didn't want to be a downer, but the past few days had been draining. Her feet moved slowly as she reluctantly headed up. She hadn't been upstairs since Enzo spent a year remodeling the building, but the limewash blue paint felt familiar. Her memory of Enzo's blue bedroom in the Weraka townhouse was still as vivid as though she'd been there yesterday.

She smiled as she trailed upstairs, where she found all four of her sisters, Enzo, and Riley Quinn dancing in the great room to the music she'd heard below. Harlow hesitated for a moment. They were having fun and she wasn't sure if she could have fun today. She wanted to, but her whole body felt heavy and sluggish, as though she were having an emotional hangover.

Larkin spotted Harlow and left the group to pull her into the living room. Everyone was singing the words to the popular song as loud as they could. Awkwardness flooded Harlow's body. She felt as though she'd forgotten how to move. Larkin took her hands and started to sway with her, singing in an exaggerated fashion that made Harlow laugh.

Slowly, her body began to move along with Larkin's. She was a terrible dancer, unlike her athletic, spritely sister, but she was starting to have fun. Larkin twirled her and Thea bumped her hip with her own. Soon, Harlow was singing along too, with the same abandon as her sisters. She felt the infectious magic of the moment in the shadows that pushed power into the filaments of magic surrounding them. Everything in the room began to glow slightly in Harlow's second sight as the tightness in her chest dissipated into the music.

The song ended and a slow song came on. Enzo turned the music down as she went to greet him. He was a little breathless as he pulled her into a hug, and looked so satisfied that it made it hard for Harlow not to smile when he ordered her to "Come chat with Riley. I want them to feel welcome."

Harlow's heart swelled with happiness for Enzo. She knew that look; he was falling hard for the talented shifter. Riley was in the kitchen, their locs wrapped in an intricate half-up style that was punctuated by jeweled gold combs. Their ears were slightly elongated, as with all the Trickster's Chosen, and they wore earrings in each ear that coordinated with the combs in their hair.

"Only part way done," Riley said, gesturing to their visage. "Thea was kind enough to offer to do my eyes."

Their voice was rich and the cadence of their words slow and measured, as though they had never been anxious or flustered in their life. Their fawn-colored eyes were long lashed and the faint glow of gold highlighter shone on their clear, brown skin. Outside of the Illuminated and Thea, Harlow had never seen such an intensely beautiful person. Or perhaps their beauty might be better described as handsome. Whichever way she thought of it, their allure was beyond just looks, but seemed to emanate from a deeper place that spoke of a truer grace, with no small helping of acute intelligence.

"It's so good to see you again, Riley," she said with a smile.

They hugged her immediately, and she felt the electric current of their empathy. It made a stronger impression now that they were in close contact. Harlow had never felt empathic power like this before. She wondered what the depths of Riley's power actually were, or if they even knew.

"Wow, that's amazing," she murmured as a wave of reassurance smoothed her frayed nerves. "You're brilliant at that."

"And you are something else... aren't you?" Riley asked, eyes alight with interest.

Harlow's eyes narrowed with wary concern. Empaths couldn't help but pick up the surface details of other people's thoughts and feelings, but only extremely rare empaths could sense things like the depths of other immortals' manifestations. From the wide-eyed wonder in Riley's eyes, she sensed they knew about her shadow magic.

"I won't say a word," Riley murmured. "But Enzo will be able to tell, too. Your secret is safe with us."

"But is it safe with the Rogue Queen?" Harlow asked.

Riley poured Harlow a mimosa, their eyes glittering with some secret knowledge. "I see no reason to tell her, at this juncture. You'll show the world soon enough, I think."

They handed her the mimosa and as she sipped it, Riley added, "But if she *did* know about you, Harlow, you could trust her to keep your secret."

Harlow wasn't sure if it was Riley's empathy at work on her, or just a sense she had, but she trusted what they said. Though it did spark a wave of curiosity about the Rogue Queen. From the very little she'd heard about the Rogue Order, asking about them would do no good. They were notoriously secretive. Her shadows pressed on her conscious mind in a warm, pleasurable way that signaled approval, though for what she wasn't certain.

Internally, she asked, *Do you like Riley?*

The answer was emphatically positive. Her magic liked Riley, and everyone in this room. These people made it feel safe and strong. She marveled at the wordless way it communicated until she noticed Riley's raised eyebrows and faint smile.

Just as Harlow was about to explain herself, Enzo brought her dress out from the bedroom, hanging it on the rack with the rest of the garments for the evening. "What are the two of you discussing?"

Harlow hugged him, opening herself up to his empathy fully and directing the shadows, *Show him in a way he can understand.*

"Oh," he said, raising his dark eyebrows as she pulled away. "Oh... Harlow. Your magic... It's beautiful."

She smiled as he kissed her cheeks. Riley's arm went around his waist and the two of them smiled at her like proud parents.

"Are you talking about me?" she asked after a moment. They were nodding as though having a silent conversation.

"Oh! Sorry, yes," Riley said, a bright smile lighting their face.

Enzo brushed a kiss on Riley's sharp cheekbones. "Easy to forget that others can't hear us. Sorry, Harls. Riley's right, your secret is safe with us. After Solon Mai, I'd love to see what you can do."

Harlow nodded, glad they knew. She had a feeling she would need allies soon, more than just her parents and sisters. Besides, Enzo had always been her family, and if he chose Riley, they would be her family too. Thea danced over and dragged Riley away from Enzo's embrace to finish their glamour.

Harlow watched them go, smiling faintly as Riley twirled Thea to the music. They were a graceful dancer, and some small part of her warned that with grace like that they'd probably be deadly in a fight. She wondered where that thought came from, tilting her head slightly as Enzo poured himself a mimosa. Finally, she said, "I like them. Things are moving quickly though, is that all right?"

Enzo nodded, watching Thea and Riley discuss their vision for Riley's glamour. "Empath to empath pairings are intense. Riley's mother was a sorcière, which as you know is very rare. Though Riley can't wield magic as a witch would, their empathy is stronger than anyone I've ever met. We immediately felt at home with one another."

That made sense, and Harlow's shadows danced at the explanation. They liked the two of them together. *Are you sure Riley's safe?* she asked. Her magic swirled inside her, comforting her with a reassuring warmth that she hoped she could depend on. She certainly wanted to.

"I'm happy for you." Harlow hugged her friend. "Will you help me get into my gown?"

Enzo looked at her appraisingly. "Are you doing your face by hand?"

"Not tonight," she replied. "I'm feeling a bit tired from the last few days."

Enzo nodded, putting his mimosa down to fetch her dress. Harlow slipped out of her sweats and Enzo helped her into the gossamer lace gown. One he had her buttoned up, she waited for Thea. Indigo and Meline were resplendent, already dressed in matching black damask ball gowns. They didn't always dress alike, but tonight they were a vision of similarities, the only difference between them the color of their hair. Meline's shone with the same honey-gold sheen as her own, while Indigo's was darker than both Thea and Larkin's.

"So Larkin is staying home?" Enzo's eyebrows furrowed with concern. "She doesn't seem upset."

Larkin was busy helping everyone put the finishing touches on their ensembles for the evening, but she was wearing her favorite sweats, her dark hair in a messy bun. She was fresh-faced and happy, nothing like the anxious mess she usually was before an event. Her eyes met Harlow's and her smile radiated happiness and ease.

"I think she's better than she's ever been. Did she talk with you about the feelings she's been having about relationships?"

Enzo smiled. "Yes, she came over early and we spent the afternoon talking. I'm going to introduce her to Avery Hargrove. Do you remember Avery?"

Harlow did remember Avery from university, a sorcière with

a gift for sculpture, who was never linked to anyone romantically. "I do. How is Avery doing these days?"

"She's great. Her sculptures are doing well in Nea Sterlis and she's touring again this winter. I think she and Larkin will have a lot to talk about. They have a call set up for next week."

Relief flooded Harlow's chest. She'd been worried that her talk with Larkin hadn't been good enough, that the fact she hadn't known the right words to say would hurt, rather than help. She knew if Larkin was able to talk with someone who felt similarly that she might understand herself better.

"I just want her to do better than I did. To understand herself better... not to suffer so much, you know?"

Enzo nodded, popping a tiny canape into her mouth. It was divine and Harlow desperately needed a snack. "Give me another."

He obliged and then it was her turn with Thea. She replaced Riley in one of the upholstered blue chairs at Enzo's table. Thea was already dressed, her slim figure clad in a simple velvet gown that fit close to her body, with long sleeves that fell off her shoulders. A tiara, sparkling with black diamonds, shimmered in her hair.

"I haven't seen that before," Harlow said as Thea sipped her mimosa.

"It was a gift from Alaric."

Harlow raised her eyebrows. "It looks expensive."

Thea pursed her lips disapprovingly. "I'm sure it was. Now, what are we doing with your face and hair."

"Something that looks like I just rolled out of bed, but elegant."

Thea shook her head. She, of course, was elegant *and* polished, her face painted in understated, classic lines, her nails pale pink ovals, every hair perfectly placed.

"I want to look a little mussed."

Thea nodded, pulling strands of magic so quickly that

Harlow barely saw her fingers move. When Thea held up a mirror for her to look in, she grinned. Her eyes were subtly smoky, and her lashes elongated past what she could hope to achieve with products, but not so dramatically that she looked overly made up. Everything else looked like her skin, with a slight glow.

"Thank you," she whispered. "I look beautiful."

Thea smiled. "You always do, Harlow. But yes, this is some of my best work."

Enzo clapped his hands to get everyone's attention. "The maters are on their way. It's time to head to the Metro."

CHAPTER TWENTY-TWO

The Metropolitan Archive of Fine Arts' marble columns were lit sparingly, but dark lanterns scattered the steps, giving the entrance to the grand old building a feeling of mystery. Photographers from every major publication and the gossips were only allowed on the sidewalk, so after walking past the column of flashing lights and shouts to turn this way and that, Harlow was free to enjoy her walk up the MAFA steps.

She'd always loved the old building, and all the art it held within, as it was one of the few places in Nytra that didn't discriminate between Orders and humans. If the art was good enough, it was here, regardless of mortality. The curatorial staff and board of directors had even shifted in recent years to employ more humans. It was slow progress, but it was *some* progress.

As Harlow walked through the arched doorway to the museum with her family, anticipation filled her. While the Solstice Gala was the apex of the season, the Solon Mai ball was considered a pivotal moment in the journey for most pairings. Typically, this was the night when the season's most prominent couples emerged and the race to the Solstice began for anyone not already matched. She'd purposely avoided making any kind of elaborate plan with Finn. Indigo and Meline cautioned her repeatedly that the best lies were told with as many grains of truth as possible, and so she'd decided to allow things to play out as naturally as she could.

Harlow was acutely aware of the way her heels clicked against the marble floors of the Metro hallways, which had been transformed to look like an enchanted forest, the boughs of the trees parting overhead to reveal a sparkling night sky. Everywhere, flowering branches wound around columns and hung from ceilings, as though an enormous blooming thicket had taken over the Metro. Tiny golden witchlights floated in and out of the dark branches, blinking slowly in and out like fireflies on an early summer evening, hinting at what was to come on the Solstice.

Interspersed between the columns of branches, hundreds of glass lanterns of different shapes and sizes glowed on the ground. It gave the dark entrance to the museum dozens of secluded nooks that many couples were already taking advantage of. Music drifted seductively out from the ballroom at the end of the hall.

From somewhere in the expertly contrived dark forest, Harlow felt eyes watching her. She stopped to look around, her dress swishing around her ankles as she stepped towards the prickling sensation of being seen by someone she could not perceive. Someone took hold of her arm and she spun to find Thea.

"Coming?" her sister asked.

Harlow nodded, following slowly as Thea led her to the ballroom, where their family was waiting. Very quickly, the twins were asked to dance; Enzo and Riley followed, as well as the maters, leaving Thea and Harlow alone to watch the dancers together. Here, the darkness of the entry hall gave way to the lush greens of ferns and branches of fragrant wisteria, dripping with blossoms. The ground around the edges of the dance floor was dotted with thick moss and lichen that led into yet another corridor of dark trees that encircled the ballroom. The same tiny golden witchlights from the hall flickered between frond and bough. At the center of the room, couples danced, surrounded by groups of people in conversation.

"There's Alaric," Thea murmured, as a raven-haired head swiveled their way.

She hesitated, as though she didn't want to leave Harlow alone. "Go to him," she said, urging her sister on. There was no need to spoil Thea's evening with the fact that she felt watched, that she felt the sinister pressure of eyes on her, even now. Thea would just worry, and she deserved an evening of romance. That was what *she* was here for after all, unlike Harlow.

Thea's smile met Alaric's and Harlow knew she no longer heard her. She watched as they gravitated towards each other, pulled by some invisible force. Alaric took her sister's hand and led her onto the dance floor, where the crowd parted to allow them room.

People stopped to stare at the figure they cut. Truly, they were the most attractive people in the room, and together each amplified the goodness and beauty in the other. The vision was so sweet in its purity that Harlow found herself clutching her heart, forgetting the feeling she had that she was being watched, if only for a moment.

And then she saw Finn. She didn't know how she could have missed him; once her eyes locked with his, she saw nothing else. He was somewhat carelessly dressed; his perfectly tailored tuxedo was everything it should be, but as usual, he refused to wear a tie. Petra was standing next to him, trying to speak to him, but he paid her no mind.

Could it have been him she felt watching her? That didn't seem right to her. The feeling she had now, with his focus on her, was nothing like the chilling prickle of warning she'd felt walking in. No, this was different. Her skin flushed hot under her gown as their eyes locked onto one another.

He pushed away from the wall he was leaning against and strode across the room, leaving Petra behind. He didn't force his speed the way she knew he could. Instead, he used his time to run his eyes over her body, causing tight longing to clench in her abdomen as he approached. He took her hand when he finally reached her and the feel of his skin against hers set her heart to pounding in her ears, as her cheeks flushed in an unmistakable blush.

"We have to go do something unpleasant," he said softly as he brushed a kiss to her palm.

"What's that?"

She followed his pointed gaze. His parents stood at the edge of the room, surrounded by people all vying for their attention. But both of them were staring at Finn and Harlow, and she felt the predatory nature of their shared attention in her bones. She had the good sense to suppress the shudder she felt coming on, but nothing could lessen the fear she felt in this moment.

But still, as much as they terrified her, this was not the presence she felt watching her earlier. The realization chilled the flush in her skin, turning her clammy almost instantly. Though most humans didn't realize it, the older Illuminated were dangerous beyond imagining. The common assumption in the Order of Mysteries was that they'd lived too long, and nothing satiated their desire for pleasure anymore but cruelty and degradation. No one could gain concrete information about them, but the rumors she'd heard were enough to make anyone ill.

Which was why the instinctual feeling she had that even they were not the threat she sensed was so unsettling. She realized Finn was speaking, tugging gently on her arm to get her attention. "We have to, Harlow. They want to meet you."

She knew he wasn't saying much else because their attention was so focused on them. The Illuminated could focus their hearing intensely for short periods of time, and it was very possible they were listening to every word they said.

"I'd be delighted to meet them," she said, forcing a smile. She wondered if, like the night of the Grove party, he sensed whatever she did about what was wrong.

"Thank you," he murmured, pressing her hand to his chest as he led her across the room. As usual, he seemed perfectly calm, at least outwardly. It was exasperating how steady he was, how safe she felt with her hand in his, even as they walked towards some of the most dangerous immortals on Okairos.

She'd have to ask him later about the feeling she had. Harlow didn't dare look for her own parents; in fact, she hoped they wouldn't join them. It was better they do this on their own, though if she could, Harlow would gladly run into the comforting arms of either of the maters to avoid this. She braced herself against the intensity of his parents' stares.

Connor McKay didn't look a human day over forty, a touch of gray at his temples the only thing to show that he was very nearly ancient—over two thousand years old, if rumors were true. Everything in his incredibly handsome bone structure was a mirror to his son's, but the similarities ended there. Where Finn was considerate under his intimidating exterior, Connor was cold and tightly wound all the way through, controlling and raptorial. If possible, Finn's mother was worse. Aislin McKay wore a simple black satin gown, her chocolate brown hair knotted into a severe chignon. She was gorgeous, and Finn's beautiful eyes clearly came from her, though that beauty was drowned in the expression of pure hunger she wore. She looked like she might reach out, snatch Harlow, and devour her.

Finn squeezed her hand as the people surrounding his parents scattered at their approach. "Mother, Father, this is Harlow Krane."

He didn't say "Mother" and "Father" in the sweet tones she and her sisters referred to Aurelia and Selene in. The words were clipped in his mouth, as though he hated to say them. Memories of bruises on his arms when they were children, as well as countless times he wasn't allowed to eat lunch, or the times he simply didn't show up to school for days at a time, played in the back of Harlow's mind. He would come back paler, with dark circles under his red-rimmed eyes, never speaking once about what he'd endured.

In secondary, it had been clear his parents expected him to join his father's real estate development firm, and when he'd applied for university, they'd been angry, but she had been proud. Like Alaric, he'd refused his parents' money after uni. It had been all over the gossips when the two of them started their own securities company, specializing in the hybridization of magic and technology. Still, they had some hold over him, though she didn't know what it was, exactly.

Harlow held out her hands in greeting, bowing her head only slightly as Aislin took them. Her hands were cold as ice, and she squeezed Harlow's hands hard enough to bring tears to her eyes. But her voice was smooth and cultured as fine silk when she said, "It is so good to finally meet you, Harlow. You are a vision."

Harlow doubted very much that Aislin sincerely felt that way. The woman was thin to the point of gauntness, as the Illuminated valued a certain kind of feminine fragility that was an unpopular beauty standard with the Order of Mysteries and the Trickster's Chosen, but all the rage with humans and vampires. Harlow could see from the slight curve of her upper lip that she was dying to make some snide comment. Connor nodded, but would not make eye contact with either of them, instead scanning the crowd, as if he too sensed a hidden menace in their midst.

"Yes," Harlow said slowly, trying hard not to pull her hands from Aislin's death grip. "It is good to meet you too."

A long, uncomfortable beat passed and Aislin released Harlow's hands, smoothing non-existent wrinkles from her opulent gown. Finn made no effort to fill the silence and Harlow wasn't sure what the expectations for her were. Her head was empty now, but for the thought that these people wanted to breed her to their son and take her family's home and livelihood. Certainly it wouldn't be strategic to mention that.

A smile spread across Aislin's beautiful face so malevolent that Harlow's stomach soured. "You two should go have fun. We will talk again soon."

Connor nodded, still staring intently beyond the crowd. "Yes, we have much to discuss about your future."

Finn visibly bristled at his parents' words, and Harlow couldn't blame him, though she suppressed her own reaction. Their statements may have been phrased kindly, but they were barely concealed threats, and neither had bothered to try to hide that fact. Finn took one of Harlow's hands, soothing it with gentle strokes of his thumb down the center of her palm.

"Wonderful," he said sharply, gripping her hand tighter, as though he feared one of his parents might steal her away. His jaw clenched so hard she thought his teeth might crack. "Enjoy your evening."

The tone of forced respect in his voice broke Harlow open. His desire to please them was as evident to her as was his clear hatred for them. Again, she wondered what it would be like not to have a family like her own, to walk through the world without people who loved you no matter what, to be alone with all the complex feelings that were obviously coursing through Finn as they walked away.

As his parents receded into the crowd, Finn's grip on her hand loosened slightly. Their palms were sweaty against one another, but she didn't let go. The hurdle they'd just cleared was significant. As Aislin and Connor disappeared from sight, the tension between them lessened enough that she recognized it for what it was: fear. They were both terrified.

Suddenly what they were doing, and the consequences for

what might happen if the McKays suspected their deception, became clear. The instinctual fear coursing through them both was an indicator of how high the stakes were. Finn's parents weren't average adversaries; they were ancient immortals with unlimited, completely unchecked power. She'd spent so much time wondering about the mysterious feeling of being watched, she'd forgotten how much rested on her shoulders.

Dizziness struck Harlow hard and she stumbled, but Finn sensed the spiral she was descending and he took her arm, drawing her close against him as they walked towards the dance floor. His body was comfortingly hard, steel against every curve of her currently melting into him.

"I don't have words for how you look tonight," he murmured. "Will you dance?"

She felt his eyes on her and she nodded, allowing herself to be led onto the dance floor and when his arms went around her, she leaned into him gratefully, glad to allow the familiar steps she'd known her whole life to take over. He held her closer than was technically necessary, allowing his chest to brush hers periodically. Slowly, the fear began to dissipate, breaking apart in her chest and floating away on the music.

Finn's grey-blue eyes met hers as she looked up, and there were oceans of unspoken words tossed about behind them. Years of longing seemed to echo the feelings she tried her best to deny. Her throat tightened, the way it always did when she allowed herself to think about what they'd lost so long ago, and she wondered, was it all just childish love? Or was there more there, something that could last longer than the flush of firsts they'd had as teenagers?

The longer they didn't speak, the closer he drew her into him. Both their breathing sped up markedly, but not from the rigor of the dance. His fingers pressed into her back as she moved closer into his orbit, letting him pin her to him so closely she felt the rock-hard length of him against her as they stepped and turned. Every nerve in her was alive at his touch and when he leaned close to her ear, his breath elicited a rush of heat between her legs that caused her knees to buckle.

His words started out as a soft rumble. "I'm glad we had these dances drilled into us as littlings." His hold on her tightened, as his fingers swept up her spine and into her hair, the rumble melting into a growl. "I don't have an ounce of blood left to operate my brain."

Harlow felt exactly where his blood had gone as he dragged her against him, her body soft and supple in his arms. She didn't have the power to think, the feel of him was so mesmerizing. Her blood lit on fire as the music swelled and for a moment it felt as though they were completely alone.

But of course they weren't alone, not at all, and this dance wasn't for their pleasure. They had a job to do tonight. She reminded herself that this wasn't about the two of them, but her family, her Order, the entire balance of the lower Orders. To keep herself from liquefying, she glanced around at the crowd, catching curious stares no matter which direction they turned. One song bled into another. "It's working—they're all buying it."

"Buying what?" he asked, his voice thick and distant.

"That my dress has seduced you."

She felt his laugh against her breasts and deep in her core, which was aflame with desire she could not quell.

"There's nothing to *buy*, Harls."

To punctuate his point, his legs parted hers and the hard length of his erection pressed into the core of her, momentarily obscured by the fan of her skirts. An involuntary moan floated from her lips. His breath was sharp as he pulled her off the dance floor and into the shadowy forest edging the dance floor. She followed without question, knowing there were hundreds of eyes watching.

Though they were partially hidden by the ferns and boughs,

she knew they were still in perfect view of the ballroom itself when he dragged her into his lap. She looked down to see he'd found a chair nestled in an alcove that was tailor-made for a tryst such as the one they appeared to be having.

"Is this all right?" he asked softly, winding a loose strand of her hair around his fingers.

"Yes," she murmured.

His voice was strained, and now alone in this little alcove, he wouldn't meet her eyes. "It's not the dress. Though the dress is very good."

She frowned, not knowing what he meant, but she didn't press him. This was all for show, after all. She wrapped her arms around his neck, feeling the crowd in the ballroom watching them surreptitiously, ravenous to see whatever they'd do next. Finn's body tensed under her, his breath as tight in his lungs as hers, his fingers skimming down her shoulders and over her arms.

"If I kiss you, would that be all right?" he murmured, his mouth moving ever nearer to her own.

She nodded and his palms grazed her hips and hair as he pulled her closer, nuzzling her neck. His warm breath on her bare skin sent currents of pleasure through her body.

"You smell fucking amazing," he groaned. "How do you smell this good?"

She turned her face so their lips brushed against each other, lightly at first, as even the slightest bit of contact sent her heart racing. A growl vibrated in his chest as his fingers tightened on her hip and at the nape of her neck, pulling her hair gently, exposing her neck to him. A feeling of primal arousal flooded her senses. She was acutely aware of his fangs, as they glinted in the dim light of the alcove.

Harlow wondered what it would be like for him to sink them deep into her neck, for him to bite her as they moved against one another. Her vision dimmed at the thought and her thighs clenched tightly around the scorching heat emanating from the center of her. When his lips met hers, his kiss was rough and fast, as though he'd been denied something for too long that he was finally allowed to claim as his own.

Her arms tightened around his neck as her fingers tangled into his hair, deepening the kiss further. She forgot a ballroom of people watched their every move for a brief second. When the hand gripping her hip began to graze up her side, toward her breasts, she remembered. She pulled back slightly, though it pained her to do so. Throbbing pleasure pulsed between her legs and she ached with need as she parted her mouth from his.

Finn's eyes were glossy with lust, his body taut with urgency. "I'm sorry," he murmured. "Got carried away."

Harlow couldn't speak, so she nodded. She had no idea how much of this was a show, his body simply responding to her soft warmth against him.

"If we left now, I think everyone would get the point, don't you?" His eyes were pleading, but what the plea was, she couldn't say. Did he want to stop, or go further?

"I agree," she murmured.

"Can I take you to my place, or yours? We need to talk."

"Yours," she responded immediately.

"Give me a minute... Standing might be a problem."

Harlow smiled wickedly. "You could always glamour yourself."

He laughed. "See, I can't even think. The way you look and smell has me..." His eyes glazed as they ran over her.

She very deliberately reached into the little bag hanging off her arm and shot a few texts to her family to let them know she was leaving with Finn. When she looked up at him through her lashes he was biting his bottom lip, mirroring her exactly. Then he kissed her, swiping her teeth with his tongue as he set her on her feet.

"Can I get us out of here fast?" he asked.

When she nodded, he swept her into his arms and she felt nothing but a slight breeze before he was setting her down in front of his car. She glanced around to find him parked at the far reaches of a back parking lot, no other cars in sight, only the stars to light their way. The usual clouds cleared to show the twinkle of the cosmos.

She didn't wait to hear anything he had to say, but pulled his hips against hers, sliding her hands up the muscles of his chest. She waited for him to stop her as her arms wound around his neck.

"Was it all for them?" she asked. "Was it just for the crowd?"

His eyes snapped open and the corner of his mouth lifted in a wicked smirk. In a flash he had her pinned against the car, his strong thighs caging hers, his hands in her hair.

"That was for them, yes," he groaned as her fingers dug into his back. "This is for you."

His kiss was tender now and would have been sweet, if the hard length of him wasn't pressed into her. Instead, the heat between them intensified as she wrapped one leg around him, angling herself so that his erection pushed against the core of her, sending waves of ecstasy through her body as they rocked against one another.

Finn's mouth opened to hers and his tongue slid suggestively against hers, telling tales of all the places he might touch. One hand cupped her breast as he ran his thumb over her obviously pebbled nipple, a hard peak straining against the thin fabric of her bodysuit. She whimpered into his mouth as he kissed her harder, sliding his hand under her dress, between her thighs, now open wide for him. When he stroked the wet spot forming on the bodysuit he groaned in her mouth.

She was surprised when he stopped, failing to pull the bodysuit aside and bury his fingers in the wet folds that ached for his touch. "This isn't where I want to do this," he murmured, the movement of his fingers slowing. "And we *have* to talk first. Would it be all right if I portaled us back?"

She nodded, rocking her hips against his fingers, which had stilled. "Do it."

Finn's hands slid away from her most intimate parts and he gripped her around the waist. He kissed her again, and when she opened her eyes, they were standing next to a dark lake, a dimly lit house behind them.

"This is your house? The place you built?"

He nodded. "But I don't want to go in just yet. Can we stay out here for a minute?"

He didn't have to ask her twice; she knew that pausing to go into the house would mean realizing they needed to talk, and she needed something else more. She sank onto the ground, pulling him down on top of her. His mouth crashed into hers as he pushed her dress up past her thighs. She spread her legs quickly, arching her back as he teased her through the bodysuit.

She slid her own hand between his legs, gripping the hard length of him through his pants. He groaned, pressing his fingers into her harder, tracing small intentional circles around her swollen clit through the thin fabric that separated them. She stroked him hard, unable to grip him as easily as she could if he were naked, but he thrust into her hands as hard as she did against his.

"You're so fucking wet," he groaned into her mouth.

"I want you inside me," she begged. "Now."

He pulled away from her and she saw in his eyes that he felt the same—that he wanted to be buried so deep in her that neither would be able to tell where they ended and the other began. So his answer surprised her: "Not until we talk. You have to hear me out first. If you haven't changed your mind, then we can do this."

Harlow saw how serious he was and reluctantly, she pulled away from him too, pushing her dress down over her knees. She struggled to her feet, reaching back to pull him up beside her, then her head tilted in curiosity as she looked at the house. Calmer now than before, she recognized it. "Why does your house look so familiar?"

Finn took her hand. "Come find out."

Finn led her up the hill to the house. The closer she got, the deeper the bittersweet ache in her heart grew. She recognized every stone, every window.

"Is this my dream house? The one you drew for me?"

He nodded. "Is it too much?"

She heard the vulnerability in his voice. The fear that she would think it was a violation of her trust. And maybe a long time ago she might have gotten angry, but now, something shifted in her, as though a key slipped into a locked door she'd never seen before. As the door inside her opened wide, she gazed at the man beside her and smiled.

"It's wonderful."

CHAPTER TWENTY-THREE

The house was an exact replica of the one she'd imagined since she was a little girl. She'd always dreamt of living in a house in the woods, rather than in the busy city. It wasn't that she didn't love Nuva Troi, but sometimes she needed quiet, distance. And this was the house she'd always dreamed of —from the peaked roof, to the arched doors, to the leaded glass windows, it was everything she'd imagined, or at least it looked to be so here in the dark.

"Can I see inside?"

He pulled her close to him, tucking her back against his chest as he spoke. "Before we go in, I need to confess. I think I built this for you. At first, I told myself it was just because I liked the house you always talked about, because it was the kind of home I wanted as a child, but never had. But once it was built, I knew it was more."

Harlow waited for Finn to continue, feeling his breath through her shoulder blades as he hugged her tightly. She lifted her face to his, resting her head on his shoulder. "What do you mean?"

"I couldn't fill it with furniture or art because I hoped

someday you'd do it your way, even though that seems impossible—I need you to know that I don't expect anything from you. If you don't want me, I'll understand and I promise, I'll help you do everything I said I would and then I'll leave you alone... But you're the reason I agreed to participate in the season. I hoped I'd see you again, and maybe things might be different."

The words tumbled out of him in a desperate way she wasn't used to hearing. His voice cracked with emotion, as he pressed his palms into the gentle curve of her soft stomach. His erection was hard against her ass, but the touch was less sexual, and more for comfort, somehow wistful as he ran his hands over her.

She looked away from him, back at the house. Some part of her knew they were crossing a threshold she might not be able to return from, but she felt reckless. Here in this moment, what she was *supposed* to be doing with Finn was far away, removed from this conversation entirely. It was as though they existed in a different world for a short time, one where she could trust him, where they might actually have a chance.

Even so, she asked, "What about your parents? Didn't they want you to?"

She felt him shrug. "They did, but I didn't know that when I came home for good, when I moved in here. All I knew was that you'd broken up with Mark, and if I was going to have another chance with you, this was it."

Her breath caught at the mention of Mark, and it felt as though poison leached into her. A memory flashed in her mind's eye: Mark calling her a slut on the way home from a dinner with friends, where she'd talked for too long to one of his colleagues about the rare book trade. There had been nothing to it; the friend was just that, a friend—but he'd screamed at her for hours when they got home. He said she'd made an idiot of herself and embarrassed him. That she was a fool to think anyone else would want her the way he did.

After that, he'd started going out to bars, parties—everywhere really—without her. She hadn't minded at first. His friends were wary of her, and it was easier to just stay home with Axel and enjoy the peace. But of course, that was when he started meeting other women. Came home smelling like them, with lipstick all over him. He hadn't even bothered hiding it. And then, eventually, he'd kicked her out. Some hidden memory of that day pressed against her consciousness, that glass wall that hid something she wasn't supposed to think about, ever.

"Where did you go?" Finn's deep voice, so steady and different from Mark's shrill tone, brought her back to the moment she was in.

"I'm sorry," she said quickly.

"For what?" He turned her, so he could see her face, his fingers tipping her chin up until her eyes met his. "What could you possibly have to apologize for?"

She shrugged, lowering her eyes.

"I mentioned Mark... Is that what's wrong?"

Harlow shrugged again, her breath shuddering through her, panic barely at bay. She shouldn't think about Mark. Not right now.

"Harls," Finn said, his voice so soft and gentle that she nearly let her panic flow, nearly let her fear take over, just so he could comfort her, prove to her that she was safe. "What happened with you and Mark? Why did you break up?"

"Because I wasn't good enough for him," she said bitterly. "We didn't break up. He dumped me. Kicked me out of our apartment. Kept my cat."

Finn's entire frame tightened, tense as his eyes began to glow with fury. "He kept your *cat* when you left?" His fingers laced through hers as he started toward the house. "Come on. We're going to get your cat. *Now.*"

The word "now" sent a shiver through her. She'd seen Finn like this before, but only rarely. He could be chilly, but he was usually calm. Now he was furious, and so lethal her skin prickled with awareness. Immense power flowed off him in waves, filling the tapestry of magic that surrounded them, lighting the threads in their immediate vicinity in a vicious glow.

There was nothing left of the vulnerable man he'd been a few minutes ago; now he was wholly the immortal predator, dangerous and terrifyingly beautiful. But Harlow wasn't frightened in the slightest. In fact, she was something else altogether. She was aroused, nearly as aroused as she'd been when he mercilessly teased her on the lawn.

His nostrils flared. He could *smell* her desire. Why had she forgotten that?

"Are you..." he trailed off, his eyes glowing.

"I already got Axel back," she said, interrupting his recognition of what seeing him so ready to help her was doing to her body. "Last week. I went to go get him when Olivia and Mark were out."

"You did?" Finn's voice was strained, as though he were almost disappointed that he wasn't going to get the chance to enact some kind of violence on Mark tonight.

"Yes, he's safe at my apartment. Larkin is staying with him tonight. I know that's a little silly, but she likes getting away from the maters and the twins and she loves animals... so, it sort of works out perfectly, since I'm a little overprotective right now."

"That's good." A shaky breath shuddered through him. "You could have asked me to help."

She nodded. "I know. But I needed to do it on my own."

Finn cupped her face in his hands and kissed her forehead so sweetly it brought tears to her eyes. "Do you want to go home and see him? We can go together, spend the night there if you want. Or I can drop you off and go. Whatever you want."

His voice shook in such an uncharacteristic way that Harlow was reminded of the conversation they were supposed to have.

"No, I don't want to go home. Axel is fine with Larkin. I want to see the house... and talk. The way we said we were going to."

He nodded, seemingly unable to speak, and led her inside. As he'd said, it was mostly empty, though there was evidence he'd been living here. His jackets, hanging on hooks in the mudroom by the back door. A single handmade mug, rinsed clean in the sink. An ironstone bowl of apples on the marble counter in the white kitchen.

Far from the open concept that many people had begun to prefer in newer homes, this house rambled from generously sized room to room. Each space was perfectly sized to accommodate a large family gathering, but there were no ballrooms, no enormous dining room, no grand halls. Only cozy places to gather intimately.

It was like no Illuminated home she'd ever been in. The walls were painted a clean, creamy white, both bright and cozy at the same time. Elegant and rustic simultaneously, the combinations of wood, stone and architectural details were immaculately chosen. She knew exactly how she'd fill the space, with rich texture and fabrics layered in light colors of alabaster, ivory and gold, with books and antiquities on every built-in shelf.

Harlow loved the dark beauty of Nuva Troi, but she wanted to fill this home with comforting light. Her shadows itched to get to work, but she shushed them. A fire burned in every hearth, springing to life from the magic in Finn's fingertips as they entered each room, and shaded wall sconces were lit dimly all over the house.

"So," she asked, "no furniture at all besides the kitchen table? Where will we sit?"

He flushed then, color rushing to his cheeks. "There's furniture in the bedroom... Or we could go back to the kitchen. Sit at the table..."

Harlow swallowed hard. He was giving her a chance to back out, to slow things down. But she didn't want to do that. She wanted to know what he had to say, and she was willing to hear it all in the bedroom. Whatever happened after that... Well, she was ready for that too.

"Bedroom," she said.

Finn swept her up the staircase in the open foyer and down a long hallway in an instant, depositing her in a room with an arched ceiling. The enormous upholstered bed was tucked into a curtained alcove. Two oversized chairs flanked the fireplace, as though waiting for them. The walls were painted the same white as the rest of the house, and all of the fabrics in the room were coordinating whites and delicate creams, just as she would have chosen. Above a primitive dresser, near the door to what she assumed was a bathroom or closet, there were nine framed sketches.

Harlow drifted towards them and when her vision focused enough to make them out clearly she whimpered, stretching her fingers towards them. They were his sketches of the house, with her handwriting everywhere, labeling things. They'd worked on these sketches for days the summer between primary and secondary, dreaming together of a place filled with light and whimsy that felt different from the world they knew. He'd followed her instructions perfectly.

"You kept these?"

She turned to look at him, standing in the middle of the room. For the first time in their lives, he appeared helpless to her, as though whatever she said next might actually break him. He nodded slowly, but said nothing, though his gaze burned with an intensity of feeling she didn't remember having seen before.

"But why?" Tears gathered in her eyes. "Why would you do this?"

"Come sit." He took her hands and led her to one of the chairs in front of the fireplace, which roared to life as she sat. Instead of taking the other chair, he sat on the floor in front of her, so he faced her.

"The last night we had together was the most perfect of my life," Finn began, his voice rough with emotion.

Harlow clutched his hand in hers, sensing that she would need the support as much as he did. She was reluctant to admit it, but that night had been perfect for her too, the world full of possibility and love. They'd had their whole future spread out in front of them and that night, she'd foolishly thought they'd spend it together.

She took a deep breath to steady herself, knowing that what came next would probably hurt. "It was perfect for me too."

He didn't miss the waver in her voice and his hand cupped her face, as his eyes darkened with feeling. "When I got home after dropping you off, my parents were waiting for me. My dad was smiling this manic smile and my mother looked absolutely feral."

Harlow could imagine it, after the scene in the ballroom at the Metro. She sensed the anger in him and squeezed his hand harder. Her knuckles went white with the effort.

"They had photos of us, Harls. I guess they had us followed? Though the photos didn't look professional... I never found out where they came from. But I couldn't understand why they were so *happy*. After all the years they lectured me about not getting too close to you—they were always suspicious about how I felt about you. They knew I was in love with you. Hells, everyone knew. It was so obvious... So their happiness... It made me suspicious."

She nodded, understanding this reaction. His parents had insulted her family so many times when they were younger that she too would have been shocked to know they were pleased by the union—as well as being instantly wary regarding their intentions.

He slid out of his jacket and flung it aside, and Harlow was momentarily distracted by the breadth of his chest and the muscles of his forearms as he rolled up his sleeves. The tattoo of the sword, snake and lilacs caught her eye again. When his arms tucked back around her, her heart slowed its thumping pace.

"Go on," she urged.

"They sat me down and urged me to keep... Gods, I can't even say it." His forehead fell to her lap in shame. She resisted the urge to run her fingers through the waves of his dark hair.

"No, say it." She wanted to know what had driven him from her, what had changed him so deeply.

"They urged me to *breed* with you. That was how they put it. Like you were an animal. Breed with you until you produced 'viable offspring.'" A strangled sob escaped his throat. She wished she could be surprised, but it wasn't surprising at all that they'd actually said it. Harlow was sure they'd said worse.

"I was so disgusted with the way they spoke about you that I argued with them. Told them I'd never use you that way. I told them I loved you, that I'd pair with you, bond with you, but that I'd never treat you the way they were asking me to."

"They just wanted us to have a baby?" Her voice was soft, but of course, given what she already knew, this wasn't much of a shock for her.

He looked up at her. "No... I mean... Yes... But by any means necessary. Whether you wanted it or not—and who the fuck knows what they wanted with our child?"

The implication sunk in. They'd tried to force him to violate her. She shook with anger. How could parents ask such a thing of their child? Especially one as *good* as Finn had been. But still, this didn't explain his actions, how he'd reacted.

"We talked about everything back then, Finn. I knew how bad they were. I would have understood," she reasoned. "You could have told me."

"Could I? Could I have said to you at eighteen that my parents wanted me to impregnate you, even if it was against your will? Harlow, I was fucking terrified. Of them, of myself..."

Anger burned a hole in her tongue, and she lashed out.

"Why in seventeen hells would you have been afraid of yourself?"

He jumped up, as though she'd struck him and turned from her, shame cowing his ample shoulders. "Gods forgive me, Harls. I considered it, for the briefest moment. I thought about what it would be like to have a child together."

She followed him to where he leaned against the hearth, his forehead pressed to the enormous stone mantel. Her arms went around his waist. "You thought about what it would be like to have a baby?"

He turned and tears were in his stormy eyes. "Yes, and in the context of the conversation I hated myself."

Harlow was perplexed. This wasn't what she'd expected to hear at all. She'd always thought that his parents might have been involved in what happened, but she'd assumed it was that they'd convinced him once and for all how inferior she was to him. How foolish he'd been for falling in love with a lesser immortal. Every choice she'd made for years after had been based on that assumption—that some fault in her had caused the first person she'd ever fallen in love with to turn cruel after one night with her.

This, though. This was something else, and her mind struggled to comprehend the enormity of the consequences that assumption had on her life. "I'm not sure I understand. You thought about us having a baby, not forcing me to do so, but only what it would be like if we had a child. You liked it, and that was terrible of you?"

Tears collected in his eyes, along with shame. "They could tell. Could smell the desire on me. Harls, they knew how much I wanted you, how much I wanted a family of my own, and I knew in that moment they'd never stop trying to manipulate us both into whatever sick plans they have."

"And what are those plans?" she asked softly, thinking of the

Merkhov book, as she tightened her grip on his abdomen. Should she tell him about it?

Before she could speak, he was answering. "I don't know. That was the last time we spoke for nearly two years. I moved into my godsfather's brownstone that he willed to me, the one in Midtown, remember?"

Harlow nodded. She remembered the place the Trickster's Chosen had left Finn when he died, but couldn't remember exactly how the shifter was connected to the McKays. Maybe she never knew.

Finn continued. "I was determined to make you hate me. I couldn't trust myself with you, not with all their fucked up shit running through my head, and I knew you'd have some clever solution, some way to solve things." He shook his head. "But you don't know who they are, Harlow. You don't know the things they've done. The things they could still do."

Harlow let her arms fall away from him. Finally she understood. She didn't like it, but it all made sense now. But for something that made sense, it didn't make her feel any better. Maybe he'd made a mistake with the way he went about things, but she'd made one after another, letting his treatment of her define her self-worth. She wasn't certain she could forgive him, or herself for all that.

"What's different about things now, then?" she asked. "Why is it safe now, when it wasn't then?"

Finn shook his head. "It's not. I'm just tired of fighting how I feel. I needed you to know what happened and make a choice for yourself. I took that from you before."

She stared into the fire. "Their goals are consistent at least. Whatever they think us having a child could mean for them can't be good for the baby, or for us."

He shook his head. "No, it can't. But I'm an adult now, and... Well, there are a lot of other things I should tell you, if you think you might want to give us a try, but they involve other people and me asking you to keep a lot of things secret." Finn inhaled deeply, his composure returning. "I can keep you safe now in ways I couldn't before."

She believed that he believed that, that he wouldn't say so if he didn't think it was true. Harlow sank back into her chair. Only one thread was left to pull. "And what about Petra?"

His head hung with remorse. "I've never hated myself so much as when I stood by and let her bully you and Enzo. I've been in therapy since I told Alaric everything."

That surprised her, but only a little. Alaric was good, through and through. Of course he'd tried to help Finn, the way an older sibling would. "When was that?"

"When I was nineteen. He found me a therapist and I still see him—through video calls now though, he's in Nea Sterlis. James is Riley Quinn's dad, an empath like they are."

Harlow was quiet. Her emotions swirled in confusing circles. She was angry he hadn't just spoken to her, explained everything. At the same time, she remembered what it was like to be that age, to be afraid of every changing emotion, to be afraid of yourself and your desires. If she was honest with herself, she couldn't say how she would have reacted if he had told her. But the abandonment and Petra's behavior still did damage that she didn't know how to undo.

He knelt in front of her, as a supplicant might. "I don't expect you to forgive me. And I don't expect you to come live here, or be with me... Or anything. I came back here two years ago, with the intention of telling you everything, and asking you to be together."

"But I was with Mark."

He nodded. "And when I saw pictures of the two of you together on Section Seven, I left. Came here. There was another house on this property then and I had it torn down. When I had the plans drawn up for this place it just sort of came out. But I never thought you'd break up with Mark, so I moved back to

Nea Sterlis. Last Yule, everyone said you were going to be engaged. I thought you'd marry him."

"So did I," Harlow whispered. "But things changed."

Finn nodded. "About that... I have something else to admit, and you're not going to like it."

Harlow raised her eyebrows.

"Do you remember Avery Hargrove?"

Her heart sank. So this was about Avery? Was he attracted to her? Her skin prickled with jealousy she wished to Aphora she didn't feel. She nodded, her mouth pressing into a grim line.

"I ran into her at a gallery in Nea Sterlis last winter and she told me a story about Mark Easton that worried me."

Surprise pulsed through Harlow, sending tiny shockwaves coursing through her. "What?"

"They were together in secondary..."

"At boarding school?"

Finn nodded. "Yes. And he was so controlling and violent that her parents had her transferred here to that academy downtown."

"Oh..." Harlow's voice was soft. She'd always thought it was her fault that Mark acted the way he did. It's what he'd said so many times, *You bring out the worst in me, Dollface. I can't help it. I love you so much, it makes me lose my mind.*

"I knew I had no right to get involved in your life, Harls, but Avery warned me that she'd heard from other women he'd been with that he'd escalated his behavior in the time since they were together... That he was worse now. When he was with her, he'd never hurt her, not physically anyway. But he broke her things, yelled at her a lot..."

His voice drifted as he searched her eyes. She knew what he wanted to ask. But there was a blank spot in her mind where that information should be. She stayed very, very still, waiting for him to continue.

"I arranged for him to meet Olivia—I knew from various

sources that she was interested in wealthy human men, and I made sure they'd meet, and that she would be primed to be interested in him." The breath he let out should have been one of relief, but he didn't look relieved. Just worried, and slightly ashamed of himself.

"How?" Harlow asked.

He shrugged. "Do you really want to know the details? It worked. I interfered, and it worked, but not the way I thought it would... I thought..."

Harlow understood then and laughed, the sound dry and brittle in her ears. "You thought I'd find out and leave him."

He nodded, guilt clouding his eyes, as though he'd just realized how he'd set her up for more pain, not less. "But something else happened instead, didn't it?"

"He was sleeping with other women before her, Finn. I didn't leave him then. I didn't think I deserved better. He kicked me out though, and it's probably the best thing that could have happened, even though it was awful."

She thought it was anyway. The glass wall between her and that memory was opaque as ever. Harlow took a deep breath. "You helped me. It didn't work out the way you thought it would, but you did help me. I don't know if I ever would have left on my own."

He was lost at sea in his own emotions, a frown furrowing his brow. Finn had always liked things to be cut and dry, bad or good, and this wasn't one of those things. What he'd done, all these things he'd done, they'd been for the right reasons, but they'd hurt her just the same. Harlow sensed he was seeing the bigger picture as they spoke, understanding the depths of how his actions had reverberated in her life for years. "I feel like it was cowardly now—like I should have come to get you."

"I wouldn't have gone," she said, her voice small and quiet. "Back then, I wouldn't have thought I deserved to leave with you, or to be protected like that."

"And now?" There was no hope in his voice.

Maybe the smart thing to do was talk about it more. Go over it all again and again until she had more information. But she'd had enough for one night. She'd need time to process all of this, understand it better for herself, but she wanted to be close with someone who loved her, someone who'd made mistakes, but had made them trying to protect her. The one thing she knew in this moment, with all the fucked up things she'd done, was that no one was perfect. No love was perfect, and sometimes people doing their best messed up. She did, all the time.

Harlow wanted what was behind that once-locked door that opened into something new. And even if she wasn't ready to fully admit that yet, she was willing to walk to the threshold and step between to see what was possible on the other side. "Now I want what I've wanted since our last night together."

His eyes lifted. "What's that?"

"To have another night with you."

Finn's jaw clenched. "Just one night?"

"We'll start with one, and then another... I need to go slow, Finn. I've done a lot of work on myself in the past few months. In a lot of ways I'm over what happened with Mark, but I'm not healed. Not yet."

"We can go as slow as you want," he said, pulling her onto the floor and into his lap. He cradled her close to him and his familiar, sensual smell filled her nose as he held her tight against him. "What about my parents? They obviously want the same things they always have."

Harlow thought of the image of the snakes in the Merkhov book. She should tell him. This was the perfect moment, but she couldn't make the words come out. She was still shaky around the edges of her trust. She could tell him as soon as she was sure of him.

"They can *want* anything they please," she spat, venomous

hatred for Aislin and Connor McKay rising in her chest. "There's nothing that says we have to give it to them."

She looked up to find Finn's eyes glowing at the ferocity in her voice. "My brave girl."

She stood, feeling restless and not at all brave, but she didn't contradict him. She needed him to think better of her than she really was right now. If he could think of her that way, maybe it might build a bridge she could cross for herself. She couldn't depend on him to make her whole, she'd have to do that herself, but it was all right to let someone help her, wasn't it?

His eyes followed her as she walked around the room, her dress swirling around her feet. The Solon Mai ball seemed eons in the past, rather than just hours ago. She felt his gaze caress her back, as tangible as if his fingers dragged over the buttons of her dress. He was giving her time, moving slow like she'd asked. She leaned against the doorway to the bathroom, watching him watch her.

He'd misunderstood her. She needed time for her heart. She couldn't reciprocate what he felt for her right now, not in the way she wanted to, but in the meantime, there were other things they could do. Other ways to build trust between them. She hadn't slept with anyone since Mark, hadn't even wanted to. But this was different: this was Finn, and she wanted him, and he so clearly wanted her too. That much she could trust with every fiber of her being.

"Come here," she murmured, so softly she wondered if he'd hear her.

He was there in an instant, but he hesitated, the heat of his body warming her. Her breath hitched as his eyes met hers. "You're sure?" he asked.

"Yes," she breathed as he stepped closer. "I'm sure."

And she was. Sure that while it might take some time for her mind to wrap around the complexity of their past, that he'd been honest with her. That he'd told her what he did at a potential cost to what he wanted most, and that was so far removed from what she'd grown comfortable believing she deserved that it surprised her. Beyond that, she was sure that tonight her body was *hers*, no one else's, and that reverent look in his eyes told her he was ready to worship it.

Harlow was absolutely certain that was part of what she needed to move forward, to trust someone to treat her with respect, to look at her that way tonight and give her freedom and choice tomorrow. But still, he hesitated, his eyes searching hers.

She reached for him, pulling him by the shirt until her back pressed against the wall and the hard planes of his body pushed into her. His eyes stayed on hers as she wrapped her arms around his neck. A small voice cautioned that he wasn't touching her, that she'd misread him, that he didn't want her. She banished it immediately. That wasn't it.

He was letting her lead. He understood that too many choices had been taken from her, that she'd been helpless against the waves of mistakes that had crashed over her for far too long, and now he was letting her be the one to take action.

Finn's head dipped towards hers as she lifted her chin, her lips parting. His chest heaved in time with hers. They were barely touching, and her body already responded to the proximity of his. She tugged his head closer to hers, and their lips met.

The kiss was slow, languid even, as she parted her lips to allow his tongue to dance against hers. Her fingers dug into the hair at the nape of his neck as he deepened the kiss further. He still wasn't touching her with his hands, but her aching breasts met his chest as her back curved, propelling her forward, greedy to make more contact with him.

As she arched hard into him, a deep moan rumbled from his chest, vibrating into her now-molten core. One of his thighs parted her legs as his hands glided up her sides, grazing the curve of her breasts, before they fastened around her waist, dragging her against him as he rocked into her. Every nerve in her body lit with the flame of his touch, heat gathering between her legs, where that thigh offered her release. But he did not press harder into her, did not bring it closer to the swollen flesh between her legs.

He kissed her hard, and each thrust of his tongue teased the release she wanted, but he offered that thigh and it was up to her to take her pleasure. She pulled him closer, parting her legs a bit more and tilting her pelvis until his leg and sizable erection made contact with her.

A moan broke free from her lips, throaty and deep as she ground herself against him. With that, he responded, grabbing her ass and pulling her against him as he aided her efforts to increase the friction between them. His mouth slid down to her neck as his fingers gripped her ass. She was openly whimpering, wordless noise urging him on.

"Come for me," he said, voice husky and low as his tongue swept the sensitive shell of her ear.

She wanted to, but she needed more. More than just this sweet agitation. "I need you inside me."

He pulled away from her, but just slightly, letting her legs lower as his hands moved. He passed a hand over the inside of his wrist, illuminating the expensive sigil embedded under his skin that protected against pregnancy and sexually transmitted disease. Her heart beat faster as she showed him her own. They were really going to do this, after so many years of waiting, of sadness—tonight they'd begin again, find a new way forward.

Finn's lips curved upward into a smile as his hands traveled to her breasts, to the hard peaks of her nipples, his thumbs sweeping across them in tantalizing circles. "Turn around," he said.

She obliged, her knees weak as she braced herself against the wall. He made short work of the buttons on the back of her dress, as he kissed her neck. "You're so fucking beautiful," he said as he pushed the dress off her shoulders.

He pulled her against him as she kicked the dress aside, caressing her breasts and then lower to her stomach. She flinched slightly and he stopped. "Are you all right?"

"It's just..." She didn't want to think about Mark right now. It was the last thing she wanted. "I... I gained weight when I was with Mark."

He froze for a moment, then turned her so that she faced him. His eyes had that predatory, dangerous look she recognized from before. "And?" he asked, his voice soft and deadly.

"And he didn't like it." Her chin began to shake and she squeezed her eyes shut. This was going to ruin everything. They'd been having a good time, and she just had to ruin it.

She heard the sharp breath he took, but his voice was steady, eternally calm, when he said, "Harls, open your eyes."

She did. He'd shed all his clothes in a mere instant, using that Illuminated speed. He was breathtaking, and she wasn't sure what he was trying to accomplish, but it only made her feel more unsure about what they were about to do. She wasn't like she was in secondary, she wasn't thin anymore, and Mark had accused her of "letting herself go."

"Look at me, Harlow," Finn commanded. "Look how fucking hard I am."

She looked, blushing slightly. His cock was thick with desire for her and he stroked it a few times, one side of his mouth lifting slightly. "That's for you. Because *I* like it—the way you look right *now*." He stepped closer, and his voice dropped lower. "That's not quite true, I don't like it, I fucking love it."

Her breath caught as he spun her around, pinning her against him again, in the same position they'd been in when she flinched. Now his hot skin pressed against hers, only the thin fabric of the bodysuit separating them.

His hands cupped her breasts, and he lightly pinched her

nipples through the bodysuit as his mouth met her neck again. "Ever since I ran into you on Mulberry Street, I've been thinking of your body, what you'd feel like if I got to touch you like this."

He pushed the bodysuit down a little, exposing her breasts to the cool air of the room and to his view, as he looked over her shoulder. "These are perfect, you understand me. I've dreamed of having them in my mouth for weeks."

She groaned as the warmth of his hands contrasted with the chilly air. He pushed the bodysuit lower, past her hips, exposing the curve of her belly. "Will you let me touch you here?" he asked as she stepped out of the bodysuit, his hands traveling lower.

Harlow's voice stuck at first. "Why do you want to?"

"Because I love the way you look, the way you feel, I love every silken curve of you, and I want you to *feel* it."

He pressed his thick cock against the curve of her ass, punctuating his words with primal ferocity. She nodded and he slid his palms over her stomach, groaning deeply behind her. "This, *this* sends me over the edge. I want to bury my cock in you," he growled as he stroked her skin.

A rush of wet heat gathered between her legs and she spread them, bracing herself on the wall. "Do it," she begged, tipping her hips so that the head of his cock pushed at her slick entrance.

"Not so fast." He laughed, a wicked noise that sent chills down her spine. "I want to see you when you come for me."

He took her hands and turned her, leading her toward the soft fur rug in front of the fire. When she stepped onto it, he kissed her deeply, pulling her to the floor on top of him. She drifted over his body, letting her skin play against his as she straddled him, dragging her wet center over his hard length and then back down again. He groaned, pushing her upright. "I want to see every inch of you."

She leaned back, luxuriating in the heat of the fire, in the pressure of his erect cock, sliding against the most sensitive part of her. His hands slid up her thick thighs, spreading them further as he traveled inward, his thumb grazing her clit for a mere moment before it dipped into the wet folds below.

As he plunged his thumb into her she arched into his hand. "Godsdamn, you are so wet," he growled.

Beneath her, his cock twitched in response, jealous of his thumb. He dragged slick desire out of her and onto the swollen flesh begging for his touch. As he traced tight intentional circles in the spot she needed him most, her legs widened and she rose to position him at her entrance.

He moaned her name as she fitted herself around the weeping head of his cock and lowered slowly onto him. He never took his thumb from her clit as he stretched into her. When he filled her completely, she began to move on him, slowly at first. His eyes burned with lust as her breasts swayed in the firelight.

She smiled as he licked his lips, lowering herself gradually until her nipples bounced against his mouth. He drew his hand back from her clit as she ground it into him. He sucked each of her nipples in turn, his lips pulling at the hard, pebbled peaks of her breasts.

Harlow's abdomen tightened in ecstasy as Finn thrust deeper and deeper into her as she rode him, her hips undulating smoothly, guiding the curve of his cock to a place inside her that made her cry out. At the sound of his name on her lips, Finn grabbed her ass, pulling her harder against him as he fitted his mouth to hers, his tongue moving against hers in time to his feverish thrusts. This was nothing like it had been the first time. That was tentative, sweet, loving. This was frenzied, desperate and wild.

She couldn't get enough of him, couldn't get him deep enough in her. And then her hips tilted a slightly different way as he pulled her ass, slamming into her so hard her vision went dark. She cried wordless pleasure as he fucked her harder, stars lighting her eyes as they found release at the same time.

When she collapsed against him, boneless and spent, his arms went around her. She listened to his heart beating, feeling satisfied, safe and cared for. He played with her hair, sending shivers through her. He was still buried in her and she felt his cock jump inside her, eager for more, but his touch was soothing.

"Do you want a snack?" he asked. "Or dinner? I could make us something."

Harlow was surprised by how wistful he sounded. She was nothing but satiated. She slid off him, feeling empty without him inside her.

"Be right back," she whispered, brushing a kiss to his cheek.

She got up and went to the bathroom, feeling his eyes on her as she went.

"There's sweats in the closet if you want to put something on."

She didn't, but she cleaned herself up quickly, and used his toilet. The bathroom was beautiful, all white marble and perfect lighting, with a tub so deep and long, it made her sigh.

"Do you want to take a bath?"

Harlow turned to find Finn leaning against the bathroom door, naked and perfect. She grinned. "Could we?"

"We?" he asked, smirking. "Yes, *we* definitely can. And then food, and then a *lot* of sleep."

His hand caressed her bare ass as he started to run water in the tub. She wrapped her arms around his waist, pressing her breasts into his back as she kissed a spot between his shoulder blades that she could reach. She was tall, but like all Illuminated, he was taller, nearly six-five, she thought. "You're a little bossy sometimes."

Finn turned, pushing hair out of her face as she tilted her head to be kissed. The sound of running water was comforting in a way that warmed her to her core. "I'm sorry about that. I'll do better. I worry when the people I—I care for—don't seem to be taking good care of themselves."

"Then come care for me," she said, perching on the edge of the tub.

He shook his head, smirking. "As my lady commands."

CHAPTER TWENTY-FOUR

Harlow woke in an empty bed, gloomy morning light blanketing her. At first she was disoriented, confused. But as her body slid against Finn's sinfully soft sheets, she remembered. The pleasurable ache between her legs reminded her further. And the sounds of the shower emanating from the bathroom brought it all back.

She got out of bed, not waiting for her brain to kick in. She didn't want to second-guess herself or even think as she entered the bathroom. There was a new toothbrush laid out on the counter and she brushed quickly, then glanced around the corner to where she had a full view of Finn in the shower.

When he saw her his skin glowed, emitting a faint light that brought a tight ache to her belly. He crooked one finger at her, grinning. "Get in here."

She obliged, stepping into the massive marble shower. He pulled her to him immediately, kissing her so deeply she was grateful she'd brushed her teeth. He'd clearly brushed his, so she had no doubt he'd been thinking of her.

Water fell from the ceiling in a gentle torrent. He turned her body so she faced away from him. "Morning, Harls. I'm happy to see you."

She felt that acutely, parting her legs as he slid against her back. His hands glided up the front of her and she realized he'd taken a bar of soap from somewhere she couldn't see. He began to slowly lather around her breasts, her nipples hardening at the attention as his free hand rubbed slow circles down her abdomen, lower and lower until he pressed his palm against her belly the way he had the night before. Today she didn't flinch as his fingers pressed into her flesh. She felt the way it affected him to touch her, grip onto her soft body. His cock throbbed against her ass as a growl of pleasure caressed her ear.

Finn's mouth grazed her neck and his fangs scraped against her. Heat built between her legs as his lips and tongue teased her ear. "You felt so good last night I thought it was a dream. I didn't want to wake you though... in case you'd changed your mind."

Harlow leaned forward, pressing her hands against the cool tile of the shower wall as water washed the soap away. "I haven't changed my mind," she said. She leaned forward further, angling her hips upward as she spread her legs. "Feel how much I want you."

The low growl that emanated from his throat sent shivers through her as he gripped her ass. "I can't believe you're here."

Finn's voice was so tender she turned to face him. His stormy eyes were full of emotion and his fangs shone in his slightly parted lips. She kissed him, letting her tongue drag across the sharp point of his elongated canines as his fingers dipped between her legs.

As she kissed him, one long finger slid into her, then two. Her hips rocked forward, plunging his fingers deeper inside her. When he drew them out of her he sucked them slowly. "I love how you taste," he murmured, voice low as he guided her to the seat in the shower.

Her heart thumped hard as he knelt in front of her. He

kissed her mouth, his tongue dancing against hers, making promises about what was to come as his fingers plunged into her once more.

Harlow moaned into Finn's mouth as his fingers worked her, gently at first, then harder as she thrust against him. His mouth traveled down her jaw, sucking her neck gently as his fangs scraped against her wet skin. She pressed her neck against them.

"I want you to," she moaned.

"Not yet..." he murmured. "Not yet."

His mouth slid to each of her nipples, sucking them to raised peaks as he used his free hand to squeeze the abandoned breast. She felt the pressure of her release as his fingers curled inside her, but he slowed as the tension mounted.

Then his head dipped lower, trailing kisses down her belly and onto her thighs, which she parted further, wanting desperately to make room for his head between her legs. He hovered above her, his breath on her most sensitive skin nearly enough to send her over the edge.

Her breath came in labored heaves as his mouth closed over her, his fingers thrusting in time to her bucking hips as his tongue lapped and sucked in turns. Her body shuddered against him, but he did not relent until she softened in his arms.

"Are you ready to get dressed?" he asked politely.

"No," she said, rising, her knees only a little wobbly. She turned from him, bracing herself against the shower wall again, flashing him a smile as she spread her legs. "No, I'm not done. Are you?"

He took her by the hips and she guided him to her entrance, which was slick with the results of his ministrations. "No, I'm not," he growled as he slid inside her, stretching her with his girth.

Harlow drove her hips towards him, increasing the power of his thrusts as one of his arms wound around her waist, sliding down to stroke the curve of her belly, moving lower to squeeze her clit as he thrust deep inside her.

"Harder," she commanded, her fingers drifting between her legs.

He moaned in response. "Does that feel good?"

"Yes," she cried as light flashed behind her eyes, as the shadows of her magic crept into her vision. He yanked her to him, kissing her neck as she quivered. He slowed his thrusts slightly now, and she felt the thick pulse of him as he breathed in her ear.

"Nothing feels as good as you," he groaned as he slid back into her, his fangs dragging against her neck.

"Bite me," she begged, clenching hard around his cock.

His hands wound through her hair and he thrust so hard into her she saw stars, the actual glimmer of the cosmos as she came against him. He called her name again and again, but his teeth did not sink into her as she went limp.

The Illuminated were an amalgamation of the lower Orders; they had the ability to change shape as the Order of Masks did, a deep talent for magic like the Order of Mysteries, and a similar body composition to those in the Order of Night, including fangs. Harlow knew that when the Illuminated were intimate that they often bit their partner, and the rumors she'd heard about the way it enhanced the pleasure of the experience intrigued her.

Finn turned her in his arms, warm water rinsing them both as he washed her hair. She felt drowsy and sated, but not quite satisfied. "Why wouldn't you bite me?" she asked softly.

He had a dreamy look in his eyes, as though he felt as come-drunk as she did. "I... I want to..." he murmured. His skin glowed still, warm against hers.

"I know the Illuminated do that when they fuck," she reasoned.

A wary look flickered over his face, so quickly she almost missed it. "They do, you're right."

"Then why won't you bite me?"

He pulled away from her. "We're turning into prunes. Let's get out."

She pulled him back. "Is it me?"

"Yes," he snapped, stalking out of the shower.

Harlow froze, her body reacting to the tone of Finn's voice immediately. A flush of shame burned her cheeks. He stood, dripping on the bathroom floor, his face twisted immediately in distress. "That... didn't come out right. Come out of the shower, all right?"

He held his hand out to her, but she couldn't move. It wasn't fair for her to hold him responsible for always speaking in a calm tone, but the way he snapped at her reminded her of Mark, and now she was stuck.

Finn's fingers grazed her chin, lifting her eyes to his. "I'm sorry I snapped. I'm a little wound up. Can you give me a beat?"

His voice was steady now, as though he knew exactly why she was stuck in the shower. She took a deep breath and stepped out, and let him wrap her in a warm, fluffy towel. There was something at work here she didn't understand. "Do you want me to wait for you in the bedroom?"

"Thank you, yes," he said, squeezing her arm. "There's a robe on the hook there."

She saw it, and knew it was his when she slid it on. His scent was all over it and she breathed it in, letting it comfort her. Harlow went to work lighting the fire and when Finn came out of the bathroom, dressed only in a pair of loose grey sweatpants, she made every effort to stay in her chair.

"Will you sit with me?" he asked softly.

She'd meant to give him a little space, but she liked that idea better. He sat in the chair opposite hers and opened his arms.

Her movements were slow, careful, in case he changed his mind, but as soon as she was within reach, he pulled her into his lap.

"I'm sorry I snapped," he said, stroking her damp hair. "What I said didn't come out right."

"It's okay," she replied, her voice tentative. "Mark was... unpredictable. I know that's not your fault..."

Finn pressed kisses to her cheeks, then her lips. "Thank you for telling me though. I'm pretty even tempered, but this, biting you. It scares me."

Harlow's forehead wrinkled as she tilted her head, signaling that she was ready to listen.

"Every time I'm inside you, I desperately want to bite you," he whispered.

"You can," she insisted. "I'm not afraid."

"But maybe you should be."

"You're not a vampire," she scoffed. "The Illuminated don't kill with their bite. Everything I've ever heard is that it makes sex... better."

That's not *exactly* what she'd heard. What she'd heard was that it made for one of the most mind-blowing orgasms ever, and frankly, she wanted that. She wanted that with him.

"Yes, that's how it usually works."

"So you've bitten other people?"

Finn's cheeks flushed red. "Yes."

Now her cheeks flushed. "But not me."

"If I bite you it will be different." His eyes fell closed and he pinched the bridge of his nose. "The way I feel about you changes things. It could change my bite."

"What do you mean?"

"What do you know about the Claiming?"

She'd never heard of it. "Nothing. What is it?"

"A brutish mating ritual between my kind. I didn't know it could happen between an Illuminated and a sorcière. In fact, I thought it was impossible, or I would have been more careful, but last night I tasted venom the first time we fucked and it scared me."

"Venom?"

He shook his head. "Not like snake venom... It wouldn't poison you or harm you, but it would bind us together in a way that would make it difficult for us to be parted."

"How so?"

Finn's brow furrowed. "It's a psychic bond. And if we were no longer in love, it would be painful for us to separate. We would need magic to revert to our original selves... Difficult magic."

Harlow's heart pounded. "Are you saying you're in love with me?"

Finn sighed. "That's complicated to answer."

"Try?" she asked, so quietly she wasn't sure if he'd heard her at first.

"I'm still in love with who you were when we were young. I get it, I don't know you now, not well anyway. But we're still connected—my heart, my body, they don't know the difference my mind does. Maybe that's what triggered my venom." Harlow nodded, understanding. "I think I could be again though," he added. "If you wanted this too. I think I could be."

Harlow swallowed hard. She couldn't lie to herself, the thought was exhilarating as it was frightening.

"You don't have to say anything about how you feel about me right now, in fact, please don't."

She could understand that impulse, and she was glad he was giving her time to think. "So the Claiming, it's reversible?"

He nodded. "But it is a physically painful process to reverse. I told you, it's brutish."

"But that's the bad part. If we were together, what would it be like if we didn't fall out of love?"

His eyes darted to hers, full of fear and hope. "It would make our joining pure bliss. It's why the Claimed rarely part, even if they fall out of love. They just screw some more, get their fix and keep going. My parents are that way. That's why they're so awful."

Harlow understood now—he didn't want to trap her, nor be trapped himself. She also understood why he'd reacted badly. This topic made him feel scared, vulnerable. Her fingers wound into his dark hair and she shifted in his lap, straddling him. He pushed her wet hair back from her face. "I shouldn't have snapped at you."

Underneath her, his hips rose to make closer contact with her as his hands ran up her thighs. She pulled gently at the hair at the nape of his neck, tilting his head back so she could brush the angles of his face with her lips. "You're allowed to have feelings. I understand everything you said." She sank deeper onto him, moving against him slowly as his hands roamed under her robe. His thumbs skimmed her inner thighs, teasing her mercilessly.

Harlow let out a tiny whimper then bent to nip his earlobe, whispering, "I'll stop asking you to bite me. For now."

As she pulled back, his eyes blazed. She was thrilled by the faint glow in his skin, the growing pressure of him against her, only the thin fabric of his sweatpants between them. She opened the robe and let it fall away, yanking his pants down as she positioned herself above him.

The dull sting of too much sex mixed with the hot rush of feeling him push into her. He was leisurely and purposeful as he dragged her down on him, stretching her aching body slightly with each increased inch. They moved slowly, looking into each other's eyes, as he moved deep inside her.

A faint scent of smoke from the fire filled Harlow's nose, mixing with Finn's scent of oud and rich amber, so intoxicating that she nearly lost her head. The rhythm and intensity of their movements increased as her hips bucked and rolled over him. Cool, dry air contrasted with the wet heat between them as he thrust harder into her. Harlow moaned, leaning back to allow the gentle curve of him to hit her in the spot that made her see the universe, keeping her eyes on his as her shadows gathered around her.

"What is that?" he breathed. "Is that you?"

She nodded as his skin lit, his lips parted as she clenched around him. "Come with me," she begged.

He pulled her hips, pushing hard into her as she cried out, her voice mingling with his. Above them inky shadows mingled with the light that poured out of him, twisting and writhing together as they did. Harlow knew he was just as amazed as she was, pleasure washing over them both in waves of light and shadow.

And for an instant she saw herself through his eyes, beautiful curves of darkness and shadow, mysterious and alluring as a new moon, dangerous and beloved. When her conscious mind snapped back into her own body, tears streamed down both their faces.

"How did you do that?" he murmured as he clung to her, kissing her over and over. "How did you channel magic that way, Harls?"

CHAPTER TWENTY-FIVE

Harlow wasn't sure what to say. She couldn't find words at the moment. Nothing like that had ever happened to her before during sex, and she'd had some truly spectacular orgasms in her lifetime.

"Are you a Strider?" Finn asked, his eyes wide with wonder.

"How do you know what that is?" she asked, voice sharper than she'd like.

Finn shook his head. "I don't know much, just that the Striders were legendary witches, a force against the Illuminated during the War of the Orders. My people are deeply afraid of them."

Her heart clenched, but she felt her magic respond. It was encouraging her, winding around her arms and fingers, soft and pleased. It liked him; it wanted to mingle with the light again.

"What about you? Are you afraid?"

A grin spread across his face. "No, I know I should be, but that was nothing like what I was taught to fear."

"What you were taught to fear?"

He nodded. "Yes, all Illuminated children hear tales of the Striders, who will extinguish our light with their never-ending darkness." Harlow's smile was faint. The Orders were full of such tales, primarily meant to scare children. For the sorcière it was the incubus, who would steal their hearts and their magic—shifters told tales of the Trickster deity, Voltos, stealing their ability to change forms. "I honestly thought those were stories to convince us to behave. But that... That was..."

"Mind-blowing?" she breathed.

He laughed, amazed as she was. "Yeah, it really was. And I feel stronger too."

"Stronger?" she asked.

"Yeah, watch this."

And without a word, they were standing on the rocky cliffs that looked over the ocean, far above Nuva Troi, both of them naked in the pouring rain. Harlow laughed as she spun. Usually portaling came with a sense of being pulled, sometimes nausea, but this had been like taking a step. "That was effortless."

"You try," he laughed.

She closed her eyes for a moment and when she opened them, they were both fully clothed, dry and standing under an enormous umbrella that Finn held above their heads. She felt her shadows sing in her blood, her fingers stained with inky, beautiful magic.

"That is amazing," Finn said, stepping close to her, winding his arm around her waist. They stared out at the ocean for a few moments, listening to the rain hit the umbrella.

"What does it mean?" she asked.

He shook his head. "I don't know, but I have to believe it has something to do with what my parents want from us, don't you?"

Fear lanced through her, cold and clammy as a dead hand gripping her heart. "I imagine it does."

"Then the stakes are higher now. Whatever it is they want, it isn't that, Harls. Or at least not that version of your magic. That was nothing my parents would want anything to do with. They want a baby, some creature more powerful than what the Illuminated can produce on their own, not for either of *us* to be stronger."

They stood together watching the rain for a long time, both of them teeming with thoughts, she assumed. Her mind was racing and she wished Thea had been able to restore more of the Merkhov facsimile. Rain thudded harder on the umbrella now, and waves crashed on the rocks below. She snuggled further into Finn's arms, grateful for his warmth.

He pressed a kiss to her hair. "Harlow, what do you think would happen if I Claimed you while whatever that was happened?"

Something wonderful. Something terrible. Harlow didn't know which. She took a sharp breath in, watching the rain. She couldn't keep the Merkhov text from him any longer. "I need to show you something. Can you take us to the Monas?"

He nodded and took her in his arms, and moments later they were in the alley behind the courtyard. This time she felt a tiny wave of nausea. "Oof," she groaned. "It wears off."

Finn stroked her arm. "You all right?"

She nodded. "Let's go inside."

He followed her, still holding the umbrella she'd made. She was pleased to find they were also still dressed. So her magic wouldn't wear off. She felt the shadows sigh indignantly, almost as though they were saying, *of course not, silly*.

It wasn't that they communicated exactly, but that she was so in touch with her magic that it was easy to feel the semi-sentient pulse of its will. She'd known magic was a force all its own before, but now she understood intimately.

When they stepped inside the house, Aurelia was waiting in the mudroom, arms folded tightly around her narrow frame, a worried expression on her face. They'd obviously tripped one of her wards when they arrived, and she'd watched them walk in. "You told him?"

How did she always know everything? As children, the Krane girls had never gotten away with anything. Selene and Aurelia both seemed to have a seventh sense precisely tuned to predicting their daughters' impulses. Harlow laughed at the way things never changed, and then shrugged. "Not exactly... He... saw?"

Aurelia barely suppressed a smug smile. "The Merkhov text *does* mention something like that might happen. Were the two of you..."

Harlow glared, cheeks turning bright red. "*Mother. Please.* I am not going to discuss this with you." Behind her, Finn snickered. She shot the glare over her shoulder to apply to him as well. He just laughed harder. *Arrogant prick.* "Finn needs to see the illumination."

Aurelia nodded, sniffing to hide her smile. "Of course." But she did not move. Her eyes went to Finn and they narrowed, appraising and cold.

Finn bowed his head slightly. "It is so nice to meet you, Archchancellor Krane. Officially, I mean."

Aurelia held out her hand and Finn took it, kissing the ring that marked Aurelia as presiding Archchancellor of the Order of Mysteries. "Be welcome in my home, Finbar McKay."

"Thank you," he murmured so softly, and with so much emotion that Harlow saw her mother's eyes narrow, assessing him.

"Go upstairs please. I'll find Mama and the book."

Harlow took Finn's hand and led him up the stairs, taking him into Aurelia's study. The room was small, lined with crowded bookshelves stained a dark green hue. Mother's mahogany desk was piled with neat stacks of notes and a small brass lamp cast a cozy glow. A heavy antique library table sat in front of the enormous windows, natural light flooding into the room through the leaded glass.

"Why does every room of your parents' house feel so much

like home?" Finn murmured as his eyes flew over the spines of the books on the shelves. His voice was painfully wistful. Harlow wasn't sure what to say, so she pressed a kiss to his hand, which she still held.

Selene cleared her throat. "Aurelia is making tea. I don't believe we've met."

Finn's hand shook in hers. He understood immediately. Aurelia was politically the most powerful Krane, but Selene was the heart of the family, the ultimate test he would have to pass. Harlow's eyes widened in shock when he fell to one knee, bowing his head. This was a position of fealty the Illuminated only took when swearing oaths. It was an ancient custom, one she had not expected to see from him, especially not today.

"I promise you," he swore, taking Selene's outstretched hand. "She is safe with me. Nothing my parents want will come to pass. I will protect her with my life."

Harlow took a sharp breath in. Her heart raced, as her shadows sang with pleasure. She wanted to shush them—this was binding. He was swearing an oath to her mother. Nothing like this had even seemed possible just a day ago.

"I accept you at your word," Selene said, her voice smooth and regal. "The next oath you take will be to her."

Finn nodded, his head still bowed. "If she will have me, I will swear any oath she asks."

A lump rose in Harlow's throat, coated with fear. *This was all moving too fast, wasn't it? Or was this the natural place for their path to take them, given all the years between them?* She tried to dismiss the feeling of the walls closing in on her. None of his promises required her to make any in return, not yet anyway.

When Selene pulled Finn gently from the floor and kissed his cheeks, the claustrophobia dissipated, realization dawning on her. This wasn't *just* about her. Finn wanted her family to trust him. No, he *needed* them to trust him, because so few people in his life ever had before, except maybe Alaric. Trust wasn't a part of his relationship with his parents. Finn had always wanted a family like hers, and given what he'd grown up with, she couldn't blame him for that.

Harlow slipped her hand into Finn's and he squeezed it hard. "Thank you," he said, and she wasn't sure who he was thanking, or if he was simply grateful.

As they settled into chairs around the library table, she wondered what it would be like to live with parents who you could not trust, and who did not trust you in return. She wondered if anyone in his family had truly loved him. From the slump in his shoulders, she thought he might be thinking the same thing.

"I'm glad you're here," she said, as Selene rose to help Aurelia with the tea tray and Thea entered behind her with the Merkhov text.

"Me too," he answered. There was an unmistakable tremor in his voice. This was as important to him as she'd suspected it might be.

As Selene arranged the tea tray, Aurelia opened the book in a cradle on the worktable. "I believe this is the illumination you wanted Finn to see."

He leaned forward. Thea had done more work on it. The image was close to being fully restored, with the coloring on the snakes' bodies showing in brilliant hues, while the egg and sphere still looked a bit dull, but much easier to make out. The most stunning improvement was the way the light and shadows coming off the snakes were interacting, twisting together. This was eerily reminiscent of what they'd experienced in Finn's bedroom just hours before. His eyes narrowed as his body stilled, his focus winnowing in a way that Harlow knew probably intimidated people who worked with him.

"Where did you get this?" No one had a chance to answer Finn. He continued speaking, his words coming out in an excited rush. "This is representative of a union between a Strider and one of the Knights of Serpens, isn't it?" He looked closer, seeing the egg, as if for the first time. His usually healthy coloring paled. "*Oh.*"

"The Knights of Serpens?" Harlow asked, gripping his knee under the table.

He nodded, glancing at her, but only for a moment. "A sect of Illuminated warriors. They came in the original envoy to protect the ambassadors. Our history tells us they fought against the Striders in the War of the Orders."

Harlow had never come across any such history of the Great War, but she understood the lower Orders and a contingent of humans had risen up against the Illuminated, attempting to force them back to their own realm. Obviously, it hadn't worked. Though the Illuminated were struggling to reproduce, they were as powerful as they'd ever been, and there hadn't been a war on Okairos since. Shortly after the war, poverty was eradicated and the strict regulation of human life began. It was a steep price for peace, in Harlow's opinion, but of course that was not the tone history took on the matter. It was practically treason to even think such a thing.

"The Striders and the Knights of Serpens were enemies?" Harlow asked, trying to understand how her people had actually fit into things.

"So the Illuminated would have us believe," Thea replied, giving Finn a pointed look. Harlow noticed the way his eyes flicked quickly away from her sister's. "But the Knights haven't been seen or heard from since the war ended. Effectively, they don't exist."

Finn shifted uncomfortably under Thea's gaze. The two of them shared some secret, Harlow realized, her stomach turning at the thought. He stared at his hands. "That's not exactly the case."

Selene's eyes snapped to Finn's, demanding he continue.

"When Alaric and I were at uni, something happened... We

received keys to an ancient store of knowledge, an invitation from the Knights of old to reinvigorate their society, which was not what we'd been told it was at all."

"Who sent the keys?" Harlow asked.

Finn shook his head. "We never found out."

That was saying something, given the work they did together at their securities company. What kind of organization could keep secrets from people like Alaric? Thea sat back in her chair, a hint of a smile playing at her lips.

Aurelia and Selene shared a concerned look. Selene asked, "Can you tell us more? About the Knights?"

Finn nodded. "Yes, because you've found this, and because of the implications... I think I can." He took Harlow's hand and kissed it, smiling faintly at her. She thought he looked anxious, but the impression passed quickly. He was far too good at masking his emotions. "The Knights of Serpens fought alongside the Striders in the war, not against them, and as punishment they were executed when the Illuminated won. On his execution day, their commander had a vision that one day the Knights and Striders would be reunited, and it would bring about an event he called 'the reckoning,' though we don't know what he meant, as he was executed before he could elaborate."

"How do you know all this?" Aurelia asked, deep suspicion etched into the lines around her eyes.

"All of the Knights' last words were magically transferred to the vault of information in Nea Sterlis that we received keys to," Finn answered.

Selene took a deep breath. "And so you are a Knight? You and Alaric both?"

Finn nodded. "Yes, and Petra. Along with a select few others, we have a network across Nytra... My friend Cian Herrington is my second and helps to run our special projects."

It was an odd addendum, like Finn was relieved to speak about someone significant to him. Harlow hadn't heard Cian's name before, but the tone Finn took indicated they were someone important.

"Your *second*?" Harlow asked. That would imply that Finn was, what exactly?

"I am the Serpens' commander," Finn said softly. "Though we do very little fighting these days, and Alaric, who is technically my third in command, handles most of our more nefarious activities."

"Which are what exactly?" Aurelia asked, leaning forward.

Finn opened his mouth to give some answer, but Selene cut in. "Where is Thea?" Her voice carried a note of panic. Everyone stopped and looked around. It was true, Thea was gone.

"I'm right here," said a soft voice in the doorway. All eyes swung to the elegant figure standing in the entry of the study. "Alaric's here too. I went to let him in. We thought you might need us both today."

Alaric peeked around the door. "Hello, Kranes! Finn," he said cheerfully, with a wave so characteristically Alaric that one might have thought they were gathering for brunch, not discussing the kind of sedition that could get them all killed.

Finn nodded to Alaric, his brows furrowing in mild confusion. "What are you doing here?"

Alaric moved into the room and tapped the Merkhov text. "The same thing you are. Protecting the woman I love."

Thea beamed at Alaric with such pride that Harlow felt the lump in her throat again. *Was this what love looked like?* "Thea?" she asked. "What's going on?"

Aurelia motioned for Thea and Alaric to take the remaining seats at the worktable as she cleared the Merkhov text and began to serve tea. Thea reached across the table to take Harlow's hand. "I'm sorry I couldn't tell you everything," she whispered. "We wanted to wait to find out if you and Finn could work things out on your own."

Harlow's brow furrowed. "Okay, we've worked things out. Could you all explain what's happening here?"

Finn looked slightly irritated, as though Alaric had stolen his thunder, but he sat back in his chair as the two got settled. When they were comfortable, Alaric looked to Finn, a question in his eyes. Finn nodded, though Harlow noted he still looked perturbed. It occurred to her that he likely spent his life rarely being questioned or challenged. Unless it came to his parents, of course.

Alaric smiled at Thea again. "Thea and I knew each other in school, as we all did, but when we were at uni we met again."

Thea's cheeks pinked, as though she was remembering something especially enjoyable. "We were both researching the Knights of Serpens, and their conflict with the Striders."

"Why?" Selene asked sharply.

Thea's face twisted apologetically. "Because I knew it was possible that one of us could become a Strider. I knew it wouldn't be me, because I'd shown all the early signs of manifestation—I was clearly not the Strider. I actually thought it might be Larkin for a while."

"As did I," Alaric murmured. "And since I'd already taken my oaths, I wanted to know more about our ancient allies, and what our shared goals may have been."

Thea continued fluidly, as though the two of them had been paired for years, which Harlow supposed they had, if they'd reconnected six years ago. "Alaric had a book I needed and we began talking. Neither of us knew the other's personal interest in the old stories at the time, but in researching our histories, we fell in love."

Something sliced into Harlow's heart. Thea had been keeping secrets from her for so long. What did all this mean?

Alaric was still speaking, "Eventually, we found the original book the triptych is from. The illumination in the Merkhov text is a facsimile of a section of the Scroll of Akatei."

Aurelia gasped. "No. You've seen it? Both of you?"

Thea smiled at her mother, and the resemblance between them was so strong they could have been twins in that moment. "We have it. Or part of it anyway. It was in the Velarius family archives, but now we have the original in the Vault."

Aurelia looked perturbed, embattled over the fact that she believed Thea should have revealed all this to the Order of Mysteries, no doubt. And perhaps she should have. It was hard for Harlow to decide. She couldn't deny she also felt the sting of having Thea keep so much from her.

Selene leaned toward Alaric, while simultaneously patting her wife's hand to console her. "Do your parents know you have this?"

Alaric shook his head. "No. My parents are more sympathetic to the lower Orders and humans than many of the Illuminated, but I haven't trusted them with this knowledge. I've been careful to hide my interest in this subject, especially after Thea and I met."

"Get to the point, you two," Finn cut in. "Tell them."

Thea's face was cool as ever, but her eyes revealed her guilt. "When we were sure I wasn't the Strider, I was sworn in. I am one of the Knights of Serpens."

"What in seventeen hells does *that* mean?" Aurelia said, her voice low and dangerous. A sorcière's first duty was always to the Order of Mysteries.

Thea shot back, no trace of her usual politeness evident: "It means that I've been *helping*, Mother. Helping to make things what they should be on Okairos. Or at least here in Nytra."

Alaric took Thea's clenched fist into his own. "What Thea is trying to say is that the Knights are committed to finding a way to bring more equity into the world, as we always have been. We know that historically, members of all the Orders were Knights, even sorcière."

Thea nodded, looking nervous. As Alaric clutched Thea's

hand to his chest, Harlow noticed the enormous black diamond shining from the ring on her sister's left index finger. She was not only paired, but bonded.

Harlow snatched her hand. "Explain this. Now."

"Oh," Thea murmured. "I forgot to take it off."

Alaric's grin could have lit a city. "We made it official last night—a priestess of Aphora performed the ritual."

Harlow's eyebrows shot so far up, she could feel her hairline move. She stole a glance at Selene, who'd been planning her daughters' bonding rituals since they were children. Mama was seething, sheets of tempestuous energy filling the room. Each of the Krane children were to be married in the Temple District in Nea Sterlis, at a date determined by one of the Order of Mysteries' astrologers, with weeks of celebration both before and after the ritual proper. A clandestine ceremony in a dark city temple was *not* what she'd planned.

Alaric seemed to sense the danger he was in and hastily kept explaining, but Harlow noticed his hands shook as Thea took them into her own. "If anyone finds out what we are doing here, we are all in a great deal of danger, as you know... Anyway, to be safe, we just went ahead and were bonded—"

He was babbling, probably due to the intensity of Selene's glare. Thea stopped him from continuing, by adding, "We'd like to have the celebrations you planned at a later date, Mama."

"Congratulations," Selene said drily, ignoring Thea's comment completely. "Please clarify why all this secrecy was necessary."

Thea nodded, continuing quickly. "Until Harlow's magic manifested, this was all just speculation. The Scroll of Akatei seems to indicate that the unification of a Knight of Serpens and a Strider will usher in a new age of magic—which we believe would effectively end the Illuminated's stranglehold on Okairos."

Alaric added, "Thea and I believe a fifth Order will be

formed through this union, that the egg symbolizes a new start, or a new power."

Harlow thought of the ease with which both she and Finn had used their power earlier in the day. Could this be an explanation for why that was possible?

Alaric continued, "Though we do not know how. The triptych is incomplete in the Scroll of Akatei as well."

Was this why Finn was so interested in her? Harlow felt as though the walls were closing in on her again. This time she could not slow it down or stop it. Her heart beat erratically and her palms began to sweat. "Did you know this?" she asked, turning to Finn. "Is this why you were so eager to ally with me?"

Finn turned to her, shock on his face. "No. I mean, I knew about your sister and Alaric, of course. But not about the Scroll." He glared at Alaric. "Why didn't you tell me this?"

Alaric sighed. "We didn't want to affect either of your choices. It's not a prophecy, Finn. It's the key to unlocking the trouble our people caused when they came here. It's only a solution, and when we didn't know about Harlow, we didn't want to introduce anything that would complicate the issues between you."

Thea nodded. "But we think your parents know. That's why we needed to tell you, *today*."

"If my parents knew all this, don't you think they'd want to keep Harlow and I apart?" Finn asked. It was a reasonable question, as it seemed unlikely they'd want to force something that would bring about the end of the Illuminated's power.

Thea and Alaric shared a look. "Well, that's just *our* interpretation of what the scroll may be saying."

Aurelia rolled her eyes. She and Thea had many conflicts over the interpretation of texts that relied on iconography and symbolism to convey meaning. Usually it was a charming quirk of their relationship. Today it made Harlow ill. Aurelia pinched the bridge of her nose. "What does it *actually* say, Thea?"

Thea looked at her hands. "If my translation is correct, it says the combination of the Knight and the Strider will produce a power unlike any other. We believe the other two illuminations show the process, much as an alchemical text might."

Finn's voice was nothing less than lethal fury, cold and dangerous. "My parents think it means we'll have a child, and that child will be the most powerful creature in history, don't they?"

Alaric sighed. "They might, but that's not the only way to interpret things."

Selene shook her head. "It doesn't matter. If that's what they think, Harlow is in danger, as would any child she and Finn might have together. We need to see the rest of the triptych, one way or another."

Harlow felt as though she might vomit. They were all discussing her *having a baby,* and no one had even looked at her, or asked her what *she* thought.

Thea continued speaking. "We think the McKays may have the missing parts of the scroll, or at least they've seen it. Tatyana Merkhov disappeared, did you know that?"

Selene pursed her lips. "Yes, I knew. Something about a plane crash, I believe."

Thea shook her head. "We think she was killed, because of what she knew, and what she published in that book. It's impossible to find intact, as you both know. We were lucky to have stumbled upon a copy in our last acquisition. I don't think the lot-owner even knew what it was."

Aurelia shrugged. "Likely not, they weren't a collector. Just cleaning out an estate."

Thea nodded. "She obviously saw the Scroll when it was complete. She knew what the triptych showed. Others might as well."

"And you think the McKays and the Velariuses are the ones who killed her?" Harlow asked.

"It seems possible," Alaric said. "We have to behave as if they did, at least until we know more."

Harlow's head spun with information, as her attention bounced from one thought to another. The room felt very small. *Was the ceiling lower than it had been a few minutes ago?*

Finn held up a hand. "Please, will you excuse Harlow and I for a few minutes?"

He hadn't even looked at her, and yet he'd known she was crumbling under the pressure of what was being said. Everyone's eyes turned to Harlow. Her skin was cold, but inside her muscles felt as though they had been set aflame.

Finn's hand closed around hers and he rose from his chair, in a motion so fluid it nearly distracted her from the internal struggle waging war on her heart. "Come with me to the terrace?"

She stood without a word, her body simply following the commands Finn guided her through. *Stand, walk behind him, follow him to the terrace, curl into a big rattan settee, sip a cool glass of water.* When she came back to herself, he was sitting at her feet, and rain poured outside the covered terrace, making the back courtyard a blur of greens, purples and golds.

"You were panicking," he said, tucking a soft cotton blanket around her knees.

She nodded, but could hardly speak. It was all a lot to take in. Finally she said, "The maters are going to kill Thea for having their bonding ritual without a big to-do."

It was good to lighten the mood a bit, it gave her room to think. Finn snorted. "You know *we* don't have to move so quickly, right? Last night was amazing, and this morning was absolutely phenomenal, but I'm not rushing this for anything, or any*one* but you."

Harlow's brow furrowed. "What are your expectations now?"

"Nothing. My only concern right now is keeping you safe.

Believe me when I say that if that means staying apart, I will make that choice. Given everything that Thea and Alaric know, maybe that would be better."

His eyes didn't meet hers, but she noticed the tremor in his hands that seemed reserved for her. *Was that what she wanted? To end things now, to remain safe? Would she even* be *safe if they weren't together?* She remembered what he'd said about his parents being willing to force her into something she didn't want.

"I think... I think I just need a little bit of time," Harlow said quietly.

Finn nodded, getting up. "I'll go then. Alaric can fill me in a bit more on the secrets he and Thea have been keeping. I'll check in with you tomorrow, if that's all right?"

She saw it in his eyes, and heard it in the clipped, businesslike tone of his voice. He thought she was backing out, that she didn't want him at all. Her hand slipped into his. "I need to breathe, Finn. That's it. Just a beat to get my bearings, okay?"

She pulled on his arm until his face met hers. A half-smile curved the corner of his mouth as he asked, "And what about the things that happened this morning?"

Harlow's words tumbled out. "It was all amazing. To tell you the truth, I was excited about all of it until it turned into a big thing. When it was just you and me, not Striders and Knights."

Finn crouched down, so his eyes were at her level. "It's still you and me. You heard Alaric, this isn't a prophecy, it's a solution, and *we* don't have to be the solution if you don't want us to be."

The idea that he would walk away, let her go, let her *choose*, made her throat clench. Air seemed scarce. Harlow closed her eyes. "I need time for my mind to catch up. This is how I am."

His voice was soft in her ear, his lips brushing her neck, while her eyes stayed squeezed shut. "I remember."

She wound her arms around him. He kissed her forehead

and was gone. When she was alone, she considered that Finn had known her almost her whole life. That he knew the way she needed time to herself to process things quietly meant something. That he respected her enough to walk away if she asked meant even more. A seed of trust drove deep into her soul and took root.

Her shadows sang at the progress she made, and she let them dance around her fingers as she thought things over. While she needed time like this to be quiet and let her brain work things through, she knew he needed to take a more active approach. Finn needed to *do* something, rather than think. It had the possibility to cause conflict between them, but if they managed it right, gave each other space to be themselves—it was possible they'd be stronger together.

Harlow took several long breaths, finally opening her eyes. The door to the terrace slid open. Thea pressed a mug of tea into her hands and curled up next to her on the settee. Harlow let the sound of the rain drown everything else out while she tried to find her way back to herself again.

CHAPTER TWENTY-SIX

"Why do you think Finn and I could do anything to bring equity to the world?" Harlow asked her sister after a time. She appreciated the company, but she wasn't going to be able to process her feelings with Thea watching her, so she might as well get some questions answered.

"The Scroll of Akatei. That's what it's all about."

Harlow shook her head. "Spell it out for me, Thea. I'm tired."

"The Scroll of Akatei isn't a written text. It's mostly images, and the few inscriptions are vague to the point of opacity and in a variety of ancient languages that are difficult to translate. Many of the images are deceptively similar to those we're used to seeing in humans' alchemical texts, which would have been the Scroll's contemporaries, but there's more to it than that. Alaric and I think it's the story of the Illuminated—what they were *supposed* to do when they came here."

"Which was what?" Harlow asked, exhaustion growing closer by the minute.

"Activate this realm's magic... for everyone."

Harlow's head hurt. "Didn't they do that, sort of? I mean,

the Orders are their children and we're all magical to some extent, right?"

"Yes, but they weren't supposed to come here and have children. They were *supposed* to come and unlock magic for everyone, making it accessible to anyone. Instead, they hoarded it for themselves, and a very small amount of the world."

Thea was obviously frustrated by Harlow's slow uptake and her tone was bordering on condescending. Harlow also got the distinct impression there was more to the story that Thea wasn't saying. She was keeping secrets for Alaric, and the Illuminated, and Harlow couldn't help but feel betrayed.

"And how were they going to do that?" Harlow asked, feeling snappish.

Now Thea looked perplexed. "We don't know. Again, the Scroll is a series of images and I was unable to restore most of them, in addition to the fact that a crucial piece is missing. It was damaged magically."

"How did Merkhov get her hands on it?" Harlow's question was more idle wondering than actual question, but Thea's eyes lit up.

"That is a really good question. One I hope we'll answer when we find out more about the triptych."

Harlow suppressed the urge to roll her eyes at Thea's tone. "Wonderful."

Thea sighed, apparently annoyed by Harlow's acidity. There was a long pause before she asked, "Are you going to congratulate me?"

"Of course. I'm happy for you both." Unlike Selene, she had nothing invested in fancy bonding rituals, or days of celebration. Still, having so much kept from her stung. "I just wish you could have told me all this sooner. Why did the two of you wait for so long?"

Thea shrugged a little, looking distressed. "I wasn't sure

what to do, honestly. When I found most of this out, you were living with Mark and it seemed like it wouldn't be a good time."

Mark. Of course Thea hadn't wanted to tell Harlow anything when she was with him. When she'd been with Mark, she'd been deemed untrustworthy, despite the fact that she'd kept all the Order's secrets. Harlow drew her knees to her chest and pressed her forehead into her hands. "Okay. That makes sense. I'm not trying to be a jerk. This is all just a lot for me, and knowing you knew all of this—plus the truth about why Finn left me—it's just a lot to take in, okay?"

Harlow hated how she'd start to melt down when things got overwhelming. In fact, she felt the tears building behind her eyes and she knew it wouldn't be long before she was hysterical; she had to get out before that started. She didn't want anyone trying to comfort her right now.

"I'm going to go home. I'll see you tomorrow," she said, forcing an evenness she didn't feel into her voice.

"Okay," Thea replied softly.

Her luminous eyes filled with tears, but Harlow couldn't stop to say anything kind. She didn't want to hurt her sister, but Thea purposely kept things from her while watching her implode. Thea was the one person who knew how much Finn had hurt her and the fact that she also could have stopped so much of that pain with the knowledge she withheld cut deep, too deep.

As she stood, Thea clasped her hand. "I *am* sorry, Harlow. I made a mistake not telling you, or at least not encouraging you to talk to Finn. Alaric and I should have tried harder to get you two to talk."

Harlow drew her hand back like she'd been stung, but Thea held on. "No. *You* should have told me what you knew. I know you're sorry now, but you knew how bad things were for me right before I met Mark. You knew and you *still* didn't tell me."

Thea held tighter, tears rolling down her face now. "I know. I'm so sorry."

Harlow yanked her hand back now, infuriated by Thea's tears, by the audacity she had to say she was sorry and expect forgiveness now. "Don't apologize. You chose your loyalty—to Alaric and the Knights. Not me, not when I was *literally* dying from how lonely and sad I was."

Thea had been the one to pick her up from the hospital. She was the only one who knew, other than Mark. She'd told Mark too. What a mistake that had been. He'd held her fragility over her head more times than she could count, reminding her that she'd lost her grip once, and that if he didn't watch her, she might again.

Every heartbeat felt like pounding a bruise and she ran, passing Aurelia and Selene in the hallway, down the back stairs and into the alley. She was on her way to Mulberry Street and Enzo's before she remembered she didn't have her phone.

It didn't matter. Her eyes blurred with tears and so she didn't see Kate Spencer, coming around the corner, until she'd steadied her. "Hey, Lo. Gods, what's wrong?"

Lo. The nickname only Kate had ever used prompted another onslaught of sobs. What in Akatei's name was Kate Spencer doing here? "I... I..." She couldn't say what was actually wrong. She knew better, even though a rebellious part of her wanted to say it all. "I had a fight with Thea."

"Oh shit," Kate said, pulling her under an awning and out of the rain. "I'm sorry to hear that."

Kate didn't ask if she was all right. Most people would, but not Kate. Kate never asked questions that had obvious answers. It was one of the things Harlow always liked best about her.

"You wanna grab a drink? We could go get some tea... Or maybe a whiskey?"

Harlow nodded and she let Kate lead her around the corner, past Mulberry onto Lupine Blvd, where there was a pub Harlow liked called the Three Besoms. When they slid into a booth, upholstered with the familiar Three Besoms crimson tartan, Harlow could almost imagine it was four years ago, and they were meeting up after work. The pub was the same as ever, all dark gleaming wood and twinkling witchlights, cozy to a tee. After a quick word from Kate, a waitress brought them both two shots of whiskey and two mugs of steaming black tea with a distinct caramel aroma.

Kate dumped one shot each into their tea, and then clinked her remaining shot glass to Harlow's. They downed their shots and then sat in comfortable silence sipping the fragrant tea. Despite being a bit damp, Kate looked amazing. Her short brown hair was freshly cut and swept away from her beautiful face, which was immaculately made up, as always.

She slid out of her leather jacket and Harlow choked up a little to see she was wearing a t-shirt from a concert they'd gone to together. Harlow didn't think before she spoke. "What in seventeen hells are you *doing* here?"

Kate grinned. "Business. Aside from having a fight with Thea, what are you up to?"

Harlow shook her head, glancing around the bar to avoid making eye contact with Kate. "Fucking everything up, as usual."

Kate's cavalier grin shifted quickly into a frown. "That's an odd thing to say."

A hysterical laugh choked Harlow. "No, *that's* an odd thing to say."

Kate tilted her head in that hawklike way she had. "Lo, you're just about the most put-together person I know. What're you talking about?"

Harlow shook her head. "Still not reading the gossips, huh?"

"I read them. What's that have to do with anything? You're still smart as seventeen hells, and beautiful as ever. What's it matter what trash like the Section Seven editors say?" Kate's grin showed the glint of her fangs. She was flirting, but just a little. "And you're seeing my buddy Finn McKay now, I hear. That's pretty slick of you."

"You know Finn?" Harlow asked, blushing a little.

"Yeah, we surfed together a lot when I moved back to Nea Sterlis," Kate said, adding, "I'm a little jealous you're seeing him though."

Harlow frowned. "You don't date men."

The laugh that erupted out of Kate's mouth sounded like a pack of wild dogs. "I meant *you*, Lo. I heard you and Easton broke up, but by the time I could get away, Riley Quinn informed me I was too late."

"Oh," Harlow said, feeling confused.

Kate took her hand. "Lo, we had so much fun together, but it's not like it is with you and Finn, is it?"

Harlow looked deep into Kate's green eyes, remembering the short time they'd spent together. "No, Finn and I have history. But we *did* have fun. *So* much fun."

Kate kissed her fingertips, sighing. "I wish it had lasted longer, but I think it might have ended badly if it had. I like how we left things. You're the one who got away, and that's a damn romantic story to tell myself... *If I'd only come back sooner, she wouldn't have paired with the most handsome man on the planet...*"

Harlow laughed, which of course was the point. Kate was great at making her laugh. They'd spent the short time they had together either screwing like bunnies or laughing 'til their sides hurt. If Harlow was honest with herself, Kate was one of the best friends she'd ever had, and she missed that part of things more than anything else.

When her laughter dissolved and she breathed normally again, she asked, "Did you leave because you knew we were a bad fit?"

"No." Kate shook her head. "It was time for me to go home and help with the family business. It killed me to leave you."

It had killed Harlow to be left, but she'd always wondered if their days were numbered. Kate had always leaned more towards polyamory, and Harlow was never quite capable of that. Not that she judged the practice, like humans did; it just wasn't right for her, and it was for Kate. It would have been a problem eventually, but this way they never had to find out.

"Do you want to go out, do something fun?" Kate asked, downing the last of her tea.

It would be nice to go do something fun, something normal, but Harlow was exhausted. She felt like she could sleep for days, and she wanted to see Axel. "No, thanks. I'm going to go home and sort myself out. Can I use your phone to call a cab?"

Kate pulled her phone from her pocket. "No service. I'll go ask the bartender to call for you, okay?"

"Thank you," Harlow said. "I'm going to run to the bathroom."

Once there, she smiled at herself in the mirror. She was glad she'd run into Kate. This conversation closed a door for her that left the one Finn had opened a shining possibility. Mark always made her feel like no one had ever wanted her but him, and that no one else ever would, but she saw that for what it was now: pathetic lies. He'd had to lie to her constantly, manipulate her into a muddled mess to get her to stay with him. He *was* pathetic.

She returned to the table to find Kate with her jacket on. "I've gotta run. Your cab will be here in five. I'll be in town for a bit for business. I'll probably see you at some of the season events, if you're going to any more."

"We'll definitely be at the Solstice Gala," Harlow said, marveling at her easy use of "we."

Kate kissed her cheek. "I'll see you then. Make up with Thea, all right? She means well."

Harlow had used the same words to describe Thea's prissy, rude behavior a thousand times. Her heart twinged a bit to hear Kate say it back to her now. She nodded and watched her ex go.

Kate was so good, so free, but Harlow didn't regret that it was over. Maybe she was free now too, or closer anyway. She tried to pay the tab, but found Kate had already done so. As she walked through the bar to the cab waiting outside, she felt watched, just like she had at the Metro. Her skin crawled under the pressure of unseen eyes, and she realized she'd forgotten to tell anyone about that. Suddenly, that seemed like a misstep.

She turned slowly, pretending to fix something about her shoe. There was no one suspicious looking in the bar. A few sorcières she knew waved from the corner booth, by the hearth, their smiles a bit cautious, but mostly friendly. She waved back. The rest of the bar was empty. Perhaps she was imagining things. Her shadows swelled inside her in a way that was new to her.

Show me, she urged them. *What am I missing?*

There it was, just slipping away—motion at the back of the bar. The heavy back door was swinging shut, very slowly. Someone had been in the back, watching her and Kate. But who? She bit her bottom lip. There was nothing she could do about it now.

CHAPTER TWENTY-SEVEN

As soon as she slid into the backseat of the cab, Harlow knew something was wrong. The doors locked immediately and there were no handles on the inside of the cab anywhere. When the cabbie turned, she looked into the eyes of a vampire—cold and milky, a sure tell they'd been drinking fresh human blood. Vampires who drank blood bank fare had eyes like everyone else.

Harlow's stomach clenched instinctually. It wasn't illegal to drink from willing humans, but she doubted that Athan Sanvier, Olivia's cousin and a baron of the House of Remiel, the high house of the Order of Night, gave a fig about willingness. He had a reputation for cruelty that never seemed to deter humans, but scared her to her core. Being alone with Athan Sanvier was the last thing in the world she'd ever choose.

"Hey there, little witch," he drawled. "Heard you were looking for a ride. I'd be happy to oblige."

Harlow swallowed hard. "Let me out, Athan, or you are going to find yourself in worlds of trouble."

He didn't respond, pulling away from the curb. She cursed

herself for leaving the Monas without her phone. "Does Olivia know you're doing this?"

Athan smiled in the rearview mirror. "I think you mean 'does Mark know I'm doing this,' don't you?"

That honestly hadn't occurred to Harlow, but now her stomach soured. Would he really go this far to get back at her for taking Axel back? Surely he couldn't care that much. He'd been treating the cat terribly.

Athan smiled again, clearly not meaning to tell her. Panic crept into her veins, thrumming like a drum that drowned out all thought. Harlow struggled to keep her head.

Think, Harlow, she commanded herself. The sun was low in the sky, which meant she had only a few minutes to escape without Athan being able to easily follow.

"Where are you taking me?" she asked.

Athan shook his head, smiling again. The smile spoke of how much he enjoyed pain. It wasn't a vampiric trait to be vicious, Kate and her House were evidence of that, but vampirism did seem to amplify certain personality traits more than others, and aggression and sadism were both commonly magnified.

In Athan's case, rumor had it that he enjoyed inflicting the kind of psychological pain that left people broken and bitter for years. No wonder Mark sent him. This all made too much sense. While she could not be compelled like a human, there was plenty he could do to torture her, if he so chose. Sorcières were not entirely immune to vampiric magics and he was certainly strong enough to overpower her physically. Her heart fluttered wildly in response to this thought.

"You don't want to do this, Athan," she warned again. "You don't want to be in trouble with the Illuminated."

Athan laughed. "Once we're through with you, the Illuminated won't be able to do a damn thing to me."

That was an odd thing to say, but Harlow didn't have time

to puzzle it out. She rolled her eyes, acting braver than she felt. "Don't be foolish, Athan. You can't do more than torture me and you know it." Murder between the lower Orders was so stringently punished that there had not been a single incident in over a hundred years.

"Who said anything about torture?" Athan breathed. She noticed one of his fingers tapped relentlessly on the steering wheel, as though whatever he had planned for her excited him to the point of perpetual motion. "You might love what we can do for you—I'd imagine a curvy thing like you is wanton as they come."

Her blood chilled. She wasn't sure what he was talking about, but his tone of voice was too sure, too confident for petty vengeance. Something else was happening here, and she very much doubted she would love anything Athan Sanvier could do for or *to* her.

"Let me out of the car," she insisted.

He ignored her. "I wonder how you'll be when we turn you. No more spells of course, but your new power will be so sweet. Promise to ride me at least once, all right?"

Cold sweat broke out over Harlow's skin as the fragments of his words fell together. What he implied was impossible. Neither Athan Sanvier nor the vampires of the House of Remiel, despite all their power, could turn *her* into anything, and certainly not a succubus. That was what he was implying, wasn't it? Harlow tried to tell herself that her imagination was running away with itself, that there was a reasonable explanation for all this. They were just vampires, after all, and vampires couldn't turn other immortals into anything else.

If there was a reasonable explanation for this, I wouldn't be trapped in a cab with Athan Sanvier, she thought.

If he'd just wanted to talk to her, he wouldn't have used this cab. Nothing good would come of this. Her mind went to war with itself, part of it trying to convince the other that the cold fear lashing through her veins was all manufactured and irrational. The other part screamed, *Get out, get out, get out.* She needed to trust herself, hard as that was. She reached for the shadows, for the inky power of her newly manifested magic, but it sputtered.

She was too afraid and wished desperately that she could portal, but she still wasn't powerful enough to blink through space. The shadows shifted within her, beyond the veil of reality. She could feel them try to help her from deep within the limen, trying to soothe her. It wasn't that she had to banish the fear; she had to accept it and master it. Harlow looked out the window for the first time, trying to get her bearings. They were headed Uptown now, toward the House of Remiel's quarters, a high-rise downtown where the hundred most elite vampires in Nuva Troi both worked and resided.

Once he took her inside, she would be subject to the vampires' will, and no matter what that would not bode well for her. *Help me*, she begged her magic. A flicker of shadow brought her back inside the car; she felt it in her fingers. Felt the threads of reality around her. The car slowed at a red light and she saw the sun was setting, streaming down 55th Avenue for the first time today. The rain had stopped.

Harlow dropped into her spirit body quickly, summoning enough power to create the simplest fix. While fear had its claws in her, she understood that she didn't need a flashy solution, just a reliable one and her wits. When the door handle appeared she willed it to be unlocked, perpetually unlocked, unable to even *be* locked.

"Shit," she whispered, looking out the front of the cab, straight into the sun. She injected as much panic as she could into her voice, which wasn't difficult, as her heart was thumping so hard she could hardly hear herself think. "What in seventeen hells is *that*?"

Athan followed her gaze, squinting in the light, his sensitive eyes unable to make much out. He reached for sunglasses in the console and she made her move. She took the newly-made handle and opened the car door, sprinting straight into the line of light the setting sun created down 55th Avenue, back the way they'd come. She knew she couldn't escape him for long, and this close to the House of Remiel there would be vampires everywhere. He was likely calling them now, if he wasn't working on his own.

She darted out of the shadows of the sidewalk and back into the street, where the sun set streams of golden light ablaze. Though vampires could technically leave the comfort of their homes during the day, even small amounts of light made it difficult for them to utilize the full range of their power. When the sun disappeared, they would be nearly as quick and strong as the Illuminated though, and in the shadows, she spotted Athan's backup gathering. They were tracking her in packs of three and four.

So he wasn't working alone. The House of Remiel supported this, whatever it was. Frantically, she sought out options. Cars honked around her as they swerved to miss her. She couldn't stand here for much longer, but the way the tall buildings blocked the light except for the very center of the street made it the safest place for her, despite the traffic.

The sun sank lower and hit the bank across the street just so, causing light to bounce off a small angled mirror affixed to the side of the building. It was a bizarre place to put a mirror, but she followed the new stream of light with her eyes. It made a narrow path through the shadows of the sidewalk across the street, hitting the door of a cafe square in the center, like a beacon.

Harlow didn't have time to be curious as the traffic lights changed and the speed of cars around her began to pick up. She had moments to make a choice and she ran, following that tiny stream of light until her hands met the heavy wooden door of the cafe. It was a strange, pale grey color. She felt, rather than saw, the vampires closing in as she pushed the door open and dashed inside.

Once on the other side of the door, inside a small enclosed vestibule, she stared at a pair of heavy wooden doors, made of the same grey wood as the front door. Could it be white ash? None had grown in Nytra for centuries, and was extremely rare, as it could kill vampires and grievously injure the Illuminated. The doors' brass handles were shaped like snakes, their scales thick and textured, like a dragon's rather than smooth skin.

Curious. She peeked out the window next to the outside door. Sure enough the stream of light was gaining strength as the sun went down, growing wider.

The vampires backed off, as if repelled by the cafe itself, but then she saw what caused the effect: the windows of the cafe reflected more and more sunlight onto the street as the sun set, and hundreds of mirrors on the surrounding buildings made similar paths of light, all leading straight here. Very curious indeed.

She turned to examine the doors again. They were inlaid with intricate silver designs. The work was beautiful, but when she engaged her second sight, she saw the spells. The silver had been wrought into ancient sigils that would make it impossible for any creature of the Order of Night to cross without express permission. She was impressed with the spellwork, which had likely been extremely expensive and utilized techniques that had been out of vogue for several centuries.

But the magic was strong. If she crossed that threshold, it wouldn't matter how dark it got outside, vampires wouldn't be able to enter. She pushed one of the heavy doors open and heard soft piano music playing inside.

The ceilings of the cafe soared above her and she saw that while the front of the building had only a few narrow windows, the back windows arched overhead, enclosing the space in steel and glass, creating the feeling of an airy greenhouse. The back of the building was enclosed in a courtyard garden, bursting with lush plant life. Inside, enormous schefflera plants sprouted out of expensive jardinieres with a deep green glaze that all portrayed forest scenes. The plaster walls were painted a fresh white and various rattan chairs, cushioned in creamy, textured fabrics, surrounded marble and glass tables. The effect was eclectic, enchanting, and *safe*.

The customers were mostly human, though there were a few shifters at a table in the far corner. People spoke softly or read books, and Harlow noticed that everyone was pointedly focused on minding their own business. This was not a place to see and be seen. As beautiful as the cafe was, she was surprised this wasn't a hot spot for socials. But she'd never seen it, not even once, and she was slightly surprised to find that no one was on their phones, or using any kind of electronic device.

"Can I help you?"

Harlow turned towards the lilting accent of the northern territories. It issued from one of the Trickster's Chosen, a tall, lithe creature dressed in a dapper, navy three-piece suit, with a sharply planed pale face and short silvery blonde hair.

She liked the look of them instantly. Their eyes were shrewd and dangerous, but infinitely calm. She wondered what their alternae was, with eyes like that. Something powerful and secretive, perhaps a big cat of some kind. Harlow took a chance that they'd help her. "I need to call Finn McKay, right away, please. Can I use your phone?"

She wasn't exactly sure why she'd used Finn's name. Perhaps because everyone knew who he was, but her deeper instinct told her there was another reason.

The shifter nodded slightly, looking out the window at the gathering group of vampires with vague disgust. At least three packs were closing in on the cafe. "Of course, Ms. Krane. I would be happy to get him on the line."

Harlow stepped closer to the shifter, taking a sharp breath in, barely noticing that they'd already known her name. She'd never seen vampires act this way, not in broad daylight anyway. Of course, she'd heard stories about this kind of behavior at night, from some of the less regulated houses, ones that allowed nests to develop and all sorts of other unruly behavior, but nothing like this from the cultured House of Remiel. And yet it couldn't be denied, the packs were in Remiel's territory and these vampires were *hunting* her.

"Ms. Krane," the shifter said softly. "I have Mr. McKay on the phone."

They followed her gaze, then pressed the phone into her hand, reassuring her. "The vampires cannot enter this establishment. Haven is a safehouse from the Order of Night."

Harlow nodded, though the words were a confusing jumble to her as she took the phone. "Hi," she murmured. "I'm in trouble."

"Are you hurt?" The chill in Finn's voice was murderous, and she shivered, even though she knew it was not directed at her.

"No. Athan Sanvier took me, but he didn't hurt me. And now..."

She didn't have to describe it to him, because he was there. He was outside, with Alaric, and they were *slaughtering* the vampires gathering outside the cafe. Humans on the street stopped to watch, though she imagined it was difficult for them to make out what was happening. Their vision was somewhat limited in comparison to her own, and even she could barely see Finn and Alaric as they moved. To a human eye, it would simply look as though the vampires' heads came loose from their bodies and rolled away as they crumpled to the ground, falling to ash as they died.

It was horrifying to watch, but Harlow's horror was tempered by something else. Arousal, yes, but something deeper as well, something deeply satisfying. When the tumult stopped, a representative of the House of Remiel, clad in a dark expensive suit, appeared in the shadows, looking furious. Alaric spoke to them, and Harlow could not recall when she'd ever seen such a hard look on his face. He was absolute power, his dark eyes glowing faintly with menace.

Where was Finn? Her eyes darted to and fro, but she could not find him. "Hey, Harls," his voice rumbled at her back. She felt the light pressure of his fingers on her shoulder, tentative as she turned and threw her arms around him.

"What did they want?" she whispered.

"Alaric is working on finding out, but they were hunting you —and that is unacceptable. The House of Remiel will be fined and an inquest into the matter will begin immediately."

His words were cold, harsh even, but his arms were warm as he hugged her. "Are you all right?" His voice was softer now.

She shook her head. The noise of the cafe began again. She'd forgotten they were in a restaurant and about the shifter who'd helped her until this moment.

"Perhaps you and Ms. Krane would like to go upstairs," the shifter suggested.

"Yes, thank you, Herrington," Finn replied. So this was Cian Herrington. Harlow understood immediately why Finn had spoken of them with such reverence in his voice before. There was something feral and immensely powerful in their presence. Immediately, she wanted to know them better.

Finn continued, "Harls, this is Cian Herrington, who I told you about earlier... and my partner in the Haven project."

Well, that explained the door handles. Harlow shook hands with Herrington as she asked, "The Haven project?"

Herrington smiled as they led them through the cafe to stairs in the back hallway. "Yes, the Knights of Serpens have been creating safe havens in neighborhoods where vampires reside— places they cannot enter—where humans are safe."

"You did this for *humans*?" Harlow asked, incredulous.

Finn nodded. "Yes, Alaric, Herrington, and I started the Haven project two years ago. We've been buying up property and creating places like this, here and in Nea Sterlis, in the hope that we might help some folks. The cafes run all day and night, and the apartments upstairs are for people who need more in-depth help."

Harlow nodded as she followed them up the narrow staircase. "And the humans... they know about this?"

Herrington unlocked a door at the top of the stairs and ushered them inside. The room was simply but elegantly decorated in shades of grey. One wall was lined with bookcases. A hardwood desk sat in front of floor-to-ceiling windows and two pewter colored velvet couches faced one another at the opposite end of the room.

"I'll fetch us some refreshments while you explain things to her," Herrington said softly. "Ric will be up in a few minutes, I suppose. Will Thea be joining us?"

Finn nodded, unfazed by the shift in tone. Downstairs, Herrington had been excessively formal. Here, Alaric was "Ric" and Thea was Thea, rather than Ms. Krane. Harlow wondered how well they all knew one another. Well, she assumed, since they were all Knights.

She was grateful for the help, but felt woefully left out. They were doing the kind of work she'd dreamed of since she was a teenager, and her sister hadn't bothered to tell her about it or include her.

"I imagine she's close by now." Finn answered, glancing at Harlow. "Alaric called her as soon as we knew where you were."

"She knows about this place?" *Of course she did. What a stupid question.*

Finn smiled. "The Haven Project was her idea."

Harlow's chin quivered. They'd all had this project together for two years—more, maybe. And the whole time she'd been doing what? Trying to have a human life with Mark? *Mark*.

Godsdamnit, it hurt to think he set her up. That he wanted her tortured, or dead? Or worse. Mark was cruel, but that didn't make sense. Harlow didn't know she was shaking until she felt Finn drape a soft wool blanket around her shoulders.

"You're in shock," he said.

She nodded. That much was clear.

"Can you tell me what happened?" He sat next to her on the couch, a respectful distance away, clearly trying to give her space. She realized how afraid he was when he wouldn't meet her eyes.

"Athan didn't hurt me. But... I think he planned to."

Finn nodded, and she saw he was shaking too. The tremors wracking his body weren't shock or fear though, they were fury. His eyes glowed with that menace she'd seen in Alaric before, faint light emanating from his irises. It wasn't like the golden light that shone from his skin when they were in bed together, or the bright pure light that had come from their union. This was something different, something deadly and cold.

"Would you hold me?" she pleaded.

In an instant, she was pulled into his lap, his arms curled around her back and hips, his legs cradling her body. He untied her shoes and slipped them off, covering her feet with the blanket that had fallen off her with the sudden movement. His hands slid into her hair, gently pulling through tangles and knots.

Harlow closed her eyes and let her head fall onto Finn's shoulder, listening to his heartbeat as his fingers skimmed her hip, the outside of her thigh, and tucked themselves behind her knee. Slowly, the shaking subsided, replaced by the awareness of his body heat and the tremble in his fingers as he smoothed her hair.

She'd been so afraid, but she'd escaped on her own power, found this place, and now she was safe. Harlow lifted her face to

Finn's, noting the cloud of concern in his eyes, but also the flare of his nostrils—he scented something of her mounting arousal, before she'd even known she felt it. But as she calmed, she realized she wanted to feel something other than reliving the fear of being trapped in the cab with Athan Sanvier. Her lips parted slightly as she grazed a thumb over Finn's bottom lip, the square line of his jaw.

He quivered slightly at her touch and as her thumb dragged down the center of his throat, she felt him swallow hard. The rate of his breath increased slightly to match her own and the heat building in her core turned molten as his hand slid from behind her knee to her inner thigh, his hands warm on her bare skin.

"Are we about to be interrupted?" she asked softly.

His stormy eyes, dark with lust, didn't leave hers and his fingers continued their journey up her inner thigh as his other hand, invisible to her, fiddled with his phone.

"They'll give us a bit... to talk..." his half-smile was faint, almost sad. "Are you really all right?"

Harlow shook her head. "No, will you help me? I have all this energy... the leftover fear and anxiety... I just need to feel safe."

"And I make you feel safe?" he asked. There was incredulity in his voice. He didn't know if she trusted him or not.

"You do," she murmured. "I was mad at Thea for keeping secrets, and I planned to go to Enzo's to talk, but I ran into Kate Spencer on my way. She took me to the Three Besoms for a drink and a talk—she asked me to come out with her, but I said no... and I forgot my phone, so she called me a cab..."

"*Kate* called you a cab?" That cold quality to his voice was back.

Harlow shook her head. "No, the bartender did. I don't think Kate was a part of this."

Finn's usually sensual mouth made a thin line. "I think you're being very generous."

Her head tilted slightly, remembering the presence she'd felt in the bar, and at the ball. "I don't think I am. There was someone else there, watching me. They were at the ball too. Whoever it is, I think they're following me."

The journey his fingers were making on her inner thigh stalled. "How do you know?" His tone indicated curiosity, not disbelief.

"I feel it, a sinister kind of pressure. I don't know how to describe it otherwise. I think my shadows make it easier for me to use my natural instinct, if that makes any sense."

Finn nodded, his expression thoughtful. "Yes, from what Alaric has told me about his and Thea's research into Striders, that does make sense. They were said to develop an almost supernatural instinct for their surroundings. Thea thinks it's likely a result of so much close contact with the aether. The more you use it, the more honed your senses will become."

Her head fell against his shoulder, suddenly heavy. "Today has felt years long."

He laughed softly, hugging her tight. "It really has, hasn't it? Did Athan say anything to you?"

"Not much. He seemed to be threatening to turn me into a succubus."

Finn snorted; apparently the idea of it was as ridiculous to him as it had been to her. "He's always been such an asshole. Did he say anything else?"

Harlow nodded. "He said something about Mark that made me think that he and Olivia planned this together."

Finn sighed. "The two of them make a terrible pair. They're beyond petty and Athan has always done whatever Olivia asked. I'm sorry... he got away."

Harlow shrugged. "Maybe this was revenge for getting Axel back and embarrassing Mark. He's always been so sensitive about that kind of thing... Oh gods, someone needs to call Larkin and check on her."

Finn soothed her. "I already did. She and Axel are fine. I have my people watching your building."

"Your people? You have *people* who do things like that? Lackeys?"

"Please do not call Arebos and Nox that when you meet them. They will be incredibly offended."

She'd never heard those names before. "Who are they?"

Finn's face closed for a moment, as though he might not tell her. Then, miraculously it opened, as if he'd just realized he didn't have to keep it all a secret from her. "Knights, siblings. They call themselves Wraiths. They're shifters, but only in the most technical sense."

Her breath caught. "What does that mean?"

"They shift *into* their surroundings."

Harlow didn't think he could possibly mean what she thought he meant. "They actually become *invisible*?"

Becoming invisible wasn't hard, in theory, if you only wanted to trick humans. But immortals had better eyesight, and a highly developed second sight. Becoming invisible to the other Orders was practically impossible, unless you could shift into the background noise of daily life. "Where in Akatei's name did you find such creatures?"

"They found me. I'll tell you the story another time." He paused for a moment, as though considering whether or not it was a good idea to ask his next question. "Can Mark be compelled?"

Harlow took a deep breath. The multitudes of ways that Mark's relationship with Olivia could go disastrously wrong played out in her head. It had been a long time since a human as much in the public eye as Mark Easton had been involved in a compulsion scandal. "It's possible. I had a protective amulet made for him, but I'm not sure if he still wears it. He probably doesn't think he needs it with Olivia."

"Since the Anti-Compulsion Act passed, it seems like humans have gotten lazy about protecting themselves," he mused.

Harlow nodded. It was true. Once, humans had practiced all sorts of rituals to make themselves less vulnerable to the Order of Night's attacks, but now they felt protected by a law that was nominal at best. There were very few ways to prove compulsion.

"How did you get out of the car?" It felt a little like he was grilling her, but she understood. Her memory of the encounter might soften over time, and any tiny detail she could remember might help them see the shape of the new threat they faced.

"I made a handle and asked for it to be unlocked," she murmured, shifting slightly in his lap. She sat up, swinging one leg around so she straddled him. His hands moved up the tops of her thighs, under the skirt of her dress.

"That was an elegant solution," he said with a smile.

It struck her how close she'd come to harm. Her magic had not yet fully manifested, and she'd been alone with a vampire who wanted to hurt her. The afternoon could have ended much differently. Finn sensed the change in her mood.

"Do you want to start doing some training with your shadows? I could help you learn to fight with them, so you wouldn't have to be afraid of monsters like Athan Sanvier."

"Will we get all sweaty when we train?" she asked, deliberately playful. She desperately needed relief from all this tension and the residual stress coursing through her.

His hands were back in her hair, pulling gently as he nipped at her neck lightly. "We probably will. Don't worry, I know all sorts of ways to get you clean again." Finn kissed her face, pulling her into a tight hug. "I'm sorry about how things went today with your family. I didn't want you to learn about the Knights that way, or Thea's involvement. I thought I'd have more than one day to make sure things were okay with us before we talked about all that."

Harlow relaxed into him, feeling the deep, purposefully steady rise and fall of his chest as she lay her head on his shoulder, nuzzling her face into his neck. "I'm not angry with you," she explained. "I'm angry with my sister. She should have told me all this a long time ago."

He didn't say anything, but he hugged her tighter. It occurred to her that what they were doing felt like a relationship. He was comforting her. They were making plans. They were supposed to be pretending, but this didn't feel like pretense anymore. They'd crossed over into the real thing. The beginning stages, yes. But a real relationship, all the same.

"You really murdered those vampires," she murmured.

"As opposed to sort of murdering them?"

She laughed. "I know I should be horrified, but..."

"You're not. And you shouldn't be. They violated every rule we live by." He was quiet, but she felt something lingering behind the silence. Something he was hesitant to say. "You know, what happened is probably enough to bring the vampires back in line... And I believe I can use the entire incident to convince my parents that their focus needs to be back on the Order of Night and away from the sorcière."

She thought she knew where his line of thinking was headed and didn't much like it. "And then what?"

"If you wanted to end things, we could. You could walk away. I have a feeling the House of Remiel pulled this today because of our relationship. I'm not sure why yet, but I'll find out... Maybe you'd be safer if we ended this now."

Her heart stuttered and she pushed away from him to stare into his face. "Is that what you want?"

Finn's eyes softened. "No. It's the last thing I want, but I feel like you're in danger and I can't stand it."

She cupped his face in her hands. "Thank you."

"For what?"

"For not being able to stand it. For coming as soon as I called. For trusting me. For being worthy of my trust. For everything."

His gaze flit away from hers as his face twisted with some internal pain. "I feel like I don't deserve to hear those things."

Her heart ached to hear him say it. "I know, but you do. And they're the truth. My truth anyway."

He pulled her close, his arms so tight around her she could hardly breathe.

"I wish we got to have a normal love story," she said, stroking his hair.

"*Love* story? Are you saying—?"

She sighed. "I'm not going to fight how I feel anymore. I think today makes it clear that we need each other."

He nodded. "We don't need to make any big declarations now."

"Okay," she agreed.

There was a knock at the door and Thea peeked in. "Everyone decent?"

Chapter Twenty-Eight

Harlow nodded, climbing off Finn's lap, though she snuggled into the crook of his arm as Thea sat in a chair opposite the couch. "Alaric and Cian are downstairs dealing with Veronica Morova. She is quite unhappy about how the two of you dealt with the House of Remiel foot soldiers today."

"Then they shouldn't have been trying to kidnap my—" he stopped short and blushed.

Thea raised her eyebrows. "Do finish that sentence, Finn."

Harlow giggled as the flush in his cheeks deepened.

"That's a conversation we ought to have in private, probably..." he muttered.

Harlow smiled and patted the hard muscle of his stomach. "It's okay. You can call me your girlfriend. I'll allow it... Or were you going to call me your *lovah*?"

Thea giggled now and Finn blushed even more. It was adorable to see him so undone by two giggling witches, Harlow decided. She brushed a kiss on his cheek and slid her hand into his, stroking her thumb down the center of his palm so he'd be reminded just how much she enjoyed being his lover. She felt his shiver of pleasure, and when he returned the gesture, she knew he'd understood.

Thea was talking, saying something about the vampires, so Harlow tried to focus. "I think they'll be talking for a while. Apparently Berith is in quite the rage and Veronica was sent to find out what the Illuminated will do next. Cian is trying to help Alaric, but to be honest with you, I think they're being too nice."

Finn grimaced. "Should I go help?"

Thea smiled gently. "That might be good."

Finn got up and pressed a soft kiss to Harlow's lips. "I'll be back soon."

She nodded, staying silent as he left the room, her eyes fixed on her hands, instead of her sister. Harlow couldn't bring herself to look at Thea.

"This all happened because you were angry with me," Thea said, accusation coloring her words.

Harlow resented her saying it, even if it was technically true. But if Thea was going to be condescending, two could play that game.

"Because I *am* angry with you," Harlow corrected.

"Fair enough. I kept things from you, but can you blame me?"

Harlow looked up then, surprised to see the ugly, arrogant look on Thea's face that reminded her so much of the Illuminated as a whole. The entire Illuminated Order wore that look constantly, like they knew better about *everything*.

"You're turning into one of them, aren't you?"

Thea looked confused.

"The Illuminated. You're just like them. Is it from spending so much time with Alaric? Is that why you're like this? So cold and callous?"

Now her sister was furious. The pink flush creeping over her ears tipped Harlow off, but the ice in her voice confirmed it.

"You were a *mess*, Harlow. When I picked you up from that hospital I had no idea how to keep you alive. Do you even remember the weeks I spent with you that summer at the cabin?"

Harlow sighed. "I remember how you helped me. And I'm grateful for it."

The summer after Kate left for Nea Sterlis, Harlow had spiraled out of control. She'd been drinking too much, doing too many drugs. It hadn't been for fun, not any of it; she'd been trying to dull the pain. And then one night, she'd taken too much of something. She wasn't even sure what, but she'd known it was too much at the time. She hadn't meant to end things, not exactly, but neither had she cared when she felt herself slipping away. Harlow didn't even know how she'd gotten to the hospital.

Thea didn't look at her. "When I picked you up from the hospital you wouldn't speak to me. They said you'd hadn't spoken once in seventy-two hours, except to make your phone call."

Harlow didn't remember much about that. The drugs they'd given her made her groggy, and she hadn't taken them again when she left. Whoever took her to the hospital had left her at a top-notch facility, but she hadn't wanted to stay, and after seventy-two hours, they couldn't keep her against her will. She'd called Thea, and they never told anyone else what had happened. They told the maters they were headed up north for the summer, and no one had questioned them.

"It was a bad start to our summer, but we had an okay time eventually, didn't we?" Harlow asked, trying not to sound petulant, but it was tiring being the sister that always screwed things up. Besides, after the first week or two things hadn't been so bad, had they?

Eventually she'd stopped wanting to die and after that her memories of that summer were golden and bittersweet. She and

Thea had swum in the lake every day, napped, read books, cooked together and when they began laughing together again, Harlow had known she would make it. That she would live. She hadn't stopped the hard drinking for another two years, but she never touched drugs again.

Thea's face contorted with grief, as though she was wrestling with herself and what she wanted to say next. Harlow thought she looked like she wanted to deliver a lecture about mental health, but she'd had enough of those and interrupted her sister's train of thought. "Sorry I'm a pain in the ass, Thea. Sorry I'm not perfect like you. But that summer was *not* so bad. We had fun."

Thea flinched at Harlow's words, as though she'd been slapped. "Fun?" she murmured as she stood and walked toward the window, staring out, wrapping her arms around her slender frame. "When we first got to the cabin, you talked about how much you wanted to die every single day, Harlow. Do you remember that?"

Harlow's breath hitched. She didn't remember that. Thea glanced at her, deep sadness in her eyes. "You said no one could ever love you. That you were fundamentally flawed somehow. Later, it was the thing that started my research into The Scroll of Akatei, into the history of the Striders... but back then..."

None of that was surprising, despite her inability to remember it. Those thoughts had lived inside her for a very long time. "But you *knew*, you knew Alaric and you knew the truth about Finn. You knew all that, you knew what I was going through, and you *still* didn't tell me the one thing that could have stopped it all."

A long silence stretched between them as Thea obviously tried to calm herself. She'd covered her mouth with her hands, and when she spoke again, her words were muffled. "But I didn't know that then... I had no idea what would help, or hurt..." Thea's voice cracked. "I was so afraid to lose you,

Harlow. What if I—" Thea stumbled forward, sobs wracking her shoulders.

Harlow froze. She'd never seen her sister lose control like this, not ever. She was incapable of moving from the couch.

"I didn't know what I could tell you and what I couldn't, but then you started to get better and I just—I just couldn't open it all up again. What if you went back to that place because I re-opened a wound that should have stayed closed? What if I lost you forever, because I made a mistake?"

The words fell from Thea's lips in a deluge of pain as she fell to her knees. Harlow moved then, freed by the understanding that Thea was a person. Not some perfectly controlled creature who did everything right, with all the answers. She was just a person, a person who got scared and made mistakes. Harlow didn't know what Thea should or shouldn't have done in that moment, only that she was certain her sister had done her best. And that knowledge was enough. Her arms went around Thea and they cried together.

"I'm so sorry, Harlow," Thea whispered. Her fingers dug into Harlow's back. "I don't love anyone in the world the way I love you. Do you understand that? I would do anything to protect you. *Anything*."

Harlow rocked them both. "I know, Thea. I know."

"And then everything happened with Mark and I failed you. I didn't keep you safe. Mama told me what you told Larkin about how you found Axel... I'm so sorry." Thea was sobbing so hard Harlow could hardly understand her.

"It's not your fault," Harlow soothed. "I should have gone to therapy—like they said at the hospital. I walked right into my pain, and I paid for it."

Thea's sobs quieted. "You don't have to be with Finn if it hurts, Harlow. Everyone will understand. We'll find another way to fix things."

"That's not what this is about. Not anymore."

Thea looked up. Her face was swollen. None of the Kranes were pretty criers except Larkin and Meline. "It's not?"

"No, I have real feelings for him. It's time for me to move on, and I think I want to do it with him."

"You're sure?"

Harlow looked around at the office, thinking of the cafe below, and the apartments and offices on this floor. The work she imagined the Knights of Serpens were doing was the kind of work she'd always wanted to do. And she wanted to be doing it alongside her sister and Alaric—but most of all, Finn. "I'm sure."

Thea's swollen eyes crinkled and more tears squeezed out. "You're really all right?"

"Yes," Harlow said, hugging her sister even tighter. "Yes, I'm doing better now."

In that moment, as she held her sister, she understood it was true. She *was* better now, and it wasn't because of Finn, or her magic manifesting, or anything else. It was because of the work she'd done on herself. The time she'd taken for herself. The months alone in her empty apartment working through things, letting herself be lonely, staying with herself, with her pain, instead of running from it. She wasn't perfectly healed, and maybe she never would be, but she *was* better. Stronger.

"Do you promise?" Thea asked as her sobs began to quiet.

Harlow nodded. "I do. I'm not in that place anymore, and it's because of you. Because of that summer. I'll never forget that."

They rested against the windows, huddled together, wrapped in each other's arms, holding one another's hands.

After a long, calm pause, Thea said, "It doesn't matter what happens next, who we pair with, any of it. You'll always be the most important person in my life. You and the sillies and Enzo and the maters. You know that, right?"

Harlow smiled, letting go of one of Thea's hands to wipe a

stray tear from her sister's cheek. "It's okay to let Alaric in. He can be a part of our family too. And then someday, you'll have babies of your own, and they'll be just as important. We can expand. Love is an infinite well."

"Love is an infinite well," Thea repeated. "I like that."

"There's enough room for all of us in this family."

"Even Finn?"

"Yes. And I expect Cian Herrington, and Riley Quinn as well."

A few more tears slipped down Thea's cheeks as she nodded. "Alaric and I are going to need a really big dining room table in our new house."

"Yeah," Harlow replied as she leaned against her sister's shoulder. "You are."

CHAPTER TWENTY-NINE

The next few weeks flew by in a blur of trying to balance the events of the season with trying to sort out what the House of Remiel had been up to when they took Harlow. Finn and Harlow went to the season's annual brunch at The Palace hotel, and made an effort to be seen everywhere from the most popular coffee shops and lunch spots to the grocery store. When she was with Finn, everything felt normal, but anytime she went somewhere alone she had the same chilling sense of surveillance as she had at the Solon Mai ball and in the bar.

Finn and Thea talked her out of calling Mark and giving him a piece of her mind. Furthermore, and perhaps more telling, Mark didn't call her either, which felt odd because he loved to gloat when he punished her. And though Harlow scraped the internet for information about him, she couldn't find mention of him having been out anywhere, with Olivia or anyone else either. Both his and Olivia's socials were silent, which was unusual. Athan, on the other hand, was busily updating the world on his rugby team's prowess.

A few of the gossips speculated that Olivia and Mark were

probably holed up in a love nest somewhere, subtly implying that Mark's humanity might be getting an upgrade soon. The thought of Mark living an eternity as a vampire turned Harlow's stomach, but it was a plausible theory, and it would explain why the whole House of Remiel was going about their business as normal.

There had been no mention of the vampires' attack, and the ensuing altercation outside Haven, in the news or gossips. Harlow was equally impressed and horrified with the way that Alaric had handled things. His securities firm had reached out to everyone involved and "made it more attractive to stay quiet."

The resources it must have taken to make something like that possible were vast, and when Harlow had discussed it with him, Thea and Finn, she began to understand that there were many things that happened in Nytra, and Okairos as a whole, that no one knew about, because the Illuminated simply erased events with money and threats. Because as rich and resourced as Alaric and Finn both were, their parents and the rest of the Illuminated had more. More power, more money, *more* of everything. So much more that it was dizzying to think of even trying to resist them when she began to truly comprehend the scale of things.

Harlow stayed at Finn's most nights, enough so that he'd gotten a litter box and a store of cat food and they'd introduced Axel to the house. The feline loved the many windows, and he and Finn seemed to enjoy one another's company. They went walking the perimeter of the property together twice a day every day, the only time Axel went outside. Harlow got a kick out of watching the two of them walking together and sent her sisters and Enzo videos and photos of them goofing off nearly every day.

The house began to fill slowly with furniture she and her shadows built. Just a chair here and there for comfort. She wanted to buy most of their things the normal way, and besides, she wasn't sure she was ready to officially move in. It was a little soon for that, but being here felt safe and good.

By contrast, her apartment, which had once been her refuge, did not. She trusted the wards on her building, but the few times she and Axel had been home to get more clothes or to simply be alone for the afternoon, she got the now-familiar feeling of being watched. That sinister pressure appeared and her shadows went wild, trying to ferret out where it was coming from, to no avail. She never felt it at Finn's and they'd agreed it was better not to risk things.

So she'd come to stay, "for a nice, long visit," they'd said, but it was all over the gossips that they were "playing house." She didn't care. They could say whatever they wanted now. The hours she and Finn spent just talking both reminded her of their childhood, and were something new altogether. It seemed they never ran out of things to talk about, their interests were so different and varied. His deeply analytical mind was always two steps ahead of things, and her big picture thinking let them look at any topic from dozens of angles. It felt good to talk to someone who listened intently when she spoke, and who she wanted to listen to in return.

Harlow hadn't been home in over a week, and hadn't checked her socials in days. Things had been blessedly quiet, near-perfect domestic bliss. She knew it wouldn't last, but she reveled in it all the same. Especially the part where when Finn did a load of laundry he'd put away her clothes in the empty half of his enormous walk-in closet and they'd started to take up a respectable amount of space. She was standing, marveling at the neat piles he'd made, when he brought her phone to her.

"You are *really* good at folding things," she mused with a grin.

He smiled, but the expression didn't reach his eyes as he passed her phone into her hands. "Alain Easton has called you seven times in the last five minutes. I didn't mean to pry, but your phone was vibrating non-stop. I was worried it might be your family."

"It's okay. Thank you." She kissed his cheek and as she did so, the phone began to vibrate again. It was Mark's father.

"Do you want some privacy?" Finn asked.

Harlow shook her head. "No."

She answered as she walked out of the closet and settled into one of the chairs in the bedroom. Rain fell in a steady sheet outside the windows, giving the bedroom a gloomy green glow. "Hello, Mr. Easton. What can I do for you?"

"Harlow?"

"Yes, Mr. Easton."

His voice was shaky. "Have you heard from Mark? Is he with you?"

"No," Harlow said, drawing the syllables out, making eye contact with Finn, who sat on the floor, adding more wood to the fire. "No, I haven't."

"I haven't heard from him in two weeks. Sixteen days. It's like he's disappeared."

Harlow didn't like the sound of that. "Have you called the Missing Person's Unit?"

"Yes, yes. I've called. They say they're doing something about it, but I don't get any updates. You know how it is..." He trailed off. The MPU was not always diligent about following up on missing humans. "I wondered if you or your parents might... Well... If you might help me."

"What are you worried about, Mr. Easton?" Harlow didn't really have to ask. She knew.

"I think that should be obvious, Harlow. I'm worried he's dead."

Harlow swallowed hard. "Does anything suggest that he might be?"

"He's dating a vampire, Harlow. I may not have approved of

your relationship with Mark, but I wasn't afraid you'd kill him. Can you help me or not?"

He really *was* worried. Alain Easton wasn't a very good father. He'd neglected Mark as a child, in favor of his work and his many extramarital affairs, according to Mark, anyway. But he did love his son. If he was worried, it confirmed her own concerns.

"I'll see what I can do. Let me get back to you."

"Don't sugarcoat anything, Harlow. I can handle whatever you find out."

"I know, Mr. Easton. I'll see what I can do."

He hung up, and Harlow locked her phone, setting it on the low table next to her chair, made from a piece of perfectly petrified wood. She and Finn looked at each other for a long time before either of them spoke.

A prominent human like Mark Easton being killed by a vampire couldn't be erased as easily as an altercation between the House of Remiel and the Illuminated. There were too many factors to control; the news would get out and upset the tentative balance between the Orders and the human world. And, as it had always been, the result would be dead humans, and dead immortals of the lower Orders. The Illuminated always came out of situations like this unscathed and seemingly more powerful than before.

"He's either dead or turned. You know that right?" Finn said finally.

Harlow nodded. "Honestly, I figured as much."

He got up. "I'm not on very good terms with the House of Remiel, obviously, but I'll have Cian make some calls. They're far more diplomatic than I am. Maybe they can get somewhere with Veronica Morova. She's at least halfway reasonable."

Harlow nodded, kissing his hand as he passed her. She knew he was going downstairs to lock himself in his office, and that he probably wouldn't just call Cian, but his other contacts as well.

Maybe even the mysterious Nox and Arebos, who she still hadn't met. She listened as he walked downstairs.

When the door to his office shut, she picked up her phone and shot off two texts. One to Riley Quinn: *Just heard from Alain Easton. Mark is missing. Any ideas?*

Finn and Alaric had been wary of telling Riley much, because the Rogue Queen was such an unknown factor, but Harlow had argued time and again that the Rogue Order's resources were untapped potential and that if Enzo trusted Riley, they should too. But this was important. They needed to find Mark and control the story before people got hurt.

She steeled herself and sent another text to Mark himself. It was worth a try to see if he'd respond. *Your dad's worried about you. He's calling in the cavalry. If you don't want shit-tons of people looking for you, text me back.*

And then she waited. She waited so long, she fell asleep in her chair. When she woke, the sun was setting and her phone vibrated in her lap. From downstairs, she heard the soft sounds of Finn on the phone in his office. She picked up her phone and swiped the screen open.

The text was from Riley, not Mark. *Have some feelers out. Nothing yet, but you should talk to Petra Velarius. Privately. Without Finn.*

Now that was curious. *Why?*

Just ask her to have coffee with you at Cerberus, downtown, and ask her to help you.

Harlow started to explain all the reasons why that wouldn't work. Why Petra Velarius was the last person in the world she wanted to help her, and how Petra certainly wouldn't be seen *downtown.* But she stopped herself and simply wrote back, *I doubt she'd help me.*

If you ask her to meet you at Cerberus to talk about Mark, she will help you. I'll be in touch if I hear anything. I can't emphasize enough that you should not tell Finn. You can use me as a cover.

Now that was downright strange, but she trusted Riley. *Okay, thanks.*

She texted Meline to see if she had Petra's number, which she did, and finally gave up prying when Harlow said she wanted to ask her where she got her hair done. Petra Velarius had enviable hair, and was notoriously secretive about where she got any of her beauty services.

When she had the number she hesitated. Was this a good idea? Petra hated her, and she hated Petra. She listened for Finn —yes, he was still on the phone. She bit her lip and typed out a text. *It's Harlow. Mark's missing. Can you meet me at Cerberus in an hour to talk?*

Petra had her read receipts on and Harlow saw the moment she read the message. There was a long pause and then the cascading dots indicated that she was responding.

I'll be there in thirty minutes. Don't be late.

Harlow was shocked. She looked down at the leggings and cozy socks she was wearing with one of Finn's plaid flannel shirts. This was going to have to do. She texted Riley to make sure they'd cover her with Finn, and she pulled on a pair of shearling boots that were tossed under the side table next to her chair. She was not cutting the most fashionable silhouette, but Petra couldn't possibly hate her any more than she already did. There wasn't any impressing her, after all.

She ran downstairs and pulled on her raincoat, poking her head into Finn's office. Axel was sleeping on his lap, and he had his feet up on the desk and his phone to his ear. She whispered, "I'm meeting Riley downtown. They might have a lead on Mark. You getting anywhere?"

He muted the phone and shook his head. Though he frowned slightly at the mention of Riley, he didn't comment on her choice to tell them what was happening. "You can take my car."

"I can't drive your car!" she hissed. "It's too fast."

He grinned. "The other one in the barn. Keys are on the dash."

She didn't know which car he was talking about. He usually parked his sports car in the garage attached to the house, next to his motorcycle. The "barn" was his workshop and she'd only peeked inside one day to see if he wanted lunch.

She walked outside. It was starting to warm up a little, finally, but the breeze was still cold. Inside the barn it was warmer, and when she turned the lights on in the garage portion of the barn, she smiled. Finn's beat-up old blue SUV, with the wooden panels on the doors, sat inside. It was the car she'd learned to drive in. Neither of the maters drove, but Finn had made sure she knew how to drive a car when she was fifteen, and he went with her to get her driver's license.

It was also the car they'd first made love in, and seeing it brought back a flood of memories. The Woody was in great shape still and it roared to life when she put the keys in the ignition. It had been detailed recently, and a book of CDs sat on the passenger seat with a folded piece of paper tucked into the elastic strap that held it closed. She opened it and read:

Thought you might need a soundtrack. The Woody won't connect to your phone, but I made you some mix CDs. —F

He'd been planning to give her the Woody. She couldn't believe it at first, but Finn had always known how much she loved the bulky beast of a car, how it made her feel safe on the road. She smiled gratefully, feeling slightly guilty to have lied about who she was meeting, but she could be honest later, once she knew why the secrecy was necessary. She would wait to listen to the CDs later. She put an audiobook of a new romance novel on her phone's speaker to keep her company and zoned out as she drove downtown.

She had a hard time finding a parking spot, and Petra was walking out of the coffee shop as she rushed to the door. "I'm so sorry," she apologized. "Parking in this neighborhood is awful."

Petra pressed her lips together, as though she was trying to suppress the disgust she felt looking at Harlow's outfit. "I hope you didn't change your clothes to meet me. Because it would be a tragedy if you were late because you changed into *that*."

Harlow rolled her eyes. "No. I came as quickly as I could. And my outfit is fine."

Petra, who was wearing what looked like couture, seemed as though she'd like to object, but she shrugged instead. "Do you want to go inside, or take a walk? It's stopped raining for the moment."

Harlow looked up at the grey sky. "Sure, we can walk."

They walked toward the river in silence. Finally Petra spoke. "Did Riley Quinn tell you to get in touch with me?"

Harlow nodded as Petra sat on a bench outside the Riverfront Park. She hesitated for a moment, but then reluctantly sat next to Petra, who smelled fantastic. Like a high-end department store, and a hothouse all at once. She looked impeccable as well, of course; though her tailored trench coat covered her outfit completely, she was perfectly made up, and her long hair was swept into her signature ponytail.

"Riley saw me here with Olivia Sanvier a few months ago. I thought no one I knew would come down here, but there Riley was. I had no idea they'd become such an integral part of our circle at the time."

Harlow furrowed her brow, confused. "Why were you worried about being seen having coffee with Olivia?"

"We weren't drinking coffee when Riley saw us."

It took Harlow a moment to understand.

"Oh... *Oh*. But why would that matter?"

Petra took a shuddering breath. "The lower Orders and the humans are so much freer about these things... But have you ever noticed how few of the Illuminated are like me?"

"Like... you?"

"I am *only* interested in women, Harlow. There are *not* sapphic Illuminated. Especially not in my family."

"Obviously there are," Harlow said softly.

Petra's beautiful face screwed into a grimace. "But it's forbidden. My parents would never allow me to pair with a woman."

"They know and would keep you from being who you are?"

"No, of course not. They don't know, and they never will. Unless you tell them. You or Riley Quinn."

There was a long silence between them.

"I wouldn't do that," Harlow said, finally. "I would never do anything like that to anyone. Not even you."

Petra wiped a tear, looking away from Harlow. Her mouth was set in an unattractive tight line. It was the first time Harlow had ever seen her look less than stunning. "Well, I'd deserve it if you did."

Harlow wasn't sure what to say to that, but she'd been honest. She wouldn't ever tell a secret like that, not even about her worst enemy. And while she didn't like Petra, she most certainly wasn't her worst enemy. Not anymore. "Do you know anything that might help us find Mark?"

Petra sighed and handed Harlow a slip of paper. "Look for him here. This is Olivia's safe house. She fucks and sucks here pretty often. If she turned Mark, it's where she'd take him to complete the transition."

"Thank you," Harlow said, taking the piece of paper and standing. As she did, she felt it, the pressure of eyes upon her. The feeling that whoever was watching did not have good intentions. Carefully, she scanned the surrounding area with her second sight, something she'd wished she'd done the other times she'd felt this. But she came up empty. She couldn't find the source of the feeling, though it did not lessen.

"I am sorry, you know?" Petra said softly as Harlow stood.

"For what?"

"The things I did to you in secondary. It makes me sick to think about."

Harlow sat back down, the breath stolen from her lungs. "It does?"

Petra nodded. "I was always jealous of you and Finn. Before he met you we were close, and then, when he met you and Enzo, we weren't anymore."

Harlow had been momentarily distracted by Petra's confession, but now she felt the presence, closer than before. She tried to appear natural, to continue the conversation as normally as she could, while sending her second sight out further. "We could have all been friends."

Petra's face twisted again. "My parents wouldn't have allowed that. I have to be perfect, and that means being above everyone else."

Her second sight came up empty again. There was nothing in the park that seemed capable of producing such a feeling, just the usual immortals and humans, and their children. She spoke more harshly than she meant to, frustrated. "So you bullied me?"

Petra's mouth opened and closed. Her eyes closed. "That's not why I bullied you. I know you won't believe me, but that had *nothing* to do with you."

Harlow turned her full attention to Petra now. Whatever the source of the threatening feeling, she couldn't suss it out. "You're right. I don't believe that."

"There's nothing I can say that would ever justify the things I did to you, Harlow. No way for me to apologize. But I *am* sorry."

Harlow sat numbly, lost for words. Petra sounded sincere. In fact, she sounded tortured. "If it had nothing to do with me, then why did you do it? I thought it was because you were in love with Finn... But if that wasn't it, then why?"

Petra stood, walking into the park. Harlow hurried after her, using the opportunity to scan the park further—still nothing. Petra walked quickly until they were standing near the waterfall at the center of the park. The noise was so loud here that Harlow worried if Petra actually said anything she wouldn't be able to hear her. When Petra turned, she understood from the look on the other woman's face that was the point.

Petra leaned in, placed her mouth close to Harlow's ear, and spoke quickly: "Aislin McKay caught me in her pool house with Melisandre Marillier when we were sixth years."

Harlow's eyes widened. Suddenly things started to make more sense.

"She threatened to tell my parents if I didn't do everything she asked. And what she asked was that I follow Finn and watch the two of you."

"You took the photos of us, didn't you?"

Petra nodded. "And then, when Finn refused to do what they wanted, Aislin said I had to bully you, make you so miserable Finn would be forced to save you from me. She thought you'd get back together. But it didn't matter how cruel I was, Harlow. He wouldn't step in. I hurt you both, and I hated every second of it."

Harlow understood now why Finn hadn't stepped in, but it still stung. The three of them were such victims of the McKays' twisted plotting, it made her ill.

"I'm so sorry, Petra. I'm sure if Finn had known, he would have done something... Helped you somehow."

Petra laughed, a dry, brittle noise. "He knew, Harlow. I was there the night his parents put the whole awful thing to him about impregnating you. And he knew about Melisandre and his mother... He knew it all. Not about the pictures, I couldn't bear to tell him that. But he knew the rest. I think he even knew about the reason I bullied you, or at least suspected. He was just *that* afraid of them."

"We were kids," Harlow said softly. "We were just kids."

She knew Petra could hear her.

"We were then, but not now, Harlow. Aislin McKay is still holding what she knows about me over my head and he's never said a word to her. Never tried to stop her. I'm not telling you this to hurt you. I'm telling you because I know what's at stake for you, and if you're hoping that Finn McKay will stand up to his parents for you... Well, I love him dearly, he's my commander, and I trust him with my life, but you should know what you're getting into, Harlow."

Harlow frowned, emotion stirring deep within her that she thought she'd left behind. "What would you do if you were me?" she asked.

Petra looked surprised to be asked, her brows wrinkling her eternally smooth forehead in a way Harlow thought was probably novel to her. "What do you mean?"

Harlow shrugged. "If you were me, falling for him all over again, what would you do?"

The immortal shook her head, her dark ponytail swishing down her back. Her brown eyes were the color of smoky topaz, and they glowed a little in the gloomy light of the park, the only thing that let Harlow know she was feeling something rather deeply. "Honestly, I don't know. I'm hurt too. I don't have a good answer for that."

Mist from the waterfall hit Harlow in the face, carried by a gust of warm spring wind. The year was turning, something that usually pleased Harlow. Winter was ending, but her heart felt colder than it had in months. In fact, her entire body was frozen. She couldn't move, couldn't think. She was stuck in the hurt of the moment and wasn't sure what to do.

Petra squeezed her arm then. "I am sorry. I really am. Please understand, this is the only way I can make amends—to tell you the whole truth."

And then Petra was gone, using her Illuminated speed to leave Harlow standing in the park alone. The pressure of the eyes watching her intensified, but Harlow couldn't bring herself to try to look for its source again; she was too flummoxed by what Petra had said. It began to rain again and Harlow didn't move. She couldn't. She just stood there getting soaked, thinking about what Petra had said, trying to ignore the feeling that she was being followed and the anger oozing in her chest like an infected wound.

Chapter Thirty

Harlow didn't remember much about the drive home, just the mounting anger building in her as she took turn after turn in the Woody. By the time she pulled into the driveway at Finn's house, rage consumed her. Old rage, rage she should have let go of long ago, but that she couldn't seem to part from for good. It was the constant in her life, the thread that tied each of her terrible choices together.

A logical part of her knew that things hadn't been perfect before her sixth year in secondary. She'd always struggled with self-worth. Something to do with being smashed between four sisters who were all extraordinary in some way, while she never amounted to anything special. But that was the moment it had all come crashing down, when she'd shattered into pieces too small to put back together again—she'd looked at that mess and *given up.*

It was the giving up she couldn't forgive herself for, and that lack of empathy for herself transferred all too easily to Finn. She walked slowly to the house, trying to let the pouring rain soothe her, but nothing could quiet the storm in her now. Finn, Alaric and Thea were sitting in the front living room together, in chairs she'd crafted from deadfall in the yard only yesterday. They looked up, startled by her appearance, she assumed.

Finn rose quickly, but Harlow's hand shot out in front of her. "Don't come near me."

He drew back, as though she'd slapped him.

She stepped into the room, her voice sharp as a blade. "You knew what she was going through." He looked lost, so she clarified. "Petra. You knew and you did nothing to stop your parents."

Finn took a step towards her. "Harls... I can explain."

She stepped back, shaking her head so hard it hurt. A headache split into the back of her skull so painful she was tempted to cry out. "No. Not unless you want to tell me she was lying. *Was she lying to me?*" The shrill sound of her voice surprised her. "Did you not know what she was going through, what she is *still* going through? Do you not know what your mother is doing to her?"

His head hung in shame and Alaric and Thea both shifted uncomfortably, but Harlow got the impression they might be confused by what she was saying. Let them ask. She wasn't going to enlighten them.

"What is she talking about, Finn?" Alaric asked, his voice gentle as he touched his friend's arm.

Finn started to say something but Harlow stopped him, screeching. "Don't you *dare* tell her secret. Not here. Not to anyone."

He flinched, but she saw defeat in the angle of his shoulders. "She wasn't lying to you. I knew."

"The bullying. You knew why she did it?"

He nodded. "I suspected."

A suppressed sob choked her. "Did you know how much it hurt her to do it?"

"I did." His voice was flat. Resigned. "It's why we stayed friends."

Thea looked as though she might panic. She clutched Alaric's arm so tightly Harlow could see the whites of her knuckles. Harlow was sure she was worried about what was coming next, and she wished she could spare her sister from this scene, seventeen hells, she wished she could spare *herself*.

But the words came tumbling out in a vicious outburst, meant to wound rather than expose her own vulnerability. "Did you know that I tried to kill myself in college? Because of how she treated me? Because of how *you* treated me, and everyone else who followed suit because of the two of you? I went to college and people were *still* treating me like shit because of you."

The things she was saying were true, but they weren't fair, or even accurate, and she knew it. *Why was she saying these things? Why was she saying them* this way? But she couldn't take the words back, not now. Her heart beat wildly as she began to panic; she was out of control in a way that was completely unfamiliar to her.

No one spoke. Axel wound himself around her legs and she picked him up. "I want to go home," she said. Her words sounded alien to her, as though someone else was speaking from within her. This wasn't how she'd wanted to tell Finn about this. She'd been angry in the park with Petra, but she hadn't imagined coming home and creating this kind of scene. Her head pounded, feeling like an icepick driving into her brain.

Thea let go of Alaric now, rushing to Harlow's side, taking her arm. Alaric's eyes widened in shock. He moved to stand next to Thea, a clear sign of support for the woman he loved.

Finn dropped into his chair. He was struggling, but she didn't know if she cared. "How can I trust you when you know that someone you love is being personally victimized by your mother? You do love Petra, don't you? She's one of your best friends? A comrade as a fellow Knight?"

He nodded, but did not form words.

"Then what in seventeen hells is *wrong* with you?" she screamed, clutching Axel. "How could you let her suffer like this?"

"I'm scared," he yelled back, then quieter, "I'm *so* scared of them."

A part of her, deep underneath all this rage, understood it. She was scared of his parents too. But she didn't know if she could forgive it, because if anyone could stand up to them, it was him. "Then how can I expect you to help me if they want to hurt me, or my family?"

Finn got up, moved toward her as though he would touch her, but she held up a hand. "Don't. Just don't. I'm going home and I don't want you to follow me or call me. I mean it."

She moved toward the door and Thea and Alaric followed. Her heart burned with shame for what she'd just done, but her pride wouldn't let her turn around and apologize. This wasn't the way to do this. Yes, she was angry, perhaps even justifiably so, but behaving this way didn't feel right. Trying to humiliate him and berating him like this wasn't who she wanted to be. *Why couldn't she just turn around, apologize and talk things out?*

Harlow was stuck again, stuck in a place she didn't want to be but couldn't see a way out of. She couldn't seem to retreat, but she could do something right. Before they could follow her out she turned to Alaric, and looked him directly in the eyes, so like Petra's the way they glowed with feeling. "I fucked that up."

He exchanged a look with Thea, but didn't respond. She felt his disapproval, and she knew she'd earned it. She'd earned her own.

"Stay with him," she pleaded. "Take care of him. I can't right now, but you can."

Alaric's eyes softened and he hugged her. "You are a good woman, Harlow Krane. I am glad you'll be my sister soon."

Harlow shrugged. "I'm not that good." She leaned into the half-hug Thea gave her. "Can you drive us home?"

Her sister took her hand and led her to Alaric's car. They got in and drove away in silence, heading back into the city. "Do you want to talk about it?" Thea asked.

"No. I said more than I should have back there."

Thea sighed. "It sounds like whatever you said was true. He admitted it."

Axel rubbed his face against hers, purring. "But why did I scream at him like that?"

Thea glanced at her, sidelong. "Why did you?"

Harlow shook with unshed tears. "I don't know. I just... Blew up... It was like all this old anger just exploded out of me. I thought I was doing better..." Her breath came in harsh gasps.

Thea reached out, taking her hand. "Harlow, *Harlow*. He will forgive you. You'll talk and work things out."

She shook her head, so angry and full of shame she couldn't think straight. "I just want to be alone. Is that okay?"

Harlow saw the worry in Thea's hunched shoulders and felt even worse, as she murmured, "Of course." It wasn't okay with Thea at all.

They stopped at a railroad crossing as the gates were going down. Harlow remembered the reason she'd gone to the city to begin with. She fumbled in her pocket, then handed Thea the slip of paper Petra had given her. "This address is Olivia Sanvier's safehouse. Petra says that's where she might take Mark."

Thea took out her phone and sent a text message. "Alaric will take care of it. If Mark's there, he'll find him."

Harlow nodded. She felt nothing but pain so deep and so close to all her old wounds she nearly went numb. In the past, she would have stopped by the liquor store, bought a bottle of something, or called one of her many connections to find drugs, but now she just wanted to go home and get into her comfortable bed and cry. The overwhelming anger was draining away, the further she got from the house. Confusion and shame coursed through her until her hands ached with the pain of balling them into fists.

Slowly she relaxed her fingers and began to force air deep into her lungs. Maybe Thea was right, and Finn would forgive her if she apologized, or at least admitted that she was wrong. She hugged Axel close, slid her phone out of her pocket, and sent a text message. Just one, because her integrity demanded she do so. *I said things I shouldn't have. It wasn't your fault I hurt myself. Please give me time to sort myself out.*

She watched as the little dots cascaded, waited for his response, but nothing came. He was doing as she asked, giving her time. Loneliness gnawed at her, and after so long being sidelined, it was ravenous. She leaned back in her seat and let it devour her.

CHAPTER THIRTY-ONE

Harlow spent exactly a week moping about what happened with her phone shut off but for the once-daily check-in she promised Selene, before Enzo showed up at her door. He had a pizza and a bag of burgers and parm fries from Gastro Lupo in his arms.

"Since you didn't answer your phone, I got everything," he said as he pushed inside her apartment. She looked behind him, half-expecting to see Riley Quinn or her sisters trailing behind, but he was alone.

Axel twined around his legs, purring in greeting as Enzo went to work getting plates out and running tap water into glasses. He peeked into her hutch and fridge, shaking his head. "So. You're punishing yourself for being shitty to Finn?"

Harlow's mouth fell open at his tone. Was he *mad* at *her*? Axel perched next to Enzo in the kitchen and together they glared at her. "What did I do to the two of you?" she grumbled.

Enzo shook his head, flinging his hands into the air. "Why is this so hard for you to get? When you do this, when you retreat like this—it hurts everyone who loves you."

Harlow sat on the bed, her chest tightening. "I needed space."

Her best friend rolled his eyes. "Yeah, and what about me? What happened with us when you were with Mark was one thing. And babe, I take responsibility for not knowing the right thing to do when all that went down, but you *cannot* disappear on me again. *Do you understand?*"

She'd been staring at her hands as he talked, but the sound of the shake in his voice caused her to look up. Grief, deep echoing grief, ricocheted on Enzo's face. Harlow leapt up, throwing her arms around him. She didn't need to be an empath to know he was thinking about how lonely he was without his parents.

"I'm sorry. You're right. I've been a bad friend."

He hugged her back and she felt the smooth comfort of his magic envelop her. "Why can't you call Finn and tell him that too?"

Harlow pulled back, sighing. She walked out onto the terrace. The air was warm and balmy today, weak sunlight filtering through the usual haze over Ambracia Bay. Enzo followed her, plopping down in the single plastic chair, munching a plate of parm fries. She stole a couple before answering.

"Because it's complicated. I went about things the wrong way, and I'm honestly not sure why I got *so* mad, but what I said stands up. Did Riley tell you what Finn did?"

Enzo smiled, slouching down in the chair. "This chair is awful," he said, disdain for the cheap plastic monstrosity in his eyes. "Actually, Petra and Finn both told me. Riley is a vault."

Harlow froze. "Petra *and* Finn?"

He handed her the plate. "*You* sit here and tell me this is a chair worth keeping." She laughed. The chair *was* awful; the other had fallen apart a few days ago, and this one was on its last legs. She let her shadows out, thinking of the plastic chairs they had at the cabin, the ones that were much, much more comfortable. The chair shifted under Enzo, until he was sitting on an exact replica of the cabin chairs.

"Better?" she asked.

"Much." She started eating the fries, a signal that Enzo should keep talking. "Yes, they asked Riley and I over for dinner. Your whole family was there, actually, and Cian Herrington."

Harlow's stomach flipped. They'd all met without her?

Enzo saw the face she was making. "You've said no to everything, Harlow. We all needed to talk about what's going on and we couldn't wait for you."

She slid down to sit on the ground, propping her feet in Enzo's lap. "Fair. So what's up?"

"No news on Mark, or Olivia. No one has seen either of them."

Harlow nodded. She'd expected as much.

"Mark's dad is gone too."

"What?"

Enzo shook his head. "If you'd been checking the news, you'd know. He's missing."

"That seems bad," Harlow said.

"Yeah... And shit gets worse... Finn confronted his parents about Petra."

Harlow felt her eyebrows raise until her forehead ached. "He did?"

"Yes. And that did *not* go well. The McKays outed her to her parents. She's out of their will and cut off financially. They paid for her apartment and car, of course. I guess she got fired from her job at their company too."

Harlow wasn't sure what to think about that. "Is she okay?"

Enzo stared off into the distance. "You know, it's weird, I've disliked her nearly our whole lives. She's always been such a miserable person to be around... But she's different now. She was *kind* at the dinner, which was at Alaric's by the way, and the food was excellent. She's staying there now. She's still a little... blunt... sometimes, but maybe that's just Petra."

"No one should have to live like she was," Harlow said, her voice quiet. "I'm glad Finn stood up for her. Did he tell her he was going to do that?"

Enzo nodded, leaning forward to steal a handful of fries. "Yes, he asked her first, and I guess she said that she'd rather face the consequences with her parents than think he didn't care enough to stand up to them. They worked their shit out." Harlow's breath caught in her throat as she bit her lip. "Can I give you some advice, Harlow?"

She lowered her eyes. "Okay."

"You should do the same. It's not your place to be mad *for* her. She told you what she did because she needed someone to tell, and she thought she was helping you. I think she feels genuinely bad that what she said caused you to be so angry with him."

Harlow's voice died in her throat for a moment, then she coughed. "I don't really know why I flew off the handle like that. I've been trying to figure it out for days. I mean, I was frustrated with him, but I was out of control..."

"You've been holding all that in for a long time."

Harlow set the plate of fries down. "Yeah, but I do actually know Finn and Petra weren't the reason things got so bad, *I am*. I've been working on this stuff for a while now. Something about the whole incident doesn't feel right."

Enzo arched an eyebrow. "You're sure you're not just repressing stuff?"

She shrugged instead of trying to convince him. There was only one way to know for sure. "You tell me. You're the empath."

He held out a hand to her. "If you really want to know, come inside."

She took his hand and let him pull her to her feet.

"You'd better get that plate, or your cat will be eating fries. I don't think they're supposed to have garlic."

Dutifully, Harlow picked up her plate and followed Enzo inside, tucking it into the oven before sitting with him on the floor. He and Axel were sitting in a patch of sunshine peeking through the haze.

"He likes you," Harlow murmured as she sat, facing Enzo.

Axel made his way into her lap as Enzo took her hands. "Breathe with me and try not to resist. Since your anger is likely rooted deep, it may take a while for me to find."

Harlow nodded, closing her eyes, trying to focus all her attention on the air moving in and out of her lungs. She felt the pressure of Enzo's magic, as he pushed deeper into her mind. Empaths, even ones as talented as Enzo, mostly read surface feelings without effort, needing to probe more deeply to uncover older emotions, or something that wasn't being actively felt.

She relaxed into the feeling, letting herself picture Enzo's gentle search as a connection between them. When she imagined it as part of the thread between them, a magical link forged by their years of friendship and connection, she felt the pressure ease off. Instead of Enzo's empathy feeling like an attack, it felt more like having a visitor.

When he let go of her hands, he sighed. "That was amazing, Harlow. Did you use your magic to help ease my way?"

She opened her eyes. "I think so." They both looked down at her fingers, which were now stained inky blue. "What did you find?"

Enzo's expression clouded. "It's strange. I found the spot where your emotions about what Finn and Petra did reside... And all I found was a deep well of sadness. Some self-hatred, but no rage, not even any anger... At least..." He trailed off, creating a hollow in his cheek as he bit it, making his prominent cheekbones look even sharper on one side of his face.

"What?" she prompted, anxious to know what he'd found.

"It's almost like there was something left over. Not a resolved emotion, that's different..." he sighed. "I'm not explaining this well."

Harlow smiled encouragingly. Sometimes Enzo got flustered when he couldn't be as precise as he liked to. She'd always found it best not to interrupt his train of thought when he was like this.

He stared up at the ceiling. "Resolved emotions are like healed wounds. They leave silvery scars, but they are healed. I can tell what they were, how deep they ran, and many times how much damage they caused. But this was something else... A remnant of rage, but it wasn't like anything else in you."

When his eyes drifted back to hers, she saw the fear in them. "What does that mean?"

He shook his head. "I'd rather not guess."

Her arm shot out and she took his hand. "Try. Please."

Enzo grimaced. "It doesn't look like it belongs to you, Harlow. *Your* anger, even your rage, looks completely different. Everyone's emotions have similarities, but they have their own signature. This didn't belong to you."

She knew he wouldn't want to answer this, but she had to ask. "What could cause something like that?"

"I'd like to talk with James Quinn, Riley's dad, before I answer that. He and Riley's mom are kind of experts about this stuff. She's a researcher specializing in parapsychology and they often work together on cases like these. Is it all right if I talk to them about what I saw inside you?"

Harlow didn't like the sound of what Enzo was suggesting might be wrong with her, but what choice did she have? If there was something inside her that wasn't hers, she had to find out how it got there and what to do about it, or there was no way she could move forward with Finn.

"Sure." She needed to change the subject. The idea that

some alien remnant of rage was festering inside her was too disturbing. "How are things with Riley?"

Enzo's face lit up with a beautiful smile that warmed Harlow to her toes. "So good. They're the best."

Harlow couldn't help but echo that gorgeous grin. "And it's *all* good?"

Enzo covered his mouth and waggled his eyebrows as he nodded. "Yes. It's all *so* good. The best ever."

They dissolved into laughter, collapsing on the floor with Axel sprawling between them. Enzo's fingers laced with hers. "Call Finn. I think he really misses you."

"I can't," she whispered, her voice suddenly hoarse. "Not until I know what's going on with me. Where all that anger came from. What if I lost my temper like that again?"

Enzo grimaced. "You are going to lose your temper again, Harlow. That boy is infuriating. People lose their tempers, get in fights, get mad. Then they apologize, make up... You get this, right?"

She almost lied and said that she understood. "Not really. There's a lot I haven't told anyone about me and Mark."

Enzo nodded. "I figured. But can I tell you that when I was looking for your anger, I saw a lot of new healing. You're doing the work, babe. You'll get there. I promise."

The floor was hard under her as she rolled onto her back. As she stared at her ceiling the hole in her memory about the night Mark kicked her out pressed against her conscious mind. "There's something I can't remember. Can you help me?"

Enzo sat up, looking down at her. "I know—I saw it. I can't help with that, Harlow. I'm sorry. Riley could, maybe, but I'm not sure they would."

Harlow swallowed as a tear spilled onto her cheek. "Why not?"

Enzo's thumb swept the tear away. "Because sometimes stuff

like that gets locked away for a reason. It's tricky business to undo it. But I can loosen some of the thorns around it, if you'd like. That way, when you work out the tangles, it should release safely."

"Okay," Harlow said, sitting. "I'd like that."

They took hands again, and Enzo set to work.

CHAPTER THIRTY-TWO

Harlow spent the next few days at home, but she answered her texts, and called her sisters and the maters, one by one. Enzo had said he'd get back to her when he heard from the Quinns about the strange remnant of alien emotion inside her. She tried not to dwell on what might have caused such a thing to happen, as the idea of something influencing her in ways she couldn't detect was so terrifying it sent her into a dissociative spiral each time she thought about it too hard. She was taking things hour by hour, but sometimes it felt like she might be stuck in this spot forever, unable to trust herself even more than she had before.

There were still no texts from Finn. And why would there be? She asked for space and he was giving it to her. When the intercom buzzed, she jumped, her heart leaping into her throat.

She pressed the button, her heart pounding. "Who is it?"

"Petra... Velarius. Can I come up?"

As if anyone else in Nuva Troi would dare be named Petra, Harlow thought with a smirk. "Sure, press your hand to the metal plate by the door, then come on up. Penthouse 2."

The light on the intercom went on as Petra pressed her hand

to the plate downstairs. Harlow pressed the green button next to it to approve Petra's presence, then ran to the bathroom to brush her teeth, changing into a clean sweatshirt as she went. When she opened the door she was surprised by Petra's appearance. Her dark hair was pulled into its usual ponytail, but instead of being flat-ironed into a satin sheet, her hair curved in natural waves, and she wore only a touch of makeup. And her clothes...

"I'd forgotten you went to UNT too," Harlow said, glancing down at their matching sweatshirts.

"It's the weekend," Petra said, cheeks flushing. "I'm trying out being..."

"Relaxed?" Harlow suggested.

"Casual," Petra corrected, laughing. "My parents actually kept most of my clothes when they ejected me from their lives and kicked me out of my home."

Harlow shook her head. "Petty."

Petra nodded. "That's my mom and dad. But believe it or not, this feels better. They hate me, but I can *be* me now."

Harlow was tempted to hug her, but she wasn't sure what Petra would do if she did. "I'd offer you something to eat or drink, but I don't really have anything."

Petra's gaze lit on Axel. "You have a kitty!"

Harlow watched in amazement as Petra Velarius dropped to the floor making little clicking noises at Axel, who looked at Harlow as if to ask, *What is this immortal fool up to?*

"You like cats?" Harlow asked as she got a bag of treats out of a drawer and handed them to Petra. "He likes these."

Petra took the treats, wrinkling her nose slightly at the smell, but grinning with delight as Axel took one after another from her hand. "My parents never let me have pets. They think animals are dirty. I've always wanted a cat. Some big, floofy monster that would love me."

Harlow understood then. Petra Velarius had spent her life isolated by her secrets, and by parents who cared more about some stupid illusion of propriety the rest of the world left behind nearly a century ago. Free from that, she was a slightly sad girl, who apparently liked cats, and women. Harlow's head shook slightly. What a shame that her parents would rather have her rich, perfect and miserable, over the sweet person stuffing Axel with rabbit treats in front of her now.

Axel pushed past the bag of treats in Petra's hand and climbed into her lap. "He wants you to pet him," Harlow said. "He likes ear and chin rubs the best."

Petra obliged, beaming at Axel. When he curled up to sleep, she looked up at Harlow, who had curled up on the bed, facing them. "So, what's up?" Harlow asked.

Petra sighed. "I... I thought I was helping you when I told you that about Finn."

Harlow held up a hand. "Please. Don't apologize. I'm the one who was wrong for getting so angry. I mean, don't get me wrong, I was pissed... But I lost my temper and made a mistake."

"Can you forgive him?"

"Have you?"

Petra smiled. "I forgave Finn before he asked me to, and we worked out the rest. When he told his parents to back off us both, it was really brave. I knew the McKays would tell my parents about me. That's how they are, they follow through on their threats. We both knew and I gave him permission to do it anyways. It was time for both of us to cut the cord. Alaric did it a long time ago when he started his company, though he and Pasiphae are on much better terms than either Finn or I will be with our parents."

"Wait... What do you mean he told them to back off us both?"

"He told them to go fuck themselves, Harlow. He shut down the bank account they opened in his name, and he told them if they didn't leave you and Antiquity Row alone that he'd make problems for them. As I'm sure you can imagine, he knows quite a few of their secrets. I tried to get him to come over here and tell you this himself, but he wouldn't. He told me not to tell you either, which of course forced me to come directly here to do the exact opposite. He's kind of a dummy about stuff like that sometimes."

Petra snickered and Harlow couldn't help herself, she joined her. "Yeah, he is, isn't he?"

"So will you forgive him now?" Petra asked.

Harlow sighed. "I'm not angry with him. I'm angry with myself. It's complicated."

Petra nodded, petting Axel gingerly, so as not to wake him, Harlow supposed. "I get that. But he's in love with you Harlow. I don't think he ever stopped being in love with you. He'd move worlds to keep you safe. Make himself miserable, if he had to. He gets a little too *focused* sometimes, and misses what might be collateral damage, but he is a good man."

"You don't have to convince me of that, Petra," Harlow said. "I already know."

"Okay, well I feel like I started something crappy between you, and I wanted to try and see if I could make it right." She looked around. "This is a nice place."

Harlow smiled, a little surprised that Petra liked it, but Enzo was right, she was different now that she was free of her parents. "Thank you. It's been good for me."

"Will you come to dinner tonight at Finn's? We're meeting to talk about some stuff your sister dug up about the Scroll of Akatei."

"Did she restore the images in the Merkhov book?" Harlow asked. *Why didn't Thea text her?*

Petra shook her head. "No, I think she's having trouble with that for some reason. This is something else. Will you come?"

Harlow nodded.

Petra looked down at Axel. "I have to go. What do I do?"

Harlow suppressed a smile, taking the cat off the beautiful

immortal's lap. He chirped sleepily as she tucked him into the blankets on her bed. Petra stood, looking around again. "This place is *really* beautiful, Harlow. What a view."

Harlow thanked her again, walking her to the door.

"Do you need a ride to Finn's?" Petra asked. "I could come get you."

Harlow shook her head. "No, that's okay. Thank you though."

She couldn't stand the thought of trying to wrangle her nerves *and* trying to make conversation with Petra for nearly forty-five minutes in the car, but there was no nice way to say that. She'd figure something else out.

As Petra stepped out the door, Harlow put a hand on her arm. "Can I hug you?"

Petra looked startled. "Why?" She clapped a hand over her mouth. "That was rude. I'm sorry. I..."

"I'm really glad you came over, Petra."

"You are?"

Harlow nodded. "Yeah. In sixth year, I used to have this fantasy that one day you'd just stop being so mean to me and we'd be friends. Isn't that weird?"

Petra's eyes filled with tears. "Not really. I used to have the same one. Where my parents knew about me and didn't care, and I got to be friends with you, Enzo and Finn." Her chin wobbled. Harlow recognized the same loneliness that haunted her chasing Petra, even now.

Harlow reached out and tugged on Petra's matching sweatshirt, something she couldn't imagine having done even a month ago. "Hug?"

Petra nodded and Harlow pulled her into a gentle embrace. When Petra's arms went around her, Harlow felt the other woman's breath shudder through her. "You get to have a whole new life now, one where all those things are true, and more."

When Petra pulled away she gave Harlow a watery smile. "We'll get there. Both of us."

Harlow nodded. "We're already on our way. See you tonight."

Petra waved as she ran down the steps. "Seven. It's casual. Don't be late."

Chapter Thirty-Three

Petra had said this dinner was casual, and she had no doubt that meant *actually* casual, unlike season events. Still, she stood in front of the racks of clothing sitting in the middle of her apartment for what felt like forever, trying to figure out what to wear. The weather had warmed just enough in the past few days to make sweaters uncomfortably warm, but lighter clothing was still too chilly.

Eventually, she settled on a plaid shirt in an impossibly soft twill fabric, tucked into a pair of vintage wide leg jeans. Harlow pulled her long hair into a ponytail, deciding not to fuss with makeup or glamour. Everyone knew she'd been having a hard time; there was no need to pretend like everything was fine.

Her intercom buzzed just as she was feeding Axel and thinking about ordering a car. "Yes?"

"Delivery for Harlow Krane. I need a signature."

A delivery? "Be right down."

She pulled boots on and ran down what felt like unending flights of stairs. Before she reached the bottom, she hesitated. What if this was some kind of trap from the House of Remiel? She slowed down, breathing deeply, reaching for her shadows.

She wasn't completely confident about using them to defend herself, but she wanted to be prepared.

As she entered the vestibule, she saw a human courier, dressed in street clothes, holding an envelope and a clipboard. Their bike was sitting outside and they were looking at it anxiously. She sighed. Just a human kid, worried about their bike being stolen.

"Hi," she said as she stepped into the vestibule. "I'm Harlow."

The kid looked at her, nodded. "Yep. Just like in the gossips."

She narrowed her eyes.

"What?" the kid said with a grin. "Everyone follows along with that shit. You're my favorite, by the way. I hope you win. Sign here."

They handed her the clipboard and she signed, trying not to be offended that her personal life had been reduced to "winning" Finn McKay. Within seconds, the kid had handed her a stiff cardboard envelope and was outside and back on their bike. A dry laugh blew out from her lungs; it was ridiculous to be recognized for doing absolutely nothing—she wasn't like the twins, she didn't work at being seen. She tore open the envelope and was about to dump its contents out on the low console table in the front hall of her building when a shifter couple from the third floor passed her coming in from the parking lot.

"Finally using your spot, eh?" the older man said with a wink. "I do love a classic."

"Hi, Phil. Marisa," Harlow replied, not sure what Phil was referring to.

Marisa rolled her light brown eyes and tucked a lock of wavy black hair behind her ears. "Come on, Phil. Harlow has better things to do than talk to an old codger like you about classic cars."

Harlow smiled. They were sweet together, but she had no

idea what they were talking about. She waved as they got in the elevator, before turning back to the envelope. She turned it over and a key fell onto the table with a note. She picked up the note and recognized the handwriting instantly.

If I can't drive you, at least I can give you a ride.
—Finn

She looked at the key again, and then walked quickly in the direction of the parking lot. The penthouse came with a nice parking spot near the door and she could see the Woody from halfway down the hall. He'd known she would need some space to fret on her way over because she'd always been this way, anxious before events. It wasn't the kind of lavish gift that most immortals would gush over. It was just an old car to most people, but the Woody meant something to *her* and Finn knew it.

Her phone was upstairs, along with her purse, so she raced back to the penthouse as quickly as she could, pulling out her phone.

Thank you, she texted Finn, not knowing what else to say.

He saw immediately and began to write back. *You're welcome.*

Harlow waited, but he didn't say more and she wasn't sure how to reply. Her stomach flipped as she put her phone down. Axel curled his long tail around her leg in comfort. "You can't come, bub. Not tonight. I'll be home soon."

She picked the cat up and he bumped his face against hers, then used her shoulder to boost himself into his tree, where he curled into a plush hammock she'd created for him near the window. Within moments the cat was asleep, his little snores drifting down to her, making her jealous for the millionth time that she hadn't been born a cat.

Her phone vibrated on the table and she picked it up. Finn. *I'm nervous about seeing you. Changed my t-shirt four times. This look okay?*

A photo came just as she was reading. It was him, standing in his bathroom in jeans and a heathered grey t-shirt that said, in faux-vintage lettering, "My girlfriend is a witch."

Harlow burst out laughing. If he'd been trying to break the possible tension between them, it worked. A small measure of relief crept into her chest, loosening the hold on her lungs until she breathed freely. She texted back. *Where'd you find that?*

A vendor on 55th. They had some with your face on them, but I thought that was too much.

She snorted and typed back. *Probably right. Humans are so weird.*

His next text came as she pressed send. *Jk. I got it.*

The photo he sent had her in tears. Someone had printed a caricature of her on a shirt, and underneath it said, "Harlow Krane: frumpy to fabulous." *Which should I wear tonight?*

Harlow shot back, *The first one.* The second was too embarrassing, even for a

family dinner. Her sense of relief that he wasn't freezing her out was tempered by her fear that something might trigger that piece of alien rage that might be left inside her.

She waited while the torturous little dots blinked. *Drive safe.*

See you soon, she wrote back, then tucked her phone in her purse.

As she locked up and headed to the car, she felt more, rather than less nervous. She knew the shirt was meant to make her laugh, maybe clear the air a little, and it had, but where did they stand? A part of her wanted to say screw it and work things out together, but her fear that something else was affecting her, causing her to react to things in ways she normally wouldn't was too frightening.

Furthermore, the memory she'd lost bothered her. Something about it felt connected to all this, though she didn't know how. Maybe unlocking it would make everything make sense, but until then it was better not to do more harm to Finn than she'd already done.

The Woody was gassed up and had been detailed since the last time she drove it. It smelled like Finn, decadent and a little like woodfire. She pressed play on the CD player, which already had something in it. It was a copy of a mix he'd made her in secondary, with all their favorite songs. It was hard not to get nostalgic as she drove through the city, rain splattering on the Woody's windshield in a non-committal way that suggested it would pour later. Her mind drifted as she drove, and she reached Finn's house sooner than she expected. She sat in the driveway for a moment. Everyone else had already arrived and she'd be walking into a group of people who knew how badly she'd embarrassed herself last time she was here.

Her cheeks burned as she bit the inside of her mouth, trying to maintain some semblance of calm. A light rap on her window startled her. Cian Herrington stood outside her window, wearing what she assumed they interpreted as "casual" clothing, but actually consisted of a pair of slim trousers and a button-down that was unbuttoned halfway down their chest in an alluring way. Their hair had been silver the last time she saw them, but today was lavender, and they wore a hint of shadow around their eyes.

She opened the car door. "Hi," she said as she got out.

Cian smiled. "I like you."

Harlow was taken aback by the blunt nature of this statement. "What?"

"You're passionate and honest. Finn's dated a lot of volatile people trying to get over you. But you are unpredictable, which is different from volatile, and I like it."

A smile crept onto Harlow's face. "Well, I'm certain I'll like you too, if we get to know one another better."

Cian's head tilted to one side as their eyes narrowed. "*When* we get to know one another better, you mean."

Harlow swallowed hard, glancing at the house. "You seem like a bit of a package deal, with Finn, I mean. And..."

Now Cian grinned, and their face was so ferocious that Harlow was tempted to step back. "And nothing. You and Finn will work things out. I'm *glad* you challenged him. He's not used to that. His parents are the only ones to ever tell him no, and they do it out of spite. Why did you do it?"

Harlow bit her bottom lip, wondering why they were having this conversation at all. But as she looked into Cian's pale eyes, something in her recognized what they were doing. They were protective of Finn and this was how they were vetting her. She was glad someone was vetting her, that someone cared enough about him to make sure she was good enough in the right ways, and she was pleased Cian found her acceptable.

"First of all, I don't like *how* I did it. I'm not proud of losing my temper that way. I'm working on it."

Cian nodded. "Fair assessment."

"But I did it because it hurt so much to hear Petra's story. I couldn't let it go."

Again, Cian nodded. "And what about the way humans are treated by the Orders? Can you let that go?"

Harlow couldn't help it; she looked around, worried to voice something like this aloud, even here. "No, I can't. I've waited my whole life to find a way to do the things you're doing with the Knights. It doesn't matter what happens with me and Finn on a personal level. We have to find a way to change things."

Now Cian's grin was positively feral. Harlow had the sudden impression that she wouldn't want to have to fight them, for anything. She was tempted to ask a *very* rude question, but she held it in. The Trickster's Chosen hated to be asked about their alternae, but she desperately wanted to know what creature lurked under Cian's humanoid form. She had the feeling they shifted into something magnificent. Cian's grin spread wider, and Harlow's heart nearly stopped as their pupils disappeared and an image of an immense silver beast covered in scales filled her second sight.

"You're an Argent?"

Cian chuckled in response, linking their arm through hers. "Aren't you a clever girl?"

Harlow was nearly stunned into silence. *Nearly.* "How... How is that possible?"

Heraldic shifters hadn't been born for over five hundred years, as the Illuminated had exterminated them in massive campaigns, since they fought against them in the War of the Orders. The Argent were the fiercest of the firedrakes, and the most deadly. Even one could lay waste to legions of Illuminated soldiers.

"We are not as rare as you might think. Of course, we must be careful who knows our secret."

"I would *never* tell," Harlow said, squeezing the shifter's arm.

"I know that," Cian said softly. "I wouldn't have let you see otherwise. There is a world beyond what you know to be true, Harlow. Tonight is just the beginning."

They'd reached the front door and Harlow took a deep breath. To think there were mysteries she hadn't uncovered yet, even after twenty-five years of being a sorcière, gave her a thrill of joy. Curiosity and deeply held interest lit a flame in her heart so bright that she felt sure she might catch fire. As she put her hand on the door Cian pulled her back.

"Do you know that the Striders fought with the Heraldic shifters in the war?"

Harlow shook her head. "No, I don't know much about them at all. Didn't everyone who fought against the Illuminated fight together?"

Cian let out a small huff of frustration. "Well, of course, but I mean the Striders actually *fought* in our units." The way Cian said "our" made Harlow wonder if they'd been there. If they were possibly that old. Her breath caught as Cian continued, "They fought in our units because they too could shift shape."

Surely, Thea would have told her this already if she'd known, wouldn't she? "I haven't heard anything like that before."

Cian leaned one narrow shoulder against the house. "You wouldn't have. We kept it a secret. It wasn't all of them, mind you. Many of the Striders couldn't shift. But some could."

"What were their alternae?" Harlow asked, using the Order of Masks' word for their non-human form.

Cian sighed. "They were the Feriant."

Harlow hadn't heard that word before, but played with the etymology in her head. *To strike, to kill, to slay*, all possible roots. "I don't know that word," she finally admitted.

The Argent pushed past her, opening the door to the house. "You will, in time, I believe. I learned it was best not to tell Striders their business a long, long time ago."

The note of finality in their voice as they walked into the house indicated that they wouldn't be moved to answer more questions, so Harlow tucked the information away for later. From the sound of things, her entire family, plus Enzo and Riley Quinn, were talking loudly in the kitchen.

Before Cian disappeared into the thick of things, Harlow pulled them back into the hall. "You know that Riley Quinn is with the Rogue Order, right?"

Cian nodded. "Yes, we know. Finn is hoping to use tonight as a way to extend goodwill to the Queen. Perhaps form an alliance."

Harlow breathed a sigh of relief. "They seem like a good person."

Cian nodded thoughtfully. "Yes, many of the Rogue joined for the same reasons the Knights were formed. They are much more willing to create chaos than we have been, but perhaps we need that kind of energy now."

That wasn't anything Harlow knew much about. She'd

spent a lot of her adult life just trying to get herself under control. She knew nothing about how to fight for justice or make societal change, only that she wanted to learn, and she hoped her efforts now weren't too late to change things for the better, for humans and immortals alike.

Cian joined the group around the kitchen table, and as they did, Finn caught sight of her lingering in the doorway. His hair was mussed as ever, and her heart did flip after flip as he approached. The street vendor's t-shirt looked good on him, tight around the arms, draping over his muscled chest. She knew he probably didn't mean to do it, but he had his hands shoved into the front pockets of his jeans and his forearms flexed in a tantalizing fashion that had her reminding herself what she was here for.

"Hey, Harls," he said as he approached. She could swear he moved in slow motion, every beautiful thing about him amplified as he drew closer.

"Hey, McKay," she replied, unable to get anything else past her dry mouth. Petra peeked around the corner and gave her an extremely uncharacteristic two thumbs up.

Finn followed Harlow's startled gaze and he shook his head at his best friend. "Sorry about that. And about her coming over earlier. I didn't ask her to. In fact—"

"I know," Harlow interrupted. "She said you told her to stay out of it, but I'm glad she came."

"You hugged her?" Finn asked as he steered her into the library, away from prying eyes. Her sisters were craning their necks trying to hear what they said to each other. He closed the door and the sounds from the kitchen died immediately, as though the door had sealed them in a world of their own. There were no books on the shelves still, and no furniture in the room. Something about the emptiness felt sad to Harlow, instead of full of possibilities as it had just a week ago.

"Petra told you that?"

Finn nodded as he sat in the window seat, gesturing for her to sit across from him. It was large enough that they weren't touching when she obliged, and this too felt sad, like lost potential.

"Yeah, she seemed sort of delighted, actually." His smile faded as he raked his hands through his dark hair, sending it in wild directions. He hadn't had it cut recently, she noticed, nor had he shaved. In his t-shirt and jeans, he looked like *her* Finn, not the person trying to please his parents and the rest of the Orders in the season. Her heart thumped hard in her chest, making her question every instinct she had about staying apart.

When he spoke, she heard the strain in his voice, but also a measure of resolve. "Harls, I thought I was protecting her, but I never *asked* her what she wanted. I just assumed, which was shitty of me."

Harlow nodded, crossing her legs and resting her elbows on her knees to cradle her chin. It was infinitely cool that he could admit the ways he was wrong so effortlessly. A little voice inside her suggested that it probably wasn't effortless, but that he'd done the work to learn how to do something she found difficult. And that voice gave her hope that if he'd done it, maybe she could learn to do so as well.

His fingers stretched toward her, but he clasped them in his lap. "You look just like you did when we were ten, learning to play chess."

Her smile at the memory felt weak. Here, in his presence, she felt like crying, though she wasn't sure why. "I shouldn't have screamed at you like that," she said after what felt like an awkwardly long pause.

He shrugged. "Maybe not, but what you said was spot on. I was a coward about the whole thing."

"But it changed something between us, didn't it?" she asked, wondering if he felt it too.

He nodded. "Yeah, I think it did."

She knew it. The way things had been going was all too good to be true. She'd screamed at him, and after a lifetime of being treated like shit by people who were supposed to love him, he was doing the right thing, drawing strong boundaries and cutting her out. She sank deep into her sadness before saying, "So that's it then."

His brow furrowed as every muscle in his body tensed. "Wait —what do you mean?"

Harlow shook her head. "I assume you want to call this whole thing off. Just be friendly... I mean, we can still work together, but..."

He leaned forward, but still didn't touch her. "Is that what you want? To stop what we've been doing?"

Harlow's jaw clenched. "What do you want?"

He looked down at his shirt, frowning and tugging on the hem. *My girlfriend is a witch.* "I thought it was pretty clear what I wanted."

Air caught in Harlow's throat, momentarily unable to reach her lungs. Surely she was misunderstanding him. "You still want that? You still want... me?"

His slate eyes widened. "Did you think getting mad at me would make me stop wanting you?"

Her eyes watered, but she couldn't answer.

"Harls," he said, his deep voice gentle as he cupped her chin in his hands, one of his thumbs stroking her bottom lip so tenderly she thought she might sob. "You are allowed to get angry. I hope we don't spend all our time yelling and snapping at each other, but if it happens, it happens. We'll make up and move on."

Harlow stared at a place on the windowsill behind Finn's head, avoiding his eyes. "I want all that," she choked out. "I just... I just..."

Finn moved her chin slightly so she had to look at him.

"Whatever it is, you can tell me. I'm not going to fly off the handle and get mad. Please, just talk to me."

She wanted to tell him everything, but she couldn't quite manage, even though she *was* trying. What if the Quinns decided that all that anger *was* actually hers? If she told him about her fears now, and Enzo was wrong, she'd look like she was making excuses for bad behavior, and she didn't want that. She wanted to take responsibility for herself. So she kept it to herself; she was accustomed to keeping secrets. Secrets had always kept her safe in the past.

She settled somewhere in between the truth and her secrets. "I need more time to process what happened with Mark. There's something in my memory, this blank space about the night we broke up. I need to figure out what happened and let go before I start something new with you."

"Okay," he said softly. She saw the disappointment in his eyes and his hand fell from her face, but slowly, back into his own lap. "Can I ask you one thing that will make me sound pathetic?"

"You can ask me anything," she said, hating to hear the strain in his words.

"If I were different, if I hadn't fucked up with the whole Petra thing, and everything else, would you still feel this way?"

"Yes. It's not about you, or because of you. This is all me."

"Okay," he said.

Harlow got up. "We should get in there."

He caught her hand. "Harls." She looked back down the line of her arm, where her hand rested in his, raising her eyes to meet his gaze. "We're still in this together, right?"

She nodded, something choking her voice. It felt wrong to walk away, but she knew that before she could move on with Finn, she had to remember that night with Mark and figure out what was affecting her emotions so strangely. Then she had to let it all go, find some way to be free. As much as she wanted that to be something they could do together, she wasn't capable of that now and he deserved better than what she could give him after everything his family put him through.

Finn's lips pressed into her palm. "I'll wait as long as it takes, Harlow."

She nodded once, tearing her eyes away from him so she could walk away. He followed her into the kitchen, where Thea had a series of printed photos spread on the table. Everyone was squeezed into the large alcove, which could barely fit the eleven immortals. Cian got up and they and Finn pulled the two chairs from in front of the hearth to the table.

Finn lit the fire to stave off the chill of the evening, which had, as expected, blown in a massive thunderstorm. Thea was explaining that they could eat after she showed them what she'd found in her facsimile of the Scroll of Akatei.

"Hey," she said when she saw Harlow.

Riley smiled up at her, tucked into the curve of Enzo's arm. Harlow looked around the table, her gaze finally lighting on Petra, who was still dressed in her UNT sweatshirt and leggings. "Hey, everybody."

The maters both smiled. They'd been worried about her isolation, and about the feeling she'd had that she was being watched, but had allowed her to make her own choices about where to stay. She was glad they were here now.

The back door flew open and everyone startled. Two tall figures stepped inside, pushing back their hoods as they closed the back door. Finn pressed a hand to Harlow's shoulder—she hadn't realized he was standing so close to her. "It's just Nox and Arebos."

With their hoods back, the Wraiths proved to be less than the gruesome creatures Harlow worried they might be. In fact, they had an ethereal beauty that couldn't be denied. They were tall and sturdily built, with skin the color of burnished amber, dark hair, and eyes that glistened with acute focus. The taller of the two had their long dark hair pulled half-up and the other's hair was cut short, with the sides shaved, but otherwise they shared many of the same sharply defined features. Clearly they were siblings, though Harlow didn't think they were twins.

"Hi," the shorter one said. "We ran the perimeter twice. The wards are good. No one is getting in." She made eye contact with Harlow momentarily. "I'm Nox," she said. "And this is my brother, Arebos."

"You can call me Ari," her brother said, making eye contact only briefly, his gaze lighting on Meline, who'd looked up from her phone. Ari grinned at Meli and she blushed prettily at him.

Nox rolled her eyes. "He's an incorrigible flirt. Beware."

Indigo looked up at the sound of Nox's sarcastic tone, her eyes immediately appraising the Wraith, and Harlow shook her head. The sillies had always been attracted to their direct opposites, and here were two people who couldn't be more unlike the two of them: the Wraiths could make themselves invisible, and the twins couldn't possibly be more visible. Indigo sat up a bit straighter, and her sweater fell off her shoulder in slow motion. Harlow was sure she'd practiced the move numerous times. Apparently it had the desired effect, because Nox was staring at her, mouth slightly ajar as she pushed a hand through her short hair.

"Gods help us," Harlow muttered to Thea.

Thea's dark head shook as she muttered, "What did you expect? They've been waiting all season to find people dangerous enough to make Mama mad and we just served two of them right up."

Indeed, Selene glared at Arebos as he leaned against the alcove, conducting a soft conversation with Meline, who was whispering so quietly that Harlow couldn't keep up. Clearly Arebos could, because he laughed as she smiled up at him through her long lashes. He crouched down, tapping his phone to hers. They were already exchanging numbers?

Harlow sighed. "Before they get engaged, start talking."

Thea suppressed a laugh, then cleared her throat, getting everyone's attention. "Right. Let's talk about what Alaric and I found when we examined the place in the scroll where the triptych should be."

Thea pointed to a section of the printouts on the table that depicted a white ash tree, with an Argent curled into its roots, asleep. "In the chronology of the scroll, Alaric and I believe whatever the triptych represents comes before the firedrake, which as we can see, wakes and joins the other Heraldic creatures in the next phase."

Larkin leaned forward, pointing to some faded swirls of color winding around the tree. "Do you think this is the same representation of aether we saw in the triptych?"

Alaric nodded at Larkin. "Yes, we think the triptych is the catalyst to all of what happens in the rest of the scroll."

"What do these represent?" Harlow asked, looking closely at the humanoid forms pictured inside small bubbles in the branches, similar to the ones Thea had restored in the first of the triptych images. Some of the bubbles were shown as cracked and the small forms floated above the tree.

Alaric grinned. "That's the exciting part. We think they might be humans. If we could figure out what happens in the triptych, Thea and I believe we'd unlock the secret to what is happening with these cracked bubbles."

"It looks like the humans are being released somehow," Riley added, squinting at the images. "But if that is the case, what would the purpose of the bubbles be?"

Thea answered, but Harlow didn't hear what she'd said. She looked at Finn, who was turning towards her, as though he'd wondered the same thing she had. Finn held up a hand. "I'm sorry to interrupt, Thea. But originally, you said you thought the triptych might have something to do with what happened when a Strider and Knight... er.... Joined forces, right?"

Thea nodded. "Yes, we think that you and Harlow might hold the key to whatever this shows."

Finn ran a hand through his hair, mussing it into further perfection. Harlow forced herself to focus. "And the tree itself? What's that represent?"

Aurelia answered. "The tree nearly always represents the web of aether in the world. The roots and the branches are an easy way to represent the threads of magic immortals draw upon."

Finn's jaw clenched. "When Harlow and I arrived at the Grove party, we both experienced something strange. With everything going on, I forgot about it…"

Aurelia's voice was sharp. "What happened?"

Harlow moved to stand next to Finn. "It was as though we were isolated from everyone else. In some kind of weird pocket of reality that only we perceived. And we both heard a scream."

Finn added, "And then magic seemed to swell, before dumping us back into our usual reality. It was unsettling."

Selene frowned. "It sounds like you witnessed a ritual from the other side of the veil."

Aurelia took her wife's hand. "I'm afraid there are some dark rituals that might be associated with the season. The Order of Mysteries has been investigating this for nearly a century, but we cannot detect exactly what is happening. We've long believed the Illuminated have some ulterior motive for encouraging the season year after year."

Thea sighed. "Why haven't you ever said anything?"

Aurelia rolled her eyes. "You and your sisters are barely adults. That's not the kind of thing you tell children."

All five Krane sisters glared at their mothers, who glared right back at their children until each averted their eyes. Harlow was the last to break Selene's gaze. "Fine. Is there anything else we should know?"

Selene sighed. "I'm sure there's a great deal we know that is connected to this. Your mother and I have been alive for the better part of a thousand years, it will take time to sort things out. And we will need to take this to the Order at some point, you understand?"

Finn balked visibly. "I think it would be better to keep this a secret for now."

Aurelia's hand flew up. "As do we, Finbar. But eventually, when we decide what must be done, we will need to have the Order of Mysteries' High Council approval. That is, if you want allies."

Finn nodded. "We do. I understand."

A long moment passed, punctuated in its awkwardness by the slow ticking of the clock above the stove. Arebos broke the uncomfortable energy, staring at the images on the table. Then he turned to Thea and asked: "What is the scroll about?"

Thea smiled, appreciative of the redirect, no doubt. "No one really knows, though there have been lots of assumptions made over the years by the different Orders."

Cian tapped the image above the tree, where the Heraldic creatures were awake, flying in formation. "My people believe this means that someday, the Heraldic Chosen will reawaken, and join forces again against the Illuminated."

Aurelia nodded. "That is certainly an interpretation that makes sense. But if I may ask, what is this alternae a representative of? I've never seen it in depictions of the Heraldic before."

She tapped a darkly colored bird that flew in formation with the Heraldic warriors: firedrakes, alicorns, gryphons and the chimaera. It looked like something between an eagle and bird of paradise, though if it were as large as the scale in the facsimile it was probably the size of a person. Its feathers were a mix of dark emerald green, blue, and black in the image.

Cian looked at Harlow when they answered. "That is the Feriant."

Harlow took a sharp breath in, just as Selene covered her mouth. "*That* is a Feriant?"

Cian nodded. "It isn't one of the Heraldic shifters at all, but a sorcière."

Indigo shook her head. "But the sorcière can't change shapes. It's not in our nature."

"It was for some of you, long ago," Cian answered, never taking their eyes off Harlow. "And perhaps will be again."

"How?" Harlow asked, surer than ever that Cian had fought in the War of the Orders. "How did they do it?"

Cian shook their head. "It was kept secret. Not because they didn't trust us, but because it was dangerous knowledge. With the Feriant Legion, we stood a chance against the Illuminated. It is why both the Heraldic and the Striders were systematically eliminated. Without them, we cannot hope to mount any kind of force against the Illuminated Order."

Harlow glanced at Finn. She knew what he was thinking, because she was thinking it too. The Knights of Serpens had been eliminated in just the same way. Could this have something to do with the triptych and their union? She couldn't bring herself to ask. Not right now while things were still so bruised between them, and she saw in his eyes that he felt the same. It was as though they made a silent promise to wait, for just a bit, to talk about that.

"And that is what you think we should be doing?" Aurelia asked sharply, directing her question at Thea and Alaric. "*Fighting* the Illuminated?"

Thea began to gather her papers. "Yes, Mother," she said, voice quiet, but steady. "I do. I think the Illuminated Order has poisoned Okairos for long enough. That's why we asked you all here tonight, to begin to form an alliance—to make a plan, and move against them, before something terrible happens."

"Like what?" Aurelia asked, hysteria in her tone. "We've lived for close to two thousand years without the kinds of poverty, war or major conflicts that plague other worlds. What do you think could happen now?"

Indigo, who'd been staring at her phone, turned it around. "Something like this?"

A video played without sound, but it was clearly the House of Remiel's building in Nuva Troi—and it was on fire, a mob of humans out front. They were being slaughtered by vampires in high definition on the screen.

"What is this?" Selene gasped.

"A livestream from a cafe across the street," Indigo answered. "Humans gathered outside the House of Remiel, demanding to know where Mark and Alain Easton are, apparently they're both missing now—it was all over the gossips earlier today—and things got out of hand. They set the building on fire, apparently, and now the vampires are slaughtering them in retribution."

The livestream was happening inside Haven. Harlow glanced at Finn, whose face was drawn. He squeezed her arm, just once. She felt as though she moved in slow motion as she looked up at him. She knew what he would say, what he would do. Time sprang back into motion and she felt as though she'd missed a chance for something, though she wasn't sure what.

"We have to go," Finn said, glancing at Alaric, who nodded. "Get there, fast," he said to the Wraiths. "Cian?"

"I will hold things down here—after I call in reinforcements for you."

Riley Quinn spoke, after looking up from their phone. "The Rogue Order is sending help as well. We'll get as many humans out as we can. Can we use your safehouse? You have one across the street, yes?"

Cian nodded. "Yes, coordinate with Nox and Arebos. You can ride together."

Alaric kissed Thea. "Stay here. The wards will keep you safe. We'll be back soon."

She nodded, but Aurelia rose. "We should help."

Finn shook his head. "Please, stay here. Make calls if you

need to, but the Knights are well prepared for this kind of thing, and I assume the Rogue Order is as well."

Riley nodded, swiping a kiss to Enzo's cheek. "I'm not headed into the fray, love. I promise. I'll go to Haven and wait. The Erynes will be along shortly."

"Erynes?" Harlow asked as Alaric and Finn portaled out.

"You can think of them as the Queensguard, if you like," Riley said, then brushed a kiss on her cheek. "We'll all be back soon."

And then Riley and the Wraiths were gone, back out into the night. Harlow's head spun with how fast they all worked. There was so much she didn't know about the Knights still.

Petra got up. "I need to go too, but there's some really nice food in the fridge and in the oven. You all should eat something and get some rest."

"Where are you going?" Harlow asked, concerned.

Petra took her hand. "I have to help too, Harlow."

"You'll fight?"

Petra laughed. "I'm not as delicate as I look." She turned to the rest of the table. "Plan to stay the night. Nobody leaves 'til Finn says it's all right. Cian, Harlow, you can get everyone settled and comfortable, right?"

Harlow and Cian both nodded. Harlow turned to the Argent as Petra portaled out. "If you need to go make calls, I can handle my family. The bedrooms upstairs?"

"All are ready for guests. Sparsely furnished, but they should find everything they need—and I believe anything else that's needed, you can help with, yes?"

"Yes," Harlow agreed, as Cian disappeared into Finn's office.

Petra portaled back in, holding Axel. The cat was calm in her arms, as though he knew he traveled with a friend. "I just thought you'd want him here with you."

Harlow took the cat, feeling wildly grateful for Petra, and glad she'd invited her in earlier so that her wards had recognized the immortal and allowed her in. "Thank you," she said as Petra disappeared again, portaling back to the House of Remiel.

Larkin sighed. "Well, this is going well."

Selene got up. "I suppose we might as well eat."

Harlow looked around, watching as her mothers pulled pans of lasagna and garlic bread out of the fridge and preheated the oven. Her family was safe. She wasn't too worried about the Knights, not after seeing Finn and Alaric decimate the vampires who'd stalked her, but anxiety plagued her all the same. *What would happen when they truly made their move? When they'd gathered all the information they could and made a decision about action?* As she sat down to eat at Finn's kitchen table, surrounded by her family, she wondered just how many evenings they'd have left together.

Chapter Thirty-Four

The next morning, Harlow sat cocooned in a blanket with Axel in the kitchen alcove drinking tea and waiting for everyone to return home. Persistent rain pelted the kitchen windows and she'd queued up a playlist of gentle piano music to play on the house speakers in the kitchen to soothe herself. Petra had texted her late into the night, saying that the Knights were headed to Haven to get the human survivors settled and not to wait up. Harlow hadn't been able to follow that advice, despite everyone else going to bed shortly after midnight.

Axel rolled onto his back, snoring loudly, as she scrolled through the news and gossips. News outlets reported on the House of Remiel fire as though it were an unprovoked attack on the vampires, justifying their actions. She looked up, blinking tears into her dry eyes. She'd been staring at her phone for too long. The little ironstone lamp on the kitchen counter cast a golden glow of light into the gloom. Harlow pulled a bit of magic through the threads surrounding her to reheat her tea and watched the rain.

It wasn't surprising that the Illuminated were working with

the vampires to suppress the truth of what happened, but Harlow was disappointed nonetheless. At some point, this tactic of covering things up would backfire. Too many humans would see the violence being perpetrated by the Immortal Orders and they would resist. Harlow feared the consequences the Illuminated would rain down on all of them when that happened.

If they could just prepare a little more before things went that far, maybe they could prevent massive amounts of bloodshed. She'd downloaded three books about the War of the Orders onto Finn's e-reader and had been skimming through them all night, trying to get a better idea of how things had happened then. The trouble was, they were all written from the Illuminated's perspective. Harlow needed better histories, better accounts of those who had resisted the Illuminated in the past. She wondered briefly if the Knights' vault in Nea Sterlis had records that might help her.

Harlow had double majored in history and literature at UNT, and when things settled down she'd always planned to get a graduate degree in one of the two. In her heart, she was a researcher, curious to a fault at times. All that had died in her when she was with Mark, and she felt it coming back to her now, the deep need to know more—to tease out the threads of history and story to understand where the narrative would go next.

Axel's head popped up and he jumped into the windowsill, hearing something she could not. She peeked out the window, but saw nothing until Petra and Alaric portaled into the backyard with Nox and Arebos. All four were clean, wearing different clothes than they had been the night before, but looked exhausted.

She ran to meet them outside, hugging each of them before asking, "Where's Finn and Cian?"

Ari explained that they'd stayed at Haven, with Riley and the humans, and that though they'd saved nearly a dozen of the protestors from the vampires, the ones who'd been saved were deeply traumatized from the attack. Finn had stayed to help get them settled. When Ari was done explaining, his hand clapped her shoulder in comfort, and she saw deep empathy in the charismatic shifter's dark eyes before he walked into the house. Nox nodded solemnly, as though she understood Harlow's silence, as she followed Petra and Alaric, who both appeared completely drained, inside.

Harlow thought about texting Finn to ask if he was all right, but his people had to be hungry and tired, so she focused on figuring out breakfast and getting them all to bed instead. A voice inside her reasoned it's what he would have done first, and the thought warmed her. Finally, she was helping with something real, something honest. Her shadows danced inside her as she went back into the house that was beginning to feel like home, despite the dull ache in her heart.

THE FOLLOWING DAYS PASSED QUICKLY, AS EVERYONE had work to do, both to help the surviving humans disappear from Nuva Troi, and to prepare for whatever came next. The twins jumped easily into the action, learning to use their digital networking skills for darker, more secretive purposes from Nox, who was apparently also one of Alaric's most talented hackers. Everyone agreed that knowing what both the House of Remiel and the Illuminated were up to was of the highest importance, and the twins were such a quick study Harlow wondered if they'd been traversing the dark web on their own for quite some time.

The Kranes opted to stay at Finn's for the time being, at least until the Solstice Gala was over. The twins created a ruse about a poltergeist problem in the Monas, which would explain their absence and the shop's closure until after the gala. Dealing with violent ghosts was a well-known pain in the ass.

"That way we'll have some time to get our information sorted and figure out how we're going to proceed," Indigo explained.

Finn agreed. The Knights had worked for the past few years on small subversive projects, but never anything as serious as the treasonous activities they were contemplating now. Moving slowly, gathering as much information as they could, and feeling out who in the lower Orders could be trusted was of utmost importance.

Arebos and Larkin formed an unexpected friendship, with Ari training Larkin in various hand to hand combat techniques and Larkin teaching him to play chess. The maters were in and out, feeling out the elders' of the Order of Mysteries loyalties and talking about strategy with Finn and Cian, late into every evening. Thea locked herself in the library most days to try and understand why she could not restore the missing images in the facsimile of the Scroll of Akatei.

Riley Quinn was strangely absent, and though Harlow asked Enzo for more information, he'd gently refused to share what he knew about the Rogue Order's involvement in the attack, as well as their help with the rescue. Harlow understood when Enzo had opted to leave Finn's to join Riley; her only question had been if he felt safe. When he'd answered yes and hugged her, she didn't argue further. He still hadn't heard anything from Riley's parents about the residue of anger he'd found in her, but he promised he'd call immediately when he knew more. It was all they could do on that front.

Finn and Harlow slept separately and she noticed he made a point never to be alone with her, though she caught him watching her from time to time, and she knew Axel still slept with him sometimes, splitting his time between them. They'd forgone the rest of the season's events, planting rumors that they were too busy planning bonding celebrations with Alaric and Thea to bother with cocktail parties. The gossips ate it up, speculating about where the ceremony would take place, and whether Enzo would design the dress.

Harlow had asked Cian if the Knights had any less-biased records of the War of Orders, and they'd gotten her everything they had in Nuva Troi, promising to get her the translated diaries of the Knights' commanders from the vault in Nea Sterlis after the Solstice. On the morning of the Solstice Gala, she'd been sorting through a very dry text on the physiology of Heraldic shifters for nearly two hours, and was beginning to feel as though her eyes might fall out of her head.

"Hey, are you listening to me?" Meline asked, snapping her fingers in Harlow's face.

Harlow looked up. Her body was antsy, but her mind had focused too hard and she felt pulled in a dozen directions. "No, sorry."

Meline sighed. "I said I think Finn should look into these three human-run tech companies, it's possible they're run by members of the Rogue Order and..."

Her sister's words became a blur. *When had Indi and Meli become such grownups?* They were twenty, after all, but she certainly hadn't been this smart when she was twenty. She smiled warmly at her sister; it was foolish to keep calling them sillies, they were anything but. "Meli, I have no clue what you're talking about. Maybe you should discuss this with Finn?"

"Discuss what with me?" he asked from the doorway to the library.

Meline glanced at the intense look he was giving Harlow, the little velvet box in his hand and shook her head. "Nope. Not touching this right now. I'm sure Ari's about somewhere."

Harlow rolled her eyes as her sister left the room. "Should I be worried about those two?"

Finn shook his head. "Arebos and Nox are great. Both your sisters are in good hands. Even if it's just a fling. I don't work with people who treat their partners like shit."

Harlow's lips curled in a small smile. "What have you got there?"

Finn blushed. "I figured I'd better show this to you before tonight. Let you try it on to make sure it fits."

They were still planning on the faux proposal at the gala, and she knew what was in the little box, though they hadn't talked about it specifically. "Okay," she said, trying to keep the shake out of her voice.

Harlow was curled in a chair that she and her shadows had created. She'd been busy creating a lot of furniture over the past few days to give everyone somewhere to just *be*, since they were all spending so much time in the house together. Finn perched uncomfortably on the arm of her chair.

"I don't really know where to be when I hand this to you."

"I think you're supposed to get down on one knee."

He smirked at her, raising an eyebrow. "I know what to do tonight. But right now... This feels awkward."

She nodded, holding her hand out. "Just hand it over."

He did so and then got up, striding across the empty library to look out the windows into the front yard, where Alaric, Arebos and the twins were tossing a frisbee around. The sun had burst through the morning gloom and the sounds of everyone having a good time were comforting to hear.

Harlow opened the little box and her heart leapt at the sight of the ring. It was simple, not at all the heavy, elaborate style of most Illuminated jewelry. A single emerald-cut sapphire, set in a gold band. The stone was large, but not ostentatiously so. She slipped it on her finger. It fit perfectly. She resisted the urge to gaze at it any longer than necessary.

Quickly, she returned it to its box and snapped it shut, not bothering to close it slowly or quietly. She rolled her shoulders, swallowing hard. This was not a romantic moment, she reminded herself. They were just working together, nothing more, until she could figure herself out. And at this rate, with no time to herself, she had no idea when that might be.

Finn turned, taking a deep breath. "So it fits?"

"Yes," she said, afraid to say anything else.

If she spoke one more word, she'd tell him how perfect it was. How the deep blue of the stone reminded her of her shadows, and the simple setting was exactly what she'd always hoped for. Her fingers ached with regret as she held the box out. She hated to give it back.

"Fits perfectly. Nice job."

He took the ring from her, and to someone who didn't know him, perhaps he'd seem calm and collected, but she saw the slight tremble in his fingers as he gripped the box. He was as affected by the moment as she was.

"All right then," he said. "I should go shower."

"Sounds good," she replied, pretending to be engrossed in her phone. The phantom weight of the ring on her finger haunted her as she listened to him walk upstairs. His footsteps were slow, and she felt the tug between them as viscerally as if it were a cord, desperate to coil back together, instead of being stretched to its breaking point.

She closed her eyes. She'd taken her shower an hour ago, and Thea would make short work of her face, hair and nails. Her dress was hanging upstairs in the room she and Larkin shared, and she barely cared about putting it on. It was beautiful, of course, but everything about tonight felt like something to get through, rather than what she'd hoped it would be a few weeks ago.

Even then, she'd known they'd probably be pretending tonight, but the possibilities would still be wide open. Things hadn't been so complicated then. The thought made her laugh to herself now. *That* had been simple? She closed her eyes, regulating her breathing and took herself back to the night she and Mark had broken up once more.

She'd been trying every day to remember more, and like Enzo had said it might, some of what she'd forgotten had grown clearer, the tangles around the dark spot in her mind loosening day after day, but she still could not reach the actual memory, and she felt sure now that she wouldn't be able to move on until she confronted whatever it was she'd been trying to forget.

As she sunk deeper into her mind, aided by her shadow magic, she saw it clearly. She and Mark had been arguing, which was nothing unusual. He'd asked her for the thousandth time to tell him something she wasn't allowed to reveal about the Order of Mysteries. *But what had it been?*

And there it was, right in front of her. She watched, as though it were an old film, the two of them flashing before her. Him and her. *How dare you speak to me that way?* Her and him. *Just who do you think you are?* She picked Axel up, said she was going to bed, and then... Nothing, she couldn't remember anything else. A slippery wall of dark glass stood in front of her. She pounded on it until her fists actually hurt, but it stayed firmly in place.

Harlow slid back into her conscious mind. She glanced down at her hands, which throbbed with pain. Dark bruises covered her wrists, a physical manifestation of the vision she had. Why couldn't she remember?

She made the long climb upstairs, and her sisters buzzed around her in a haze of actions she barely registered. Her mind was stuck in front of that glass, seeing her own eyes glowing back at her in the dark.

Thea's voice broke into her quiet reverie as she gingerly held Harlow's hands in front of her face. "What happened here?"

Harlow looked up. "I've been trying to remember the night it ended with me and Mark."

Her sister sucked a sharp gasp in. "And in remembering, these bruises appeared?"

Harlow nodded, tears filling her eyes. "Every time I return to the memory, it's like there's glass in front of me, between me and what I can't remember. I was pounding on the glass in my vision just now." She sighed, exhausted. "I shouldn't have tried, but Finn showed me the ring for tonight... and I thought..."

Thea shook her head, dismissing something about what Harlow said. "I know what you thought, but do you not remember these bruises?"

Harlow's frowned. "No? What do you mean?"

Thea held them up in front of the mirror Harlow was seated in front of. Thea had finished with her hair and makeup. "When I found you, you were pounding on the back door to Mark's building, sobbing. Your hands and arms were bruised, *exactly* like this. I'll never forget the shape of those bruises. Your knees and legs too. You were all banged up—you said you fell..."

Harlow shook her head. She didn't remember any of that. Just waking up at home, in the attic, in her old bed next to Thea's the next morning, with puffy eyes. She hadn't been injured.

"You really don't remember?"

Harlow shook her head. "Tell me."

Thea crouched in front of her, looking up at her with luminous eyes. "I asked you how you got hurt and you said you fell down the stairs on your way out. You said you were crying too hard and you tripped. I asked why you were pounding on the door, but you were in so much distress that I couldn't understand you." Thea sighed, as though the memory was physically painful for her to recall. "I took you to a healer right away. Kylar Bane. You don't remember?"

"No," Harlow said. "Wait, Kylar Bane? The healer they found in the river last winter?"

Thea nodded. "Yes. Are you saying you don't remember seeing her? I left you alone with her for a while, because you kept trying to talk to me about what had happened and you were so upset she couldn't treat your wounds."

Harlow shook her head. "I don't remember any of that. Just waking up the next day."

"Shit," Thea swore. "I never thought to ask you... But it is strange that she was killed so shortly after treating you, isn't it? At the time, I thought it was because she was helping humans to have unplanned children, but now..."

Harlow nodded. "It's too much of a coincidence. We should look into it as a part of all this. I'll talk to Finn about it tomorrow. We just need to try to get through tonight first."

Her sister's arms wrapped around her. "Did Mark hurt you, Harlow? I'm sorry, I know I should have asked sooner. But did he?"

Harlow looked at the floor. "He didn't hit me ever. But he broke things that were important to me. It wasn't like he was flying off the handle and throwing a random glass, or anything like that. He chose things that were special to me, and broke them."

Thea's grip on her hand tightened.

"And once I woke him after a night he'd spent out with other women. He was supposed to be at a meeting with his father. He was going to be late. So I tried to wake him up, but he wouldn't rouse. I shook him, I was worried something was wrong with him. So I dumped a glass of water on him and he woke up."

"You don't have to talk about it, if it's too hard."

Harlow shook her head. "I want to say it. He woke up fast, so fast I don't even really know how it happened. One second he was dead to the world, and the next he was awake, and he had me pinned to the wall, his hands around my neck. He was calling me a bitch, and there was just *nothing there* in his eyes. I think he was still drunk, or maybe on drugs, I don't really know. But I got out of his grip and locked myself in the bathroom with Axel. I stayed in there for hours until he left."

"How did he explain that?"

It was a logical enough question to ask, Harlow supposed, but it just proved that no one had ever treated Thea that way. Harlow was equally glad that her sister had no frame of reference, and consumed with envy. Thea had spent the majority of her adult life being cherished by one man who was utterly *good*, despite his parents and his upbringing. Alaric would never think to pull Thea apart over and over, just for the pleasure of seeing her wounded.

How wonderful it must be to be so unmarred, she thought wistfully.

"Nothing. He pretended it didn't happen when I asked him what happened. The other times, when he broke my things, he'd apologize, but that time he acted like I made it all up."

"Oh, Harlow." The pity in Thea's voice was unbearable. "When was that?"

Harlow's eyes drifted back to the floor. "About a month before he kicked me out."

"Why didn't you tell me? Or the maters?"

Harlow laughed, finally making eye contact with her sister. "Because every time I told him I would tell someone, he said, 'Tell them what?' and then he'd remind me that everyone who'd ever loved me left me, that he was the only one who stayed. He reminded me for days on end, until I stopped pushing back."

Thea's body tensed, hearing the things coming out of Harlow's mouth, things she was sure Thea thought didn't happen to girls like the Kranes, with families who loved them and happy childhoods. She had to end this conversation. She had to stop thinking about all this and play her part in the terrible evening ahead.

"I didn't think anyone would understand when I was in it. It's taken me months to sort this all out for myself. But I am fine now." Harlow stood, smoothing her robe. "I'm going to get dressed. Could you give me a minute?"

Thea looked like she wanted to say something else, but she

just nodded and left the room. Harlow slipped out of her robe and into the dress Enzo had so lovingly made for her. It was the deepest shade of sapphire blue, so dark it was almost black, with a neckline that plunged between her breasts. It was simple in every way, but for the sleeves that trailed off her shoulders and would drag on the ground behind her, draping beautifully in a cascade of weightless feathers. When she'd first seen it, she'd loved it. Tonight, she couldn't wait to have it off and be snuggled in bed with Axel.

She was struggling with the zipper when Thea returned. "Oh, thank goodness you're back, I can't quite—" She looked back over her shoulder to find Finn, in just his trousers and tuxedo shirt, untucked and unbuttoned.

"Thea asked me to come help you." His voice was rough and she saw the awe burning in his eyes. "Are you trying to kill me with this dress?"

Harlow was so exhausted from her afternoon of memory that she barely had the energy to feel. She definitely had no energy for banter, so she smiled weakly. "You're immortal. You'd be harder to kill than I'd like."

"Harls," he said, his knuckles brushing her cheek. "Thea said..."

"Please," she whispered, as she turned away. "Please. Can we not right now?"

She met his eyes in the mirror, and as the hollowness of her gaze registered in his, he nodded. She felt his fingers, warm and gentle as he zipped her up. His arms went around her waist, and she had no energy to decide if it was a good idea or a bad one.

"Lean on me," he said.

"What?"

"Lean on me. Now, tonight. Let me help you." He pulled her closer, his arms tightening around her. "Let me keep you safe."

The weight of what she felt sunk into her slowly as she

relaxed into his chest. He wasn't asking her to talk, to tell him anything. He wasn't asking her *for* anything. He was asking to be there for her, and for the life of her, she couldn't find anything wrong with accepting that offer. All her reasons for staying apart shattered as she let him hold her. Her shadows danced with joy as her resolve to do things on her own weakened, as though her magic came alive at the thought of letting him help her.

Strange, she thought to herself as she melted into Finn's embrace. He stood so still behind her, not tense, but almost afraid to disturb her as she relaxed into him. *I do actually feel better.*

They could do what they needed to do tonight. Pretend, if that's what they needed to do, and tomorrow... Tomorrow she could let him help her. They could call the Quinns together, ask what it would take to unlock that memory and free her, find out what that remnant of emotion was and solve it. She knew Finn would help her and she was tired of trying to do things on her own. When she'd decided, it had seemed like the best plan, but now she knew she needed help, and he was offering it. Tonight, they could get through the finale of the season, and tomorrow they could have the future back.

"Okay," she said, sliding one of her hands into his and then the other, turning in his arms to face him. "I'll lean on you." She didn't qualify it with a timeframe. She meant what she said. She would lean on him. Whatever came next, they'd do it together.

His eyes lit with an unspeakable joy. "Let me go grab my jacket and then we can go."

She nodded, and sank back into her chair, depleted. Harlow didn't know how they'd get through the next few hours, but she was determined to get tonight over with, because tomorrow her future could finally begin.

CHAPTER THIRTY-FIVE

The Solstice Gala was held each year at Nuva Troi's massive botanical gardens. Tonight, the Jardin was lit with thousands of tiny witchlights, giving the hundreds of topiaries and enormous mosaiculture figures scattered throughout the grounds an even more surreal quality than usual. Everywhere Harlow looked, flowers had burst into bloom, filling the air with a heady natural perfume. Beds of irises created a wash of blue as they entered the enormous, elegant conservatory. Finn's hand stayed firm against her back as they moved through the crowd.

The rest of her family would arrive separately. They'd agreed that since the big distraction of the evening would be Finn's proposal, that it would be better not to socialize together. That way the others would more easily observe the crowd's reaction to Harlow's acceptance—the McKays and Velariuses, of course, being of particular interest.

"Lo, you look *stunning*."

Harlow turned to find Kate Spencer looking fairly stunning herself, in a white pantsuit covered in thousands of sparkling sequins. Her slender, athletic body was accentuated by the cape that fell from her muscular shoulders to the floor.

Finn grinned and the two of them hugged. "It's great to see you, Kate. Why haven't we gotten out on the water?"

Kate ran her eyes over Harlow. "I heard you've been busy."

Finn's arm was relaxed around her as she watched them interact. They seemed to genuinely be friends. Something warmed in her chest at the thought. That meant that if she and Finn were together, she and Kate could have a friendship of their own. Nothing like that had been possible with Mark. He'd been even more jealous when he understood that her attraction wasn't limited in the slightest by gender. Everyone had become a suspect after that. She lost track of what Finn and Kate were saying as she watched the crowd swirl around them.

The conservatory was warmer than she'd like—too many people, too much movement. The now-familiar feeling of being watched crept over her skin, causing goosebumps to raise on her arm, despite the heat. Next to her, Finn tensed, as though he too sensed something amiss. Finn's eyes slid to her bare arm, and the pressure of his hand on her waist increased.

Kate's eyes followed his and her voice was low when she asked, "What's wrong?"

"I don't know yet," Finn murmured. "Dance together while I get some drinks?"

Harlow nodded, wondering at how easily he trusted Kate. How quickly they'd fallen into an attitude of camaraderie. How had they achieved that? Kate's arms slipped around her waist and they joined the dancers at the center of the room.

"What's going on with you and Finn?" Harlow asked, keeping her face pleasant and her voice low.

Kate raised her eyebrows. "Jealous?"

A little laugh bubbled out of Harlow's chest. "Nope. I'm glad of it."

Kate's gaze softened. "Me too."

The energy in the room was shifting. Harlow felt a ripple of anxiety wash over her, and then aggression. She found herself wondering if Kate might be lying to her, if she and Finn were keeping secrets from her. Maybe they'd had a relationship in Nea Sterlis, when Finn was at Aphelion. As they turned on the dance floor, her suspicion grew. Her cheeks flushed. Had they planned this? Was this all a ploy to humiliate her?

Her shadows flickered inside her, soothing her, cooling the heat building in her. She blinked. Kate was watching her carefully, concern in her eyes. "What's going on, Lo?"

Harlow tried to stay calm, but her emotions spun out of control. "I honestly don't know. You still only like women, right?"

Kate laughed, loud and hearty. "Yeah. I don't see that changing anytime soon. Why?"

Harlow shook her head. "I just had the strangest worry that you and Finn might have something going on..."

The concern deepened in Kate's eyes. "That's not like you. You've always trusted people *too* much, in my opinion."

Enzo's words echoed in her mind: *This was something else... A remnant of rage, but it wasn't like anything else in you.* Of course. Whatever was happening now was the same as it had been in the park with Petra. A tiny seed of her real feelings had magnified, amplified to an irrational level she didn't actually feel. Except that she did. The emotions coursing through her *felt* real.

Something stirred deep within her memory, as though beyond the comprehension of her conscious mind, things were beginning to come loose and pull together to make a larger picture. Enzo's words played over and over in her mind, and suddenly she thought of the book she'd been cataloging the day she'd first visited Enzo's atelier. What had it been? *Lore of the Lilu.* Panic broke loose in her and though she tried to stay calm, Kate obviously knew she was distressed.

Before Kate could ask questions, she asked one of her own.

"What immortal creature can change the emotions of other immortals?" she said softly, knowing all too well that Kate would know the answer immediately. Empaths could smooth emotions, or impart some of their own feelings in those they were close with, but they couldn't actually change anything anyone felt, or make their feelings more intense. This was something different, something menacing and wrong.

"No..." Kate breathed. "It's forbidden. Not even the House of Remiel could make an incubus. It's impossible... The Illuminated made sure of it—they screen for Gene-I in the mandatory screenings at the monthly donations. Whole human families have been wiped out because one member carried Gene-I."

Harlow resisted the urge to ask Kate how she knew that. For obvious reasons, vampires always knew more about how the screenings at the Night's Own Blood Banks worked, and what was done with that information. They didn't have time for that conversation now. "How long would it take for a human to make the full transformation?"

Kate spun Harlow in time with the music, and Harlow couldn't help but be impressed with the calm exterior she presented. "About six months. Maybe nine for the incubus to grow to full strength, and until the last few weeks of the transformation they'd appear as a human would. But Harlow, even if they could make one, why would they? The incubi were uncontrollable, nearly unstoppable at full strength, even for the Illuminated."

Harlow nodded, then pulled Kate off the dance floor. "We have to find Finn. Now. He isn't by the bar."

Kate grabbed her arm. "Tell me what is going on here."

"Athan Sanvier and the House of Remiel tried to kidnap me a few weeks ago. He implied that he could do something terrible to me. *Change* me."

Harlow searched the room for Finn, or Alaric, or anyone in her family, but they were nowhere to be seen. Kate's brow furrowed, watching her. "Okay, but we'd know if Athan were an incubus. He's the worst kind of vampire, but Harlow... That's not something he could hide. Not for hundreds of years. And besides what would he do to you—*No*."

She glanced back, shaking her head as Kate realized what she had. "Only an incubus can turn a sorcière into a succubus. I thought he was being cruel, using our biggest fears against me, but maybe he was telling the truth..."

It had been foolish to dismiss his threats so quickly, impossible as they'd seemed at the time. Harlow began to move through the edges of the crowd. If none of her family or the Knights were inside, maybe they were outside. She tried to appear casual, but she was tugging on Kate's arm rather hard as she walked outside, onto the lawn that dropped off in a steep hill towards the lake.

Behind her Kate murmured, "And only a witch can become a succubus. Fuck, why didn't I see this coming?"

Harlow looked back, confused. "Why would you?"

Something flickered across Kate's face in the moonlight that Harlow couldn't identify, and she didn't have time to worry about it. Sounds of a struggle came from the lake. Harlow started towards the noise, but Kate gripped her arm. "Don't go down there without backup. Just wait here and I'll get help, okay?"

Harlow nodded as Kate pushed her gently behind an enormous oak. Her face was stern as she tapped Harlow's nose. "You promise you'll wait?"

She nodded again and Kate used her vampiric speed, disappearing back into the conservatory in the blink of an eye. As soon as Harlow knew she was out of range to keep tabs on her, she started towards the lake. There was no way in seventeen hells she was leaving her family in trouble. If that's what was going on here, she would find a way to help them.

Her heels sunk into the soft ground, so she slipped out of

them, hiding them under a blooming lilac. She snuck towards the lake, pausing every so often to duck behind a bush and listen. She was sure she heard Mama's voice, as she got closer, though she couldn't make out what she was saying.

As she rounded a corner in the hedgerow, she got her first sight of them, a group of hooded figures, holding on to a handful of the people she loved most in the world. Her sisters and Enzo were nowhere to be seen, nor was Alaric, she noted with relief, but they had the maters—and Finn.

How in Akatei's name were they holding him? Why didn't he portal out?

She squinted, trying to see better. It took two of the figures to hold Finn, but he wasn't struggling. One of them had what could only be a white ash stake positioned above his heart. Her chest clenched. It couldn't kill him, but if they staked him, it was hard to say what might happen. No Illuminated had suffered that fate for so long, it was impossible to say exactly how it might affect him.

Harlow took a few steps backward, thinking to go back to the conservatory to find Alaric, and perhaps Kate, though she wasn't sure exactly how Kate could help. She backed into something—no, some*one*.

"Dollface. So glad you could join us."

Mark. Fingers dug viciously into her arms and all went dark.

CHAPTER THIRTY-SIX

When Harlow came to, she was woozy. An acrid smell of burned wood filled her nose. Her head ached as though she'd been drinking for hours. She struggled to open her eyes, move, anything, and found her arms were restrained. Voices were arguing nearby, only slightly muffled.

A feminine voice complained, "You were supposed to get them *all*, not just her and Finn." *Was that Olivia Sanvier?*

"All we need is them."

That was definitely Mark. Harlow fought against the restraints as she struggled to open her eyes. They were heavy, too heavy.

"But now someone knows we took them. That wasn't the plan. Aurelia Krane can make trouble for us."

"You're worried about the wrong people," said a groggy voice. Finn.

Harlow forced her eyes open and her vision swam. She watched as Mark Easton backhanded Finn hard enough to make his body strain against the chains that held him. His face was bloody and beginning to bruise. How was Mark strong enough to harm him? No human could hit one of the Illuminated hard enough to bruise them.

They were in a dark room. Everything in it was dirty... No, sooty. Were they in the burned-out House of Remiel? She looked around as much as she could in the dim light. Her vision was still unfocused, as though she'd been drugged. In the distance, she saw shallow windows. They were in a basement. Probably the House of Remiel's basement, given the red velvet of the chairs that surrounded a scorched table at the center of the room. She'd only been to the House of Remiel a few times, but the red velvet was ubiquitous and memorable. Her throat hurt as she swallowed.

As Mark turned towards her, her entire body went cold and rigid. *How could she have been so stupid? Why hadn't she put this together sooner?*

Mark had turned into a thing of nightmares. His once-brown eyes had turned a muddy shade of red, his skin gone pale with an unnatural grey undertone. He was the thing under the bed that little witches feared: an incubus who could steal her heart. No, that wasn't right. That was just a children's story.

She wracked her brain trying to remember exactly what kind of danger she was in, but her mind was still cloudy... Then she remembered. He could turn her into a succubus, a creature whose only purpose in life was to seduce and drain the lifeforce from their victims. All her magic would disappear, everything she was would disappear.

A wave of fear washed over her, intensifying until she was so terrified she vomited, the bile burning her sore throat. *Had she already vomited?* She looked down to find her dress was already stained.

"Dollface, you ruined your pretty dress," Mark said with a fiendish smile.

There was nothing left of the boy who'd held her hair when

she puked in uni. She'd thought he'd been a monster when they ended things, when he wouldn't let her have Axel back out of spite, but she hadn't known how bad he could be until now. Now, it didn't take an explanation to see that he was perfectly willing to harm her. She glanced at Finn's bloody face. Her and Finn both.

She vomited again and Finn struggled towards her, the chains binding his hands above his head clanging, causing her ears to ache. "Get her some water," he growled.

"No," Mark said, hitting him again. "The little bitch can soak in her own stench."

"What have you done to me?" Harlow asked, her voice coming out in a croak. She had to distract him from hitting Finn again.

Mark turned to her, his ugly red eyes narrowing as he focused on her. In a flash he was in front of her, stroking her cheek with his icy grey fingers. He was nearly as fast as one of the Illuminated, she'd hardly seen him move.

"I haven't done anything to you... yet, Dollface. You need to be awake for the ritual. But now that you're up, we can get started."

Olivia Sanvier stepped out from the shadows, her arms curling around Mark's waist. The look on her face was one of pure malice. "Now that Heifer Harlow is awake, what games should we play with our fattened prize?"

Mark smiled, but didn't answer. Harlow saw something in his expression that belied whatever he truly felt. *Was he annoyed with Olivia?*

Olivia stepped forward. "She's already so pathetic, with her stupid little cat, and her frumpy clothes... Gods, even Enzo Weraka couldn't do something to make her look glamorous." Olivia's moonstone eyes locked onto Harlow's. "Why *are* you so pitiful, Harlow?"

Hot tears slipped down Harlow's cheeks. She was furious,

and when she was angry, she often cried. It was a weakness she'd hated, but now it seemed to fill a purpose. As tears splashed onto her dress, she saw the revulsion it evoked in Olivia. Anything to stall them. She had to think of a way out of this before they began whatever infernal ritual they'd unearthed to turn her. She had the terrible feeling that her first feed as a succubus was meant to be Finn. She couldn't let things get that far.

"Ugh. She's crying." Olivia slapped her face, her nails dragging across Harlow's cheek, drawing blood as she went. "What do *you* have to weep about, you spoiled little cunt?"

A roar erupted from Finn's throat. He seemed to be fighting some unseen force. Mark was manipulating his emotions, pushing him somehow. Harlow didn't know the technicalities of how an incubus' power worked, just that they could control what anyone felt, and the Illuminated were not immune. He was torturing Finn. If only she'd dug deeper, paid more attention to *Lore of the Lilu* when she had it right in front of her. Or any of the dozens of books in the Monas that explored the taboo lore of the Order of Night's most dangerous creatures.

A sob choked her as Olivia hit her again, this time in the stomach. She doubled over, letting her head fall forward. She *had* to think, buy them some time. Outwardly, she cried harder, since it provoked Olivia. Inside, her shadows roused. The sounds of Finn's cries of rage and pain lit something within her that seemed to block some of the effects of Mark's power.

If she could distract them, she might be able to get free. And then what? She hadn't trained to use her shadows in combat. She wouldn't even know where to start. Fear gripped her. She was tempted to shove it down, but her shadows didn't like that. Instead, she leaned into her fear, embraced the idea that she was scared. *She was scared because the man who'd hurt her, the people who'd hurt Axel, were hurting Finn.*

And she *loved* Finn. She was *in* love with him. Her future was with him, doing the work he'd started with the Knights of Serpens, and these two would not take that away from them. Her magic swelled within her as her fear transformed into something else. Something she could *use*.

Olivia punched her in the jaw. Either she wasn't trying very hard, or something about Harlow's magic protected her from the full impact of these blows. Finn wasn't faring as well. Whatever Mark was doing to him was wearing him down. His skin had begun to dull, losing its usual faint luminescence that hinted at his power. She wondered how long they'd tortured him before she woke up. It was obvious Mark and Olivia meant to kill him, and turn her into a mindless beast, but why? This was all too much just for the sadistic pleasure of being cruel.

"Why are you doing this?" she asked, injecting as much fear as she could into her voice without sounding as though she was putting something on. She still wasn't sure what to do. She needed to keep them distracted, see if she could get Mark to pay attention to her, rather than Finn.

Olivia laughed. "Are you really so stupid?"

Harlow sobbed quietly, lowering her eyes as though she was frightened. "*Why?*"

Fingers gripped her chin, Olivia's nails dug into her face. "We're going to stop you and the golden boy here from spawning whatever little abomination the Illuminated want."

That was it? The Order of Night believed, as the McKays did, that a child begotten between them would be some kind of powerful creature. It all made a sick kind of sense. The Order of Night wouldn't just kill them, they'd turn Harlow into a succubus to prove that they could. To prove that they could still make the most volatile immortals Okairos had ever known and wreak havoc on the world. This was all some stupid power play between immortals.

Mark turned as Finn sagged against the chains. Finn's eyes

fell shut and Harlow fought panic, waiting, watching his chest. His lungs expanded, but his breath was too shallow. Olivia's phone buzzed and she stepped out of the room, her voice muffled as the sound of her footsteps died away. Harlow reached inside herself. She needed to do something now, while Olivia was gone, use her magic to help them both.

Mark's voice broke her concentration. "No babies for you, Harlow. Just an eternity of fucking and sucking."

Her heart sang with pleasure at the idea, but only for a moment. Her shadows fought it off at the source, understanding dawning on her. He'd been following her, influencing her feelings. Planting seeds of doubt, rage, and gods knew what else in her. But now that her shadows knew where the threat was coming from, they fought it. She felt better almost immediately, but she couldn't show that. She felt the influence of Mark's power, its intention, and she arched her back, moaning softly as she pushed against her restraints.

It created the desired result. Mark's lips curved into a seductive smile. "Just like that, Dollface. Wait until you see all the ways I can make your body sing for me."

Finn's eyes met hers as he raised his head slightly. He was in pain still, but she saw that like her, he'd been exaggerating how hurt he was. As Mark turned back to him, he grinned at Finn, his new fangs glinting in the dim light of a lantern as he patted Finn's cheek. "Poor boyfriend, maybe I worked him too hard that last time. That little show should have made him very angry."

Mark walked over to Harlow, caressing her cheek. "I missed you, Dollface. But now we're going to be together, forever. No more Order of Mysteries. No more stupid witches. Just you and me."

Olivia returned to the room, fury written all over her face as she glared at Harlow. "And me."

Mark smiled, looking for a moment like the handsome co-ed Harlow had fallen in love with. "Of course, Liv."

His voice was smooth. Too smooth. Harlow wasn't sure why Olivia didn't hear the lie in his words. She knew that tone all too well. The vampire princess was pouting now, and he wandered over to her, soothing her with touches and words. "We'll break her together. Use her up and then turn her. And then..." Now he stroked Olivia's jawline, planting kisses on her neck. "Then we'll feed McKay to her." So she'd been right, after all. Mark's hands roved over Olivia's body as he whispered, "You'll see, Liv. It'll be fun."

"Yes," Olivia said, her voice full of a desperate need for approval as she wrapped her body around Mark's.

Now who was pathetic? Still, this interaction gave Harlow time to try to figure out what to do to get them out of this. She sank down into her mind, the way she had before when she called up her shadows, but the glass wall that hid the suppressed memory of the night Mark kicked her out rose up in front of her instead.

In reality, Mark wrapped his arms around Olivia's waist, one hand sliding into the front of her pants. "Does that feel good, baby?" he crooned as she lapped Harlow's blood off her fingers.

"Yes," the vampire moaned. "Harder."

They weren't watching her, enraptured as they were with one another. Inside her mind, Harlow stood in front of the glass. The tangle of thorns that had been there before was gone now. The wet sound of Mark pleasuring Olivia broke through her ability to concentrate.

"Tell me about how you hurt her," Olivia begged. "Tell me about the poor little witch's fall down the stairs."

"Shut the fuck up," Mark said, his voice shrill. Harlow's entire body reacted to that tone so violently that Olivia's words almost didn't register. Almost. *The poor little witch's fall down the stairs.*

What fall?
What?
Fall?

In her second sight, the glass wall splintered into a million shards and she slid easily into the hole in her memory, living it again.

They were standing on the backstairs at Mark's apartment. Their apartment. Above, the moons were waning, barely emitting enough light to see by. The flickering light at the back door made her head hurt. Her eyes were swollen and tired from crying. She had a bag of her clothes slung across her chest and Axel was yowling in his carrier.

"Can't we work this out?" she pleaded. "It doesn't have to be like this."

Mark shook his head. "You'll always choose them over me, Dollface. My questions were innocent, but you proved I can't trust you."

"Innocent? You asked me to find out how to make a succubus, *Mark." Her voice was harsh; she hadn't even tried to modulate it into a tone he'd like better. This was a mistake she'd been making more frequently lately, and now she knew he'd make her pay for it.*

His hand flew towards her and she stepped backwards, almost falling down the steep concrete stairs. He caught her before she fell, tearing Axel's carrier out of her arms.

"Thanks," she said, quiet, but still not in the tone she knew he'd prefer. She wasn't going to grovel anymore. They could work this out in a healthier way, she knew it. Things had been good once, hadn't they? He was just going through a hard time.

"It was only a question, Dollface," he murmured. "But you overreacted, like you always do. You always have to make something out of nothing."

A part of her immediately believed him. Immediately lapped everything he said up. She was *overreacting, wasn't she? But there was a hard glint in his eye that scared her. Something about him was different than before. Something fundamental had changed, but she didn't know what. Her head tilted as she stared at him. She knew he was seeing someone else. He'd done it before, but this time something was different... but what?*

Mark watched her as her body instinctively shrank from him —something was wrong *with him—rage built in his shoulders and tensed muscles. Rage beyond anything she'd ever seen in him, flowing off him in waves that almost felt like* magic. *How had she missed this about him? What was she seeing?*

"Get out of here," he snarled, pushing her hard.

Her feet flew out from under her, and her spine hit the concrete steps as she fell, tumbling down, until she hit the ground with a hard crack to her skull. When she looked up, he'd gone inside, taking Axel with him. What had that been, that power he'd emitted? Had she imagined it? He'd taken her key and she had no way to get in now. Not without using magic, and she was too afraid to use any of her meager powers against him.

She looked down at her battered legs, sobbing, and crawled up the steps. Surely he was waiting on the other side of the door. He'd done things like this before to teach her a lesson. If she begged hard enough, he'd open the door and at least she could get Axel. Harlow crawled up the stairs and began to beat her hands against the door, begging him to open it.

Harlow's eyes opened slowly, her mind clear. He'd been turning, even then. Olivia, and whoever else was involved with this nightmare, must have turned him shortly after they'd started seeing one another. *How had she missed it? Had there been other signs?* She shook her head a little. Now was not the time for berating herself. She could feel guilty later.

Mark and Olivia were still going at it in front of her. The memory had come loose too late. She wanted to scream, but that wasn't going to help her, or Finn, now. Her shadows stirred within her, coming to life with her fresh clarity.

It wasn't too late, now she was free. Something inside her

that had stayed shut tight since that night had opened, and she was finally free of Mark Easton, once and for all. She'd been afraid to use magic on him back then, but she wasn't now. The trouble was how to use her shadows best.

"Fuck me now," Olivia begged. "Make her watch."

"No," Mark replied, his voice rough. "Let's turn her, and then we can watch her destroy McKay."

Olivia pouted, rubbing her ass against the front of Mark's body, writhing seductively as she rode his hand. Harlow knew she didn't have much time. Mark would get his way, because he always got his way. She went deep inside herself to where her shadows waited patiently.

No more chains, she directed them with new confidence. *No more chains for me or Finn.*

The threads of aether surrounding the chains pulled apart, softly, slowly as they disintegrated into nothing.

Olivia cried out again. "Fuck me, baby. Make her watch."

Mark spun Olivia to bend her over the large, sturdy table at the center of the room. Harlow didn't have time to watch them too carefully; her arms were free, the chains truly gone. Across the room, Finn stumbled but caught himself as the chains disappeared. He was far worse off than she was, and she saw it then, the splinters of white ash protruding from his chest.

He shook his head once, looking down at them. He didn't need to say anything for Harlow to understand. He couldn't help her fight them off or portal them out; the white ash was affecting him too much. If an Illuminated at the height of their power would struggle to fight an incubus, how would she fare alone?

"I told you what I wanted, Olivia," Mark growled. And before Olivia, or Harlow for that matter, knew what was coming, he twisted the vampire princess' head clean off her shoulders. Her body fell to ash. Harlow only saw it in her peripheral vision, because she was watching Finn, watching the helplessness in his eyes turn to resolve. He motioned for her to come to him, one finger barely crooking towards him.

She didn't have time to consider the horror of what Mark had just done, or the realization that she and Finn were very likely next. She had to move. It was a risk. Mark still had his back turned, but any motion would alert him to their freedom. Harlow trusted Finn though and she ran for him, sliding into his arms as she tripped on the hem of her dress. He dragged her up, turning her so she faced Mark as he twisted around.

A look of surprise crossed the incubus' face, seeing they were free. Then he laughed. "I don't know how you got rid of those chains, Dollface, but it doesn't matter. You can't get away. Neither of you can. And now that Olivia is gone, we're going to have some fun together."

Finn's arms went around her waist, his mouth at her ear. "I figured out how the Striders shifted. Trust me?"

She nodded once, knowing he referred to the Feriant. If he knew how to help her shift, it might be the only chance they had, because otherwise, even with her shadows, she knew she couldn't handle him.

Mark's head tilted, his eyes narrowed. "What are you whispering in my dolly's ear, McKay?"

"I'm saying goodbye," Finn said, his voice clear and strong.

Mark laughed, sinking into a half-burned chair, apparently unconcerned by this. "Should I kill him first, Dollface, or do you want him to watch us after I turn you?"

Something about his transformation had deranged him. The way Mark laughed, how easily he'd killed Olivia, made her think the transformation to an incubus was different than a vampire's usual amplification of personal qualities, good or bad. Though, of course, it was possible this was Mark's true self.

Finn's grip on her waist was firmer now as he pressed her against him, careful to keep her back from the shards of wood in his chest. "I'm sorry, Harls," he murmured. "I didn't want it to be this way."

Mark's head fell back as he laughed, his eyes closing in apparent mirth. "Boo-hoo, he's sorry." Mark's laughter rang through the burned-out basement. He turned from them to face the table he'd bent Olivia over only moments ago. Whatever power he had as an incubus was so great that he didn't care that the two of them were free. His shoulders shook with laughter as he began to adjust a series of instruments laid out on the table. Harlow hadn't seen them before, but now she recognized them as a set of tools any sorcière would know: he was preparing for a ritual.

"Say your goodbyes then." He waved his hand at them, as though what they did didn't matter.

Mark may have misunderstood Finn, but *she* knew what he'd meant. He'd wanted this all to go differently. For them to figure this out together. She wished she could tell them that they still would. That if this worked, they'd never be apart again—she had to believe there was still time for all that. Harlow's eyes fell closed and she tried to relax as much as she could into Finn's hold on her. Whatever was coming, she knew she couldn't react, or Mark would spring into action.

Finn's fangs slid into her neck, venom burning through her as he pulled blood from her in several strong draws. Euphoria lit her soul, even through the pain. Lightning fast, he spun her, using the last of his energy to bite open his own wrist, pressing it to her mouth. She was only confused for a moment. When his blood hit her tongue, her shadows sang.

"What the fuck are you doing?" Mark screamed, turning at the sudden movement.

Harlow did not stop, pulling mouthful after mouthful of Finn's blood into her. Her power shifted, grew, fluctuating within her in such a way that she vaguely remembered what it felt like to get high. This was so much more. She was connected to the center of the limen, the space between all worlds, the dark home of the aether. In this moment, she was connected to the heart of the limen, deep in its swirling depths. Just as she felt the attention of the heart's inhabitants begin to turn her way, her spirit form pulled back, just enough to keep her safe.

Finn's voice broke her heady reverie. "I *told* you." There was so much unbridled arrogance in his voice that it caused a feral grin to spread over her face. "Saying goodbye."

Harlow stepped out of Finn's arms, raw magic pulsing in her veins, racing through her. Her shadows danced with pleasure as she healed completely. She wasn't sure what the mechanics of shifting were, but as it turned out, it was much like anything else with her manifested powers. She just had to want it enough. And she *did* want it. More than anything in the world, she wanted an end to this.

"Goodbye, Mark," she said, just as her mouth disappeared. Her humanoid body dissolved into something avian, lethal and without a shred of doubt about what to do next.

Her new body launched at Mark as he stood, mouth hanging open as her razor-sharp beak ripped into his throat, one of her talons making short work of his bowels. The stench was unbearable as his guts spilled out. Ichor spilled in her mouth, dribbling over her beak as she snapped ferociously once more, severing his head from his body completely.

She let go of the body, letting it fall. It didn't turn to ash the way a vampire's would, but the flesh disintegrated all the same, leaving behind Mark's skeleton. Her wings longed to stretch free, to fly out of this place, but she was too large for the door. A rustle behind her caught her attention. She turned, a long trill emanating from her throat.

Finn stumbled against the chair Mark had been sitting in. Finn. He needed her help. She shifted from talon to talon awkwardly. *I can't change back*, she said, speaking directly into Finn's mind.

He smiled, as he pulled splinters of white ash from his chest. "Give yourself a second to come down from the high." He was remarkably calm, given the fact that she was an enormous bird. She watched him pull the ash from his chest. "Fucker splintered that stake and then shoved these into me one by one. Really glad you were out for that part of things."

Her head tilted, and she knew how much of a bird she was in that moment.

"I may have cried a little," Finn said with a grimace as he yanked a particularly large splinter out, tossing it to the floor. His tuxedo shirt was torn open; underneath he wore a shirt that said "Cat Dad Extraordinaire" on it. The humor in his voice soothed her.

"*What are you wearing?*" Her voice came out of her mouth. She looked down at her very humanoid arms and legs. She was stark naked.

Finn looked up. "Is it messed up that I think you look *super* fuckable right now?"

She laughed, but tears streamed down her face at the same time. "We have to get out of here. This is the House of Remiel, right?"

He nodded, yanking another splinter from his chest. "I think that's the last one."

"Can you portal?"

He paused, then shook his head. "Not yet. But the good news is that we're in the basement." He stripped his ruined tuxedo shirt off, tossing it aside. "We're near the garage. We can take one of the vampires' cars."

Harlow nodded and started for the door. Finn caught her arm. "Slow down." He pulled his t-shirt off. "Much as I'm sure I'm going to regret this, can you please put this on so I can concentrate on getting us out of here?"

She took the t-shirt, yanking it on quickly. It covered her ass well enough. "Good?"

"No," he said softly, pulling her into his arms. "Not yet."

His mouth found hers. The kiss was gentle at first, then as she wound her arms around his neck, the intensity grew, heat building between them. When he pulled away, she felt his reluctance in the grip he still had on her hips. "Okay, now we can go."

CHAPTER THIRTY-SEVEN

They found the garage, behind a heavy metal door. "I guess this kept the cars from getting blown up in the fire?" Harlow remarked as she helped Finn pull the scorched door open.

It was concerning how weak he was, but she didn't say anything. Neither of them addressed the room they'd set on fire before leaving. "It'll be obvious they didn't die in the original fire," Finn had said as they left.

Harlow knew it was true, but there was nothing they could do. What she'd done...What *they'd* done... It was unthinkable. She'd turned into a giant bird and murdered her ex-boyfriend, after all. Sure, it was self-defense, but Harlow doubted that would matter much in light of her transformation into a mythical creature that had been hunted to extinction.

Finn pointed. "That one. Can you drive it?"

The sleek, black sports car was intimidating, but she nodded. "You want me to drive?"

He stumbled. "I think you're going to have to. I can get the car started if we can't find the keys inside, but then I'm going to need time to recover from the white ash."

Harlow helped him into the car, wondering if it had ever been driven. It still had a delicious new-car smell. There weren't keys anywhere that she could find. Finn pressed his hand to the dashboard, closing his eyes. The car revved to life and he slumped a bit in his seat.

"I'll be fine," he said, taking her hand. "Just get us home as quickly as you can, all right?"

She nodded, finding the garage door opener as she pulled out of the spot. There was no one around in the dark garage. Only one light near the exit flickered as though it was shorting out. She remembered the twins saying that the electrical had been damaged in the fire. As she pulled up to the garage door, she prayed to Akatei and Aphora that it would open.

Gods all bless them, it did, and she sped out of the garage and into the dark night. Outside it was pouring rain and she pulled into traffic. She wished she had her phone, but of course, it had been lost somewhere along the way, as Finn's probably had been as well. She glanced over at him and his eyes were drooping.

"Should you stay awake?" she asked.

He shook his head slightly. "No, sleep will help. Are you okay to get us home?"

Harlow nodded. They'd talked about what to do if anything went wrong, not that they'd anticipated anything like this. The plan was to meet back at Finn's, where Larkin had stayed home with Axel for the evening.

The streets were nearly empty, likely because everyone was home or at bars watching coverage of the Solstice Gala. It was only eleven o'clock. They hadn't even been missing for four hours. She took a risk and increased her speed, knowing everyone would be worried about where they'd gone. Soon, they were outside the city limits, past the suburbs and onto the road that led to Finn's house.

When she crested the hill, she cried out. Finn woke up. "Shit," he swore. "That's..."

"Our house," she breathed, hitting the gas as hard as she could. "Our house is on fire."

Panic flooded her and she felt Finn's hand on her thigh. "Pull over. I think I can portal us the rest of the way." She pulled over and he directed her to a small grove of trees. "This is part of our property, just pull into the woods. I'll send Nox and Ari back to deal with the car later."

She raced to the other side of the car to help him. He was still so weak. "Are you sure about this?"

He nodded. "Yes, just... hold on tight, okay?"

She did, and they blinked between, appearing on the driveway.

"Finn," she screamed as he fell to his knees.

Hands pulled him from her and she took in the inferno. Indigo and Meline ran towards them, and Alaric and Cian were already tending to Finn. The maters were nowhere to be seen, nor were the Wraiths. "Where's Larkin?" she shouted. "Where's Axel?"

No one seemed to hear her and she started toward the house. Hands yanked on her arm. "They're in the barn with your parents." She looked up into Petra's eyes. The girl threw her arms around her. "Thank all gods you're both okay," Petra murmured.

Alaric and Cian helped Finn into the barn, where the rest of her family, including Riley and Enzo, sat in folding chairs, wrapped in various blankets, despite the sticky heat. When Finn was settled in a chair, drinking from a bottle of water, he motioned for her. "Come sit with me," he said.

She hesitated. "I don't want to hurt you."

"You won't," he said, pulling her down into his lap. "I'm mostly just tired. A big nap and I'll be fine. I need you close."

She snuggled into his arms as he whispered, "They're going

to want to know what happened. Are we talking about the big bird?"

Harlow nodded. "I think we have to."

And so they did, everyone listening in silence. Harlow didn't know if it was the horrors of the night, or just general shock, but for once, her family was quiet. No one asked a single question. When Aurelia simply nodded, accepting everything they'd said, Finn asked, "Where are Nox and Ari?"

Cian answered. "They're containing the fire. We can't do anything about the house. I'm sorry."

Finn nodded. "What happened?"

Larkin shook her head. "I don't know. Axel and I fell asleep watching a movie. He woke me and the house was on fire. I called Mama and everyone came home. The fire department never arrived."

Alaric shook his head. "Fuck them, seriously. Fuck them."

Harlow frowned, looking to Finn for answers. He dragged a knuckle over her cheek, soothing her. "My parents. They have a tendency to do things like this as retaliation for betrayal."

He was so casual about it. His parents had set fire to their home, nearly killed her sister and Axel, and he sounded as though he wasn't the least bit surprised. All the things he'd told her about them started to add up. How scared he'd been of them, how worried he'd been they might hurt her. This was why, because he wasn't shocked that they'd burned his house to the ground for standing up to them. How was his heart intact? This wasn't the time to talk about that. Later, when they were alone.

"They could have killed my sister," she murmured.

"Not that I think they care about that," Alaric said, "but likely they assumed she'd be at the gala. They don't pay much attention to the intricacies of other people's lives."

Petra nodded. "He's right. It's likely they were sending a message, not trying to start a war between the Order of Mysteries and the Illuminated."

Harlow reasoned that the McKays simply didn't care who was hurt, so long as their message of intimidation was received. She wasn't going to argue with Alaric and Petra about that. Not right now. "What happened after we were taken? Did Kate find you?"

She noticed a look pass between Enzo and Riley. Alaric shook his head. "No, none of us talked to Kate."

Aurelia said, "Alaric and Cian found us, but not before the vampires portaled out with you. The two vampires who were holding us are in custody and being questioned."

"The *vampires* portaled?" Harlow asked.

"Incubi can do that," Selene commented, her face thoughtful.

"But... At the House of Remiel, it was just Mark and Olivia. And *she* wasn't an incubus. You're sure *both* of them portaled, they weren't touching?"

Aurelia nodded. "I'm afraid so. There are two of them."

"That is very bad news," Finn said quietly.

"What do we do now?" Larkin asked.

A long silence passed, while everyone thought. Harlow wondered how any of them were reasoning through this. She was dead tired, and hot. The barn was humid and the sticky air made her more agitated than she'd like to be right now. She squirmed in Finn's lap. He pressed a kiss to her sweaty cheek.

"I think we go home," Selene said finally.

No one looked particularly interested in that idea, not even Selene. With the McKays out for vengeance and the Velariuses not too far behind, going home—to any of their homes—felt dangerous. But it seemed to Harlow that no one else had any ideas about what their next move should be.

Cian held up a hand. "There is another option."

They all turned to look at the shifter. "What's that?" Aurelia asked.

Cian shifted in their folding chair, uncomfortable under

Aurelia's imperious stare. "We could catch the night train to Nea Sterlis. Maybe we need to visit the Vault. Get some distance between us and Nuva Troi for a while."

"What's the Vault?" Enzo asked.

"Technically, it's the Knights of Serpens original records space," Finn said. "It's under Cian's family home in Nea Sterlis."

"You don't have to come, if you want to stay," Harlow said to Enzo. "My guess is that this might all blow over for you if you put some distance between us."

Enzo shook his head firmly. "No. I go where my family goes." Riley took his hand and they smiled at each other. "Besides. I've been wanting to scout some locations for a shop in Nea Sterlis and who wants to suffer through a Nuva Troi summer?"

Harlow couldn't argue with that. Nuva Troi was crowded, humid and blisteringly hot for the months of Juli and Aout; things were only going to get worse from here. By contrast, Nea Sterlis was filled with sea breezes and a warmer climate for the entire year, so it was always refreshing in the summertime. After everything they'd been through, why not get away for a while?

"What about the Monas?" Meline asked.

"We'll have to close up shop for a while," Aurelia said. "The building should be safe enough, I should think."

"We can say Harlow and Finn got engaged, and we're going to Nea Sterlis to celebrate," Indigo said brightly. "It makes a romantic cover story."

Thea cleared her throat. "Maybe we should say that Alaric and *I* eloped, and you all came with us. That would make a better story, and as it's very nearly true, I think it might work better."

Thank you, Harlow mouthed to her sister, who nodded in return.

Nox and Ari returned as Indigo booked sleeping cars on the

two a.m. train to Nea Sterlis. "The blaze is out and we cleaned the vamps' car and left it downtown," Ari said.

Nox handed Harlow a bundle of clothes. "It's just sweats, and they're mine, but I thought you might want something else to travel in."

"Thanks," Harlow said, ducking into the barn's bathroom while Finn gave the Wraiths their orders. They were to keep an eye on things in Nuva Troi and meet them in Nea Sterlis in a month. No communication in between, unless they came in person.

When she came out of the bathroom, everyone was piling into cars and driving away. "I'm sorry about the house," she said as she got into the Woody's driver seat.

"Me too," Finn said. He was wearing a new t-shirt and his tuxedo pants, holding Axel in his lap. He craned his neck to watch the house for a long time as they drove away.

Chapter Thirty-Eight

When they reached Ambracia Station, valets took the cars to board in freight, and a concierge led them to their private sleeping cars. Enzo, as always when boarding a train, looked nervous, but Harlow was pleased to see Riley whispering something to them that made them smile. Her best friend waved as he stepped into the private room they would share and Harlow had the distinct sense Enzo would be all right.

Before she could go inside the car she would share with Finn, Petra pulled her aside, taking Axel from her. "I'll take this little monster tonight, if you like."

Harlow nodded, kissing the cat on the head as he purred loudly at Petra. "Thank you. I need to take care of Finn."

Axel rubbed his face against Petra's. He knew who would spoil him, and he seemed happy enough to go with her. Petra rubbed her nose to his, then turned to Harlow. "He needs to rest, Harlow. *Really* rest."

Harlow nodded sleepily. "Me too. I don't think I can keep my eyes open much

longer. I promise I'll let him sleep."

"He's going to kill me for telling you this." Petra sighed, and wiped a sheen of sweat off her forehead. "White ash can do some serious long term damage. He needs to shift and rest in his true form."

"All right," Harlow said slowly, not understanding.

Petra patted her shoulder, then covered a yawn. "Just tell him what I said. See you in the morning."

Harlow stepped into the car, just as the train began to move. She shut and locked the gilded mahogany door. The twins had fretted about having to ride in the second-class private rooms, but Harlow didn't care that they didn't have spacious suites. That they had privacy at all felt like a precious gift right now.

Finn was using their tiny bathroom, showering from the sound of things, which meant there was just enough room for Harlow to stand, alongside a double bed and a chair near the window. Much like the rest of the train, the second-class cars were lavishly decorated. The chair she sat in was sublimely comfortable, covered in a dark blush velvet with a pattern that made her tired vision swim. The bed looked comfortable, but a little small for the two of them, and it was tucked under an unfortunately low dip in the ceiling. When Finn came out of the marble bathroom, he was clean and looked like he might fall asleep on his feet.

"Wish we'd been able to book first class," he muttered as he hit his head on the low doorway. "I barely fit in here." The train picked up speed as he sat down on the bed, indenting the blue velvet linens. When she didn't respond, he kicked her lightly in the shin. "What's up?"

"What is your alternae?" she asked. "I've always heard that the Illuminated can shift, but I've never seen one actually do it. What's yours?"

Finn flopped onto his back, and his head sunk into the mountain of pillows behind him. "Fucking Petra," he growled.

She got up and crawled in next to him. His arm went around

her as he drew her close. Without thinking, she wrapped her leg around his, as her arm went around his middle. The way he played with her messy hair felt comfortable and sensual, all at the same time. "Yeah, she's such a bitch, wanting you to get better fast."

Finn's arm slid under her head as they turned toward each other. He kissed her sweetly, pulling back before either could deepen the embrace. "This is my alternae."

Harlow sat up, banging her head on the ceiling. "Fuck," she swore as he pulled her back down. He kissed her head, pulling her to his chest. She was confused; alternae were usually animal forms. They could be hereditary, though often there were other factors at work in what a shifter's alternae manifested as that Harlow didn't truly know. The ways of the Trickster's Chosen were mysterious to humans and the other Orders, as they were quite secretive. "What do you mean this *is* your alternae?"

Finn shrugged. "This is the form I wear all the time. My true form is underneath."

"Why?" she asked.

There was a long pause. Harlow waited patiently, listening to the steady noise of the train picking up speed.

Finn's eyes were dark in the dim light of the train car, his breathing even, but slightly labored. "If I tell you this, there is no going back. We can break up, but you will always be bound to me by this secret. Are you ready for that?"

What Finn didn't understand was that there was no going back for her, not now. Not ever. Like him, she had no idea what was ahead for them personally, but he had opened up her world in a way that she couldn't walk away from. His fight was hers, from here on out, and she wanted to know everything.

"I don't want to go back," she said. "Just forward, together."

She wanted to kiss him, but she didn't. The moment seemed too solemn for that. What they agreed to now was beyond love or lust, or just them. She felt the weight of that bearing down on her and accepted it without question or doubt.

When Finn spoke, his voice was marked by a distant quality, as though he had never spoken these words aloud. "The Illuminated are hiding on Okairos. Not that we get too many travelers from elsewhere, but it was decided when we got here that we'd never show our true forms in public, just in case."

"Hiding from what?" Harlow asked.

"The rest of our people. When we left our world, we were supposed to come here, wake magic, and begin training your people to fight in our wars. But the Illuminated that came in the original envoy were tired from the endless wars on our home world. They decided not to return. The way we got here was dangerous, and my parents didn't think it was likely that they'd be followed."

"Your parents were among the original envoy?"

Finn nodded. "Yes, and Alaric's parents, though none of them were bonded at the time. They were the leaders of the envoy, coworkers, essentially. When they arrived, the envoy was in terrible shape. After a few months here, they decided not to awaken magic at all, as it would alert their home world to their progress. While they were less worried about being followed, they knew their people would feel the shift in the balance of power."

"How?" Harlow breathed, amazed by the idea.

Finn shook his head. "I don't know. It's a secret they've guarded carefully, and it's likely that what I just told you is only part of the truth. Only my parents, Petra's and Alaric's were actually there. The rest are dead now."

"How many came with them, originally?" Harlow asked.

Finn sighed. "A legion, if what I was told is true."

Harlow's heart beat erratically. *And only six were left? What had happened to the rest of them?* Likely, many had died in the War of the Orders, and of course the original Knights of Serpens had been executed, but still. Only six of the original Illuminated remained. It seemed strange.

Finn continued. "Make no mistake, Harlow. My parents and the Velariuses, they are evil, but they are a lesser evil than those who ruled the planet they left behind. They'd endured centuries of pointless wars before coming here. It's why they were determined to keep the peace on Okairos instead, create a paradise. But you see the way it turned out."

"They had good intentions once," Harlow murmured, the rhythmic vibration of the train soothing her.

"They did," he murmured, yawning.

"So, if we awaken magic, will we broadcast something about Okairos to the rest of the galaxy? Something bad?" The thought was worrisome.

She twisted slightly to see his face. Finn shook his head. "To be honest, I don't know. It could have consequences. It's why we need to proceed carefully. But I don't think Okairos can go on this way, do you?"

Harlow shook her head, exhaustion creeping in. There was so much she didn't know, didn't understand. Part of her was frustrated that she had been kept so sheltered, so in the dark about all this. A more reasonable part of her understood the complexity of the problem. These secrets were dangerous for her, or anyone, to know.

Finn shifted next to her, his hand sliding up the back of her shirt as he pressed kisses to her eyelids and cheekbones. "Petra's right. If I don't want to spend the rest of the summer recovering, I'm going to have to sleep in my true form. You have to promise never to tell anyone about all this."

"Does Thea know?" she asked.

Finn yawned again, nodding. "Yes."

"I promise," she said, propping herself on her elbows. "Show me."

"You're sure?" he asked, hesitating.

"I am. We're in this together, so let's be *together* all the way, okay?"

His fingers traced the lines of her face, and she felt the aether in the room begin to move. He changed slowly, the pale shade of his skin turning to something nearly opalescent, a very light blue color. The dark brown of his hair deepened into ebony, with a bluish sheen. His face was mostly the same, but the angles of his jaw and cheekbones were sharper, and his teeth seemed larger, especially his fangs. In fact, he was larger overall, his limbs visibly longer, including his hands, which she took in hers as his fingers lengthened.

Aside from these changes, he was still obviously Finn; he looked much the same. Or at least he did until he rolled over. Three pairs of enormous wings sprang out as he rested his head on his muscular arms, which were covered in shimmering scales. "It's been a long time since I shifted," he said, watching her face carefully.

The wings were beautiful, closely resembling a firedrake's, she thought. In fact, from the scales to the wings, he very much resembled something distinctly draconic. She wondered if this was a part of what drew him and Cian together, if Cian felt more at home with someone who looked like this underneath their humanoid form.

"Am I hideous?" he asked, his eyes drooping heavily.

"Not a bit," Harlow said, pressing a kiss to his forehead. He needed to sleep, and she needed a moment to herself. "I'm going to clean up a bit."

"Shower's tiny," he murmured, already mostly asleep.

The bathing chamber was opulent, though, as Finn mentioned, tiny. Harlow peered at the blown glass tile in the floor, shaking her head. Such artistry was inspiring. She undressed and stepped into the narrow marble shower. The hot water flowed over her body, creating a tranquilizing effect, even as her mind raced. She washed absently with a finely milled soap that smelled like summer at the seashore. Everything she'd ever known about the Illuminated was wrong, and she tried to puzzle pieces together that blew her mind.

It wasn't that the people of Okairos were ignorant of the existence of other populated worlds; they learned about their existence in school. But the nearest was too far to travel to, even by spacecraft, and no other kind of reliable intergalactic travel had ever been developed. But of course, that was probably because the Illuminated had stopped any progress on such science. What had Cian said? *There is a world beyond what you know to be true, Harlow. Tonight is just the beginning.*

Of course Cian knew this secret, and looking back she understood that they had been sure she'd eventually know as well. Cian Herrington could be a good friend if she let them, she thought. She rinsed her hair, watching the grime of the night swirl around the drain and out of sight. As she got out of the shower, she couldn't bear to put Nox's clothes back on, so she wrapped herself in a towel.

When she entered the bedroom, Finn was fast asleep. His clothes had disappeared, folding themselves neatly on the chair, and he was covered to his waist by the blankets on the bed. His wings fluttered slightly in his sleep, but for the most part looked relaxed.

She crawled into bed. There wasn't much room for her with his increased size and the wings, but she was too tired to care. Something velvety stroked her arm, sending delicious shivers down her spine. Harlow looked over her shoulder to find one of Finn's wings wrapping around her, as his arm drew her into his side. She lost her towel as he moved her, but couldn't say that she cared much. Her skin flushed with wanton need as it made contact with his.

"You're back," he murmured in her ear as she reached out to shut off the lamp next to the bed. Every nerve in her body came alive as his hands made slow, languorous swirls around her breasts and belly, moving lower by the moment.

"Yes, and you're supposed to be sleeping," she said when the room was dark, curving her body to make as much contact with his as she could. One hand slipped between her thighs, teasing her.

"I napped while you bathed," he whispered. His voice was nearly the same, but seemed to have dropped another octave, and even at a whisper its depth vibrated within her as he murmured, "Now I'm *very* awake."

He moved next to her, covering her body with his in one fluid motion. In this form, he was even faster than he usually was, somehow even more graceful. His legs tangled with hers, their skin sliding against one another as he kissed her neck. Above them, his wings moved of their own accord. As his mouth reached one of her breasts, closing around her nipple, she reached up to stroke one of the arms of the wing closest to her. He shivered with delight.

"You need rest," she murmured as he sucked gently on her nipple, his fangs dragging sinfully over her skin.

"I need to be inside you," he replied, kissing her protests away. She needed him too. Every part of the day had been painful, hard, and confusing.

Her legs spread for him as he slid down her body, trailing kisses until he reached the center of her. His mouth closed over her clit, two of those extra-long fingers sliding into her. She moaned at the feel of his tongue tracing circles around her swollen flesh.

She pulled his head from her gently. "I don't want you exerting yourself. Come here."

He glided against her, his skin like silk in this form. She reached between them to take hold of his cock. That was bigger too, she noted. Big enough to make her wonder just exactly how this might feel. But his fingers still traced wicked circles around her clit as he kissed her deeply, his tongue dancing against hers as he moaned in her mouth.

She spread her legs a bit wider, guiding the head of him to her entrance as he moved his hand to brace himself above her. "Go slow," she murmured against his mouth. "I don't want you to wear yourself out."

He pushed into her, stretching her slowly, as warm, wet heat flooded her core, slick desire guiding him into her. Above her, his eyes glowed softly in the dark. "You can't believe how good this feels," he said, his voice rough. "I've never been with anyone in my true form."

"What you did earlier, to help me shift into the Feriant, was that the Claiming?"

she asked as he inched deeper inside her.

"No," he moaned, distracted by her. "That has to be during intercourse." He

slowed his descent into her, looking into her eyes. "You'll know when I Claim you. It will be both our choice, and you won't mistake it for anything else."

He thrust deep into her, taking her breath away with the sweet ache of him. He stopped then, pushing her damp hair from her face. "I'm so glad it worked. You were amazing tonight. You saved us both."

"I'm glad it worked too," she said, arching into him, drawing him further inside her as she clenched hard around him.

His movements were slow and steady as he rocked against her, his glowing eyes never leaving hers as she ground herself against his pelvic bone, her breath coming in quicker gasps each time their bodies met. Ecstasy of a new kind bloomed in her as the air around them filled with magic.

She stroked the arm of his wing again, then pressed her fingers lightly to the spot between his first set of wings. He cried out with pleasure as he moved in her, his mouth meeting hers in a desperate kiss as he came hard, his body shuddering with pleasure.

He didn't stop moving when he'd found his release, their wet spend creating more lubrication as he increased the strength of his thrusts. "Slow down," she murmured, worried about his condition. "It's all right. We can sleep, if you're tired."

In the dim light of the train car, she saw him grin. In this form, his smile was feral, alien and familiar at the same time, and her arousal mounted higher. "I feel so good, you have no idea. It's easier to heal in this form. My alternae slows everything down for me." His hand slid between them to rub her clit. "Let me fuck you," he growled in her ear. "*Please.*"

She was caged by his enormous body and she loved it, loved feeling his strength return, and the heat of his need for her. Underneath him, she drew back from him, feeling empty as she released his cock. She flipped onto her stomach, then raised herself up on all fours under him. He let out a primal noise when he realized her intention, his cock sinking immediately into the wet folds of her as his hands slid to her breasts, which he squeezed as he thrust hard into her.

His fingers worked her clit as he bent over her back, purring. "When it's time, when we decide it's right, I am going to Claim you over and over in this form. I'm going to sink my teeth into your neck."

Finn's other hand stroked her throat, showing her where he would bite her. She clenched around him, eliciting a noise from him so loud she was sure the entire train could hear. His free hand slid from her neck to her breast, pinching her nipples hard. She cried out with the pleasurable bite of pain. "And here."

"Where else?" she whimpered.

He flipped her onto her back, his fingers gliding between her thighs as he hovered over her, dragging his wet fingers towards her core. "Do you want me to bite you here?" he asked, tapping the inner crease of her thigh.

She nodded and he lowered his mouth to the spot he'd touched. His fangs dragged across the spot, stinging slightly. His velvet tongue lapped at the spot they scratched. Harlow's hips raised to meet his mouth as Finn's fingers moved closer to her center, tracing her sensitive flesh, wet from their encounter.

"How about here?" he asked.

"Yes," she begged as his mouth teased her.

The train rocked beneath them, bouncing her heavy breasts as he forgot about the game they played and dragged his mouth over her clit, plunging his tongue deep inside her as he drank her in. His fingers followed and she felt the sting of his fangs against her sensitive flesh and was surprised by how much she wanted to feel that bite of pleasure on her most sensitive skin.

He slid his body up hers, his lips capturing hers, the taste of her in his mouth as he thrust hard into her. Stars exploded behind her eyes, her shadows dancing with the bright light that he emitted as they came together, all six of his wings spreading taut above them as he cried her name.

When he slowed, she saw a glimmer of tears in his eyes that she knew were echoed in her own. She hugged him tightly, and spoke without hesitation. "I love you."

The quiver of his heartbeat against hers told her the depth of his reaction. An echo of the orgasm they shared throbbed between them, where they were still connected. Finn's hands dug into her hair and he kissed her deeply, thoroughly. When he pulled out of her, she no longer felt empty. He filled her with his words.

"I have always loved you," he said, with so much feeling that she thought she would sob at the sound of his voice. "And there is nothing in this world, or any other, that could make me stop."

Her kiss was tender as she left the bed to clean up. When she returned from the bathroom he was fast asleep, his breathing deep and slow. She watched him emit a faint glow, and saw that the wounds from the white ash on his chest were gone now.

Harlow's eyes were heavy as she crept into the space he'd left for her, his arms and legs, and wings, closing around her as soon as her skin made contact with his. When she fell into a deep and dreamless sleep, she did so knowing she was safer than she'd been in years, cocooned in their love, lost once, but now found.

CHAPTER THIRTY-NINE

When she woke, the train was still moving, but it was day. She was alone in bed. The bathroom door was open, and as she rose on her elbows, she saw it was empty. The window shades were drawn, but light streamed in from outside.

Just as she was about to get up, the door opened, and Finn walked through, his humanoid alternae back in place. She missed his true form already, but he looked better today. In fact, he looked to be in perfect health. He was also dressed in a luxurious looking white cotton t-shirt that clung to his chest in a tantalizing way, and a pair of linen pants that weren't quite his style. When she sat up, she saw he wore flip flops and held a large paper shopping bag. He looked sexy, but far, far too preppy for her taste.

It took everything in her not to laugh as her eyebrows raised. "That's quite the outfit, McKay. All ready for your seaside vacation?"

He smirked playfully at her. "It was what they had in the shop. I got you something to try on. Larkin helped. We should be in Nea Sterlis in an hour. We slept through most of the trip."

The bag he held must have clothes in it. She yawned, still sleepy, but she felt clean and refreshed. The horrors of the Solstice Gala felt like a dream. Harlow blushed when she realized she wasn't dressed, and Finn was staring, leaning against the bathroom door, a seductive look playing in his eyes.

"You don't have to dress, of course," he said, pouncing on her at lightning speed. "We could have breakfast here."

"There's nothing to eat here," she countered. She *was* hungry, and she needed tea.

"I beg to differ," he murmured in her ear, pulling the covers down further to trail kisses down her throat and breasts. "Though, we *have* already been accused of keeping others awake last night."

They both dissolved in laughter and he hugged her tightly as she cuddled into his open arms. Here in their nest of pillows, she felt like happiness was a true possibility. The memory of the previous night, of Mark and Olivia marred that feeling.

"I killed Mark," she said, her words sticking to the roof of her mouth.

Finn's arms tightened around her. "You did."

She thought about it for a moment. "I don't feel bad. Is that wrong?"

He loosened his grip on her and raised himself up on one elbow, playing with her hair. "No," he said slowly. "He was going to destroy us both. That was very obvious. And you were quick about it. Do you think he planned to offer either of us the same clean death?"

Harlow shook her head. "Will I be in trouble?"

Finn sighed and her heart sank. There would be consequences, she knew that. "I just got off the phone with my father."

"What?" she yelped. "Why would you speak to him?"

Finn sighed again. "He called, Harlow. He knew where we

were and he called here directly. I couldn't very well not take the call in front of a train full of people. I'm sure he knew that."

"What did he say?" she asked quietly.

"That whatever we'd done at the House of Remiel was justified, that it was cleaned up and that he and I are square. He said that he and my mother will back off, leave us in peace, leave the Order of Mysteries in peace. He said we should enjoy our summer."

Harlow's heart pounded in time with the sharp sound of each of Finn's words. "That is altogether too easy."

Finn nodded. "The worst part is, he meant every word. I can always tell when he's lying. The trouble is, *why...* Why back off now?"

They lay together in silence for a few moments, listening to the train. Muffled sounds of people moving about distracted Harlow for a time. "They got what they wanted. Or at least they think they did. You told them we were together, right?"

He nodded.

"Then they think they have us right where they want us. They think they engineered all this. Why do they think we killed Mark?"

"He congratulated me on eliminating my competition. He thinks I killed Mark because I was jealous. And before you ask, I don't think he knows about the incubi, and I didn't tell him."

Harlow nodded slowly. "That's good. We bought ourselves some time."

He turned to her. "We did. Speaking of that, I have something for you. Do you want to get dressed first?"

"Sure," she said, slipping from his arms, letting him watch her as she pulled out what he'd bought her. A long linen dress and a pair of flip flops were inside the bag, along with a silky set of panties.

She turned, watching him watch her as she pulled the

panties on, and then the dress, which was comfortable and loose, but very low cut. He moved in a flash to the edge of the bed, his long arms drawing her between his legs.

"You're so fucking beautiful," he sighed, his hands skimming the line of her generously curved hips. She ran a finger down the tattoo on the inside of his forearm, her eyes flicking up to his when his muscles tensed in response to her touch.

"Lilacs are my favorite flower," she said, almost feeling shy.

He caught her fingers, kissing them. "I know."

"And this moon is the same as the symbol on Akatei's temple."

He nodded, his face grave. "It is."

A small frustrated breath escaped her lips. She wished she could just ask him what it meant, but that seemed rude.

"I got this the year I found out about the Knights, Harlow." He drew a long breath in. "I wanted a reminder of what I was protecting. What I gave up my chance at happiness for."

"Oh." The single word couldn't convey everything she felt in that moment. Nothing could. "Did joining the Knights help?"

He stared at the window shade. "Yes, it gave me purpose. Something else to focus on, besides losing you."

She traced the lines of his face with her fingers, memorizing him in all his smoldering glory. She was the one with dark liminal magic, but he was the one who lived in the shadows. They complemented one another well, the perfect mix of dark night and golden dawn.

"We are going to have a good summer, you know that?" he said as her fingers brushed over his chest.

She nodded, pressing a kiss to his lips. They were warm against hers. His hands closed around hers, and a small velvet box appeared in her palm. She broke their kiss and looked down.

"You still have this?" she murmured.

He nodded slowly. "I'd like us to go out there and make a show of my proposal."

"Okay," she replied, knowing that it was the right thing to do. It would complete the charade, maybe even buy them a few more weeks or months of time to figure out their next move.

"Before we do that, I want you to know something, though. If you say yes now, everything I say out there will be real. I know it's probably fast, but..."

She interrupted. "Yes. I want it to be real. This is already real," she said, her palm against her heart. "I love you, and I don't care if it's fast. We've waited years for this."

Finn took her hand and kissed her palm. "Then come on, everyone is waiting for us." He bent down, sliding the flip flops onto her feet, returning the velvet box to his pocket. When he looked up at her, his face was relaxed and serious.

They left the tiny car that had begun to feel like the whole world to her; she let out a little gasp as the windows in the hallway let in a view of the coastline. Unlike the dark blue roiling waters that surrounded Nuva Troi, here the ocean was calm, and a deep aquamarine, with sandy beaches that stretched along the coastline as far as the eye could see. The train was rounding a huge curve as they entered the dining car.

Outside the windows, the white buildings of Nea Sterlis were stark against the rocky coast and myriad evergreen varieties that dotted the shoreline. The Alabaster Citadel that housed the Temple District rose high above the city, contrasting sharply with the dark sky. A storm was moving in, but perhaps it would pass quickly and they'd dine under the stars tonight. Harlow hadn't had the opportunity to spend more than a few days in Nea Sterlis, and she was looking forward to spending at least part of the summer in the Alabaster Citadel's many libraries.

Finn squeezed her hand, bringing Harlow's attention back inside the train. Her friends and family sat together at a small cluster of tables, already drinking tea and eating baskets full of buttery croissants. Harlow's mouth watered at the sight of them, but Finn shook his head, a smile curving one corner of his mouth as his fingers laced through hers. There were plenty of other people in the dining car, and most of them at least pretended to mind their own business, though Harlow thought at least one human couple was trying to take photos of Thea and Alaric. She reached for a chair and Finn stepped in front of her.

They were taking up the aisle of the dining car. She glanced back at the servers, worried they'd be upset, but she saw the trays of sparkling wine they held and their grins, and understood. Slowly, she turned to face Finn, her cheeks flushing as her heart beat so loudly she was sure the whole car heard.

"Hey, Harls," Finn said, the sound of his deep voice quieting all conversation in the car. He didn't say anything else, but dropped to one knee, taking her left hand in his. She saw him struggle for words, his throat bobbing. She brought his hand to her heart, a tear escaping, rolling slowly down her cheek as she nodded at him. A big speech wasn't necessary; they'd said everything they needed to in private.

He took the velvet box from his pocket, pulling her hand back to his level. "Be my girl?" he murmured, his voice rough with emotion.

"Forever," she agreed, as he slipped the sapphire ring onto her finger.

The dining car exploded with applause and cheers as he stood, sweeping her into a kiss so deep she was almost embarrassed to have her family witness it. *Almost.* In the background, she heard Aurelia comment to Selene, "I think we can stop worrying about Harlow drying up, my love."

"Indeed," Selene replied, sniffling a bit.

When they turned to take their seats at the table, the maters beamed with pride. Everyone talked at once, as was the way with her family, and she knew as she made eye contact with each of them that they understood the proposal was real, that she was finally happy.

Cian got up from the table to take a call, clapping a cool hand over her shoulder as they went. "Welcome to the family, Harlow," they said as they left the table.

"You too," she replied, smiling at Finn as Cian walked away. "Welcome to my family."

EPILOGUE

Rain pelted the sea, thunder crashing as lightning lit the sky. The speedboat bobbed on the waves, as Aislin McKay's skin turned a sickly shade of grey. "Why in seventeen hells did we have to meet here?"

"You know perfectly well why," Pasiphae Velarius said, her usually pleasant voice sharp as the boat sped further away from shore. Aislin didn't answer, but glared at Pasiphae before running to the bathroom. The sounds of her retching echoed through the cabin, punctuating each crash of lighting outside.

"Where is your husband?" Connor asked the Archchancellor, as his wife returned to the table, wiping her lips with a silk hanky.

"None of your godsdamn business," Pasiphae said, every inch the leader of the Illuminated. "Show me the photos."

Connor spread six photos on the mahogany table. The cabin of the speedboat was well appointed, like everything he owned, including his wife, who looked positively wretched but was at least outfitted well for the occasion in a dress that hugged her narrow frame.

A tiny whimper in the corner caught his attention. "Quiet,"

he commanded, his gaze narrowing at the creature, who shivered in the corner.

Aislin rolled her eyes. "I'll never understand why you need to bring your pets along at times like these."

Connor shrugged, tapping one of the photos to redirect Pasiphae's attention. "This is the one that shows the teeth. The bodies were burned, but you'll notice these are not the usual formation we see in vampires."

Pasiphae's mouth tightened as she looked closer. "No, they are not."

"We have a problem," Connor said.

Aislinn rolled her eyes. "Finn took care of it." Her skin was turning green now as the boat rocked wildly in the storm. "We *had* a problem, and now we don't."

The back of Connor's hand met Aislin's cheek before she could flinch away. "If I tell you we have a problem, *we have a fucking problem.*"

Aislin's eyes burned with hatred. Pasiphae sighed, exhausted by the two of them. They'd be fucking in the bedroom before she could get off the boat, of that she had no doubt; the Claimed were all the same. "What exactly *is* our problem then, Connor? I agree that it's not ideal that the vampires have regained the knowledge to create incubi, but as Aislin notes, the creature was destroyed. Your boy destroyed him. You know as well as I do that Gene-I is rare in humans. It's unlikely they'll be able to replicate their results."

Connor pushed a manilla folder across the mahogany table. Pasiphae's eyes glazed over with boredom. "Why am I looking at an MPU case file?"

"The dead incubus," Connor said, pointing to the photos of the burned bodies in the House of Remiel basement, "is Mark Easton. That case file is the MPU report on his father, Alain Easton, who is still missing."

"Oh," Pasiphae remarked, sipping her whiskey. "That does present a problem."

"It does," Connor growled.

"How did they get past us?" Pasiphae mused.

"Money, status... The Eastons have been buying their way out of their blood donations and family planning for generations," Connor said, his lip curling in disgust.

Pasiphae shook her head. "Our own corruption will be the death of us, Connor."

He rolled his eyes at her, clearly impatient to get on with things. "What's more, my people found traces of white ash on the floor of that basement. There's no way Finn killed the incubus on his own. Harlow Krane was with him."

There was a pause as the implication marinated, each of the women turning over the possibilities in her mind. "Impossible," Aislin said with a scowl. "That little cunt couldn't have helped him out of a cardboard box."

"Easton's head was severed," Connor replied. "Torn clean off his body. Finn couldn't have done that at full strength, not to an incubus, especially not one that was newly made. Unlike vampires, they're strongest in the first months of their reborn life."

"So what did this?" Pasiphae asked.

Connor sat back in his chair, glaring. "The *little cunt* is a Feriant."

"You don't know that," Aislin replied, getting up and pacing.

"No," Connor replied. "I don't. But I'm going to find out."

Pasiphae nodded. "We'll get people on it immediately. They all went to Nea Sterlis for the summer. We'll have them watched."

Aislin shook her head. "You'd better. What we buried in Nea Sterlis is too—"

"You don't need to tell me my business, Aislin," Pasiphae said, cutting her off. "I know the stakes as well as you do."

Connor rolled his eyes as the two most important women in his life glared at one another. "Enough arguing. Let's eat."

Aislin smiled, blinking across the room in an instant. "Come now, pet," she crooned to the human cowering in the corner. "It's time for dinner."

Outside, the early summer thunderstorm raged on, the sound of screams lost to the waves crashing against the rocky shore.

GLOSSARY

Aether: An elemental energy that is both life-giving and that generates magic.

Akatei: Patron goddess of the Order of Mysteries.

Alicorn: A heraldic shifter. An alicorn is a unicorn with wings.

Alternae: The non-humanoid form shifters turn into.

Aphora: Akatei's sister. Goddess of beauty, art and love.

Argent: A silver firedrake.

Bonded: Married.

Chimera: A heraldic shifter. Can appear as a combination of several different animals, but most usually has the body of a lion, a scaled tail tipped with poisonous spikes, and a pair of horns that resemble a goat's.

Firedrake: A heraldic shifter. Much like a dragon, a firedrake has the ability to breathe fire. It has two hind legs, and wings that can be used to fly, or operate as arms.

Gryphon: A heraldic shifter. Has the body of a lion, the head of a golden eagle and feathered wings.

Heraldic Shifters: Shifters thought to be extinct that have humanoid forms and alternae that resemble mythical beasts.

Often used in heraldic imagery to depict supernatural strength and nobility.

Incubus: A vampiric creature that feeds primarily off human and immortal fear and other strong emotions. Has the ability to manipulate emotions and is physically stronger than vampires and the Illuminated.

Pallyra: The ceremonial robes of the Immortal Orders.

Limen: The space between worlds, the spirit paths, the home of the "heart" where all aethereal energy comes from.

Mater(s): A word that means "mother" or "mothers."

Nea Sterlis: A city in southern Nytra. Home of the Alabaster Spire and the Temple District, which are known as the "citadel of the gods."

Nuva Troi: A coastal city in the Midlands region of Nytra. Home to the seat of the Immortal Orders, functionally the capital of the world. All of the most powerful immortals have homes in Nuva Troi.

Nytra: The most powerful country on Okairos.

Okairos: The planet that *Dark Night, Golden Dawn* takes place on.

Paired: Being in a committed relationship. Being paired does not necessarily imply monogamy.

Raia: Mother to Akatei and Aphora.

Solon Mai: The vernal equinox.

Succubus: A vampiric creature that primarily feeds on sexual energy. Only a sorcière can be turned into a succubus, and only an incubus can turn them.

Voltos: The Trickster deity and the patron deity of the Order of Masks. Voltos is genderfluid, and shifters are their "chosen" people, said to be blessed with Voltos' ability to see beyond natural perception and change forms, thus the common moniker "the Trickster's Chosen."

Author's Note &
Acknowledgements

I want to thank my mom for letting me watch so many soap operas as a kid. For a long time I misremembered, thinking that my first "dream profession" was to be a marine biologist. I'm glad I remembered this year that my actual first dream profession was to be a soaps writer.

The thing I love most about soaps is that yes, there's a lot of romance, but there's usually a lot of drama as well. And that drama is often a delightful mix of the interpersonal and something external, be it business, politics or otherwise. Growing up on soaps meant that I understood that romance was a big deal, but that all sorts of things could get in the way of a romantic relationship: family, your job, and wild plot twists.

Writing fantasy romance is like coming home to who I really am and I'm so happy to be here. It took me a while, but here I'll stay. Now, let's get to the part where I name names, because a book takes a village to publish.

Thank you to: Nikki Colinarez and Sara McCormick, who have loved this book so ferociously from the start and who cheered when I said I was writing something spicy. To Holly Karlsson, who walks through life with me in ways that I can never quite say thank you enough for, thank you for loving my writing.

To Nicola Hastings who picks up on the stuff I miss, time and again. To Maria Sclafani, who asks the best questions, and Annie D'Orazio, who reads even when she doesn't have the time. To Sarah Guthu, who is such a great creative sounding board, and Victoria Mier, who's talked to me for *hours* about this book. Thank you Lindsay Holt for making Duke and Duchess again this year, tea powers all I do, and that one fueled this book.

To Kenna Kettrick, who just keeps pushing me to be better, and who I trust so much with my stories.

To Christin Engelberth—where do I even start? Thank you for loving my wildly detailed briefs. Thank you for always making me feel like my project is as important to you as it is to me. Thank you for being such a wonderful artist, but really, more than that, thank you endlessly for being such a good friend.

Thank you to all of the Book Tour Gals. You may not know this, but on the day things fell apart, our group DM made me feel like I'd be able to pick myself and the book back up again.

To Doug, for the room of my own, and who taught me that love truly is an infinite well.

And last, but frankly most importantly, thank you so much to the early readers who loved this book from the get-go, who said they'd love it if we covered it with a paper bag, who love Harlow, who think Finn's a bit dreamy, who are crushing on the elusive Kate Spencer—thank you endlessly to all of you.

Everything I do is for y'all. Thank you every single day for making me an author. Thirteen year old Allison finally thinks I'm cool because of you.

beware what lies

BENEATH
THE
ALABASTER
SPIRE

BOOK II OF
THE IMMORTAL ORDERS
TRILOGY

COMING
FALL 2022

Printed in Great Britain
by Amazon

84298494R00235